Reading the Signs

A Paranormal Love Story

Reading the Signs

A Paranormal Love Story

Thomas Ramey Watson

Barn Swallow Media

READING THE SIGNS:
A PARANORMAL LOVE STORY

 **Barn Swallow Media**
Denver, CO

Copyright © 2016Thomas Ramey Watson
ISBN: 0-9818430-3-4 (alk. paper)
ISBN-13 978-0-9818430-3-2
LCCN: 2016917856

Although inspired by actual events and characters, certain elements are fictionalized. However, the protagonist's experiences as a university professor and an Episcopal campus chaplain are very close to the author's own. So are the paranormal happenings, many of which are echoed in his more clearly autobiographical book of poetry, *Love Strings.*

LIBRARY OF CONGRESS CATALOGING-IN-PUBLICATION DATA
Reading the Signs: A Paranormal Love Story / Thomas Ramey Watson. p.cm.
ISBN-13: 978-0-9818430-0-1 (alk. paper)
1. Magical Realism. 2. Paranormal. 3. Mysticism. 4.Christianity 5. Spirituality. 6. I. Title.

Cover design by Mnsartstudionew
Barn swallow photo by Roger Lindsay

Author's Note

As always, I want to thank a number of people who have been supportive throughout the journey, especially Alan Naslund, Carolyn Plummer, and my sister Vickie. Spirituality writer, editor, and friend, Dianne Arcangel, has been phenomenally helpful, advising me through a number of hurdles. My editor, Michael Kaye, has also proved thorough and insightful, and Kitty Brodrick has been an invaluable copy editor.

None of us walks alone. I am grateful for all good folks who have listened and offered help and encouragement along the way. I am also thankful that our current shocking and appalling political climate has brought to the forefront the manipulative tactics used by power mongers who rise to the top in so many fields. Sex often becomes a favorite method to gain power over others who serve to gratify the desires of the perpetrators. When sex is denied, or withdrawn, they do not hesitate to destroy their prey. In the past, victims of such acts were encouraged to keep their mouths shut and move on, as if that were easy. It is not. Sometimes it is not possible. The perpetrators' wounded egos and need for revenge must not be underestimated.

Vision

The bells of St. Elizabeth's, loud and dissonant, blended for a moment before becoming strident again. They brought back memories of studies in Italy. There, such bells rang out from the landscape and tumbled across the hills into cerulean seas. Here, in Denver, the sounds reverberated across campus to snow-covered peaks and reminded me of melodies rising from chaos.

I walked toward the church. The sun shone brightly. A blizzard had blanketed the city the week before, but this morning felt warm. The snow had almost vanished, even in shaded areas. Overnight, the grass had turned from straw to dewy green. Crocuses were bursting into small purple, white, and yellow stars. Like Persephone, spring had returned from Hades, decked in flowery gowns of green. The cycle of life had begun again.

From the sidewalk in front of St. Elizabeth's, I heard a voice. It was coming from the roof. My eyes traveled up the grey granite blocks to a white statue of Mary, a bouquet of roses carved in her hand. I moved my eyes to the stained-glass window behind the statue. The voice came from there. I was sure of it.

I stood still and concentrated. I shifted my consciousness slightly to the right. Mystical experiences were not new to me. I'd experienced a number of these phenomena over my thirty-three years. As a professor of English, I specialized in the Great Philosophical and Theological Tradition of the Western World. I'd read the mystics and saints. I was also the Episcopal chaplain for the colleges sharing the Auraria campus.

The apparition of an old woman floating in mid-air appeared near the rose window, a smaller version of those adorning the great cathedrals of Europe. Like a mist moving across the building, her body looked translucent, as fragile as rice paper. Her white hair was pinned at the back, with loose strands falling about the deep wrinkles of her face. Again, she called my name and began to speak in a language that sounded like Russian. She gestured for me to come closer.

I listened more closely.

The old woman shifted to Russian-accented English. "Please help my granddaughter," she pleaded. "Sherry needs your help, Dr. Jones."

I searched my memory. I couldn't think of a Sherry on my lists of students, colleagues, or acquaintances.

The old woman descended, sweeping past the granite stones of the edifice, and took hold of my arms. She pulled at them with a tugging that wasn't as strong as that of a flesh and blood human being. I felt her nonetheless.

"Help my Sherry!" the woman cried with greater urgency.

Just then, I heard the voice of a young woman about my age. I turned to see a living person bending on the sidewalk in front of the church. She was buckling the ankle strap on one of her pumps. She looked up and saw me. "Hello," she said. "Beautiful day, isn't it?" Her voice, like an oboe, reedy, pleased my ear. The highlights of her shoulder-length auburn curls glinted in the sun. Her skin tones were creamy, her eyes a warm brown.

"Sherry's a good girl. Don't forget that when she tests you," the old woman interjected, tugging at me from behind.

The apparition disappeared.

The woman I guessed was Sherry straightened up. I would have sworn she'd also been observing the spirit of her grandmother.

"I'm Sharon," she said. "Some call me Sherry, but I prefer Sharon—at least, at this time in my life."

I laughed. "So you've been going through different phases. Nothing unusual there."

"You sound like my psychiatrist," she replied.

Her grandmother's warning sounded in memory. *Her psychiatrist*, I thought. Sharon hadn't said her therapist or counselor, but her psychiatrist. Many of us sought counseling when needed. I certainly did.

If she needed a psychiatrist, rather than a lower-level counselor, I wondered if I'd be up to those tests.

"So far, March is acting like a lamb," she said. "Usually it's our blusteriest month."

"The blizzard came in February," I replied. "We'll have to see if March keeps frolicking on the green."

"To keep the pastures green, we need moisture," she replied. "Even if it does come as blizzards."

The bells let out another sound, only two notes this time. *Dong dong.* "Each bell is dedicated to a certain saint," I said. "I've forgotten which, but there's a plaque in the vestibule that tells."

She nodded. "I heard about them from my grandmother. She's been dead a long time now. St. Elizabeth's was her parish. That's when the building stood in the midst of the original neighborhood of little, wood-frame houses. One of them was hers. She liked to talk about the Gold Rush camps of the 1850s just over there."

She pointed toward Confluence Park.

"So your grandmother hung out with the gold panners." I managed to keep a straight face. "She must have lived a long, long time."

Sherry laughed. "And I'm eighty."

I grinned. "You sure don't look it. But your knowledge of Denver history is far greater than mine."

"I spent lots of time with my grandmother. She constantly instructed me, especially in matters of the faith. Even though Russian was her first language, she was always going to Mass, hanging on every word. That's how she learned English. Priest talk was what she knew best," Sherry said. "It was always, 'Father Joe says this, the Holy Father says that.'"

"My family sometimes attended services, but I can't say we were preoccupied," I said. "We didn't even go every Sunday."

"That's why you haven't rebelled." She smiled.

I noticed she was shivering. I was about to ask if she was cold, but she was wearing a coat. I was wearing only my green corduroy jacket, and I was plenty warm. Was she troubled about something? If she had some dark secret, I needed to beware and keep my foot near the brake pedal, no matter how attracted to her I was.

"One Lent I examined my life to discover what I'd give up as my penitential act that year," she said. She smiled. "I gave up guilt. I've never touched it—or church—since."

"That's a new one," I said and smiled.

A long string of bells sounded again. "They're so noisy," Sharon said, covering her ears. I noticed her elegant nails, the same coppery red as her lipstick.

"They indicate that all voices, in varying degrees of expertise, echo the one voice that created all by divine *fiat*," I explained. "The Gospel of John begins, "In the beginning was the Word. The Word was with God, and the Word was God; all things were made through him, and without him nothing was made. Because of the Creator, the Master Poet, the Maker of Song, all words will finally draw harmony from discord. Sharing his creation, his song, all voices discover meaning as they find themselves in him."

Sharon shot me a rather incredulous look.

I nodded. My face didn't change. My eyes remained steadily on her.

For a few moments, she said nothing, as if trying to soak in what I'd said. "I remember why I stopped going to Mass," she remarked. Her hands fidgeted on the buttons of her chestnut-colored coat. "From what I've heard, fiats and harmony are contradictory."

She'd understood more of what I'd said than her words let on. I was sure of that at the time. The energy that I felt coursing like electricity through my body made me think I certainly wouldn't mind instructing her on both esoteric and mundane things. This, I knew, was what Dylan Thomas meant by his lines, "The force that through the green fuse drives the flower and drives my green age."

"I'll explain later," I said. "What I told you was a very short digest of St. Augustine's theory of signs, or semiotics. He believed all signs are ultimately verbal. We are unable to live without verbal formulations. My scholarly writings are about his profound influence on Western literature, especially of the seventeenth century."

"I don't know that I'm up to hearing more," Sharon said. She seemed primed, ready to help the flow of my essential self right into her. Only later would I realize that Sharon knew far more about me and my work than she was letting on.

I tried to read her face, but couldn't tell if she was being serious or teasing. "By the way, my name is Ted," I said.

"I'll call you Theodore. Theodore sounds so much more sophisticated than Ted."

"Ted is just fine," I countered. I worried that this signal might mean she'd be another woman who insisted on turning me into something I wasn't. That never worked. I glanced at my watch. "I'm free for a couple of hours before I teach my class on Spenser's poetry. Let's grab a cup of coffee at The Market. I like its wide variety of freshly brewed coffees, four or five flavors—"

"And croissants," Sharon added. "I'll bet you're some lecturer," she said, pausing to laugh. She shook her head dramatically and clucked. "You're open-faced. Good thing you're built like a linebacker, or the brutes would run over you. I have a real estate showing on Seventeenth Street in a few hours, so let's get that coffee."

She led me by the arm toward the wide expanse of Speer Boulevard. On the other side of multiple lanes, lay the quaint shops lining Larimer Street, surrounded by the skyscrapers of downtown.

"I prefer the sidewalk tables," I said. "I like to think I'm sitting at an outdoor café in France. Have you been there?"

"Lots of times."

I wasn't sure whether she meant she'd been to The Market or to France. I decided not to ask. I was too intoxicated by her perfume—something sweet and spicy. The name floated near the surface of memory, although I couldn't put my finger on it.

We stepped out onto Speer Boulevard. We were jaywalking, but there were no cars in sight. Suddenly, a red Camaro careened down the road and headed for Sharon. At the last moment, he swerved and sped on.

She jumped back to the curb behind us. She crossed herself, leaving me in the street, heart racing.

"I thought you were a lapsed Catholic," I remarked. "Why'd you cross yourself?"

"I don't know," she said, trying to catch her breath. "Maybe I'm more of a believer than I'd thought." Her jaw hardened. "But I don't think so. I don't want anything to do with Christianity."

Oh great, I thought. I felt a spasm in my belly just to the right of my navel. Sharon had no idea I was a chaplain. This budding relationship was in danger of being nipped by a spring frost.

When we got to The Market, all the sidewalk tables were taken, but we found a spot near the window inside. Forced indoors, we sat in what had once been a huge department store. Now, it was a food emporium. We sipped our two allotted cups of almond coffee, sweetened with a little sugar, and Sharon devoured a chocolate croissant. I picked at an almond one. I wanted to make the pleasure of eating it last.

Sharon's energy was electric, magical, but I worried about her grandmother's special appearance begging me to help, helping to establish an immediate connection, but warning me that Sharon would test me. I also worried about her supposed rejection of everything to do with Christianity. Organized religion was troublesome, but I had few issues with mere Christianity. I sipped my coffee. She referred to her psychiatrist. Would getting involved with her pose a serious threat?

Instead of confronting these matters head on, I brought up my love of Europe. "After earning the Ph.D., I backpacked most of Western Europe for six months."

"I've also visited many Western European countries," she replied. "I really want to explore further." She smiled seductively.

"So do I," slipped out of my mouth. "I mean, I want to explore the world," I added. I didn't want to sound like I was trying to seduce her.

Sharon smiled knowingly. "You're the most fascinating man I've ever met," she remarked. "I feel you will open new avenues for me."

"Right," I replied, "ones with Camaros careening down them."

"Speer's a Boulevard." Sharon laughed. "You have no idea how I've hungered for a gentleman and a scholar."

Sharon was pretty, intelligent, and a good conversationalist. Nor was she deficient in her ability to compliment me on qualities that I held dear. All my life, I'd hoped for a lover who was not only pretty but an intellectual and spiritual companion. I'd made a horrific marriage when I was twenty. Over a decade later, the recollection of that union still made me shiver.

"I should tell you I'm the Episcopal chaplain for the Auraria campus. I'm not yet ordained," I said, pausing to gauge Sharon's reaction. I was known as an open book, although I was rarely so candid from the start. In the first few minutes, we'd jumped into the deep waters of personal and intellectual revelation, but that, I thought, had occurred because of prompting from the other side. I'd felt an immediate and intimate connection. Sharon's manner and looks certainly hadn't swerved us from that course.

Sharon didn't stop smiling. Her eyes remained fixed on me, her face and posture open.

"I specialize in the theological aspects of English literature, especially the great religious writers like Milton, Donne, Herbert, and Vaughan." There, I'd said it all—blurted out the most dangerous truths about me and my interests.

"I gathered there was something like that going on," Sharon said, her voice calm. She put her hand on my forearm. "If anyone could help me regain my faith, it would be you."

I felt an electrical charge shoot up my arm to my heart. Perhaps her grandmother had more in mind than my helping Sharon.

"Are you single?" she asked.

"I've grown used to it," I said. "My relationships have been few but miserable. I've stayed away from anything hinting of love for years. I've got a career, rather two careers, to worry about."

"I'm alone too." She slumped. Then, straightening up, and, with an impish grin, she added, "I'm free all afternoon—after the showing."

"Unfortunately, I have my class to teach. I've only missed teaching a couple times in my whole life."

"How about when you finish? I want to know you better."

"I have to run off," I explained and looked at my watch. "I had no idea how late it was." I felt my jacket pocket to make sure the book of Spenser's sonnets was in it. "I'm going to be late! I've got to put in some office hours afterwards."

"Are you rejecting me?" Sharon asked, her mouth turning down at the edges.

"I really do have to go," I explained, my anxiety flaring. I stood up to leave, almost knocking the table over.

Sharon jumped up and deftly caught it with both hands. Nothing broke. She extended her arms as if she wanted to embrace. I suddenly remembered a married church woman who'd insisted on kissing me goodbye after a party at her home. I'd turned my cheek, but with her hand she turned my face back to her and insisted I open my mouth so she could really kiss me. Her husband stood only a few yards away.

I was embarrassed and frightened at how quickly things with Sharon had turned intimate. I nervously grabbed one of her hands and started shaking it. I felt like a trained dog. My face felt hot. I blushed.

"Ted, you make me feel strong, like a real flesh and blood being," she said.

"I'm glad I don't seem like a ghost."

Sharon's eyes pleaded. "Could we meet tonight? In a public place?" Her lovely mouth opened as if to swallow me.

I felt as if the cameras were rolling. An important scene was being filmed. I felt terrified. My thighs trembled. I knew the feeling well, although no one had ever remarked that they'd noticed. I hid inside my six feet two inches and one-hundred ninety pounds. I made myself talk about issues that most people preferred to ignore. Folks seemed to believe I never shrank from anything.

"Yes," I said, feeling more at ease with meeting that evening, "let's meet tonight."

She placed her hands on my shoulders and turned me in the right direction. "Breathe," she commanded. "Center. You won't spin out of control."

I quickly stepped outside, with her hot on my trail. "Go back. I've got to teach!" I laughed. I headed toward campus on the other side of Speer.

"Where?" she called, waving at me. "Where are we meeting?"

"The Denver Center," I called. "Eight o'clock." I broke into a sprint, my heart pounding. I had to dodge several cars. Class was supposed to have started ten minutes ago.

Song

With Sharon's presence—her touch, her face—pervading my consciousness, I took up a discussion of Spenser's *Amoretti* with my class. Inspired by the Love attributed to God, the sonnets, "little loves," are meant to be echoes of the Love that is always, beautiful, and true.

On special occasions, the numinous shines on creation, granting those who are open moments of insight into deeper realities. I recalled sitting on a bench on campus not long before meeting Sharon the first time. A sparrow lighted beside me. It turned up its head to look at me. For a moment, I felt as if we were seeing the world through each other's eyes, connected by a profound curiosity that informs creation. Blake saw the world in a grain of sand, Julian of Norwich in a hazelnut, and I in the eyes of a sparrow.

That profound connection had been sparked with Sharon. The feeling that all is being woven into some sort of web—with a great mystery at the core—was manifesting in my consciousness again.

My mystical experiences had helped me understand why in God things enjoy true being, no matter the ravages of time and appearance. This is the Christian Platonism of the West. Spenser's little loves were inspired by his lady, who acted in a Christ-like role as a mediator of flesh and spirit, just as Sharon seemed now to be mediating flesh and spirit for me. Like the risen Christ, or perhaps *in* the risen Christ, she seemed to assume a role greater than mere human.

As my students and I explored glimpses into the eternal in Spenser's poetry, and applications to our own lives, I imagined us tapping in to this energy and bursting into song. The lyrics and tune were there—just beyond the reach of earthly touch and hearing, waiting to be called down into this realm.

> That doth argue you
> to be divine and born of heavenly seed:
> derived from that fair Spirit from whom all true
> and perfect beauty did at first proceed
>
> He only fair, and what he fair hath made:
> all other fair, like flowers, untimely fade.

Caught up in ecstasy, my soul tuned to something greater than myself, I finally remembered to glance at the clock. We'd run over-time by thirteen minutes. My students had also seemed caught up. I grabbed my book and quickly dismissed class.

I noticed the leaf-buds on the elm and maple trees scattered about campus. The sparrows on the roofs and eaves looked sweeter and more delicate than ever, as if they'd been renewed by spring. On the lawns and in the flowerbeds, robins hopped about, tipping their heads to the side, listening for worms.

The distant mountains appeared deep blue, capped by snow. Those nearest sprouted firs, pines, and spruces more lush than ever from winter's heavy snow. I could see the aspens leafing and ready to whisper to all who would listen.

The trees reminded me of the tree full of angels that sang to Blake as a child. When he ran to tell his mother, she promptly beat him for having such insight. But that didn't matter—not in the larger scheme of things. Blake knew his mystical experiences were all that mattered. The real world—that which was of God—lovingly influenced the world that most saw, forming and reforming it.

The light of Christ shone over all things, renewing them, making them whole. In this theophany, I walked toward my office in the St. Francis Interfaith Center, a structure that cradled St. Elizabeth's.

I opened the door, bolted up the stairs, and greeted Louise, our receptionist with a warm smile. By the time I'd walked down the hall to my office, I'd discarded my English professor role and put on my chaplaincy. Keenly sensitive in my amorous state—not only aware of the books on grieving, relationships, and God on my bookshelves and the students' papers on my desk—I was mindful of what seemed some deeper magic at work.

I kept pondering how my involvement with Sharon would play out. What it would mean in the tapestry of things? Anxious, I hoped that my powerful feelings were more than infatuation and what I'd perceived was no illusion. She seemed genuine. I'd almost given up the belief that I would find an earthly love that was strong and true—certainly one that would last. But Miracles still happened. Their rarity made them more precious. I was open. I spent the rest of the day in euphoria.

That evening, I parked at the Interfaith Center. With a mixture of hope and anxiety, I walked toward the Denver Center for Performing Arts. I saw a couple dozen people milling about, some individually, some in pairs, and some in small groups. I should have been more specific in my directions, since the Denver Center covered a large area composed of several impressive glass, stone, and steel buildings. I walked and breathed deeply. I tried to allay my fear that Sharon would stand me up—or that we wouldn't find each other, even if she did show.

I stood in front of the multiplex Cinema, looking up at the marquee. *E.T, the Extra-Terrestrial; Sophie's Choice; The State of Things; The Year of Living Dangerously.* "Hmmm," I muttered, "no chance of Cocteau's *Beauty and the Beast.*"

I heard Sharon's voice behind my ear, as her hand lightly touched the arm of my ski jacket.

"Reading?" she asked. I turned to see that she held a plaid blanket of blue, green, and plum under her left arm. With her right hand, she held a grocery bag up against her chest.

"Yes, I was reading the signs," I replied, taking the bag from her. I looked inside. It contained a bottle of Beringer Gamay Beaujolais and two little paper cups, like you get in kindergarten.

"You're always reading the signs," she remarked. "I like how your green jacket brings out the green of your eyes."

"I like your chestnut-colored coat for similar reasons," I replied. I felt wrapped in what I realized was her Cinnabar perfume. I could breathe this every day.

Although we had been apart for only a few hours, I'd missed her. Why we seemed so united, so familiar, I didn't know. Perhaps we'd been together in past lives, if such things existed. Perhaps we were meant to be together, and I was tapping into what would be, stepping out of time and space as we normally perceive them.

I glanced at Sharon's face as we walked down the steps toward the grassy area along Speer Boulevard. I slipped on a patch of ice and hit the cement. I had been sort of galloping, I realized, not holding the hand rail. For a moment, I imagined the stars singing, as on the first night of creation. I'd almost passed out.

"I must have been trying to recreate Blake," I said, coming to.

Sharon dropped the blanket and bent down to check on me. She turned my face toward her and checked my pupils to see if they were dilated. "I hope you don't have a concussion," she said, feeling my forehead.

"My head hasn't been normal since the doctor used forceps to pull me into this world. I don't think I really wanted to enter. I must have been aware of what a mess it was."

Sharon hugged me to her in a way that seemed maternal. She patted my back and rubbed it gently. "There, there, my child," she cooed.

After a few moments of breathing the night air, I realized that I did feel a little bruised. I got up to walk and hobbled a bit, but I hadn't sprained an ankle or broken anything, even the bottle of wine.

Taking my arm, Sharon helped me out to the grass near the solar fountain bordering Speer Boulevard. "I wonder if we shouldn't take you to the emergency room to be checked out," she said.

"Really, I'm sure I'm all right," I insisted.

She turned me toward the street lamp and again examined my pupils. "They look fine," she said. "They're still contracting when the light shines in them."

"Shining light on every situation helps us see better," I said.

"Wait while I spread out the blanket." She signaled to me, "Sit down."

I sat, and, gracefully, she joined me. Removing the paper cups from the bag, she handed me the bottle and corkscrew. "Open the bottle," she said.

I poured. The wine was a jeweled, lightly bodied red with a fruity bouquet.

"To us," we toasted.

"To lives filled with deep and abiding happiness," Sharon said.

"To synaesthesia and all metaphors, mixed as they might seem." And after only a few sips, I felt drunk. "For all will be harmonized in God, the Creator, the Poet, the Author of all."

After a few cups, Sharon took my hand and traced our lives, laughing, across my palm.

"Do you see any perils or pitfalls?" I asked.

"None."

I drank a little more. I envisioned us walking in milkweeds and foxtails in mountain meadows near Eagle, Colorado. For her, I would descend to valleys, snow-covered, dark. My need to adore had found a local habitation. Within God, and within God's presence, we would embrace a wholeness rarely grasped by humanity. Elevated from disparate noises, our hearing, like our sight, would be cleansed. We would be turned into harmony, woven into God's poem, his song.

Several cars honked on Speer. I looked up to see a near-accident. Three cars had managed to swerve around another that had come to a sudden halt.

"It never ends," Sharon said. "Even though you're driving along carefully, someone does something unexpected."

Later, when we kissed goodbye at Sharon's car, a mist moved in and draped us, diffusing the city lights. For a moment, things lit up in a soft, pink glow. As the soul wears the body like a garment, God garbs himself in creation.

Sharon's words about the near-car accident came to mind, as if a quiet warning. Something unexpected always happens. Sometimes the crash is avoided, sometimes not.

Trusting the Gut

I woke the next morning with an awareness that we typically project our hopes and dreams onto someone who has excited us. It's strongest in the beginning—until reality breaks through. I had counseled enough people to know it's never wise to rush into things, no matter how good you feel.

I felt some anxiety. The wine and the music of the angels, not to mention the fall, the night before may have induced a state of delusion rather than vision. I decided for our next date that Sharon and I had to meet either at The Market or another public place, without any Beaujolais. We felt enough intoxication with just ourselves. Without rushing, we could continue to explore the possibilities of a relationship.

Unannounced, Sharon dropped by my office that afternoon. I looked up from my desk, first glimpsing her shapely legs walking toward me. She had such a sense of style. The reddish brown color of her low-heeled pumps with little ankle straps matched her hair.

I doubted that she'd announced herself to our receptionist. Rather, Sharon had paraded down the second floor hall that was open on the side to the great space capping the first floor. She knew where my office was. I'd told her. She sat down in the chair across from me.

"I don't think this is a good idea," I told her, putting aside the papers I was grading. "Your presence is too distracting, too easily observed. Every noise on this floor carries out into the open space and echoes there. The wall of windows behind me invites anyone in the friary next door to look in."

Sharon looked crestfallen. "You could pull the blinds and close the door," she suggested.

"Oh, wouldn't that look good," I remarked. "You know we're tempted to do more than talk. Closing the door and blinds would only make Louise and others even more eager to stand outside the door and listen." I paused, trying not to hurt Sharon's feelings. "Only holding hands and looking deep into each other's eyes proves more than I can bear," I explained. "You know I want to tear your clothes off."

"Well, I keep telling you to do just that," she answered, her voice low.

"Please, don't tempt me," I said. "In my counseling, I tell people to lay a solid foundation for good relationships. Those take shared vision and values. To see if we have them, we mustn't rush sex."

"If we go too slowly, we might discover something that keeps us from erecting," Sharon remarked.

I laughed. I couldn't resist.

She phoned me daily over the following weeks but didn't stop by. If I'd not heard from her by evening, my anxiety would be so great that I would phone her. Not one dependent by nature, and especially by training, I felt that I needed at least to talk with her, even if I didn't get to see her.

"You could do more than that," Sharon replied.

One night at eleven, she phoned. I'd talked with her only a few hours before. I was sitting at my desk, grading papers and doing some research.

"You could have it all—my voice, my lips, my body, my soul," she answered, "if only you'd say the word."

"Only say the word, and I shall be healed," I said, echoing the words of Holy Communion, Whether she knew it consciously or not, she was leading me in that direction. "I told you, I'm not ready. You're not either. But that doesn't mean we can't see each other."

"You wouldn't tear off my clothes," Sharon said.

"Nor would I let you take them off. You know why we're going slowly," I reminded her. I turned around to look over the bookcase-lined the wall behind me. I wanted my copy of

The Oxford Dictionary of Saints. "I quickly became intimate with my first ex-wife. You know where that landed me."

"Out the door on your ass," Sharon replied.

I laughed at her directness. "I need to get to know you better. I need a sounding board, someone I can trust to keep my best interests in mind."

"Ted, I'm really not sure I have your best interests in mind," Sharon responded.

I couldn't tell whether she was being serious or teasing. I stopped searching for the book and looked back at the papers on my desk. "You know my deepest instincts, located somewhere in my gut, are causing me worry over my career paths," I said. "My stomach feels as hard as a basketball."

Sharon laughed. "Just make sure it doesn't start looking like one."

"Frankly, I don't really know that I have the energy to invest in a relationship until my professional life gains some clarity," I said. "I've had two serious relationships. Even the second became serious right away. I should have been devoting my attention to my studies. My careers have suffered for it. I don't want to repeat the pattern."

"I know you're not on a tenure track and get no benefits," Sharon answered. "After you finished your Ph.D., the market was depressed. Your experience and publications should now help you land something better."

"I hope so," I answered. "I'm sending articles and poems out all the time, even placing some."

"You're rewriting your dissertation so you can publish it as a book," Sharon said. She knew the story. I'd told her. "The Dean of the Cathedral should come through with a salary for your chaplaincy when you meet with him on Friday. He said he would, if you'd move your ministry base to the Cathedral. It seems things are moving into place. I don't see as high a barrier between us as you do. "

When Bishop Lane had appointed me the Auraria chaplain in the fall, the Episcopal Diocese of Colorado agreed to give me health insurance while my home parish paid my office rent of fifty dollars per month. Because students typically did not—often, could not—contribute financially to campus ministry, the Diocese of Colorado had cut out funding for college chaplaincies. We had to seek it ourselves. "Every other major denomination has salaried chaplains on the largest campus in Colorado," I complained. Nonetheless, I had to search for my own funding. Friends suggested approaching the Dean of the Cathedral.

"You must have faith," Sharon said, certainty in her voice.

"I thought you'd given that up," I reminded her. "You're sounding more faithful than I." I paused to muse. "I wonder if the Dean really plans to help. He's new. No one knows for certain what he's like. In my eyes, he seems most interested in building projects and flashy music programs that get media coverage."

"People remember monuments to ego," Sharon replied, letting me get back to my work.

I put the phone down. I decided to fix on hopefulness, instead of barriers and empty monuments.

A week later, on Friday, April 1, I climbed the stairs to Dean McDougal's office in the granite building behind the Cathedral. I knocked on the imposing, dark oak door. My anxiety was running high. The complex was meant to echo the imposing Gothic edifices of Cambridge and Oxford. I knocked harder because I didn't think I'd been heard.

A deep male voice from inside said, "Come."

I opened the door to find a chunky, blond haired man of middle age. He stood behind a massive oak desk in a dimly lit, cavernous study lined in oak paneling. Pictures of his wife and children sat prominently on his desk and on oak tables about the room. I towered over him by at least six inches. I noted that he managed to give me a quick but close look up and down. Then he motioned for me to sit across from him in one of two leather upholstered chairs which stood near the stone fireplace at the far end of the room. The lights were off.

The only light filtered in through the leaded glass panes of the windows.

The Dean moved from behind his desk to take the chair facing me. He sucked in his gut and sat down. He introduced himself. He tried to continue speaking in a deeper, more masculine voice than was natural for him. I wanted to urge him to use his natural voice.

The Dean's vision dropped to my ankles, which he paused on, then moved slowly up my legs to my crotch, where he stopped. He wasn't listening to what I was now saying about needing funding. He was drooling. From the crotch, his eyes moved up to my chest and concentrated there. He wasn't looking at my heart chakra. I knew exactly what women meant when they complained of men who molested them with their eyes. I found myself wanting to suggest, with more than a little sarcasm, "I have a face. See, up here. Think of raising your eyes to heaven."

At the end of the interview, McDougal shook my hand firmly. "I'll see that you get funding for your ministry. I want you to join the exciting ministry of the Cathedral team. We're moving full speed ahead with more building projects than you can dream and working on organ and choir recitals, as well as a national Arts Festival. We need your help with that."

Despite McDougal's encouragement and promises, I continued to have doubts. Knowing that I was not in a hurry to get ordained—not until I knew it was right for me— McDougal said he'd put me "On the fast track. The church is a kind of club, you see. Without ordination, you'll always be looked on as an outsider."

I knew he was right. I had observed the club mentality. I was not sure, however, that his was a club I wanted to join. Jesus and the prophets, both before and after, always stood outside the institutions—of faith, government, and education. Because of their standing at the edge, they saw things more clearly than those on the inside. They too suffered for not being members of the clubs of their day.

I talked with various friends at the Cathedral.

"You must join the team," Dr. Beecham, one of my old religion professors remarked. He and his wife were active Cathedral members. She wrote for Episcopal publications, while he had recently retired from the University of Denver.

Mrs. Beecham urged me to join too. "We'll make our pledge to your ministry. We'll see that others do too."

"You'll be at the epicenter of the Episcopal world," Dr. Beecham said. "The times are changing. The Cathedral is no longer asleep. Excitement is in the air."

When I hinted that McDougal did not strike me as someone totally on the up and up, even close friends brushed aside my concerns. Most changed the subject. Of course, McDougal was a man of fine character. He had studied at Cambridge University in England and came highly recommended by those in the know.

"He's married with children. Yet he eyed me up and down," I complained.

"Don't make too much of that," another of my professors, an ardent Episcopalian whom I'd regarded as a mentor, exclaimed. "The Dean is bold, outgoing, and is bagging huge pledges from all kinds of individuals and corporate sources, many of which had pledged only pennies, or none at all, before."

"The Dean has big plans for the Cathedral; you can feel the energy—progress—in the air," Mark, the Choirmaster from Oxford, remarked. "You can be part of it, if you don't hold back."

"You must jump in," one of the Associate Rectors urged. "Vacillation is the cause of so many failures."

I sometimes felt as if the sales pitches were just that, pitches. On Sharon's urging, I moved my ministry from what had been my home parish in the suburbs near the University of Denver to the Cathedral. I would join the team. I hoped all those people urging me to do so were not mistaken.

In my academic world, the University English Department had appointed a new Chairman at Christmas. As a non-tenure track professor, I had not been able to vote. I was not considered a faculty member in the full sense. For people like me, and there were a dozen and a half, there were no guarantees, no rights, no benefits, and no protections.

The new Chairman, Dr. Jeroboam Spet, was a scholar. Of that I was glad. Some, however, indicated privately that they didn't trust him. That was not unusual. People were drawing lines in the sand. Either you were for them or against them. Sides had to be taken. Everything everywhere was becoming politicized and the university seemed especially marked.

So far, Spet had been decent to me. I had nothing to complain about. I tried never to form judgments without firsthand observation.

Spet had complimented me on my teaching and my writing. He'd visited my classes. "Jones' mind is sharp but flexible. His scholarly writing is admirable, clear, in-depth," Spet wrote of me in a letter of recommendation for my job placement file. "He is well liked and enjoys uniformly positive student evaluations."

Spet then recommended me for a sudden opening that came up at the University of Idaho. The English Department Chairman there phoned a few nights later to ask if I would take it. The position was to begin in June, not much notice, he admitted. While it was not a tenure track position, he expected it to become a tenure track opening the following year. "The new job description would be written with you in mind," he promised. "By law, we must advertise, but in the description we would give you the edge by describing your specialties."

I hoped instead to find a tenure track teaching position around Denver, perhaps even where I was. I was publishing more than many of the tenured and tenure track faculty. Even with doubts about ordination, I wanted to give my chaplaincy the chance to take off. The combination of English professor and campus chaplain suited me.

And then, of course, there was Sharon. More than anything else, I wanted to nurse that relationship. The more we interacted, the stronger my feelings for her grew. She stirred my imagination. This, I kept feeling, was the woman I'd dreamed of and found. Her hair, her eyes and face, her touch, her voice. Her legs and the way she walked. Her wit. Like a sparking fuse, she lit me.

I did not go into every detail of my decision with the Idaho Chairman, but I graciously declined his offer, telling him that "I just can't think of making such a big move right now. I have too much going on here in Denver," I explained. "But please, keep me in mind for the tenure track position. Things change. I need several months notice to make big changes. Not long ago I bought a renovated town home in the Highlands just west of downtown Denver. I'm very involved."

The Idaho Chair assured me, "We shall."

For a moment, I relaxed. I could at least feel good about someone who held power over me. From all the evidence, Dr. Spet had been on my side. In him I had one person in power who admired me for the right reasons.

Washington Park

I chose to concentrate on Sharon. She inspired me to write several fine poems, full of striking imagery and sensual detail. She gave my life the human anchor it needed because she understood my work. She'd told me she had an M.A. in English. "I wanted to go on for the Ph.D., but I lacked the discipline," she explained one day over a glass of wine at a little French restaurant in Larimer Square. "You have to stay humble and kiss too many asses."

"More than in real estate?" I asked.

She nodded. "Academia is much more Byzantine. You're dealing with highly intelligent devils who expect you to be at their mercy, even putting out for them if they want you. They destroy you if you fail to do what they want." She put down her glass and looked me straight in the eyes. "Ted, I'm not easy unless I respect someone. I have to feel something. I don't just put out to get ahead."

I nodded. "I'm glad to know that." A waiter walked past. I took a sip of wine.

Sharon genuinely appreciated my work. Necessary for the writer, since few of us write for ourselves alone. No matter how small the audience, how much the world turns to coal, we need to believe that we have at least one person who appreciates our efforts and us.

I reached into my back pack sitting on the chair beside me for a poem that I'd composed comparing the wet stones and angles of the Denver Center to Tours in France. "I titled it 'Meditation'," I said and read the beginning to her:

I stood with you
under the arches
of the Denver Center,
the damp stones rising
in myriad angles.
The changing light,
the grey subtleties
reminded me of Tours . . .

"I haven't been there yet," Sharon said. "But those lines make me want to visit." She blushed. "With you."

Our waiter returned. He asked if we wanted another glass of wine.

"No, I think one is plenty for each of us," I said. The glasses were big as fishbowls. I didn't want to get tipsy. I knew I might not be able to hold out if I did.

"Let's visit Tours later this year, even if only for a few days," Sharon said, placing her hand on mine. "I hope by then you won't mind sharing a room," she added, demurely.

"Only a room?" I asked. I got up, deciding that we needed to go for a walk, and we headed out.

One green day shortly thereafter, Sharon and I agreed to meet in Washington Park for a picnic lunch. It was mid April and warm. Everything was green. Chickadees were trilling up and down the scales. Sparrows were chirping, and doves were cooing.

Sharon had packed a basket with Jarlsberg cheese and Black Forest ham on dark, seeded rye, along with a nice bottle of merlot. We sat on her plaid blanket to eat. We said very little. We didn't need to.

After lunch, Sharon walked to the edge of the lake. There she bent to feed the mallards crusts from her sandwich. Eagerly they swam over to feed.

"My grandmother escaped the Ukraine," she said on her return. "She spoke English mixed with Russian."

I nodded.

"You already knew this, didn't you?" Sharon asked.

"You're completing the sketch," I replied.

"Gramma taught me to count by using ducks—one duck, two ducks, three—white, and brown, and mottled."

"My grandmother, who raised chickens, taught me to count by counting them," I said, "as well as the horses and cows of my grandparents' ranch in northern Colorado."

Suddenly, a vision of myself as a grown man, standing with my grandmother came upon me. Grandma's hair was no longer white but golden as the wheat near harvest, golden as it had once been when she was young and blooming. Her blue eyes were shining as the Colorado sky.

My grandmother and I, now grownup, stood—with me at least a head taller—in the midst of ripening wheat fields beneath a lapis sky. The west was heaped with down-filled clouds.

In the vision, I glimpsed Sharon, also grownup and smiling, with her tiny grandmother, walking hand in hand through the fields toward us. They came from the east, the direction of the sun rising over the horizon. Here, I knew, is the intersection where earthly time rolls into eternity. All that has lacked meaning is made clear. At last we understand the language of signs and see the patterns woven by our lives.

"With my body," Sharon began, loosing her grandmother's hand for mine, "I thee worship."

"And with my body I worship thee," I returned, priesting the ancient sacrament of marriage by kissing Sharon's fingertips, her eyelids, and then her mouth. I was again intoxicated by her perfume.

My vision dissipating, to be replaced by earthly sight, I watched Sharon bend to feed the ducks—white, and brown, and mottled. The meridian sun fell in a glinting and took residence in her hair. It filled me with light.

I thought, *My God, how could I love anyone more? I'm supposed to help her—look what I'm getting in return.* My heart felt like a supernova. "Rise to adore the mystery," bristled in my mind, "the mystery of love."

I knew that I'd found gold. My entire being was charged. The blood throbbed in my veins.

When Sharon returned to the car, she had tears in her eyes. "I want to feel safe again, loved," she confessed. "I hate the aching loneliness that's engulfed me for so long." I'd intuited that she'd felt vulnerable, but she'd finally said so herself.

All I could do was hold her, rock her on my lap like a child. "Sherry," I said. "My Sherry, my own." I more fully understood the words that her grandmother had said to me when she'd manifested there at St. Elizabeth's. No wonder she'd asked me to help her granddaughter. Sherry's grandmother had given herself and her time. She'd made Sharon feel safe.

I wondered about Sharon's parents—were they too busy, too caught in their own conflicts—perhaps making money, seeking power, or just surviving—to attend to her? What about her brothers and sisters? Was her family as unawake as my own?

"Do you believe in lucky threes?" Sharon asked, as if from nowhere. She looked up at me, placing her hand on my heart.

"That depends on the game," I responded. Her eyes were huge, deep, and warm.

"We've known each other for several weeks now," she said, moving her mouth close to whisper in my ear.

My heart was pounding.

"I hope you're ready."

I said in a low voice, "Yes," and nodded.

The Necessity of Symbols

On the eighteenth of April, six weeks after we'd met, Sharon and I arranged to meet at her house "to explore the nature of love," as she put it. Before leaving my place, I went out into the common area behind my town home. In the slant light of late afternoon I picked several roses of varying hues—two Chicago Peaces, two Tiffanies, and two Pascalis—and a few sprigs of baby's breath. I felt my passion, and my anxiety, rise with each heartbeat. My breath quickened; my thighs were beginning to tremble. My face felt flushed.

Buddhists argue that we must wake up and become fully conscious, fully aware of ourselves and our surroundings. For a moment, I wished that I could remain a little more asleep. Constant prodding does not make one comfortable.

When I drove into the Cherry Hills neighborhood where Sharon lived, I realized that I could no longer just imagine the spacious, custom built home on carefully landscaped and manicured acres where she lived. The area was gated with a warning to all who might enter that we were being watched. If we had no business there, we were to leave at once. I fully realized that I could never begin to afford the luxuries to which she was accustomed. If Sharon wished to love me, she would have to settle for more spiritual and intellectual riches.

Sharon's surroundings also brought back my earlier concerns over the roommate that she'd mentioned in passing now and then. His name was Brad, she'd said. He was just her roommate, she'd assured me. The house was his; she paid him rent.

When I gave her a certain look, she smiled. She assured me, "The rent is in the form of American currency only.

There's no other payment. We have a housekeeper come in every morning. And a groundskeeper twice a week. Brad is more interested in the housekeeper than in me. Besides, I make great money selling commercial real estate. I treat those male clients' extended tongues like red carpets."

"Oh," I said. I'd changed the subject in my mind, so I didn't hear more.

I hoped Sharon was telling the truth about Brad. I wanted to believe her. Having a roommate of the other gender was not unusual, but still, the thought of it knotted my stomach.

When Sharon answered the door, she was wearing a simple, black, floor-length gown with a scooped out neck and a single string of pearls. Her ample breasts with piqued nipples were nicely framed. She was clouded in perfume. "All dressed up and plenty of places to go," Sharon remarked, warmly. She threw her arms around me in a firm hug. I tried to preserve the bouquet that I was holding by moving my hand out to the side.

"It used to happen all the time, but lately Brad's been a homebody, way too much the homebody," Sharon complained. "Thankfully, he's overseas now, negotiating some corporate concern."

I suddenly felt underdressed in my fern green corduroy jacket, green and blue plaid shirt, and khaki pants. I found myself wishing that Sharon didn't bring up Brad at all. I hoped that my Lagerfeld cologne, also spicy, with a hint of bitter underscoring the sweet, was acceptable.

Sharon turned around so she could escort me inside. "Un Bel Di" was playing in the background. "Butterfly sounds like Victoria De Los Angeles," I said, "not because I'm such an opera aficionado, but because I have the same recording."

"You're sharp," Sharon said. "I knew you'd know."

Interfering with Puccini were the sounds from at least two television sets blaring from other rooms.

Shortly after Sharon and I stepped onto the marble floor of the massive foyer, she kicked off her shoes and began to kiss me. She stood on my shoes so that she was tall enough to reach my mouth.

"I love kissing you," I said, pulling away to speak, "but I know the roses you hold awkwardly at your back will go limp if they don't get stuck into some water."

She laughed and said, "Believe me, I know all about dipping the wick."

I was glad she didn't expand on the metaphor. I feared what would come out next.

As Sharon raced off to find a vase, leaving me to hold the flowers, I was glad for the time to collect myself. Maybe I could breathe. I watched as she rushed away for a vase. She did have a lovely back, not to mention her sweet behind and shapely legs. *Actually*, I thought to myself, *I like every inch of her*.

While waiting, I peeked under the coats tossed over what appeared to be a statue in the foyer. It was the Henry Moore sculpture of a woman with a hole in her belly—a copy, I assumed, although I wondered. A couple of prescription bottles had been tossed inside the hole. *Weird*, I thought and dropped the coats back on the statue.

Sharon rushed back. She held a large, leaded glass vase filled with water. She took the flowers from me, plopped the stems into the vase, sat it on a marble topped table in the foyer, and started leading me toward the bedroom.

My bladder felt full. "I need to go to the bathroom."

Sharon directed me, hardly unlocking her grip as she walked me there. I almost had to push her aside and shut the door. I was tempted to lock it, but I refrained, thinking she'd hear the lock turn. The bathtub, sink, and toilet were emerald green, the designer faucets gold.

Out of curiosity, I quietly opened the medicine cabinet. I spotted more prescription bottles and a vial of what I assumed to be cocaine. Making no noise, I closed the medicine cabinet and stood at the toilet.

Sharon flung open the door. "What's taking you so long?" she asked. She looked at me standing there. "I love watching men pee," she exclaimed. "What a nice cock you have, especially the head," she began. "It's so nice and round, and pink. Does yours get really red when it's hard?" she asked. "I'll bet it does. You're light skinned and blush like a peach."

I didn't know what to say. I guessed she was high. I noticed a change in the sound of the pee. It no longer seemed to be splashing in the toilet bowl. I looked down to find myself peeing on the purple streaked tiles below. "Oh great," I said. "Sorry."

Sharon said, "Never mind, just hurry up. Do you think we could do it here on the floor? I've never done it on this bathroom floor."

Wondering what bathrooms she'd had sex in—and what might happen next—I tried to collect myself by ignoring her questions. I shook off, zipped up, and walked toward the sink to wash my hands like a good boy.

"By the way, I think water sports can be fun." She reached down, pulled off my shoe as I was washing my hands, and tossed it into the corner beside the bathtub. "We may end up in that tub ourselves," she laughed. She began ripping off my other shoe and socks, and then moved upward, as she pushed me from the bathroom into the bedroom.

The room was as big as many living rooms. A TV blared from the far end of the bed. A news show was on, showing rubble and bodies blasted by bombs in the Middle East somewhere.

Nearing the bed, I almost took a tumble but managed to catch myself. "Do you think you can turn off the TV?" I couldn't hear my own voice, let alone Sharon's.

"I don't care about anything, definitely not TV," she said. "I just want that big cock in my mouth, like a breast to a starving baby." She reached over and yanked down my pants. My boxers came with them. She bent down and pulled them from my legs, tossing them across the room.

I felt myself shrinking. "It isn't that big," I said, looking down. It seemed as small as a week-old pickle.

"Who cares?" Sharon asked. She pushed me onto the white lace duvet that covered a feather bed. She let go and, like a madwoman, hurried over to punch the off button on the TV set. She ran back to me and dropped her gown, leaving only her black lace bra and panties. I still had my shirt on. She almost ripped the buttons to pull it off.

She pounced on me, knocking the breath out of me. Again she grabbed my cock with such wild abandon that I feared she was going to rip it off and tack it over her bed as a trophy. She'd remove that ugly black and white painting from the wall and nail it there *in memoriam*. Everything was too fast, overwhelming.

Suddenly, she started screaming. "You don't love me! I'm too fat!" She was looking at my cock, still limp in her hand.

I looked down. It didn't surprise me. I couldn't handle too much going on at one time. I never could. But I'd never thought a thing about her weight before then—except to notice that she was not model-skinny, for which I was glad. I was certainly not skinny myself, never had been, and probably never would be.

As she cried, I began to see her through her own eyes. Yes, Sharon's stomach was not so firm as a Playboy model's. I began to notice patches of cellulite on her thighs. I couldn't help it. I didn't want to notice. I loved her. Of that I was certain. "I love you regardless!" I blurted.

"Just leave! Get out. Out!" she screamed, clutching her breasts with her arms. She ran to hide herself behind the drapes at the window.

I noticed a small red stain on the drapery material. I wondered if it was blood. "You realize by standing in front of a window you're showing your body to the world, don't you," I asked.

She wept.

"Just, calm down," I said, trying to calm myself. I walked to the window and tried to take her in my arms.

She wrapped herself more tightly in the drapes and refused to change her tune, no matter how much I tried. I wondered if she'd pull the drapes off the rods. "I hate priests," she added, in another burst of tears. Just as I thought I was going to be able to take her in my arms, she let go of the drapes and ran to the corner of the room. She turned her back to me and wailed.

I had no idea what exactly she meant by her remark about hating priests. "What do you mean?" I asked. "Please turn around and face me." I handed her gown to her.

She refused to take it. Instead, she wailed louder.

"I'm not a priest," I said. "You know I'm no priest. I'm a lay chaplain, not ordained."

"You may not be ordained, but you're still a priest. In God's eyes you're a priest. You know it. So do I. God chooses. Man recognizes what he's done."

"Man, oh man, am I confused," I said. "Where did that come from? All the things you said you've rejected come rushing out to be dumped on me. I don't think you realize how you've played into this mess." Even though I was trembling, my hands unsteady, I kept my voice low.

After more failed attempts to touch and hold Sharon, I sighed and put my clothes back on. I went to the bathroom to rescue my shoes and socks.

By the time I returned to her, she had her gown back on and was glaring at me.

I turned and walked slowly, heavily, to the foyer. I put my hand on the latch of the front door. It felt icy. My whole being had gone from sheer light to lead.

I slowly turned the latch and opened the door, hoping she would come to her senses and talk things through.

I heard her walk down the hall. She neared. I thought she was about to embrace me—to acknowledge our mutual faults—but she pushed me outside, hard. "Out," she said.

Still in shock, I sat down on the steps and wept. I didn't know what else to do. I was confused. Words—deeds—nothing mattered. It was as if she'd gone mad. Images of the vial of cocaine and prescription medicine bottles flashed in my mind. I wondered if that explained her erratic behavior. I just didn't know. I didn't associate with drug users, didn't do drugs myself, so I really didn't know what to think.

Eventually, I pulled myself up and drove home on Speer Boulevard through a sudden downpour. Although the West had still been a little orange from the last traces of day, I could see little light now. The weather seemed all too appropriate. My tires were beginning to hydroplane. I could hardly see what I was passing on the road. I wished I were a machine—press the accelerator and go—faster, faster. No emotions. No thoughts.

My tears burned as I sped down the road, the water whipping about the wheels and up under the car, making it slip and sway roughly, back and forth, side to side. I could feel the water lashing the undersides of the car, threatening to keep me from getting to my own house across town. There, I would open the door and find no one.

Near the Denver Center, a cop pulled me over. He wrote me a ticket for speeding twenty miles over the limit. I deserved it. When he told me I could appear at court in person, even plead not-guilty, if I was so inclined, I thought about becoming obnoxious, so he'd throw me in jail. At least I wouldn't spend another night alone.

"Thank you, Officer," I said instead and wished him a good night. "I hope you have someone waiting for you," I muttered under my breath.

Then I remembered my dog, Tray. She was waiting for me. She wasn't very affectionate, but she'd be there, probably nesting in my bed. When she finally heard me home, she'd come down the stairs, wanting to be fed and let out. At least someone depended on me.

I arrived at the L-shaped brick building that spanned a corner lot. It was built in 1890 as an apartment building and turned into town homes in 1980.

I put the key in the lock, opened the door, and called out. After a few minutes, Tray lumbered down the stairs. From her groggy manner, I guessed she'd been sleeping in my bed on wadded up pillows and bedding that she'd turned into a nest. She was a blonde, black-masked Afghan, on the small and boney end. Lying on the floor, even though carpeted, wouldn't have felt good to her.

"So, my little Goldilocks has wakened," I said. "I know, if I'd stick around more, you wouldn't sleep so much. At least not quite." I pet her, fed her, and took her for a quick walk around the block. After all these years, she knew the routine.

After we returned to the house, I knelt on the hard floor beside my bed. I couldn't think of anything else to do. "I thought you gave me Sharon," I said to God, trying mentally to reconstruct the details of how we got together.

I wept. Getting the woman in return for helping her was not what I had been promised. It was Sharon's grandmother, not God, who asked me to help her Sherry. I had to acknowledge that, no matter how great the pain. "I guess I misread your intentions again," I said to God, growing a little less angry. "You didn't say a thing."

"Sharon told me she was lonely, until I came along. I was lonely too. She made me realize how lonely. Sharon was the reason that all my pedestrian notions of house and home and family were going to come true. I knew it in my bones," I muttered. "God, I never made the mistake of medieval lovers—substituting earthly loves for you. I know that earthly loves fade. I know the fate of Troilus." I was talking to myself—and Chaucer—more than God.

My knees were hurting. I tried to shift my weight. I glanced at the moonlight glinting through the lace curtain on the window and tried to steady myself.

"But why, why can't I have Sharon?" I cried, another wave of grief passing through me. I thought about Spenser, how he believed that his lady Elizabeth proved that earthly loves can be rooted in Christ and reflect him. Such loves redeem. Such loves show that earthly love doesn't have to oppose heavenly love, as is so often reflected in the literature of the Middle Ages. Spenser's age was the Renaissance, the Age of Exploration and Discovery—of continents, the universe, and spiritual realms. People were marrying for love; even priests in the English Church and Protestant denominations were allowed—often encouraged—to marry. Along with these discoveries, went excitement and greater hopefulness regarding the possibilities of this world than expressed in the Middle Ages.

"Sharon, I love you—" I blurted, hoping that somehow my words would imprint the air and carry my intent for miles to her home.

I felt Tray's nose touching, ever so slightly, my neck. I reached to stroke her head. She dropped down beside me, laying her head heavily on my lap. She sighed. I was sorry that I'd so neglected her. I got her at a very bad patch in my life, shortly after my ex divorced me. Tray was an emotional replacement, something to love me unconditionally. But she suffered because I was such a wreck for years afterwards, made worse by having to move out of state for graduate studies and jumping through all the hoops getting my doctorate required of me.

"I'm sorry, Tray," I said, stroking her head. "You aren't nearly so unresponsive as I tend to think you are."

I lifted Tray onto the bed. Carefully I got in beside her and drifted into a netherworld of images and dreams.

Waking

It was nearly nine in the evening. Spet stuck his head into the cramped staff mail room. "Ted, could you please help me move an electric typewriter bolted to a table into my office? He pushed his wire frame glasses up on his nose with his right hand.

"Sure," I said. I put down the mail I'd been reading.

"You must have played football in high school."

"No," I answered. "I'm not very sports minded."

"Then you must have played in the band," Spet said. "To fit in, you small town kids always play sports or play in the band."

"I played trombone for years, but I dropped out in my sophomore year. However, I sang in choirs all the way through."

"I have a bad back," Spet said.

I wasn't sure why he told me that. Maybe he was trying to indicate why he didn't appear at all strapping in middle age, but skinny and bent, with a chest that tended to cave in.

During the awkward transit of the table and typewriter through the narrow hallways and into his office, Spet placed his hand over mine. "I'm glad you're here to help," he said.

I noticed a change in the sound of his voice. It seemed more hushed, darker in tone. The pressure of his hand was distinct. My hand grasped the edge of the table, so I'd thought it a mistake that Spet would soon realize and correct. But he made no attempt to remove his hand even when we got into his office.

Applying a little more pressure, Spet squeezed. The skin was soft but his grip was strong. "You're one of the most intelligent and talented people around," he said. It was unlike

Spet to be so complimentary. From the eye contact he was careful to make, and maintain, I guessed he was up to something. Usually Spet's eyes darted about, as if keeping careful watch on his surroundings.

"I plan to see that you get literature classes," Spet said, still keeping eye contact. "Just as I did this spring. Without all the grading that writing classes involve, you'll have more time for your own research and writing."

Spet gazed deeper into my eyes. I remembered the rumors that floated about his affairs with students, despite his marriage and young children. His secretaries exchanged looks when one of his "special friends" phoned. One told me they'd been ordered to put such calls through to Spet even if he was in conference with a Dean or even the President. Right after I was hired, one of my faculty friends hinted that Spet was not to be trusted. When I asked for details, she clammed up. Then she changed the subject. It occurred to me now that she was afraid of him.

A red flag was flying here too. I figured that I should have paid better attention to those warnings. Spet was my Chairman. I needed his endorsement and support, even more than those with tenure.

Perhaps if I made little of this incident, acting as if it had never occurred, Spet would be a gentleman and let it go.

Spet knew I wanted a permanent, tenure track teaching position. Surely he would remain supportive of me. Like him I was a scholar. The reality of my being in a very vulnerable position rang clearly again.

Spet finally let go of my hand. He broke eye contact. Casually he asked, "Are you going away for the summer?"

"I'd like to," I said, "but I can't afford to take time off. I have to work. I don't get the perks that go along with tenure track positions."

Looking down his nose, Spet reminded me, "You should have taken the University of Idaho position that I recommended you for."

"I just couldn't do it on so little notice," I told him. "Not long ago I bought a town home. My ministry, even if I don't get ordained, is an important aspect of who I am."

Spet scowled. He hated religion. Everyone knew that. By Spet's orders, the department secretaries were allowed no religious expression on the premises, even their desks.

"I'm hoping to get my ministry secured. To do it I have to become more involved at the Cathedral, not just on campus. That means I must spend more hours away from things I consider central." I did not tell him that I was not yet getting any money from McDougal, whose promises of a salary continued but produced nothing.

Spet looked away toward the shelves that lined the walls of his book-and-paper-strewn office, as if he were looking for a title. Like some other scholars that I'd come across, Spet could not separate moderate to liberal Christians from fundamentalists. We were all the same to him—narrow-minded, delusional hypocrites, always ready to impose our self-righteousness on others. He seemed totally unaware that his own extreme position negating religion was just as narrow.

If he sabotaged me, he could run me right out of my profession. He'd done it to others. I'd run into a few who told me pieces of their dark tales. All my years of preparation, all that money spent on getting my education, would be washed away because of one bad man.

"I'm sure you have to get home to your dog," Spet said, almost sneering.

Taken aback, I stuttered, "Yes, I do need to feed and walk her. And myself."

It Still Felt Personal

When I got the courage to phone Sharon, she refused to talk, hanging up on me without a word.

Teaching even my favorite authors quickly became a chore. "What a difference a day makes" kept coming into my mind—like a dirge twisted from its original, happy, context. "What a difference a day makes when you're sad and your heart is lying on the floor."

I wrote several letters to her to try to explain my behavior. I soft-pedaled questions about hers, hoping she might open up if I took most of the blame.

My stomach was still hard as a basketball, and sometimes I felt familiar contractions to the right of my navel. When they were strong, they caused me to feel like bending over in pain. When they became unbearable, I took Librax, an anti-anxiety drug with a smooth muscle relaxer for a spasming colon.

I didn't want things to happen the way they had. I was worse than ever about being able to perform. Not that I'd ever been good at it anyway. But my ability to trust had been damaged. I didn't know if I'd ever get over that.

Sharon had added shame and distress to a burdened past. I was sure that my ex-wife had done a good job initially with her guilting me into marrying her for taking her most precious commodity, her virginity, something I wasn't at all sure she possessed from all the sex talk she'd made. Like Sharon, she too had offered herself. But being the devout and good young man that I'd been, I prayed for forgiveness and soon found myself feeling love for her, then saying, "I do. I do."

After marriage, she once confessed, "If it isn't sinful, it isn't exciting." Yet, I'd destroyed her faith, according to her. Her parents loved to repeat that fact. Her family's Christianity seemed something they could take off and put on as the mood struck.

In some ways, Sharon's conflicted views toward the faith reiterated the necessity of working through such issues with one I wanted to love. Although we move away from the people manifesting them, the issues go with us.

Five weeks, and five letters, later, I still had no reply from Sharon. I'd hoped that showing my vulnerability might evoke some positive, nurturing response. In later letters I enclosed some of my poems. I hoped that, somehow, I could touch the right nerve, reopening some channel of communication between us. Even if we were not to become lovers, we could become friends, even distant ones.

When I finally got up the courage to phone, Sharon said, "Please, don't call me again or write."

I glanced at the copy of *Paradise Lost* on my desk. I reached to touch it. I had to transform my pain.

I visited St. Elizabeth's, where Sharon and I had met. I went inside and knelt before an altar. I lit a candle. Since the Virgin seemed somehow involved in this, at least standing there with her roses, heavenly flowers, in the background as a witness, I asked her to intercede on our behalf.

Sharon had once confessed that, before she'd left the church, she'd felt especially close to Mary. "I loved to pray the Rosary," she said. "Mary understands our humanity better than Jesus. After all, she was a mother. She was fully human, not God in the flesh, but God's chosen instrument, blessed among women." I knew this was a standard Catholic explanation for veneration of the Virgin, but it still felt personal.

I tried honestly to wish Sharon the best—to envision her happy and whole, surrounded by sweet scent and song. I could not bring myself to envision her with any other man.

Then I let her go. I envisioned her walking away and disappearing over the horizon.

When I rose, I decided to channel all returning emotions connected with Sharon into writing. I turned out some of my best work, "my holy scriptures," I began to call them. Sharon's muse had not failed.

> You took my hands—
> my palms are stained cerise,
> my fingers—the petals of a rose.

I sent the poem to a journal, where it was quickly accepted for publication.

In the Wind

Temperate spring coiled into the dry heat of summer.
Because we'd had no rain, unwatered grasses were turning
straw-like, a fire hazard ready to be ignited by the random
cigarette, unattended campfire, or lightning strike. Those who
could water had to attend to their gardens daily.

I'd decided to go into the university only to teach the one
course that had been available to me. I had to beg for that. It
gave me a couple thousand dollars. Now and then I checked
in at my ministry office. I was on call in case of emergency,
but little was happening. The Dean still had not managed to
find me any salary.

I spent more time tending the townhouse gardens. The
roses, especially the red ones, in the common area behind my
unit, looked as if a blow torch had been turned on them. I
planted more roses, carnations, and lilies, oriental and Asian.
I weeded and tended the gardens.

Gardening allowed me time to meditate, to center, to
keep anxiety at bay. Tray could be outside with me. I had her
hair cut short in a puppy cut so that I didn't have to worry
about brushing out knots every day. I kept her hair away from
her eyes by tying it back into a topknot with a rubber band.
She could see me, and I could see her eyes. They were nice
eyes, warm brown, and expressive.

Even when I thought I had suppressed all hopes of seeing
Sharon again, I found thoughts of her returning at the oddest
moments—as I pulled weeds or tended the garden, as I
stepped out of the shower, as I bent to feed Tray, even as I
stood on the front step turning the key in my lock.

As time passed I became convinced that I would see
Sharon again. She would smile and walk toward me through

what seemed a dark fog, open-armed, calling my name. We would embrace, knowing finally that we were meant for each other, our lives inextricably linked.

I continued to see this image—in fact it got stronger and came more often as the weeks passed through the summer.

I continued applying for suitable tenure track teaching positions as I heard about them. But jobs dwindled to nearly nothing as summer droned on. That was no surprise, since even last minute non-tenure track openings for the coming fall were hardly to be found. The big push would build for hiring at Christmas for the following year.

My doubts about Dean McDougal and the way he was managing things at the Cathedral did not go away. Every time I came into contact with him, he managed to implicate someone in some kind of questionable behavior. "You don't want to associate with him. They say he's infected," he told me, clucking his tongue. "He isn't going to be long for this world if he isn't careful about the company he keeps," he said about another, shaking his head as if saddened. And about someone else, "He won't be an elementary school teacher much longer. He takes too much interest in the boys." He winked and straightened his collar. His fingers looked like sausages.

One Sunday, McDougal gave a rousing sermon about the scourge of AIDS without ever saying the word, AIDS. He was always careful to skirt around being direct; nothing was spelled out. I could see that his method might seem good mannered, less shocking to those of dainty sensibilities than the bald truth, but to me it often seemed less than honest—often, downright devious.

Whenever I asked, McDougal promised to see that I'd get funding for the rent and supplies as well as a regular salary for my work, things that still hadn't happened. "I'm working on it," he'd say. I'd only received small contributions of a hundred or two or three hundred dollars now and then from a few parishes, mostly my old suburban one. From those moneys, I was expected to pay rent and it was never enough.

One night, McDougal caught me near the altar after a special service I'd attended. He looked me up and down with a hint of disapproval. "You need to get involved in the Cathedral ministries, not just your campus ministry. I require this of everyone," he said, "even if their ministries are off site. What Cathedral duties can you take up?" His eyes darted from wall to wall. Everyone else had rushed away. They wanted to get home.

McDougal's paranoid streak seemed stronger than usual. I wondered what had happened to make him even more fearful about who might be lurking.

The Dean probed my history for talents and experience.

"I sang in choirs all the way through high school and even into the first year of college," I said.

"You can join the choir. We can always use more men. All these nelly queens are so unreliable. What do you sing?

"Second tenor."

"You can also work on some sort of literary outreach, bringing in writers for conferences," he   added. "I want you to move your volunteer creative writers' group from the campus to the Cathedral. You can hold it in one of the impressive great rooms in the Cathedral proper."

"I thought the big rooms here were all booked with various activities," I said. I looked off at the rood screen to avoid his holding my gaze for long.

"They are," McDougal said. "The Diocesan offices are just across the parking lot. They don't have much going on over there. But we at the Cathedral envision a great gulf lying between us, like that between paradise and sheol," he remarked. I'd heard the same sentiment from the Choirmaster. Paradise, in their minds seemed to be the cathedral, and the place of the dead, the Diocesan offices.

"Are you dating?" McDougal asked,

"Well," I hemmed and hawed. "Sort of."

"What kinds of fun activities do you like?"

I drew a blank. I wondered if he wasn't getting ready to ask me on a date.

His wife breezed through.

He turned away. The conversation was over.

The next morning he phoned to ask me to lunch. "I'll treat you to my favorite—Tante Louise, a fancy French Restaurant on East Colfax."

I couldn't afford such indulgences, so I only vaguely knew of the place. I tried never to be tempted by things I couldn't have.

At Tante Louise, overly mannered waiters seated us and then gave us handwritten menus in French, without prices. I had no idea what to order, not because I couldn't understand the dishes, but because I always tried to order less expensive to moderately priced plates.

"Everything is very expensive, and very good," McDougal said.

After being served an aperitif that he ordered for us both, he smiled seductively. His voice warm, his manner unctuous, he said, "I don't desire that you want for anything."

I kept thinking how I was wanting the promised office expense money and a salary. Instead, my reply was more general. "I want you to make good on your promises," I said. Perhaps he would understand the less direct approach, just as he practiced. Maybe that would appeal to him.

By our third lunch, also at Tante Louise, I told McDougal, "I really am uncomfortable being taken to such expensive restaurants. There are many people right here in Denver who can't afford food."

"I assure you," McDougal began, "that you needn't worry your little head about it," he said. "I have discretionary funds to cover these treats. You must look at them that way, do you understand?" His eyes met mine. He tried to hold my eyes. He reached for my hand.

When he'd told me not to "worry my little head," I'd felt he was talking to me as a lecherous old man talks to an innocent woman he's planning to seduce in some eighteenth century novel. But, as he went on, I felt that I was being viewed as even less human, more like a dog in training. I moved my hand off the table and consciously looked away, breaking McDougal's gaze.

Although I wasn't getting any other benefits, I still felt guilty about such lunches. I saw so many people on the streets who lacked decent clothing, food, housing, and medical care. Some carried everything they had in bundles; some in backpacks. If a street person were lucky, he or she had all their possessions packed into a stolen grocery store cart. "I pass these people every day. Many people fail to recognize them as human beings," I said.

"Our Lord says the poor will always be with us," McDougal intoned. "We must remember such wisdom," he said, with a sigh. He ordered dessert wine and chocolate mouse for himself, knowing that I would resist such indulgences.

The Dean certainly did not seem to know much about the poor. After all, the Cathedral had paid his down-payment on a great, modern home with a circular drive and a four car garage in Cherry Hills. They saw that he and his family, consisting of wife, dog, cat, and several small children, had the best of everything. I doubted that he even *saw* the poor, even in passing. In his eyes, they were stick figures wearing rags.

I thanked McDougal for lunch, as before, but I kept my distance. I divulged as little personal information as possible. I remained vague about dating, love, and what I liked to do for fun.

I kept thinking, that, even though married, McDougal was hoping "to know me better," as he often put it, in ways to which I was not open. Regardless of his power, he did not attract me. That was probably part of my allure. He was not used to people who did not kneel before him.

Men in the choir gossiped that McDougal's wife, Mo, was mannish and naïve. They said he was "Collecting a stable of young men who could be counted on in times of need. There are plenty of them to go around," they tittered.

In Boulder, one of the tenured professors in the University of Colorado's English Department was said to have raped one of his women students. He'd been accused of it twice before, but he'd managed to get off the hook. He was a tenured, prominent scholar. He knew how to turn the blame upon some crazy female underling. She was merely making things up to get back at him, he had argued.

Since I had not been present, I didn't know the facts firsthand. But I had my suspicions. I'd heard the University was paying out hundreds of thousands in out-of-court settlements to stifle such cases. This was not, I was assured, an isolated occurrence. I wondered how long it would be before I heard that the church was doing the same.

Did the men who rose to the top think they were running sex clubs instead of churches and places of higher education? I thought about John Donne, in one of his more dubious similes, comparing the true church to a woman,

> Who is most true and pleasing to God then,
> When she is embraced and open to most men.

Clever yes, but it's smarmy, especially when you press the comparison toward the literal—where it wants to go. The Church is not, and was never meant to be, a prostitute, although I was all too aware that Jesus was right: the violent bear away the Kingdom of God. They did in his day. They still do.

I knew I couldn't go on this way, with everything up in the air, and so little money coming in. If I didn't get more income, I would lose my home.

Bread of Heaven

In August, I was invited to a party given by a former student, Laura Cameron. A middle-aged "wild woman," as she liked to refer to herself, Laura was married to a prominent surgeon in town. Laura and I shared the same Sagittarian birthday, and she always made a great deal of that, calling us twin souls, "born a few years apart." To have her in class certainly livened things up. Despite her joking, and often bizarre comments, she was reliable and intelligent, someone whom everyone warmed up to and trusted. They easily projected their maternal ideals onto her. Because of these qualities, I playfully asked Laura to "Take every course that I teach."

"Well darling," she said. "I'll see what I can do."

But I worried about accepting the invitation to her party. I didn't have the right car, the right clothes—or even a Gold Card. She promised, with a wink, that her guests were "fascinating people, including several eligible women about your age."

"Are they single?" I asked.

"Some. Some are," she answered with a wink. "I'm sure there will be eligible men there too, if you decide that's what you want." She changed her tone to one more maternal, and a little scolding. "You're far too picky, darling."

I parked my car in an obscure spot at the bottom of a hill a number of yards from the Cameron home. As I'd entered the development, I'd wondered if I'd have to pass Sharon's home. Fortunately, they lived on opposite ends of the development. I also did not have to pass McDougal of the Cathedral's house. All my ghosts seemed to live here.

With some foreboding, I trekked up to the Cameron grounds, walking the curved driveway past BMWs, Volvos, Saabs, Audis, a Rolls Royce—and one Mercedes. As I stepped up to Laura's door and rang the bell, I found myself meditating that the word *Mercedes* derives from "mercies"—more fully, "Mary of mercies."

I greeted the butler and stepped into the marble entryway. I felt like a classical statue in a modern art museum. I looked to see if Laura, like Sharon, had a Henry Moore statue displayed somewhere in the spacious foyer. I didn't spot one.

I caught sight of myself in a full mirror framed in heavy and intricately worked gold leaf. My best sports coat looked a little worn, especially about the elbows. At least my pants were nearly new, lint-free, and pressed.

Because the narcissism was making me nervous, I cut short my observations, making myself join the crowd back in one of the grand living areas. Several people were smoking cigarettes. A bong was being passed over on one side of the room, filling the air with the sweet heavy smoke. I saw that some were also passing a brandy snifter full of what I assumed to be cocaine. I'd never seen people snorting in real life, only in movies.

I made small talk with several guests. Trying not to think about my notion that Laura's friends were friendly but not people I'd be comfortable with for long, I glanced across the room toward the wall of windows facing the swimming pool. Just as I did, one of the sliding glass panels opened, and Sharon and Brad entered the room, hand in hand. I knew Brad from several photographs I'd seen around his house. They were smiling, although Sharon, upon closer examination, looked a little nervous, out of place. Sharon looked like a jewel: her flowing silk gown of emerald embroidered with intricate floral designs on the skirt emphasized her eyes and set off her auburn hair.

The woman next to me confirmed my suspicion with her assurance that they'd been "together for years, off and on, that is. Two light bulbs," she said. "Actually more like neon lights—neon signs."

I didn't like the comparisons. I stepped away from the woman before I heard more. Although I'd wanted to believe that Brad was just Sharon's roommate, as she'd told me, I knew now just how blind I'd been.

Brad was of moderate height—shorter than I by three or four inches—but of a similar husky muscular build. I wanted him to possess a square and determined jaw, or perhaps knotted and heavy brows beneath a low forehead—some feature that I could fix on and hate. But I couldn't find any terrible flaw in his demeanor. Despite his height, he looked fairly kind and intelligent. His eyes were clear, his face clean. He too was wearing a sports coat and dress pants, although probably not from a men's fashion outlet, like mine.

A woman was blocking my way. "Excuse me," I said. "I need to leave."

"Why would you want to go?" she asked, smiling. She was older, grey haired, wearing elaborate gold jewelry that looked custom made. She scanned my face. "You don't look well," she said. "You're a little green about the gills."

I confessed that I'd fallen for the woman who just walked in. "Her," I whispered. I nodded in Sharon's direction

"Oh you mean Sharon?" The woman moved in closer. She seemed interested in gaining information.

I nodded.

"By the way, I'm Lauren, as in Bacall," she said. She offered me some champagne from the bottle she was holding. Her hands were bejeweled with several rings set with huge diamonds and sapphires. "Here, this will put some color back in those cheeks. Be sure to try a couple lines of that," she added, pointing to a clay pot sitting on the counter. It was filled with little packets of what I assumed to be cocaine, although they might have been some other drug that I didn't know.

"Thanks, but I have better visions on my own," I replied, hoping that I didn't seem too judgmental.

"Brad and Sharon fight like cats and dogs," Lauren explained. "Sharon likes Brad's money. You know what he likes." She ran her fingers down the gold necklaces that followed the down-to-the-waist neckline of her gown.

My chest went leaden. "She told me that they were just roommates."

Lauren laughed. "Sharon's the type who says what people want to hear, especially when you're intelligent—and male." She smiled, all too smugly for my taste. "Brad isn't exactly Mr. Boy Scout either. Many people here have had affairs, some with each other." She paused. "I think you're rather naïve, aren't you?" she observed.

My stomach was spasming. If I had not taken a Librax an hour before the party began, I would have been bent over in pain

"Oh Ted, Ted Jones, how good to see you!" Sharon called. She'd spotted me from across the room. I didn't want to look at her—but my eyes trained on her voice. Brad seemed nowhere in sight.

Here, I realized, was the vision that I'd been having for months. While the room wasn't darkly foggy in a literal sense, it certainly was spiritually so.

Sharon rushed over, hands extended, smiling. She kissed me full on the mouth—as if nothing had ever gone awry.

"What's wrong?" she asked, realizing that I felt like a corpse. "You're as icy as the dead." I couldn't embrace her. "I'm dying—that's what's happening," I muttered.

"Relax, Ted. You feel like a body pulled from the morgue." Sharon refused to let me go.

"I know," I managed to say. I kept trying to pull away, but her mouth reawakened memory. I was imprinted by those kisses, the feel of her mouth and tongue, the taste of her saliva. I wanted more. My body cried out for all that I'd not enjoyed.

"Know what?" Sharon asked, her eyes searching my face. She seemed innocent, although nervous. I wondered what she was trying to hide, other than the fact that she wasn't single.

"That you have a lover!"

Sharon laughed. Not a cruel laugh, but an amused laugh—as if she'd just watched a puppy trip over his tail.

"Sharon, I never lied to you," I said. "Why didn't you tell me the truth?"

"You didn't ask the right questions," Sharon said, her nervousness visibly rising. She averted my gaze. Taking me by the arm, she turned and began to walk me outside. I figured she wanted to avoid a scene. Being the practiced seductress that she was, she knew how to turn things to her advantage.

Once outside, we moved away from the cars and people. We came to a halt before a waist-high brick wall, somewhere on the far grounds of the Cameron estate. No one so far had found their way out there.

Sharon asked me to help her up onto the wall.

Placing my hands about her waist I lifted as she jumped up.

"That's better," she said. Her face was now on the same level as mine. She pulled me close, her legs gathering me into the loose folds of her skirt, as her arms had earlier enfolded me.

"You said Brad was just your roommate," I replied, wanting desperately to be inside her.

"He is," she said, pulling me closer. "You know the necessity of appearances."

"I know the necessity of symbols," I corrected. I could feel her pulling my energy in. "You promised me that there wasn't any love between you two."

"There isn't," Sharon said, her voice leaden. "That's never been truer—now, more than ever."

Her hand found my zipper.

I realized I had an erection. "I wanted to die when I thought how I'd failed you," I said. "Don't you understand?"

"Ted, I'm bad in bed. Believe me," she said, her gaze earnest. "Do you want me to come over to your house and show you?" She unzipped my pants. She started to bend. I knew what she was about to do.

"Sharon, don't degrade yourself. I'm not good in bed either—that ought to be obvious. But we could learn together," I said, pleading, half-heartedly pushing her mouth away. "Practice helps. I love you. Do you love me?" I blurted, getting her head pulled high enough to let her bury it in my chest.

She held me tightly. Her tears wet my chest. "I love your poems," she whispered. "They're beautiful, too beautiful for me." For a moment her muscles relaxed, then stiffened again. "So are you."

I pulled away. I couldn't take any more. I stopped my ears. No more Siren's songs. With measured pace, I walked across the lawns and roads to my car. My body rang like a bell. Every bone in me rang that I had a lover. My mind said no, how could I have a lover when Sharon had Brad? But my bones, my bones —

Casting Your Bread

Three days after the Cameron party, Dan, one of my former students, phoned me at the office. It was mid-afternoon. He had just finished his Masters in Engineering at the University of Nebraska. Because he'd majored in English as an undergraduate, he'd had to spend a year and a half taking the prerequisites needed to get into the program. But he'd made it. He'd come to Denver for his first job. I'd taught him in a couple of classes several years ago when I was a graduate student.

We chatted. He remarked on the hot weather. He'd thought it was going to be cool, even in August, since we were a mile high.

"Yes, Dan, it snows most of the year, except for one week in July," I said. "Or so some people think." The heat had moderated a little with days now in the high eighties instead of the high nineties. The nights brought harbingers of fall, temperatures that dropped into the sixties and fifties.

I glanced out into the enclosed yard of the Franciscan friary below, wondering when Dan would drop in. He promised to do it soon. The chickens were clucking about, pecking for grubs and worms in the grass.

Shortly after I took office space in the St. Francis Center, I wrote a poem inspired by the place. I pulled it out to read it again:

Easter Morning

The bells of St. Elizabeth's ring out the hour:
the high voices, dedicated to certain saints,
ring first; the low, to sturdy others, take up the call

and bid us rise
and come away, away.

The rooster crowing in the friary yard
reminds us that we've strayed.
Here loveliness, like poppies, fades
and passes quite away.

Come, the bells of St. Elizabeth's say.
Eternity signals in every hour,
bids us climb, and ring
this bright and one, eternal day.

Although ever-cautious about placing too much stock in this world, I had been fairly optimistic about the possibilities of my life and my career at that time. The poem showed it, although it lacked the complexities of my better work.

I could probably get another poem out of the scene, maybe a story, something more literary and profound. To do so, however, I would, as Wordsworth formulated, have to experience strong emotions. Then I could recollect them in tranquility.

I laughed to myself. My life held only moments of tranquility, and I had to push to open up those.

"Hi," a familiar voice said. "Some office space you've got here. What a beautiful building."

I looked up from my desk to see a big, although rather embarrassed, smile stretching across Dan's face. He had appeared in my office doorway as if manifesting from air. "I didn't expect to see you so soon," I said.

"I was calling from the receptionist's phone," Dan said. He squinted, as if trying to see my face more clearly. "You must be getting a lot of sun," he said, commenting on my still rather sunburned demeanor.

I recognized Dan but barely. He had always been quite thin, the bones in his face and shoulders prominent. He was now filled out, muscular. He wore blue jeans and a royal blue polo top that matched the blue of his eyes. With dark, almost black, hair he was stunningly handsome.

I stood up to walk around my desk and greet him.

Dan reached to hug me to him.

He seemed a couple of inches taller than I'd remembered. My face was on the same level as his.

"I'm sure you've noticed that I've beefed up," Dan said, as if reading my mind.

"Have you grown in height too?" I asked.

"Yeah, I seemed to have experienced a spurt of growth soon after I got my B.A," Dan exclaimed. "In every way."

"You look healthy, happy, and handsome," I remarked. "How's that for heaping on the alliteration?"

"I'm working out daily and eating well—lots of fresh fruits and vegetables and whole grains, no red meat." Dan paused. "And, I'm not so oppressed as I used to be. I've come into a stronger sense of self."

I gave him a quizzical look, waiting for more.   I wasn't one to jump to conclusions. Letting things unfold was my preferred way of being.

Dan laughed. "I'm free, free, at last," he exclaimed, taking a deep breath, as if expanding into the room.

The extra height and mass suited him, both inside and out.

Dan told me where he was going to work, but it didn't mean a lot to me. A large engineering firm downtown. He was staying with friends while he looked for a place to live.

"Do you want to have dinner?" he asked. "I have money now."

"Well, that's good. More than I can say about myself," I remarked. "How'd you manage that?" I asked. "You just graduated."

"Selling my body," Dan answered.

For a moment, I paused to wonder. He certainly could be telling the truth. Then I shook my head. That wasn't Dan. He was highly ethical. "But one never knows with today's college students. Buying and selling, we lay waste our powers."

Dan laughed. "Oh yes, Wordsworth. Nice sonnet. Had any strong emotions lately?"

"I was just thinking that I needed to look for some—ones that I could recollect in tranquility."

"Give them time," Dan said. "I can't imagine you without passion."

"Oh, I've got passion, but it seems I'm always in tumult." Always curious, I returned to the previous subject. "Maybe you should tell me more about selling your body."

"Women drool over me. They never used to. Often men do too," he said, and paused. He gave me a quizzical look.

I wondered if I'd been staring at him myself. If I had, I'd not been aware of it. "Some men drool over me too," I said. "But in my case I can't figure out why. Besides, they're always the wrong kind." I laughed.

"I caught a little spark in your eye," Dan said, moving closer. He put his face up close to mine.

His intelligence and sense of play engaged me. I often found him reminding me of my younger self. I wondered what would come next. I was being teased, and that was fine, but I felt my foot near the brake, just in case.   "I've never had an affair with a student," I added. "Not even a former one."

"I believe you," Dan said. "But you must have been tempted." He paused. "Remember when I told you that if you'd been a girl I would have kissed you?"

"Yes, vaguely," I said, recalling that he'd had too much to drink when he said so.

"I wanted to kiss you, right there, right then, no matter who saw. You were my ideal."

I laughed, a little nervously. "Right, some green graduate student trying to teach those only a few years younger than himself the profundities of literature and life."

"We were on the same wavelength," Dan remarked. "That doesn't happen often."

"I know." Dan's energy was strong and sexual, I realized. "One woman I dated told me I was her standard. Just before she announced that she was getting married."

"To someone else?"

"Yes, you've got to be a real poodle to fall for that one." Dan laughed. I wondered if he was going to pant.

"To get involved with a student is a dangerous move, even if the student is willing. It puts both the student and the professor in jeopardy. The dynamics change."

"You might even seesaw back and forth in the struggle," Dan added, playfully. He continued his game. He moved to the window to look down at the chickens in the friary yard. "I hope they aren't frying chickens," he said.

It took me a moment. "No, they're friary chickens." I laughed. "I'd forgot how quick your mind is, able to pun without the reference being obvious."

"Sharpened by a Master," Dan replied.

"Getting back to the subject of a professor getting involved with a student," I began. I felt we needed to clarify the issue. "If you have a falling out, someone is bound to get hurt. More than in a relationship between equals."

"Is there really such a thing?" Dan asked.

"I admit that's a good question."

"Well, that's why I never kissed you," Dan added.

"That's also why I didn't let you," I said. I laughed.

"I'm taking you for dinner," he announced, ordering me to gather up my things and follow. "It's five, and I'm starving."

I insisted we go Dutch. I gladly would have paid, but because my own financial situation was still not secure I thought better of it. It seemed that Dan had indeed managed to save some money.

While waiting for a table at Zach's, a Fern Bar located several blocks east of the Capital, Dan remarked, "To tell the truth, I rather enjoy being a sex object. In the past, I never considered myself attractive. I was raised not to give much thought to my body," he said. "It's sinful, or potentially so," he reminded me. "In Adam's sin, sinned we all," he reminded me. "Strict Calvinist that I was."

"It was only after the Fall that sex became selfish and destructive, devouring," I said. "That's what Augustine, whom Calvinists distorted a bit, actually said. Milton follows suit. He shows that Adam and Eve's sex life was full and fulfilling before the Fall, the envy even of angels, who can step inside each other at will, their spirits blending. Angels enjoy a higher form of what humans are always searching for." I paused, watching Dan's reaction. He moved his feet and shifted his weight almost imperceptibly.

"I knew that would get you going," Dan teased. He flexed a little seductively. His strong sexuality had always struck me as innocent. Now, I was not so sure.

"Some minds are also tempting," I countered. "Some hearts as well."

"You always liked mine," Dan replied, his meaning ambiguous. As the host led us to our table, Dan whispered, "What about you?"

I explained that a few people seemed to respond to me once I'd hit my late twenties. "Before that they were few and far between. Unfortunately, it's usually the wrong people—involved women and married men."

"You too?" Dan remarked, with a laugh. He confessed that the same types seemed inordinately attracted to him. "I can never figure out why."

"Our magnetism draws them, and we're perceived as safe. I guess," I added. "The whole issue of peoples' sexuality, or at least how they act it out, puzzles me."

"Leaning over the table, ferns of various sorts drooping above and on every side of us, Dan said, "To be truthful—much as I like the attention—I wish they'd look to someone else for their experiments."

"I know what you mean."

"I've never been involved with someone who was married, and I don't intend to start," Dan said. "Are you still single?"

I laughed. I thought about Sharon. I still wanted her, but every bone in me said she was too screwed up.

"I guess that answers my question. I'm single too," Dan said.

We ordered our food, a huge plate of nachos with grilled chicken, black beans, and salsa to share, and returned to mundane topics.

"I was surprised that I didn't have a harder time getting my first job," Dan said. He commented on the trend to hire women and minorities over white males.

"I not sure what I think about that. I certainly believe in equal opportunity and believe that balance in everything, both outside us and inside, is essential."

"But look at how much trouble you've had getting a tenure track position," Dan remarked. "Some of that must be because you're white and male."

"Probably," I said. "As well as not holding a Ph.D. from an Ivy League, or a major state university. My Dissertation Director's connections were lost because of her alcoholism. The job market was depressed when I completed my doctorate." I strung out the possibilities. "I've hoped my publications, including a book that a major university press has expressed interest in, would offset those weaknesses."

"You do traditional studies, not trendy work," Dan said. "That makes you one of those dreaded dead white males, or at least a proponent of them," Dan observed. "I hear that the non-tenure track teachers have asked you to represent them to the rest of the department."

I nodded. "I know I'm putting my academic career further on the line by agreeing to represent non-tenure track faculty. Those with the power, the tenured, don't like to share it. It suits them to have slaves who teach the required courses and for only a pittance. That preserves the goodies—the upper level courses and most of the salary pot—for them. But the non-tenured people, mostly women, by the way, asked. And I agreed," I said. I gulped down a cheese-covered chip. "I've been working for years to integrate my intellect with my life, to take a holistic approach to all. Seeing clearly calls for action, which is probably the biggest reason so many people prefer to wear blinders."

"What will you do if you get shut completely out of academia?" Dan asked.

The idea brought chills. I shrugged. "I'll be out on the streets."

"Not with me around," Dan said. He winked.

"That may be happening anyway." I took a deep breath. I didn't like to think about the possibilities of losing everything. "I guess I'll have to find yet another career, or two," I said. "And not as a street walker."

"I told you, I'll be your superman." Dan laughed.

I laughed but didn't pick up on his lead. "I can't imagine a life that isn't centered on teaching literature and writing. Worse, would be a life without integrity."

"Here, have a nacho," Dan ordered, sticking a mound of cheese, chicken and bean covered chip in my mouth. "They're getting cold."

I chewed but began to talk before I'd completely swallowed. "According to Aristotle, you only possess a virtue when you have been tested in ways that demonstrate that virtue, and passed." I began to choke.

"See what all that theory does," Dan said. He whacked me on the back.

I felt something dislodge from my windpipe. "Until then, it remains potential." An image of Sharon flashed on my mind. I saw her opening her door to greet me. She smiled. She was wearing her elegant black gown, the string of pearls caressing her breasts.

"I'm surprised you didn't ask where I heard about your career dilemmas," Dan said. After a short pause to sip some water, he confessed to feeling guilty for being deceptive. Blushing, he said, "Father Norbert told me. He thinks you're wonderfully idealistic and project a strong, innocent sexuality that the unbalanced misread."

I laughed. "Is that the reason?"

"You never run away when someone needs to take a stand. He likes those qualities, but he worries about the consequences. Moses never made it to the promised land."

"That was left to Joshua," I said. "My ministry team colleague Viv says I'm like a rat terrier," I said turning the serious edge toward humor. "I see a rodent, start yapping and nipping. I don't give up till I've grabbed 'em." I yipped once, bared my teeth and growled, just for the effect. I found myself in high spirits, even without alcohol. I felt embarrassed.

"Good thing we didn't order any drinks," Dan said. "You'd be dancing on the tables."

I calmed down, becoming somewhat rational again. "I really don't believe Viv, however, because, my body just doesn't fit a rat terrier's. But all of us frame our discourse according to our experience, as Viv likes to point out."

"I think Father Norbert's right," Dan said. "Those who run the world do so by taking advantage of people. They know the right words, but you can be sure they have every intention of keeping those under their thumbs voiceless and without power."

I nodded. "The violent still bear away the Kingdom of God," I remarked. "Flannery O'Connor was right."

"So was Jesus," Dan wryly commented, remembering the one whom O'Connor had quoted. "You pointed that out way back when you taught me. I've also heard it as, 'people still try to seize the Kingdom by force.'"

"That too," I said. "The metaphor goes backwards and forwards in time. That is the Christian way of handling significant events. They read all by the light of Christ. He makes all things meaningful—and present—in him."

"I can see you've really been delving into that theory," Dan said.

I nodded. "That's expected."

Dan looked me directly in the eyes. "You have no contractual protections from those who would hurt you. You've only been at the university for a little over a year," he said. "They can dump you as easily as they dump the food they ate last night."

I nodded. "But I consider myself to be following a higher calling, urged upon people of faith. I'm walking on eggshells, both in my teaching and my ministry."

"That Dean of the Cathedral sounds like a wild man," Dan said. He sipped water. "I heard about him too. Father Norbert kept trying to pull your receptionist away from the edge of telling all, but she couldn't hold back. She told me lots about him."

"Months after agreeing to all but one of McDougal of the Cathedral's demands, I'm still without funding. The Cathedral finally caught up on my ministry office rent, which is only fifty dollars per month. Nothing."

Dan shook his head.

"I still haven't seen one cent of the pledge money promised to me by my old professor and a few other supporters at the Cathedral—lost, I figure, to McDougal's discretionary allowance. Thousands of dollars are rumored to be spent on dessert wines and fancy gifts for himself and special friends."

"I'll bet they're special, all right," Dan said.

"Lately, McDougal is preaching with more than a little audacity that people must watch what people do instead of what they say. 'We shall know them by their fruits,' he said last Sunday, quoting scripture—a commentary that evoked tittering in the choir. Many of us had to cover our mouths and turn away from facing the congregation to hide what threatened to become hysterical laugher."

"Does that man really have any idea what he's confessing?" Dan asked, almost choking on some guacamole.

"Or is he hiding the purloined letter in plain sight, knowing that most people will never see it there?" I said.

Dan asked why I couldn't get ordained and become a full time chaplain somewhere.

"After being at the Cathedral, I'm less and less sure that I want to join that club."

"It seems remarkably stupid that the Diocese has stopped funding campus chaplaincies," Dan said, shaking his head.

"The Diocese has decided that since students cannot pay their own way, as individual parishes can, campus ministries are not worth funding."

"If the church loses its youth," Dan said, "who will later join local parishes and foot the bills?"

I nodded. "I get the idea that the church believes they'll come back to the parishes later, whether they've been ministered to or not. Because of some sort of miracle," I added. "Like Balaam's ass."

"I've heard some asses make a lot of noise," Dan said.

"Seems like many are attracted to the Cathedral," I said.

"Instead of joining the Episcopal Church, they'll flock to the evangelical churches."

"They're the only denominations growing, while the rest of us wither on the vine. Easy answers, big promises for material wealth and miracles on earth—and even bigger rewards in heaven. All without much sacrifice," I said. "Never mind that these are not the teachings of Jesus or the prophets. Like Bonhoeffer, the true Church argues that grace is not cheap. Faith can never be separated from works."

"If you have faith, your life shows it," Dan agreed. Dan told me that he'd joined the United Church of Christ. "Because they're still Christian, but they've stepped into the twentieth century on social issues. Few other denominations seem able to get their acts together and remain true to historical Christianity."

"I would be more apt to become a Quaker," I added.

"Hardly anyone nowadays knows much about them."

"They were more visible during the War in Vietnam. Everyone knew who the Society of Friends were then, even Dick Nixon," I said. "Dick was a Quaker by heritage, although he managed to go against every sacred principle on which they stood."

"He was a real Dick," Dan laughed. "Maybe we'll have to have another Vietnam, or worse—some sort of debacle—

to wake people up." Dan remarked, "Eating all that cheese and guacamole with salsa and corn chips was a sensual experience."

I laughed, and shook my head. "Am I responsible? Did I teach you this? Tricky Dick and sensuality following on the heels of each another. The logic seems skewed, the signs contradictory, at least at first glance."

"You made me infinitely, or is it infinitesimally, aware of the rich symbolic layers of everything we say and do," Dan remarked. "Tonight's dinner was layered, like everything I share with you."

"I wonder if such signs can be deconstructed," I mused.

"Traditional sign theory does not date deconstruction," Dan replied.

"How'd you know that?" I asked.

"I recall it from the days of yore," he said.

"I didn't know I talked about that then."

Dan placed his hand on mine. "You'd be surprised what we talked about."

"That makes me worry," I said, feeling an electric charge passing through my hand and arm. "But, as Freud says, sometimes a cigar's just a cigar."

"Oh, English teachers," Dan intoned.

"We all should be taken out and hung." I laughed.

"Don't they do that under oppressive regimes?"

"Intellectuals are the first to go," I remarked. "We're dangerous. We expect people to read and use proper grammar and syntax, and, most of all, to possess a pleasing style." I ended this also-skewed comment with a laugh. I wanted to make sure Dan realized that I was meaning not to hit on the qualities of a true intellectual at all.

"I was just thinking that maybe I should join the Cathedral choir with you," Dan said. His ironic tone made his words seem tongue in cheek, although I was not certain. "According to Louise, I can really check things out," he said, and laughed. He winked. The St. Francis Center secretary Louise had evidently tempted him by promising that the

Cathedral was "a colorful place, full of high drama and intrigue."

"I can't believe how much Father Norbert and Louise managed to tell you in a short space of time," I said.

"I'm like a reporter," Dan said. "I know how to get the scoop."

I nodded. "You'll have to be prepared to give five or six hours per week of your time, on average, for choir practice on Thursday nights, for church services on Sunday morning, and for concerts, not to mention special practices," I warned him. "And, if you are chosen to sing solos, you can be sure you'll need to give even more of your time."

"Like blood."

"Spiritual vampirism is the idea," I said. "But the soloists are paid. They're professionals."

"You're trying to locate some writers to bring in for the Arts Festival in the spring?" Dan asked. "All this on a volunteer basis?"

"I had the promise of being put on the payroll right away." I was certain Dan would hear the hollowness that had crept into my voice.

He said nothing.

I thought about telling him that I'd also started a Writers' Group that met monthly at the Cathedral, but I could not bring myself to tell him more. This was but another way that I was spreading myself thin, taking on too many responsibilities, trying to help everybody, do everything, write, teach, do research, minister, counsel, sing in the choir, represent non-tenure track faculty, get writers in for the Arts Festival--all without proper pay for my efforts, by either the university or the church.

I couldn't even love. That too was denied me. I imagined myself groping for Ariadne's saving thread. But my hands turned up empty. I couldn't see a thing. I could only sense the Minotaur hiding at every turn.

Something had to change.

Marriages

"I figured Dan would provide some good distraction," the St. Francis Center Receptionist, Louise, remarked. She winked.

"Dan's just a friend," I said, hoping to steer Louise in the right direction. "A good friend, but there's nothing more."

"Well, you're more centered with him around," Louise said. "It's good you haven't seen Sharon for weeks now. She wasn't the one for you. She kept you in turmoil all the time."

"So do all the tasks I find myself straddled with."

"You took them on," Louise reminded me.

"Yes, because I'm trying to better myself professionally," I said, "with both the church and the state." I tried to clear the early snow from my coat before I walked further into the building. I'd just driven back from the Cathedral in a sudden blizzard that had barreled down from the arctic into Canada, into the mountains over to Denver, and spread out onto the Plains. So much for my chrysanthemums and roses, which were at the height of another cycle of bloom in mid-October. The snow was so heavy and wet that still fully leafed branches were broken and down everywhere—on lawns, streets, power lines, and houses and garages. Because the weather had been so mild, the trees and bushes had only begun to change colors, so the damage to the vegetation was great.

"You've also got quite a Savior of the World thing going on," Louise said.

"I don't need more turmoil in my life. You're right about that. Both of my careers provide plenty. Rather, the people in power do." I'd just had another "discussion" with McDougal. I was not having any luck getting nationally known writers to agree to come to the Cathedral for the Spring Arts Festival. I did not think that five hundred dollars with housing and round trip plane fare was tempting. He assured me that I could do it. All I had to do was be more convincing. "Tempt them with the mountains. If they have any religious commitment, and they should, remind them of their obligations to the Christian faith—or humanity, if they're Jews or something else."

"I have a hard time being convincing when I'm not sure what they'll face when they arrive. Will you fail to come through with reimbursements, just as you've failed to fund my ministry?"

"I've told you," McDougal responded, "I'm working on that." A handsome new parishioner caught his eye. "I've got to go introduce myself to him," McDougal gasped, scurrying off.

"You were telling me about the Arts Festival," Louise reminded me.

"Oh, sorry," I said. I forgot that I'd brought it up. "We might have to deal with area writers."

"That wouldn't be so bad," she said. "You could showcase yourself."

I snorted. I laughed and turned to walk back to my office. I looked at my calendar. I'd forgotten that I had an appointment with Spet. If I hurried and managed not to slip on the ice, I'd be only a few minutes late.

"He's expecting you," Jill, the departmental secretary said.

I rushed to Spet's office. "You're seven minutes late," he said, looking at his watch. He stood at the door, as if ready to leave for something more important than myself. "Because of a worsening budget crisis, your Advanced Writing course this spring will have thirty-seven students, some of whom will not have met the prerequisites."

"I can hardly wait," I said. Only a year before, no writing course had more than sixteen students. In the spring, writing courses had been bumped to eighteen. Over the summer, they'd jumped to twenty-two. I was given two writing courses that fall, not one literature course. To be assigned writing courses in the spring, at least one of which would have thirty seven students, was outrageous. I was being punished because Spet thought I'd rejected him. Before that night, he'd said he was going to help me, was going to see that I had more time to research and write. He was going to give me literature courses, which I loved teaching far more than writing courses.

"Don't count on getting any more literature courses," Spet added, staring down his nose to look over his glasses at me. "You'll be lucky if you get a Writing 102 for your second class," he added. "You may only get basic writing. In fact, you may get only one course in the spring." He turned and picked up a book. "Are you looking into another career?" he asked, ominously. He moved back into his office and sat down at his desk.

I thought he wanted me to sit down. Instead, he ignored me. He picked up the phone and dialed. Soon he began to talk with someone as if I weren't there.

Clearly, I'd been dismissed.

The cold wind outdoors bit my face. I pulled my jacket close and shivered. I couldn't remember winter weather that rushed in more ominously. It had been a year of extremes, both internally and externally.

As I passed the friary, I glanced down at the snow blowing and gathering in heaps against walls of the chicken yard. I wondered what the poor chickens did in such weather. How did the priests protect, feed, and water them?

I didn't have much time to ponder the question. I just couldn't keep up with everything.

I had to see a counselee who would be waiting for me. He was having faith issues, wanted to believe but having a hard time.

I had another after that. She was new. From our phone conversation, she seemed to be having relationship problems.

The last counselee, named Mary, was the worst off. She'd been molested by her father. I'd seen her a few times already.

"Are you sure you don't want to see someone with more training than I?" I asked. "I'm no expert."

"No, she answered. "You're the only one I trust with such information. I've kept it a secret for forty years, and it's ruined all my intimate relations." After her third divorce, she'd finally come back to school to finish the degree that she'd begun a few times before. She looked off in the distance, as if trying not to feel any pain. Her troubled brow, eyes, and mouth told a different story. "But it's interfering with my ability to concentrate. I can't turn on the TV without hearing about someone's incest, or pick up a magazine without reading about it."

Finally, I locked up my office. All my colleagues had left a couple of hours before.

At seven, I arrived at home, and fed Tray. I heated some baked chicken and scalloped corn in the oven, and then took Tray for a walk in front of the building. It was too cold to stay out long. I worried about her paws getting frostbite.

I graded papers the rest of the evening and managed to do some reading for class.

At one in the morning, I stood at the sink upstairs. I was finally ready to try to get some sleep. My doorbell rang. I wondered who in the world would be ringing so late and in such weather. The roads were slick. The sidewalks were treacherous. The temperature had hit fifteen degrees during day, and it was zero by midnight.

I hesitated, wondering if someone hadn't come to my door by mistake. Maybe it was a prank. In my neighborhood kids sometimes rang a doorbell and ran off. Drunks wandering through the neighborhood sometimes stumbled to someone's door and hoped to be let in. Given the weather, that seemed most likely.

The person at my door laid into the bell, ringing and ringing again, insistently.

I pulled the curtain to the side and looked out the window. I could only see the shadow of someone cast in the snow by the porch light.

The ringer was persistent. I heard what sounded like crying, but too muffled, too distant to make out clearly. I still could not get a look at the person directly. I wished he or she would step back so I could get some notion who was standing there.

Troubled, I walked downstairs, with Tray following.

By the time I yanked the frozen door open, I found no one there.

Tray indicated that she needed to take a walk. She was right. I'd forgotten that she needed to empty her bladder before she slept. Wearing my pajamas, I bundled up, put on my snow boots, and grabbed her leash.

Outside, I wondered if we would see a drunk at another door down the street ringing and calling to get in. That would ease my mind.

Tray didn't manage to do anything, so we walked further down the street. I had to be careful. I wasn't good on ice, and it was slippery. Tray wanted to walk around the corner. There she found something that smelled interesting. She was able to squat and relieve herself.

I turned and headed back. Just as Tray and I turned the corner to return to the house, I noticed someone standing at my front door again. It looked like one of my neighbor's girlfriends. Every now and then one of a string of them—drunk, or high—would ring my doorbell, thinking that it was Sam's.

By the time Tray and I got there, the woman had gone. I saw her walking to her car several houses down and across the street. To my surprise, she was able to move fairly quickly.

As the car passed, I realized in the light of the streetlamp that underneath a cover of snow was the green BMW that I knew well.

I called out "Sharon!" I waved—and called—but to no avail.

She drove on, the exhaust billowing clouds of vapor behind her. For several minutes I stood shivering in the arctic air, thinking perhaps she'd turn around.

Not knowing whether I should phone her—since Brad might be around—I decided to drop her a note composed in the early hours of that day. I could not sleep. I worried about her. "No matter how angry I was, no matter how hurt, I will always love you and wish you well," I wrote. "I thought I had to let you go." I did not say anything about my botching her attempt to visit. I hoped she'd tell me what was wrong without my prying it from her.

A few nights later, I woke about two a.m. I had been fast asleep. Tray was stretched out on the floor beside the bed, still fast asleep. Someone was standing in the bedroom doorway. It was Sharon—rather, the spirit of Sharon. She was crying, shaking like a frightened rabbit.

I wondered what was going on. And what to do. I had no idea how to proceed, since I hadn't experienced anything like this before. Finally, I decided to lift the blankets and try inviting Sharon's spirit into my bed. I knew it was Sharon. I had no doubt about it.

For a few moments Sharon hesitated, but she nodded, and crawled in. I held her. Clearly there was a presence, less substantial than flesh, but nonetheless present. I felt her. Some time around dawn, she disappeared.

From that night forward, each night for the next week or so, Sharon's spirit would return, just as that night. Strangely, the incarnate person never answered my letters. I sent her several notes, trying to ascertain what was happening.

When I finally got up the nerve to phone, I got a, "Sorry I'm not able to take your call" recording on her answering machine. No message that I left was ever returned. Yet several more times in the early morning hours of the following weeks, more sporadically, her spirit appeared in my doorway and got into my bed. She was always silent, shivering.

It had not occurred to me to try talking with her spirit. I later wondered if she could have—would have—replied if I had.

Worn Out

Term exhaustion was setting in much earlier than usual. It was caused by diligently grading papers and exams and preparing for classes, coupled with extra practices and services that Cathedral choir members were required to attend.

Special concerts were to start at Thanksgiving and go through Christmas Eve, Christmas Day, the Twelve Days of Christmas, New Year's Eve, and New Year's Day, stretching through the other holidays in the spring. Fortunately, many of the same pieces would be performed at each. Still, we had to know them all, each and every one.

By then, I was sure that I needed to let the search for national writers go. I didn't have the funds or the pull to bring them in. We needed to invite area writers to the Arts Festival instead. Locals seemed glad to participate. Regional exposure never hurt anyone. I would read from my own poetry during one of the sessions, another item that I could add to my resume.

But my stress was making itself known. Not a day or night went by that I didn't take a Librax every eight hours. Even then, a dull ache just to the right of my navel never left me.

At the end of October, we experienced a break in the weather—a welcome, sunny and crisp clearing from the winter which we had been experiencing for a couple of weeks. Suddenly, the sparrows were flitting about on the sills outside the windows and chirping again.

Fully embodied, Sharon showed up on my doorstep during the noon hour. I was home, grading papers because I could concentrate with few interruptions there. I invited her in. She looked pale, tired, and she'd lost quite a bit of weight.

I took her coat, asking if she would like a glass of wine, coffee, or something to eat. I didn't have anything special around, but she was welcome to what I had.

Stooping down to pet Tray, she declined. Then she sat on the couch beside me and said, "I just got out of the hospital."

"I hope it wasn't something serious," I said.

"I was in rehab," she said. "Cocaine. Everyone thought I was going to die. It was bad," she said, "really bad." She lifted both sleeves of her dress to reveal needle tracks going up and down her inner arms. Her pale skin was still black and blue.

"You shoot up?" I cried. I saw her wince when I spoke of it in the present tense. "Shot up," I corrected. My voice was loud, I knew. I tried to turn down the volume. "Are you crazy?" I asked. My colon began to spasm, just as it did when I was really stressed. Every conscientious person was afraid of getting AIDS; we'd heard how it was transmitted through sexual intercourse and intravenous drug use.

"Do you want to die?" I asked, unable to keep my mouth shut. I could imagine Sharon dying in such a grisly manner, still shooting up as her body wasted away, her hair fell out, and Kaposi's blotches spread over her arms and legs. The clenching of my gut made me double over.

"Sometimes," she said, without facial expression. "I did—I did want to die and be over the pain."

Jesus, I loved her. I had before God promised that I would give my life as a ransom, a ram for Isaac, if it would do any good—if I could release her. At that moment, I silently reiterated that promise, never meaning it more. I told her, "I promised to give my life for yours," I said. "I made a solemn vow before God."

Sharon nodded, her eyes full of tears. "I know. I heard you in my spirit," she said. "Take me to the bed where we've been sleeping." She reached out and touched my face, tenuously. Her hands were cold. She leaned over to kiss me gently on the forehead. She placed her hands on my chest. "I cannot always tell the difference between hallucinations and reality. My psychiatrist has been trying to help me sort it out. He's not closed to paranormal experiences, but he wants to be certain it isn't something else." She paused, looking down at the floor. "When I am in really bad shape, I leave my body. I've been doing it since childhood. I'm sure of that. This time, I came to you. I know it as well as I know my name."

I froze, thinking of Brad—thinking of AIDS.

Sharon nodded. "Please, Ted, love me." She scanned my face. "I'm not infected. At least nothing has shown up in all the blood tests so far. You alone understand me. You've proven that."

I could not answer. I held her, there on the couch in my living room, and rocked, and rocked, and rocked. But I could not take her to bed. It was obvious that she knew as well as I that we'd spent several nights there, my body and spirit with her spirit.

She whispered, "I don't trust people."

I said, "I don't easily give my trust either."

She said her psychiatrist had read my poems and notes to her. "He told me he'd always wished for someone who could love as deeply and truly as you." She paused. "He's never found that person." She glanced off into space. Telling me this was hard for her. She wasn't used to being so vulnerable. "He urged me to stay near you. He tended to believe that my so-called out of the body experiences were some sort of projection of myself, rather than actual experiences of my soul leaving my body. But," he added, "observation, and time, will tell."

I was silent. Words failed me.

"I need to go," Sharon said. She got up.

I followed. I took her hand. "I don't want you to leave," I said, finding my voice, "not now, not ever." I held her hand for as long as possible before she pulled away and hurried down the front steps to her car.

Ice Cream

One warm and starry evening Dan stopped by unannounced. He brought a quart of mixed gelati flavors from a
new gelateria that had opened in Cherry Creek. "I've been
thinking about all those 'empires of ice cream.' I think we
ought to eat some of them up."

He made me laugh.

"Food therapy," I remarked. I invited Dan in.
"Everything begins on the spiritual and symbolic level," I
said.

I offered to get out bowls and spoons, but Dan said, "It'd
be more fun to eat it right out of the container. I don't think
you have any germs that will hurt me," he added.

"But you might have some that would hurt me."

"I also doubt that," Dan responded. "I'm never in close
contact with anyone."

"Still virginal," I commented.

Dan nodded. He never would tell me if he was a virgin or
just virginal. So I took the safer route and referred to him as
virginal. The reality was really none of my business. If Dan
wanted to tell me, he would.

I was not one of those moderns who thought that youths
ought to run out and have sex just for the experience. In my
youth I read all the *Playboy* advice about doing it if it felt
good and hurt no one. But my own experiences along that
line had left lasting scars. When you're young and naïve,
you're apt to take things very seriously, especially sex. After
you get broken in, in every sense, you may no longer care.

"When you're ready," I advised, "you can proceed." I
never went to the opposite extreme to say that people had to

be married to have sex. But both of parties did need to be mature enough to handle the emotional ties that often result.

"I've been doing some soul-searching since I left Denver," Dan said. "I'm learning to accept myself."

"I would have sworn that you'd passed that test with flying colors," I teased. "For some people such a statement, however, is rationalization for bad behavior. I can't imagine that you've got too much to accept,"

Dan raised his eyebrows slightly. "Well, you must know what I mean," he said. He swallowed a spoonful of pomegranate gelato. "Mmm, just right."

I shrugged.

Dan stuck a spoonful of pomegranate gelato in my mouth.

"Well, you've known me for several years now and you never guessed?" he asked. Dan paused, his voice lowering. "Didn't you wonder why I'd never had sex?"

I was beginning to think that he was going to tell me he had some physical problem. "You used to be awfully bony, but that's never put off anyone before, not that I know of."

Dan laughed. "I'm coming out of the closet. You never guessed I was gay?"

"Oh," I said. It didn't surprise me, but I'd not really worried about it. People make too much of sex—at least in this country. "When you specialize in literature, and you do a lot of counseling, you realize that sexuality is best characterized as a spectrum. Hardly anyone is fully gay, or fully straight," I said. "Although people usually tend toward one or the other end of the spectrum, a significant number find themselves somewhere in between, at least over an entire lifetime."

"Well, I always knew, but I couldn't admit it," Dan said. "I was afraid of going to hell, I think. I felt like I was defective."

"The whole point of redemption is owning our defects—faults, weaknesses, whatever we term them—so they can teach us. Learning from them, we move toward wholeness."

"I remember you told us that the word *holiness* shares the same root as *wholeness*," Dan laughed. "You often reminded us of that."

"You can never get too much of the truth," I laughed.

"You're not going to reject me then?" Dan asked. "Many of my old friends, and most of my family, have shunned me. They're strict Presbyterians."

"Why would you think I'd do the same?" I asked.

"When I suspect that others are not fully straight themselves, they prove all the more rejecting," he replied.

I nodded, knowing all too well what he meant. I thought he knew me well enough to know that I wouldn't reject him to try to cover my own sexuality issues.

"I haven't had sex yet, but I've wanted to," Dan said. "Isn't lusting after someone the same as having them, at least according to Jesus?"

"I know what the Bible verse says, but do you believe it? I have the feeling Jesus was exaggerating to make the point that people who think themselves better than others still have sin in their hearts. Laws have always held that those who carry out wrongdoing are worse than those who merely contemplate it. So have theologians." I paused. "But, you're still operating under the notion that being gay is a sin."

"Well, I've pretty much overcome that. I'm sure being gay is a condition," he said. "Now, I'm wondering if acting on such urges is wrong."

"Do you believe God gave you the capacity to love, but only to love those of the other gender?"

"Maybe sexually," Dan replied.

"But is that for you a complete—real—expression, of all you feel?"

Dan shrugged. "Well, I haven't felt much yet. I don't know that I will," Dan said. "I wonder if I lack the capacity to love, at least in a deep and real way."

"I often doubt how great a capacity to love any of us naturally possesses," I said. "That capacity is developed through testing."

"This is probably the best defense for God's allowing evil that I know of. Without evil—without temptation—without the ability to fail, as well as pass—we cannot grow into the full image of God."

"It just seems like the testing could be a lot less—" Dan paused, stumbling for words.

"Painful," I supplied.

We both laughed.

"Look, the chocolate hazelnut is melting," Dan said, indicating that we'd better dive in. "I think I'm tasting your saliva," he said, holding his spoon out for examination before him. "It's awfully salty.

"I think you're tasting Tray's saliva," I replied, pointing to Tray who had been standing at his side and breathing eagerly on his spoon. "I wouldn't be surprised if she didn't lick it when we weren't looking."

"Here I thought it was your saliva," Dan said, still laughing.

I rolled my eyes. "I thought you liked saliva."

"Well not hers," Dan replied.

I shook my head and laughed. "Such a flirt." I paused, noting Dan's expression. "I was talking about Tray." Tray certainly seemed to have come alive again. Increased attention, not only from me, but from friendly people who dropped by, had made a difference.

"The owner of my company is strongly attracted to me. She's been open about it," Dan said, smiling, with more than a little satisfaction in his voice.

"Oh," I said. "I wonder where you would actually place on the gay-straight spectrum. Klein and Wolf refine Kinsey's sexual scale so that we're invited to look at whom we desire to have sex with, whom we want to socialize with, whom we feel emotional connections with, and so on. A fuller picture always complicates things, but it's far more truthful." I was watching Dan's face to see how he was reacting. He seemed okay with it. "Is she making things uncomfortable?" I asked, thinking about McDougal and Spet.

Dan shook his head. "She's been open, but she's promised she'll never act on it," he said. "She's old enough to be my mother, and it wouldn't be professional—it would hurt relationships at the office. She's admitted that. But she's breathtakingly beautiful, with a great figure, really intelligent. Everyone respects her."

"That's the reason," I said. "She takes responsibility for her issues."

"She's had years of therapy," Dan replied.

"Oh, well, that explains it," I said. "Here's a little information that you can file away for future reference. Dog's saliva is supposed to have therapeutic properties. It encourages and speeds healing. That's why in ancient times people used to hope that dogs would lick their wounds, especially if they were too poor to afford doctors."

"I'll remember that—in case you wound me." Dan smiled.

Close

November had been sunny and warm, like much of the fall. I decided to leave school early. Although I wanted to be outside that Friday afternoon, I went home to get some work done without interruption. I needed to send out some teaching applications before I missed the deadlines. I also needed to work on my publications. They had to take high priority if I ever was going to work myself into some sort of permanent position.

The phone startled me. It was Sharon. Her voice was clear, full-bodied, like the weather. She invited me over. "I want you to see my new condo in Washington Park. I moved out of the Cherry Hills house." Evidently, things really were over with Brad, as she'd said at the summer party.

I went. Sharon's complexion was again creamy. Her eyes shone and her bearing was straight. The other views were fine. You could see downtown from one side and look out over Washington Park on the other. Sharon ordered in from a local Chinese restaurant that delivered.

After a dinner of mu shu pork, moo goo gai pan, rice, and egg rolls, Sharon urged me to stay the night.

Without hesitation, I said, "I can only stay part of it. I have to get home to take care of Tray." One of Sharon's cats peeked out from behind the couch. "Tray will be all right for a few more hours. We went for a walk before I came over. But I can't leave her alone the whole night."

"I understand. In fact, I honor that," Sharon said.

I literally felt my heart warm. I so needed someone who honored me. "Tray's being a good dog, probably because I'm being a good companion person," I said.

Sharon nodded. "My cats aren't acting out, now that things at home are calm," she said.

"If something is important, you make time for it, no matter how busy or distracted you are," I added.

Sharon smiled sadly. "During my time in rehab, my Persian starting tearing out his hair," she said. "He had to be shaved." He came out of hiding and lurked like a cowardly lion in the corner. "Poor shorn thing," I said, wincing. Without his hair, he looked only a shadow of all that he was meant to be, and he knew it.

When I asked about Brad, Sharon said her anger was still too great to talk about him. "Even to think about whether there'd ever been any love between Brad and me. He was such a jerk. You can never begin to guess all the ways."

"I'd just as soon not hear them," I replied. "At least not now." I was reminded of the woman I'd dated in graduate school named Fae. That was some time ago She was witty and made everyone laugh. She was also pretty, with copper curls. But just as soon as we started to get intimate, she'd launch into stories of the men that she had dated. They always involved some sort of weird sexual happenings that freaked me out, even though I never could bring myself to tell her so.

When she started getting verbally abusive toward me, and it happened fairly early, she told me it was because I reminded her of her father. He was educated and a gentleman. He started having an affair right after they'd married. Her mother never let him forget. Her wrath was never far away. They didn't divorce. She preferred to make life hell.

"I can see the idea troubles you," Sharon said. "Do you want to talk about it?" she asked.

"No," I answered.

Sharon laughed. "I can understand that too."

She reached to take my hand. She held it to her mouth and gently kissed it. She looked into my eyes and said, "I do love you Ted Jones, more than life itself."

"With my body, I thee worship," I said.

"And with my body I worship thee," she said. She knew the lines of holy matrimony from the old Anglican prayer book. In Orthodox churches, the bride and groom are crowned as part of the process of deification meant for all who are faithful. In Christ's mystical presence, all who endure to the end will be taken up into the godhead.

Sharon stood. My hand still in hers, she led me to the bedroom.

The bed was opened. Red and white rose petals were strewn upon the white lace embroidered sheets and pillow cases. Their scent filled the entire room.

I touched Sharon's hair. She touched my cheek. We finally made love. She gasped again and again. She called my name. "I'd walk the fires of hell for you," she said.

"Even if I descend to hell, thou shalt be there," I echoed.

Sharon looked at me and laughed. "In that Psalm, David is talking to God. He says God will be with him wherever he finds himself, even in hell," she said. "I told you, I'd walk through hell for *you*."

"Well, God will be with you even there," I said, breaking into laughter myself. "If you descend to hell, you'll need God's company."

Sharon suddenly became quiet, distant, as if she were separating her consciousness from her body, and from me.

Here, I'd been feeling totally connected with her at last, far more deeply and fully than I'd felt in her weeks of haunting me at night. She had become embodied. But she seemed to disembody herself again. She felt no longer present. She turned away. She began to masturbate, bringing herself off not once but several times.

We'd made love, but she had to culminate her sexual experience on her own. "Sharon—Sharon," I said. What in hell were we just doing?

She continued to ignore me. Finally, she turned back to me. She put her arms around me. With her head on my chest like a buoy, she fell asleep.

I was left to lie awake and wonder about everything. How I would manage to carry on with Sharon when I was searching for another teaching position or a post-doctoral fellowship. If I were fortunate enough to land a position, I would probably have to move again. How could I ask Sharon, who had a good job, to move with me? I didn't know that she'd come with me anyway. Besides, Sharon and I were not ready to settle into a live-in relationship. I was not even sure that a sexual relationship had been established, given what happened afterwards. I'd thought we'd participated in the sacrament of marriage, priesting our vows ourselves. But then she turned away. And back again to sleep.

Too many questions about Sharon, about us, remained. *Oh, poor Tray.* I had to get home to her. Thinking I was driving home, I must have fallen asleep.

When dawn colored the east with brilliant reds and oranges and yellows, Sharon whispered that she didn't want to leave me ever again, even to go to work.

I woke, startled. I wasn't at home with Tray at all. "I've got to check on Tray," I said, getting up to leave.

"I'll call in sick," Sharon said. "You go home and take care of Tray and come back. Or I'll come to you," she said. "If they fire me for my absences, I don't care. I'm one of their best salespeople, working from commissions only, so I don't really worry about it. I can always find another job, if I have to."

Both of us had a brilliant idea. I reached for Sharon's phone. I called Dan. "Could you do me a big favor?"

"How big?" Dan asked. He laughed. "Your voice sounds awfully husky, like you've got sex on your mind."

"Take Tray for a good morning walk and love her up. I'm with Sharon."

"Oh," Dan said, as if surprised. "If need be, I'll take Tray home with me tonight."

"I'll let you know later."

"I'll take Tray around with me on Saturday errands," Dan said, sounding yet more comfortable with my news.

Tray loved to ride in the car, especially with Dan. She rode in the back seat, with her right forepaw on the arm rest, just as if Dan were her personal chauffeur.

When I hung up, Sharon got out of bed, grabbed her white robe, and sat in the little upholstered chair across the room. It too was white. As if diving into the abyss, she said, "I've got to tell you I was molested as a child by my priest, Father Joe. He was fresh out of seminary. He was charming, so good looking," she said. Her breath was labored. "My mother adored him. So did my grandmother."

I suggested moving to the living room. I grabbed my shirt and pants and put them on.

We sat on the couch. The mallards were waddling across the grass toward the lake. We could see them from the wall of windows.

"He molested my older brother too. He made me promise not to tell anyone. So did my brother," Sharon said. "Before long, Father Joe stopped doing my brother. But he kept molesting me."

All I could say was, "oh," at several junctures in her confession. I didn't pump Sharon for information. She told me, "The abuse went on until I was twelve. It began when I was eight."

For twenty years, Sharon said she had never said a word to anyone. "My brother and I are no longer speaking because I've insisted on telling," she said. "I finally told my mother. She went into complete denial. 'How could you?' she said, slapping me across the face. She accused me of making everything up."

I nodded. "The scenario is all too typical, from everything I've heard and read. I know well the pattern of denial in abusive families," I said, recalling my own family dynamics. *"No, you didn't see that,"* my mom, my grandmother, and my great aunt would say. *"You misunderstood. That never happened." Whack, my dad was going to knock some sense into me. Kick, "I'll teach you."*

Punch—"You goddam brat. Shut your mouth. Stop your crying. Do it! NOW, or else."

"It wasn't what you thought. You've forgotten how it was. Your dad didn't mean it. I didn't say that. Have you seen the tulips coming out in the garden? The daffodils down the street are really nice this year. Spring is on the way."

Sharon continued, squirming a little. "If I wasn't making it up, Mother said, I'd seduced Father Joe. *He* was the innocent victim. Her own daughter, I, was always a whore."

Things in Sharon's family had become so strained that she was planning to spend Thanksgiving and Christmas alone. "I won't celebrate Thanksgiving," she said. "I'm having Christmas dinner at the Parker House. I'll tell the waiter I'm Jewish. It won't be the first time."

I reached out for her hand. She pulled it back.

"For most of my life, I've been trying to pretend the abuse never happened," she said. "I've tried to escape in various ways, including drugs,"

I continued to listen intently. I said next to nothing. I was losing the feeling in my feet from sitting so still for so long.

"My psychiatrist is trying to help me stay in my body. He wants to help me sort fantasy from reality," she sighed.

I tried not to let Sharon's disturbing revelations interfere with our relationship. Nonetheless, I couldn't help but brood over what had happened to her. The molestation and family issues explained a great deal about the behaviors she'd exhibited. I hoped her psychiatrist had a good grasp of the largeness of reality, how it includes both the physical and spiritual realms, which must be brought together and integrated. From what Sharon had said, he seemed to have some insight. I hoped that it was not merely talk so that he could subtly force her into some mold where she had to deny her spirituality.

But her psychiatrist had encouraged her to see me. If he had been trying to force her into the physical plane alone, I doubted he would have done so. He would have told her to avoid me. I hoped he realized that I would stand in the way of any plan to reduce—rather than deepen and integrate—the various planes of reality. To do that she did need to sort reality from fantasy. He was right about that.

"I first started leaving my body while I was being molested. I could escape that way. Returning was always the most frightening aspect of the experience," she said. She shook her head hard, as if trying to get dirt out of her hair. "Every time my spirit went back into my body, it gave me a jolt, even physically. Psychically, I would often become confused over what was fantasy and what had actually happened. Doing drugs didn't help."

"Nor did my brother." She knotted her hands into a tight ball as if to keep them from striking out. "He told me to stop imagining so much. People have always wanted to pull me back to their notions of reality. They want to make me like *them*. My brother told me the reason Father Joe kept molesting me was that I was exciting. 'You know things. Next to you, I was boring. Everyone was,'" he said.

Sharon started to stand up but quickly sat back down. "I'm dizzy," she said.

"You look pale, better breathe deeply for a bit," I advised. I knew she was reacting physically to the stress of confession.

"I asked my brother if he thought my being female might have been part of the reason Father Joe kept having sex with me."

"That crossed my mind too," I said. My feet were asleep. I tried to move them, but they felt dead. I tried to stand up but felt as if I were walking on stumps. I couldn't even tell that I had anything past my knees.

"You're going to fall," Sharon said, urging me to sit down. "You're having a physical reaction too." She pulled her robe tight and grabbed the plaid throw from the back of the couch. "I'm freezing. I know the process."

"The feeling in my feet and lower legs is totally gone," I said, hobbling around the room. "I've got to wake them up."

"I wish I could feel totally gone," Sharon said, her voice flattened. She was rummaging around inside her being for some rags of self. When she began again, she'd found more feeling. "'No,' my brother replied, 'that guy didn't care. He liked it all. He was an addict,' he told me. 'I've met others he screwed. That's how these guys get their kicks. If someone didn't offer resistance, or something that excited his imagination, he got bored and moved on to someone else. You were exciting. You tried to stop him. But you also told him about your out of body experiences, and that fascinated him. 'Remember?' he said."

Sharon thought her experiences, even though a child's, seemed to Father Joe to confirm the existence of a soul that could be separated from the body. I knew that my own experiences with Sharon had helped me to believe as well, for I knew that they were more than mere projections of a troubled mind.

To relate my own situation to the priest's, however, made me uncomfortable. I stood at the window, looking out. A duck taking off from the lake caught my eye. I was no molester. But, still, I understood his interest in the paranormal, in looking for signs, and trying to understand more.

If, however, what I experienced was some sort of projection of Sharon's psyche and not her soul, as her psychiatrist tended to believe, I could accept that too. His theory, however, did not work so well to explain away my experiences with the dead, such as Sharon's grandmother. Granted, I didn't have lots of those. But there were some. I trusted myself, and what I experienced.

My faith had been tested in many ways, and it always seemed to pull me through. With greater knowledge, my understanding of the language of signs grew ever more complex, as I did.

Sharon's masturbation, her inability to really connect with me—and stay connected—was also explained. I'd read enough to know that such behaviors among those abused as children were common. Most professionals, however, would explain away what Sharon and I both knew to be actual out of body experiences as "imagined, not staying in reality, aspects of her dissociation due to severe and prolonged trauma."

Almost right. But reality, I remained convinced, is multileveled, more multi-dimensional and complex than most of us realize.

I returned to the couch and sat down beside Sharon again. She allowed me to take her hand. "I want to locate the priest who molested you and have a good talk with him." I paused, searching inside myself. "The more I allow myself to consider him, the more I want not just to talk with him but to do him real harm," I said. "You don't incorporate qualities that someone has by having sex with them." I paused. "Well yes, most of us do," I said, having an inner dialogue with him. "But you don't have sex with a child, or with somebody clearly your inferior in age or station."

As a youngster the priest had probably been molested himself. I knew that from my studies too. My anger grew more complex and mixed with sympathy. "In his twisted way, Father Joe probably thought he was loving you and the others in the best way he knew how," I said.

"Yes, I think so," Sharon said, thoughtfully. She squeezed my hand.

I squeezed back. "He probably entered the priesthood to search for wholeness by ministering to others in good ways, thus ministering to himself. Not a bad thing. At least he would have been trying to do good."

"He was very young when he began training as a priest," Sharon said. "He'd never dealt with his own sexuality."

"He probably stopped developing psychologically when he was an adolescent," I said, "at least that's the theory. People who do that seek out others at about the same age that they stopped developing."

Sharon laughed. "He would have been only a boy."

"Everyone looks for wholeness, says Jung, no matter how botched the attempt. I believe him. I'm doing so myself. If you love someone, you begin to share their vision, to incorporate their qualities. It's like taking communion. It's only holy when you are ready to surrender to the real thing."

Sharon leaned into me and put her head on my chest. The sunlight entered the room and lit up her hair.

I recalled my prophetic dream of several years before, just as I was entering the process to become a priest.

I rested on a hard wood pew inside a cathedral. I sat near the altar, not in the front row but ten rows back.

"Judgment is coming," a deep voice boomed. The air felt electrical, as it becomes before a lightning strike. The hairs on the back of my neck stood up.

When a man dressed as a bishop, wearing a gold miter, appeared and sat on his throne to the right of the altar, people in various parts of the congregation started popping up like jack-in-the-boxes to announce their good deeds—all that they'd done in God's name.

I found the phenomenon deeply disturbing.

The more people bragged, the more I tried to make myself inconspicuous. I lowered my shoulders and head, trying to slump down in the pew. I hoped I could become invisible. My deeds, like my motives, were mixed. They always had been. I was becoming ever more aware of my Shadow, my dark side, how apt each of us is to project the dark, and act it, without being conscious of what we were doing.

Scattered throughout the cathedral I realized that some others, not many, were also hunching down in the pews. I began to mumble the words from the Service of Holy Communion. "Oh Lord, I am not worthy so much as to pick up the crumbs under thy table, but say the word only, and I shall be healed." One by one a few began to go forward for communion, trying to ignore the majority, who were still braying about all they'd done in the name of God.

Finally, I stood up and proceeded to the altar, the focal point of earth and heaven.

I looked over the large platter of wafers set before me. There was no priest, I noticed, no special ceremony. Everyone administered communion to him- or herself.

Again I paused, thinking of the implications.

Some wafers were flat, like fish food. Some, however, were large and round. I noticed that these looked like giant pearls.

One of the spherical hosts caught my eye. Something about it beckoned. As I looked, the milkiness of the surface began to clear. Inside, I saw the legs of an *alpha* linked with those of an *omega* that had been turned upside down to join with the *alpha*. At the very center, as if buttressing the entire structure, was a cross.

Before I knew it—I did not swallow—the sphere was inside me—and I was inside the sphere, standing, looking out, just as I was also looking in. My vision was double, one eye on earth, the other on Heaven. That is the essential tension of every life that longs to be whole. We act here, but always with something greater in mind.

Because I was increasingly seeing through Sharon's eyes, just as she was seeing through mine, our vision was also double. We'd stepped inside the pearl of great price. Just as we'd taken it in, it had encompassed us. We had one eye on earth and the other on Heaven. I'd been called into her life for a greater purpose. She'd been called into mine.

"The dancer, the dance, the singer, the song—all turn, and turn into One, the circle that knows no beginning, no end, the point of all that is, was, and will be," I said. I mused on my vision and stroked Sharon's hair.

"I'd like to think we gain inner sight," Sharon said, embroidering the metaphor.

"By it, we gain knowledge of paradise and the beatific vision. You read about it in my writing on Milton, didn't you?"

"Or in your article on motion in Herbert's *Temple*," she replied. She looked up at me and smiled.

"Paradise." I bent to kiss her. There in the calm of togetherness, we breathed. We were.

Hosts

By noon things felt increasingly uncomfortable. Sharon and I had shared enough for the time being. Without speaking, we both knew we felt exhausted by the intensity of our encounter.

Sharon said, "I think I want to run some errands, maybe go in to work for a little while."

"I need to get home to see my dog," I said.

When I arrived, I found Dan playing with Tray in the common area outside behind the town homes. She was even running, as he chased, and then she chased, a ball, something I'd not seen her do in years. She did not run very fast or more than several yards, but she did run. She even managed a yip of joy now and then.

"I didn't expect to you until Sunday," Dan said. He smirked a little.

"We needed a break," I said.

Dan gave me a quizzical look but did not pry. He walked over to me. Handing me the ball, he said, "Tell me about the Puritans and their views of sex."

"Yuck, it's kinda wet," I complained.

"Sex'll do that to ya," he said.

"What prompted your request?" I asked.

"I read something you wrote about the Puritans. People have told me my views of sex were Puritanical. I thought Puritans had a negative view of sex overall," he said, "even in marriage."

"That wouldn't be incarnational. The Protestant view of sex, including that of the Puritans, is that God gave us pleasures to enjoy rightly. For instance, they loved their beer. A wife could haul her husband into court to force him to have regular sexual relations with her, just as a husband could demand that of his wife. The Puritans believed that regular, loving sex in marriage prevented Satan from tempting them to seek such lawful delights elsewhere. "

Dan kept gazing at me. "What did you do differently?" he asked, looking me up and down.

"I don't understand your question," I said. "What did I do differently regarding the Puritans and sexuality?"

"Something about you is different, but I can't place what." Dan started sniffing me. You have a faint odor. It isn't how you usually smell. It's very subtle, something kind of musky."

"Here Tray, help Dan out," I called, encouraging her to sniff at me too. I must have looked rather embarrassed because Dan blushed.

"Does sex make you smell different?" he asked.

"Well, probably," I said. "Sharon has different soaps and shampoos too. I did shower."

"It isn't shampoo or soap I smell," Dan said. "It's something more subtle. Actually," he said, blushing rosy red by now, "it's kind of turning me on. So is thinking about you and Sharon and what you got up to."

I stepped back. "Well, there are subtle odors that we put out to attract the other gender, I've read. Especially during hormonal peaks."

"It must be my inner woman," Dan whispered, as if rather surprised at himself. His face turned beet red.

"Or mine," I said, turning the situation into a joke. "Now Tray, I hope you don't get turned on too." I suggested we to go back inside. "I don't want the neighbors hearing too much."

I decided to return to Dan's question about the Puritans as we walked back inside. In the kitchen we put on the kettle for tea. "The Puritans were not prudes," I said. They saw sex as a good thing, but only within a marriage between one man and one woman. Outside of that, sex was dangerous, an instinct to be tamed like the wilderness, the fallen world that lies outside the shining City on the Hill. Hawthorne, who felt guilty about his Puritan ancestors' rigid belief system, specifically their persecution of witches, embraced Transcendentalism to try to go beyond them. He hoped people trapped by such beliefs could learn from their mistakes and grow."

"That's part of the American Dream," Dan said.

"Or nightmare, depending on your cast of mind," I said. "The Puritans stressed examining yourself to see if you could detect signs of having been granted special—or saving—grace. They believed the modern idea that "I'm saved and going to Heaven" was presumptuous. That's the position of the entire mainline historical faith, by the way."

"I remember Calvin got his ideas from Augustine. Both said God grants special—saving—grace to those he'll save. To Augustine, God neglects to grant such grace to those who'll be damned. Calvin says God also chooses those he'll damn." Dan took the kettle from the stove and poured boiling water on the tea leaves in the pot I'd prepared.

"St. Paul first explored these issues. Paul's positions on this and other things don't always seem consistent. Sometimes the pot is made to be busted up and tossed in the trash. At other times Paul advocates choice. Thus, the varying strains of Christian theology, all based on the Bible."

"That's the position of those who believe in free will—God grants grace to all who ask for it," Dan said. "To some people, like me, such ideas are relevant."

"I agree. Now let's move to the living room and drink some tea. We can meditate in silence for a little. I'm kinda worn out."

"I'll just bet you are," Dan said. He winked. "Tray, grab the pot," he said, glancing down at her. He took it in his hand.

I took two mugs in mine and followed Dan and Tray into the living room. We sat near the front window on the couch.

"Maybe we should light the fire in the fireplace," Dan said. "It's chilly in here."

"I don't keep the thermostat very high. I have to conserve on utilities," I said.

Dan opened the gas to light the logs in what had once been a coal fireplace. He struck a match, held it to them, and they took off. "That's better, although it's a tiny fire. Reminds me of *A Christmas Carol*."

"People may not think very theologically, but the issues are still with us," I said, finding my words again. "We like to go along with our lives without giving the problem of evil much attention—until something bad happens to us, or to someone we love. Then we find ourselves taking up the old questions again. Evil then seems more than mere talk. It becomes a force to be reckoned with," I said. "Then we ask, do people choose evil, or is it thrust upon them? Are they seduced into choosing it? Are there truly bad seeds among us, people who are somehow predisposed to do evil? If so, who does the predestining, God, or some other force, such as Fate or Karma? Or is the cause merely one of defective genes that have been the result of some evolutionary or biological accident?"

"In that case, no over-riding, larger purpose, or cause, could be blamed," Dan said. "It's just the way things are." He patted Tray's head.

"Looks like you've got yourself a companion," I said.

"Is it possible to resist evil and choose good, especially if there is no larger, over-riding purpose at work?" Dan asked, moving the discussion on. "Would it be worth it? Would we seek to do good as its own reward?" Tray looked up lovingly at him.

"Talking about theological issues has at least taken some of the heat off you and me," I said.

Dan glanced over at the fire and smiled a telling smile.

"But you know we can't let esoteric discussions keep us from addressing issues we have to entertain," I said. "We dare not pretend they don't exist or switch topics to ones that are more comfortable because less personal."

"Academics are good at that," Dan said, smirking a little.

I smiled and nodded, pouring us both more tea.

"Some day we're going to have to talk about what's going on between us," Dan said. He looked squarely in my eyes. "But not today," he said and laughed. "I don't want to mess up a good day."

Disconnect

Sharon stopped answering her phone. Although I left messages, she didn't return calls. She'd not seen me since our tryst in her condo. That was near the start of the month. We'd had one conversation on the phone two days later. We'd talked of spending Thanksgiving together. At Sharon's urging, I extended our invitation to Dan, but he said he was going to have dinner with friends. He and his family were still not on the best of terms. I avoided my own family during holidays. To visit at such times was only asking to be swept back into the same old family dynamics that I had spent years learning to stay out of. Such dynamics are particularly strong and peculiarly deadly during the holidays. The vast gulf between people's expectations of what *should* constitute family get-togethers and what actually takes place does not help. My family and I did better visiting at other times, especially if they came to see me on my turf.

Sharon's latest bout of ignoring me underlined my conviction that I had to search out other jobs, wherever they were, since I could not count on a stable relationship with her. For awhile I'd thought that I could endure teaching writing classes only, which I would be assigned in the spring. I preferred teaching literature; I did not have to be constantly critical, at least about weak writing, but could pay attention to the great ideas and the complex problems that arise in good, if not excellent, writing.

I just knew that kicking me down to being a writing teacher only was part of Dr. Spet's retaliation. The budget problems provided a convenient excuse for making my life harder. When I was on his favored list, he saw to it that I taught literature courses, even ones that excited me, courses that were in my areas of specialization.

If the university had stopped sexual and other forms of harassment before they got out of hand and became law suits, typically settled out of court, plenty of money would have been available to hire more faculty and offer more classes. If the university cut budgets for administrators, who multiplied like rabbits, no matter how serious the budgetary crises, more funds would have been available for faculty as well.

But then, universities—and churches—like family systems—do not like to address problems openly and come up with solutions that work. That was exactly why Spet and McDougal of the cathedral had gotten away with all they had. Spet was smarter and more careful than McDougal, and held one of the highest ranks in the faculty, although McDougal could always claim his being a man of the cloth and rely on excuses made on his behalf. He held the most prestigious position of any outside of Bishop Lane in the entire Diocese of Colorado.

In my campus office, Dan and I sat talking about this. "Which, I wonder, will get away with the most, and for the longest time?" I asked.

Dan had made his long-promised, long-planned visit to the Cathedral. "As I was walking out the door, right in the midst of a line of parishioners who wanted out, McDougal took my hand and looked deeply and longingly into my eyes. I thought he was trying to hypnotize me."

"No doubt," I said. "Like a vampire. Part of his dominance and control act."

Dan raised his eyebrow. "The Dean asked what my name was. He even wanted to know where I lived. He wanted the address and wrote it down in his day timer."

I laughed. "Planning to make a pastoral visit, I'd guess."

"He asked for my phone number," Dan said. "And what I did for a living, and what had brought me to Denver and, more important, to the cathedral. 'Why, God is at work here. You can feel the electricity in the air,' he gushed, with his slight lisp. Then McDougal leaned in and whispered, 'Many men feel it in their groins, a kind of tingling that goes up the whole spine,'" Dan related.

I saw him actually shiver, starting in his groin. "With me it was, 'Most men feel it in their thighs,'" I said.

"He was taking so much time that some of the parishioners broke out of line and walked around us to get outside," Dan said. "'I thought the spine was in back,' I said to McDougal. I looked puzzled, as if I just didn't get it," Dan related. "But he smiled. I swear he even blushed—and replied, 'the energy goes around. You know, what goes around, comes around.' He was so silly that I had to stifle my laughter."

Even telling me about this provoked laughter, first in Dan and then me. In fact, I got the giggles so bad that I had to get up and look out the window. Once I gained control, I turned to face Dan again. His face was red from laughing. "Sounds like he was hoping you'd ask him out on a date," I said.

"I told him a little of the truth, mixed with lots of lies." Dan got out of his chair to act out the scene. "I decided to make my getaway by turning around and walking toward another exit." Dan turned abruptly and walked to my office door. "The Dean dropped everything. He motioned to another priest to stand in his place and greet people, while he scurried after me. The leather soles of his black patent leather shoes kept slipping on the waxed tiles."

"Too bad you didn't start running," I said. "You'd better come back here, sit down, and not make so much noise, before Louise comes to check out the commotion. "If you'd run off, maybe somebody would have noticed."

"I doubt it. People there seem like they're in some kind of trance," Dan said. Instead of sitting, he decided to stand at the window. "I tell you, I wanted to run, but I didn't think it was appropriate. The Dean caught up with me and grabbed my arm. 'You forgot to give me your phone number!' he said. So I gave him a phony number that I thought up on the spot," Dan said, laughing. "He was far, far too excited when I told him I was an architect. 'Oh, you erect things,' he said, stretching to put his face as close to mine as he could."

"I can just imagine that."

"But, even on tiptoe, he came up to my neck," Dan said, laughing, lifting himself up in imitation of McDougal. "I suggested he might get better lifts in his shoes. Then I broke loose again and hurried to another exit, with him hot on my heels. This time he slipped, but he managed to catch himself before falling. I noticed some of the men from the choir were standing off to the side. They were watching and laughing,"

"They were probably taking bets on whether he'd slip right into you on purpose—he winds up in your arms, and you look into his eyes, and the whole world knows it's love, true love at last!" I joked.

Dan's face turned pale, then changed to a yellowish green. He looked like he was going to vomit, saliva leaking from his mouth.

"Careful," I said. "Louise will have to arrange for a rabies shot if she sees that."

Dan wiped his mouth. He sat down in the chair.

"They say he also likes to make late night calls to handsome young men," I winked. "You didn't tell him where you lived, did you?"

"I lied about that too." Dan paused. "But I did make the mistake of giving him my real name."

"Oops. You may have a night visitor after all," I said.

"I'll bet he can get my address from the telephone operator."

I nodded. "You'd better call up the phone company and have your number unlisted."

Dan jumped up to grab the phone from my desk. He lifted the receiver.

I decided to tease him. "But if you're looking for power, hooking up with McDougal might overcome the strongest denial mechanism," I replied.

Dan put down the receiver, thought for a few minutes, and then asked, "Is power really such an aphrodisiac?"

I answered, "Of course. You know how attractive I am."

Dan laughed. He wondered if he ought to trap McDougal in some sort of compromising position. "I could videotape it," he said, his face brightening. He leaned over and whispered into my ear. "We could use it as leverage."

"I've seen movies about this," I said. "But I think the ones who got even by trapping the cad were women. If you're male, people wouldn't want to think about it."

"Or believe it," Dan replied. "It would be entirely my fault."

I nodded. "Probably. However, I do need leverage. I just got notice that the rent hasn't been paid for months on my ministry office, as McDougal promised. I don't have office space in the English Department because they don't have any extra room in that little house. They were only too glad to hear that I'd use my ministry office to see students regardless of the reason. Spet's strict adherence to the separation of church and state didn't seem to matter in this case."

"Spet is probably glad you aren't around to prick his conscience," Dan said.

"Now that he realizes he can't prick me otherwise," I said. I stood and glanced out the window. "I would truly miss the views of downtown and the friary yard if I had to move back into the little house where non-tenure track faculty share tables in what had been the living and dining rooms."

"I can't believe McDougal's antics toward me weren't noticed by other priests and staff," Dan commented. "There were lots of them around. They must have realized he was chasing me from door to door. Each time he caught up with me, he was so winded he could hardly talk."

I couldn't remember when I'd laughed so heartily.

"By the way, I've met someone. I think we're becoming serious," Dan said.

I wheeled around to look at Dan. "Where'd that bombshell come from?" I asked, feeling rather stunned. "Do you think he's stable?"

"He doesn't strike me as very horsy," Dan replied. "He's also an engineer, so we have a lot in common. We haven't even open mouth kissed."

"Boy, am I glad to hear that. No sharing of germs that way," I said. I decided I'd better laugh so Dan knew I was giving him a hard time.

"Both of us are dedicated to the ideal that we should wait until we are in a committed, monogamous relationship."

"You're going against all the stereotypes put out by the far right, as well as the gay media. All gay people do is have sex, you know. Why, every bit of brain is located in your genitals."

"More so than everybody else?" Dan wisecracked. His face became serious. "That's why we're dedicated to waiting. We want to prove to ourselves, as much as everyone else, that real love waits."

"The government must be adding something to the water, or releasing it into the air," I joked.

The phone rang. It was Laura Cameron, inviting me to a party.

I told her, "Laura, you know I really like you, but I really am not comfortable with your friends."

"Oh Darling," she said, sounding terribly disappointed.

"But thank you. I appreciate your thinking of me."

"I promise you, Darling, to try not to shock you," Laura replied. "I'm moving past that. Bud and I are trying to have a baby, so we have to become respectable—and responsible. We're sorting out our friendships." She laughed.

"I seriously doubt you can pull that off."

Laura then invited me over for lunch. "That way you won't have to run into any of our decadent crowd," she said. "We can spend the entire afternoon catching up. Besides, you need to relax. Every time I talk to you, you're a ball of nerves. I worry that you're going to have a stroke or a heart attack."

I didn't want to worry about something else. Other friends had commented upon my nervousness too. I tried to make a joke of it. I said, "If you were getting screwed by both the church *and* the state, you would be nervous too."

"Are you having any luck with your job search?" Laura asked.

"Only nibbles," I replied. "I'm still wondering if I'm going to have to change careers. To what, I don't know."

"Well, you'll just have to become a famous writer," Laura said.

I remarked that I needed to get back to Dan. "He's here consulting me."

"Oh, I see." She laughed. "Now I know you can't see my face, but you can imagine it. So I'll say, don't do anything that I wouldn't do, wink, wink."

House Call

I agreed to have lunch with the Camerons on Friday. Laura made me laugh. Crazy as she might seem, I knew she really did care about me, and about others. There typically was method in her madness. We shared the same birthday. She always said that's why we were so much alike.

"Oh, boy, I hope not," I would reply, partly in jest. I would take the afternoon off and drive out to their home.

When I got there, I found a note taped to the front door, saying, "Ted, come in."

I opened the door, stepped into the foyer, and called out. The intercom on the wall came on. Laura's voice announced, "We're in the bedroom. Take the hall on your left, then go in the door at the end."

Bud and she had obviously been playing. Both were lying naked on the disheveled bed. Although the house was elegant and neat, the bedroom was not. Clothes lay everywhere, on the cherry wood floor, in heaps on the dressers, and on the end of the bed that seemed the size of a small home.

"Here darling," Laura said, patting the side where the sheets were bunched up. "Have a seat. You won't catch anything. You're so nervous. I really worry about you."

"Well," I began, "it isn't every day that I'm invited into someone's bedroom."

"But we're friends. Besides, priests have to be woken up," Laura laughed, "given a good dose of reality every now and then. That's what Rajneesh teaches. We lived in his community for a few years, you know. We had the wildest sex we've ever had."

"I'm pretty wide awake, I think, but thanks," I replied. "I often muse how much I'd like to go back to sleep. I'm so tired."

"Darling, were you ever asleep?" Laura looked me over head to toe. "I'll bet when you were three you were noticing far more than anyone ever wanted you to."

"My family didn't like what I saw," I said, remembering. My mom would try to console me, and stop my dad from attacking me, but she would always deny the truth of what was going on. Or, she'd try to change the subject and distract me with pleasant thoughts. At the end of her tack, she'd quote Scarlet O'Hara's, "Tomorrow is another day."

I decided to divulge only the basics in answer to Laura's assertion. "In first grade it was discovered that I couldn't see the black boards, so I was prescribed glasses. I'd suffered serious headaches for years before that," I said. "Even as a toddler I'd noticed too much, and was far too curious for my family dynamics."

"One becomes myopic in response to being told that he does not—must not—see the bigger picture. Seeing what's before one's nose is plenty," Laura said. She scrunched up her eyes. "Now, where, oh where are my glasses?" she said, raising herself to look around the room. Her breasts flopped a bit on her chest. Her nipples were pert. She lay back down.

I laughed. "I've read that. It makes sense."

Bud finally raised himself on his elbows. "Hello," he said, and brushed across his penis with his hand. He was still hard. It wouldn't stay down.

I noticed a vibrator with a little bird at its base lying beside Laura's hips. I stared a little more closely. The bird seemed to be positioned so that it would turn in small arcs, while the rest of the wand vibrated and turned in larger circles. Toward the base of the main wand was another little probe, stationary.

"Do you like the new toy Bud got us?" Laura asked. "The little duck is supposed to stimulate the clit when the donger won't do."

"It looks dangerous," I commented, wincing a little at the thought.

"You think so?" Laura asked. She laughed. "I suppose you might get some tissue wound up in it, flesh, I mean. That's why you marry a doctor. He can stitch things right up and ring your bell again." She laughed. "Did you know, Darling, that vibrators were first used in doctors' offices at the beginning of this century? Masturbation was commonly prescribed for women." She paused, pregnantly. "But it was only to be performed by a trained professional."

Bud laughed. "Such services comprised up to eighty percent of some docs' practices."

"You'd love that," Laura said, tickling Bud's thigh. "Here, Miss or Mrs. Whatsyername, let's get you plugged in. That's a good girl. See how much better you feel. Maybe we should give you a hysterectomy while we're at it." She paused, and then looked wide-eyed at me.

"Darling," she said, staring into my eyes, "you're so uptight. As I've told you, you need to get out more."

"Well, I'd better shower and get to the hospital. I teach this afternoon," Bud remarked, excusing himself as he got up from the bed. "You and Laura have all afternoon for yourselves," he said to me. He turned and left the room. I noticed how hairy his ass was. At his age it was still firm. I heard the shower start in the bathroom.

"How's your love life?" Laura asked, still lying uncovered on the bed. "I hear you and Sharon are seeing each other again."

"We were. I thought we'd made some real breakthroughs, but I haven't heard from her in awhile." I paused. "I'm afraid it's still off and on."

"You scare her," Laura said. She raised herself again. She located her glasses beneath a pillow and put them on. "That's better. I can see you."

"Everything scares her, from what I'm seeing," I said.

"You've read lots of literature about Americans who suffer from intimacy issues, you told me so yourself."

I nodded. "They're legion."

"That's why Buddy and I have sex all the time," Laura replied. "We don't want to develop any intimacy issues ourselves."

I laughed, and added, "I don't think having sex often is necessarily the solution."

"It certainly doesn't hurt."

I agreed. "When you have a bond, sex is great," I said.

Laura assured me that she knew that. "I was testing you, seeing if you understood intimacy," she said. "But even with a bond, Sharon can't let go and fuck. It scares her, brings back all her pain. That's why she and Brad got along. He doesn't demand intimacy because he wouldn't know what to do with it. And she couldn't give it."

"But—"

"I know you love her," Laura said, taking my hand to comfort me. "I think she loves you too." She stared off at the wall, and then returned her gaze to me. "But you can't expect too much—"rather, you *mustn't hope* for too much," Laura warned, her voice growing tender. She petted my back maternally. "You demand people's full and conscious attention."

"I know that." I nodded. "Not just in class or on exams and papers, but in daily life."

"That makes you difficult, Darling," Laura reminded me. "Most people don't want to open themselves up that far. They can't," Laura explained. "It scares the hell out of them."

"It scares the bejeesus out of me too. But I know I have to press forward if I'm ever to move forward."

"That's why we keep coming back to this planet," Laura said. "We reincarnate to get things right."

"Tell you what," I said, "you can keep coming back to this purgatorial place if you want. But I want to move on to a better realm, preferably paradise."

Projections

Ron, the Director of Writing, called me into his office. "One of your women students, Liz Herren, has filed a complaint that you continually exhibit prejudice toward her," Ron said. "'He dislikes women,' she writes."

When Ron got riled, his manner became overly precise, almost prissy. He'd look and sound like a woman barely able to suppress her rage. "She demands that I react strongly and swiftly to her charges." Ron paused. His jaw was set, his eyes blazing. "These are serious accusations."

From my representation of the non-tenure track teachers, mostly women, I'd noticed that Ron and Spet made lots of noise about being supportive, especially of women. However, neither in actuality was. To say they were feminists lined up with official university policy. It was politically correct. But to be supportive in real ways requires putting aside the mask and balancing oneself within and without, so that one could in actuality treat others with dignity and justice.

"I have no idea what's going on with Liz," I said. "Often, bad students who get the grades they deserve will make up excuses, blaming the professor, just as they've blamed earlier teachers and parents for their own laziness and lack of insight."

Ron began to snort, as if ready to tear into me.

"But Liz isn't a bad student," I said. "While she isn't brilliant, she's doing solid B or maybe B+ work. She has to work hard, make lots of revisions, but she's doing well. Anyone who wants to write has to learn to revise, rethink, rewrite, and revise some more. That's painful, like life."

"I'll remind you again how serious such charges are," he said, the vein on his forehead throbbing. "She accuses you of having a deep hatred of women," Ron remarked. "In our day, that is the kiss of death," he said, his voice icy, the vein on his forehead threatening to burst.

One of our faculty members, Pam, a very popular teacher who could not praise her students enough, always seemed to know how to get what she wanted from Ron. She went on the attack first, totally fearless—and Ron responded like a whipped puppy. I really wished I could be so audacious.

"If I hated women, I would never have agreed to represent the non-tenure track teachers, who, I would remind you, are mostly women. I certainly stand to gain nothing professionally for doing so. In fact, I was well aware that doing so would likely damage my standing with the administration, which has everything to gain by the exploitation of slave labor. It was, and is, however, the right thing to do."

"Well, I will continue my investigation," Ron vowed. "Meanwhile, you need to be more aware of what you're doing." He ended our meeting by rolling his chair back behind his desk, and becoming cool, distant. His face went soft, almost blank.

"I'll try to figure out what went on," I said, rising to leave. I refused to be intimidated by Ron or anyone else. If Ron could use women to do his dirty work, to slave as teachers and secretaries paid pennies, he, like Spet, didn't mind a bit. Ron's and Spet's objections to the contrary, and there were plenty—we heard them when the non-tenure track people organized to take their voices and gain some rights— meant nothing. Ron and Spet could complain all they wanted about their own dismal wages and benefits. And Spet could complain till bears tore him to pieces that someone with his brains should have been teaching at an Ivy League University, not some backwoods of the west. Who really hated women was obvious.

With my student Liz, something more was going on. I was not sure what. I needed time to figure that out. Although he said he'd continue his investigation, Ron didn't seem genuinely interested in being a neutral party. He'd made up his mind. This was the perfect opportunity to crucify me. Spet could be rid of the thorn in his paw at last.

Evidently Liz had told some of the students in class that she'd filed a formal complaint against me. Some approached me about it. I told them what I knew. "We'll have a chat with Ron ourselves, on your behalf," my student Susan said. She appeared to be heading up my group of defenders.

Ron listened. Right after their visit, he called me back in. "How dare you talk with students about a formal complaint," he said, his face turning red with rage.

"They're also involved. They're my witnesses," I said. I shrugged, maintaining my cool.

"You're being insubordinate. You don't send students over in your defense," Ron said.

How I wished I could be like Pam and fly into a rage. But I responded, "I did not send them. They were standing up for me of their own accord." I paused for effect. "But even if I had sent them," I said, "it certainly seems well within my rights. If you make false accusations, it is my duty to see that they are corrected."

Ron did not respond. He picked up a book lying on his desk and started reading.

"I would remind you that you told your colleagues that we were welcome to write to the personnel committee on your behalf when you were up for tenure," I said. "I did so. I doubt that many others did. As you know, my recommendation was glowing. Before you got tenure, you were very earnest, intelligent, and hard-working. You were most careful to listen to those who worked with you, and always exhibited an even hand."

In private, I talked with Liz. "I really don't believe that I'm prejudiced against you or anyone else, certainly not women. I respect you. I know you work hard on your writing."

Liz became less defensive. Although she said nothing, her face and manner softened.

"I would remind you of what I tell all my students at the beginning of every course," I said. "I expect more from you than I think you can deliver, and promise to take that into account at the end."

Liz's manner softened more. Her mouth became less set.

"If people really work hard, keep revising and rewriting, and participating in class, showing me that they're working hard to improve by struggling with the materials, I always give them the benefit of the doubt. It is certainly possible to receive an A or A- for your course grade, even if a strict average only grants you a B or a B+."

I could see Liz's mind working. Her eyes became less despondent.

"My theology is integrated into my life. I believe in grace," I reminded her. "Liz, I'd like you to help me figure out why you responded as you did. There's some reason for it, and you'll be better off by understanding it, so that you might prevent it from happening in the future."

Liz agreed. "I'll try," she said. By the end of the week, she had things figured out.

"My ex-husband's first name was also Ted. He wanted to become a writer more than anything," she confessed a little sheepishly. "I always wanted to be a writer too," she said. "Nothing I ever did—writing, reading, housework, rearing our kids—was good enough for him. He was always critical. He intended to keep me in my place as the little woman who depended on him. He let me know *he* was the one who was going to be the writer, not me. Everything I wanted was of little importance compared to him." She paused. "I think I had begun to see you as my ex-husband. At first it was cool to have a teacher named Ted. But as you criticized, I grew more resentful. I wanted revenge."

I nodded. I thanked Liz. "Liz, I think you've come to a good understanding of the issue. I applaud you for having the courage to explore things with open eyes and let me know what you discovered," I said. "Good job."

I walked over to the house where Ron's office was located. I related Liz's insights to him.

Ron nodded, dismissively. I surmised that he'd already heard from Liz. "I don't need to hear anything more from you," he said.

"Gee, you were so ready to impale me not long ago," I replied. "I would again remind you that I was elected to represent the non-tenure track faculty. Most are women. If I were so prejudiced against women, they would certainly not have elected me."

Ron shuffled through some papers on his desk. "I have tons of papers to grade," he said. "It's almost the end of the term. The budgetary crisis is growing. I've already given too much time to your matter." Ron started pulling certain papers from the piles to grade first.

I wondered if he planned to grade his best students' work first so he could to set the standard for the rest. Ron had to keep in the good graces of the Chair. To do that meant treating me more and more shabbily. If Ron didn't toe the party line, Spet would find a way to get back at him. Ron couldn't be fired, since he had tenure, but Spet would see that he was denied promotions and raises, even demoted.

Prior to Ron's getting tenure, he had been the most responsible and level-headed Director of Writing that I'd worked with. He eschewed the formulaic, write-by-numbers, approach that was the vogue in many English Departments, preferring a more thoughtful, individualized approach to every paper. He stressed genuine critical thinking instead of superficial dash.

I was not sure that I should have gone out of my way to write letters of support on Ron's behalf as I did. I even encouraged colleagues to do the same, since there was some doubt as to whether the higher ups were going to grant him tenure.

A picture of Ron's young son came to mind. Still a toddler, he was the apple of Ron's eye. Ron loved his other children too. Something about the boy troubled me, but I couldn't quite put my finger on what. I tried to look with my internal sight to see what might be wrong. I saw the boy growing taller, running toward the horizon, but falling down, limp as a rag doll.

I had no idea what to make of the vision. For a moment, I wondered if I were wishing evil upon the boy and his family. But I knew better. I was certain that wasn't it. It came to mind that when we sell our souls in order to get ahead, everyone around eventually pays for this act. So does the offender.

I asked God for special grace and protection for the boy and his family. Whether my habit of praying for people in trouble truly made a difference, I didn't know. I hoped it did.

Thanksgiving

Dan and his new friend Rick knew that I didn't return to my home town to spend the holidays with my family. Neither of them planned to spend Thanksgiving with their families. Since Sharon had still not communicated with me, they invited me to spend the holiday with them. Because both of them lived in one bedroom apartments with small kitchens and not many appliances, dishes, and pans, I suggested that we have a potluck at my house. "We can spend the morning cooking and then eat our feast in the afternoon," I said. "That way, Tray won't have to spend her holiday alone."

I had heard that Rick worked out, but was not prepared for someone so tall and bulky. His muscles were so large that he practically popped out of his shirt and pants. In so many ways, he and Dan were flying in the face of conventional notions. They certainly didn't look like wimps. But then, I knew that lots of gay men were starting to bulk up and break various stereotypes, sometimes on purpose, sometimes because they never fit them in the first place.

Tray jumped up on Rick, as if he were her long lost friend. Dan said something about her "Lusting after someone new, even first thing in the morning."

"Morning sex is best, you know," Rick intoned.

"I wouldn't know," Dan answered. "She's never jumped on me."

"She must like the way you smell," I said.

Dan and Rick had brought a turkey that we would stuff together, put into a cooking bag and wait for, while cleaning the house, setting the table, and preparing a relish made with fresh cranberries ground with oranges, walnuts, and celery.

Rick said that he was a whiz at sweet potatoes and brown sugar. Dan was going to make a pecan pie.

"I certainly am glad we all learned to cook," I said. "I'm going to put some regular potatoes into the oven, along with a few whole yams, all in their jackets. I'll also make some scalloped corn. I don't like the overly-sugared foods that many Americans devour for the holidays."

"He needs to watch his weight," Dan said.

"You've got that right," I said. "Really sweet foods also make me feel sick; so do greasy ones."

In something of a Southern accent, Rick remarked, "Well, honey, we'll have to cancel our plans to ladle on the butter, the lard, and them bacon drippings."

"Ted, have you still never been drunk?" Dan asked. He hauled an assortment of liquor packed in a cardboard box into the house. "Here's a bottle of cranberry liqueur, a half bottle of Chivas Regal, a couple of bottles of good wine from France, a bottle of Mumms, a bottle of Remy Martin, and a bottle of Cointreau. Now, where do you want to start? We're going to get you drunk."

"Brought your whole liquor cabinets, did you?" I joked. For a moment I worried about everyone getting drunk, not just me.

That soon passed, however, as I saw that neither Dan nor Rick drank quickly or heavily. Except for an occasional sip, they let their glasses sit idly on the countertops as we prepared our feast.

Rick decided to make some fresh bread. He had to run out to the nearest convenience store for yeast because I didn't have any. "You can say lots of bad things about queers, but we know how to cook," he said, returning to put the ingredients together in a big bowl. He kneaded the bread and covered it with a cloth so it could rise. Like an expert pastry chef, he didn't even use a recipe.

Dan and I prepared some stuffing from a mix. We liberally added chopped celery, onions, and chicken bouillon before we placed the mixture into the turkey and in the cooking bag around it.

When the doorbell rang, Dan answered it.

I heard him greet and invite someone in. Who in the world would be there on Thanksgiving, I wondered. I moved from the back of the house to the dining and living area to see who was there.

There in the foyer, holding two bottles of Beringer Gamay Beaujolais in each hand, stood Sharon. She looked wonderful, eyes bright, glowing skin.

I took the wine. "I sure didn't expect to see you, since I haven't heard a word for weeks."

"Unreliable me," Sharon said, smiling. She handed her coat to Dan. "Do you know there are nuns going in and out of the two units near the alley?" she asked.

"Mother Cabrini and her nuns used this building as their mission headquarters near the first part of the century," I said.

"I meant nuns' spirits, of course," Sharon said.

"I have no idea which units they used, however," I said. "The nuns might have used the entire building."

"I'll bet it was just those units," Dan said. "I trust Sharon's psychic insights," he explained.

"Whether the spirits were the actual spirits of nuns still going in and out of the building, or whether they had somehow imprinted the air with their energy, I don't know," I said. I wondered what had prompted Sharon to show up unannounced. She was probably feeling lonely. If I had had to spend the holidays alone I would have been all right. I'd done it before. But for Sharon to do so might send her off on some kind of binge.

Most of the food preparation was finished. We had only to clean up the countertops, put things away, and run a couple of loads of dishes through the dishwasher. "I'm not a good cook, but I help with cleanup," Sharon said. She found my wine glasses and poured us each a glassful.

"She doesn't want to poison us," Rick mocked, winking at Dan.

"I'm sure you guys have eaten worse," Sharon said, "even if true love waits."

"Ahem," I said, half joking. "You guys act as if you're old friends. Rick's no doubt heard something of Sharon from Dan, but I've never said a thing about Rick to Sharon. I'm not sure I've said much about Dan either." I glanced at everyone's face, trying to read them. I wondered if people had plotted behind my back.

"You said enough that I could fill in the blanks," Sharon responded. She raised her glass for a toast. "I know Dan is one of your favorite former students, so we shall toast to old friends."

"And new friends," Rick added, raising his glass, as Dan and I followed.

"By the way," Sharon began, "I want you to know I'm everyone's sexual orientation. In fact, I've considered becoming a lesbian."

"Not another political lesbian," I said, rather tongue in cheek. I recalled my first trip to Europe. I met many women, especially in Holland, who had thrown over men because "men were dominating, obnoxious, and hurtful toward women." They were only too glad to let me hear about it. I figured they let all men know.

"I've also thought of joining up with a gay couple as their sexless mistress," Sharon explained. "I do better without sexual involvements, and I get along with gay men."

"That's because you're perverse," I said.

Sharon gave me a surprised look—until she realized I was teasing. "Well, I am kind of perverse," she responded. Dan saw to it that we didn't let Sharon move into self-accusation by saying, "Well, most everyone I've ever gotten to know was somewhat perverse, barring myself."

"Hey, I'm not perverse," Rick said. "We're even waiting to have sex. No one dare call us perverse."

"You are? You're actually waiting to have sex?" Sharon asked.   She put down her wine glass and leaning forward to hear their story.

"You told them true love waits," I said.

"It just came to mind," she said. "I was being clever, I thought."

I sensed that she seemed somehow too interested in Rick and Dan's line of thinking. As I examined myself, I knew I was afraid that she'd use this as an excuse for not having sex again until we were sure of our love.

Rick and Dan explained their reasoning.

"Well, I think they have some good reasons not to consummate their relationship until they're sure," Sharon said, turning to me. "I wish I'd been strong enough to wait."

"If I'd have done that," I said, "I'm not sure I'd ever have had sex at all."

All three of them laughed.

"Maybe moving into a building where nuns were headquartered was no accident," Dan said.

"Well, maybe I *would* have had sex with Sharon," I said. I paused, smiling. "Somewhere along the line."

"I've also thought of joining a gay couple for sex," Sharon said. She seemed in a confessional, or provocative, mood—I didn't know which.

"Would you have to love them first?" Dan asked. I wasn't sure if he was being serious either.

"I think we've had enough of the shocking and perverse for now," I said. I called Tray over. "This dog needs more attention. She's coming out," I paused, "of her shell. I'd hate to have her retreat because of being shocked and ignored." I petted her then encouraged her to make the rounds for attention. "I'm not being ignored," I said. "But I am feeling rather shocked."

By early evening I felt exhausted. I wasn't used to having so many people around, everyone asking questions, commenting, expecting witty repartee.

When Dan and Rick finally left after feasting on leftovers, Sharon and I talked about the holidays. Although I'd sent out some letters in response to several job openings around the country, I was not sure that anyone was going to ask me to job interviews during the Modern Language Convention in New York City right after Christmas.

I concluded that I'd rather spend the time with Sharon in Denver than fly to New York and hope. Sharon suggested we spend a couple of weeks in Europe during my Christmas break. Sharon would also take the time off. "Business is slow around Christmas," she said.

I finally said, "I don't think I can afford it. I can barely afford a trip to New York."

"I spent Christmas in Vienna once. Brad and I spent a lot of time in the hotel drinking and doing drugs. But we did get in some skiing in the Alps and some waltzing." She paused, a sad look coming over her face. "Most of the time was spent in the hotel, though." She slumped a little in the chair. She seemed to want to talk about this experience, although her physical expressions made me realize that her memories were painful.

"You don't need to talk about it," I said, "not unless you want to."

"I had really wanted to attend a ball on New Year's Eve and waltz in the New Year, but Brad was too stoned to leave the hotel room. I threatened to go by myself. We had tickets. I even threatened to find a partner on the street."

"I've spent a fair number of Christmases and New Year's Eves by myself, which really wasn't a whole lot different than spending them with my mates," I said.

"The holidays are supposed to be such happy times, such family occasions," Sharon whispered.

Noticing that she was starting to cry, I thought perhaps we should change the subject. "Let's walk Tray."

Sharon glanced at her watch and realized it was later than she'd thought. "I have to be up for a big showing in the morning," she said. "I'm so sorry, but I have to go. If I'm going to pay for our trip to Europe at Christmas, I have to close this deal. The commission is big."

"Oh, you're going to pay for it," I said. My mind was relieved.

After Sharon left, Tray and I walked a few blocks by ourselves. The night wasn't cold at all, in the thirties from a warm westerly wind. Half talking to myself, half to Tray, I wondered if the relationship with Sharon would really gel. Dan and Rick said they'd be glad to dog sit if Sharon and I ever wanted to get away. To know that Tray could spend time with friends that she liked was comforting, although in some small corner of my consciousness I worried about leaving her. She was getting up in years. I didn't want to remind her of my earlier neglect.

Cut Offs

The day after Thanksgiving Sharon phoned. I was home, sending out more job applications and trying to figure out how to tell the Cathedral that I wasn't doing a thing more for them unless I got my promised salary.

"I've reserved roundtrip tickets on a TWA flight to Cairo," she said. "That should be exotic enough for us. I charged them to my AMEX."

"I'll come up with the money for hotels, as long as they aren't lavish," I said. "Since I'm very careful with my money, I think I can manage it."

"If you need help, or we decide to splurge, don't hesitate to ask," Sharon said. "I make plenty, as I've said. I'm glad to squander some on worthy causes."

"I've never spent much on hotel rooms in my travels abroad because I spend little time in them. I get out and see things. Nor do I take tours," I reminded her. I decided I'd better stop typing, or I'd have to go back and rip up what I'd just written. I didn't do well with more than one task at a time. "I like to meet locals and get to know them."

"I know," Sharon said, laughing, "You feel too protected from life as it is really lived when you're with other tourists who are being herded like sheep." She paused. "You may be sorry for that position in Egypt. At least, that's what I've heard."

"You'll protect me," I replied. Her generosity felt good.

"Be sure you get to the doctor immediately for whatever shots are recommended—hemoglobin, tetanus, and whatever else they recommend, maybe malaria pills. I'll do the same. If visas are required we'll have to rush those too. I can pull strings. I've done it before. I have friends."

An hour later, Sharon called back. "Visas are required, but we can get them at the point of entry."

After that, Sharon became silent. She didn't phone. She didn't return my calls. I dropped by her condominium, but she didn't answer the buzzer.

Whenever we made some breakthrough toward intimacy, she seemed to become a ghost. Had she started doing drugs again? Had she experienced some kind of psychotic break? I had no idea.

I began to wonder if she'd found someone else, someone who would not require so much from her. I couldn't blame her, but I wanted to know. At least, that way I could move on—or try to.

She'd shown up at Thanksgiving, even though signaling she wouldn't. Would she reappear like this again? It had been ten days.

I was walking between campus buildings, thinking about how long to give Sharon before trying another tack, and what that other tack might be, when I ran into Dr. Spet. I had no desire to talk to him, but he said, "Hello." He wasn't unfriendly. His manner was cool. "Do you have any job interviews for MLA this year?" he asked. He looked me over, and then his eyes darted about, as if on the lookout for anyone who might be listening.

"Only ten or eleven colleges and universities advertised positions that might be suitable for me, but they don't seem overly interested in my candidacy," I answered. "A few have asked for my references, but I've not had any calls for interviews at MLA."

Spet's scenario was typical. He started by seeming to be interested and caring, yet something sinister, lurking just below the surface, quickly took over. "You ought to think of your Ph.D. as a carousel ticket," Spet responded. "If you don't get on the horse quickly, your ticket soon expires," he said. "The carnival moves on."

I listened in silence.

"If I were you I'd retrain. Go back to school and take a degree in library science. You might like being a librarian," he said, watching to note my reaction.

Again I was thrown for a loop. He was suggesting that I look for another career, but why as a librarian? My other career choices had something to do with books, although they were more people centered than library science. I could excuse Spet for not knowing me well enough to figure that out. It was perhaps something that he would have done if he had not become a professor. His people skills were notoriously weak. Yet, I was suspicious of his intentions. His inability to move up to an Ivy League university had been a terrible disappointment. He let everyone know it. I felt like asking him about that. I could probably couch the blow in the velvet glove of concern myself.

"By the way, I've been reading some of your poetry," Spet said. Again his eyes searched me, and then spied over the area, as if on the lookout.

"Oh, thanks," I said, feeling caught off guard. I was glad that I hadn't said something nasty to him after all. Perhaps he had not meant to turn the knife, as I'd thought.

"You have some talent," he said, carefully, thoughtfully, pausing as if he were formulating his next sentence. He looked down his nose at me.

"I've worked on it. I'm not one of those people who turn out brilliant material on the first try." "You do know, don't you, that you're no Yeats," he said, searching my face for a reaction.

Again I was puzzled. Why would I want to be Yeats? Why would anyone want to be? I liked Yeats a great deal, but his high rhetoric was not mine.

"Milton is not a great poet," Spet added. He was really laying on the criticism. "He's too religious to be great."

I glanced at my watch. "You'll have to excuse me. I have to get to my office."

"I know you're very religious too," Spet said.

"I have a student waiting for me," I said. I was not even going to try to answer Spet's crazy criticisms.

Spet smiled his tight, little smile, his eyes still looking me over as if looking for clues about my inner life, still darting about us, watchful of who might be around, who might be wondering what we were saying, what we were plotting.

"He does this to raise our deepest fears. He hopes to cause our mechanisms of self-damnation to kick in," an old faculty friend from another department had warned. "He needs to imagine that everyone is a character in a novel of international intrigue," his personal secretary, Shana, had only a few days before remarked, when she and I and the departmental secretary, Jill, found ourselves alone in the English Department. "That lends meaning to his otherwise empty life. He has no real friends. Lovers, yes, family, yes— but no friends," Jill chimed in.

Jill said, "I've had three requests for your job placement file, which I sent out." She got up to check to make sure no one had come in. "I thought I heard the front door," she explained.

"At least two people called to talk with Spet about you," Shana said. "He called up three search committee heads on his own."

"How'd he know who to call?" I asked.

"He checks to see who's asked for your files," Jill replied. "I keep a list."

"He puts nothing in writing, leaving you to think that glowing letter of recommendation he showed you and added to your placement file is still how he views you," Shana said.

"Ron does the same, nowadays, anyway," Jill added. "Devils learn from each other."

Ron, I figured, would not have gone along with Spet if he hadn't known what would happen if he didn't. Spet's manner, his ways of assassinating character and talent, and his suspicious behavior and darting eyes, reminded me of the Dean of the Cathedral's. Even though Spet hated religion and McDougal was a supporter, both used others in every way they could. If we refused to go along with them, to flatter and worship them, we were further abused.

When I turned the corner to my office, I saw Sharon standing outside, waiting for me. She smiled widely, openly, as if there had been no distance between us, no time lapsed between our Thanksgiving tryst and the present, fifteen days later.

"You're always throwing me," I said, shaking my head. I couldn't help but smile. I said, "I thought you'd moved too near the edge of a flat map of the world and fallen off." I was glad to see her. I would always be glad to see her, even if I was also annoyed.

"I try to keep you off guard," she said. "Don't you know human relations are like engaging in a game of chess?"

"I try not to think of them that way."

"You'd do better if you would. Trust me. I'm very successful, as you know—"

I started to interrupt, but she stopped me by placing her finger on my lips.

"I'm very successful *in business*; I started to say, because I look at things as chess games. You've got to outmaneuver your opponent," Sharon said. "I saw you with that thing called your Chairman. He's a weasel—long nose, beady little eyes that dart about to see what mischief he can get up to next. People look like what they are inside," Sharon said. She paused, searching my face, my eyes. With eyes full of pity, she looked at my mouth, as if ready to kiss me. "I would never claim to be successful in love," she said. "You have no idea how hard this is for me. How frightening."

I thought of all the imbalances in modern life, all those business successes that were lousy at relationships. Then, there were those of us who were not very successful at either.

"Now kiss me, you fool," Sharon said, removing her finger from my mouth, "and show me that you love me." She kissed me long and deep.

I pulled away for air. "I really can't be seen in such passionate embrace outside the Interfaith Center," I said. "It would give the wrong impression. Most people have no idea who you are. You might be one of my students. If they assumed that, I'd be deemed guilty and sentenced."

"OK, let's walk over to The Market," she said, taking my arm and turning me around. "I've decided that I'd like to go to France. If we run into cold weather in Paris, we can hop a train to the south. Provence is pretty mild even at Christmas. I like Aix. We could also visit Lourdes, for healing."

As we neared Speer, we passed a man holding a sign saying, "Homeless, Please Help." Internally I was searching out places where I could suggest that he go for food and shelter, but found my thoughts interrupted by Sharon's comments.

"Get a job," she snapped. "Make yourself useful."

Shocked by her attitude, and words, I became silent as a stone. How in the world was some unkempt homeless man supposed to get himself a job? Doing what?

"You think I shouldn't have said that," Sharon whispered, as we walked in a steady but tomb- silent pace across Speer, arm in arm. "I know how you feel even without your saying a word."

"Well," I said. But I said nothing else. I didn't know what to say. I hoped she'd blurted out those words without pausing to get hold of herself and think. She was not heartless. She was troubled. Disturbed people have a hard time being compassionate.

Here I was sounding like my grandmother. She excused everyone, even criminals, as my granddad, the hard-bitten cynic, liked to point out.

"I get so tired of all these people bleeding everyone for sympathy and money," Sharon said. "Most of them don't work because they don't want to work. They'd rather live in a box under the bridge."

"Your reasoning is awfully breezy," I said. "Your attitude is worse."

"You're darned right. Those winter winds give you pneumonia. If that doesn't kill you, some lunatic with a knife will slit your throat."

"What about the people who are on the streets because of mental disorders and addictions that prevent them from working?" I asked.

"I know that's what some people say," Sharon answered.

"The government keeps cutting mental health benefits, closing down facilities where people can get help. No one deals well with mental illness, especially chronic mental illness. It's too costly."

"I hadn't thought about that," she said. "I have great insurance. It covers eighty percent of my psychiatric visits, meds, and hospitalization, with a $2,500 out of pocket cap."

"You're lucky," I said. "You're insured. And insurance companies are trying to get rid of that kind of coverage. What if you didn't have it?"

"I'd find myself begging for money and food on the streets," she answered. She stared thoughtfully at her feet. She stopped dead in her tracks. She opened her purse and started rummaging through the contents.

Finding some bills she left me and ran across the street to locate the homeless man.

I stood on the corner with my mouth open. One thing was clear—I never knew what Sharon would do next.

When she returned, she was beaming. "I gave it all away," she called. "I emptied my purse. Wasn't it *Magnificent Obsession* where that guy crashes into Jane Wyman and blinds her or something, so he spends the rest of his life trying to do good?"

"Something like that," I said.

"Well I gave away every cent I had, not only to that guy but to two other street people who were talking to him. I feel so good," she exclaimed, beaming.

I laughed. "I suppose I'll have to buy the coffee."

"You're the man," Sharon said. She hooked my arm in hers and walked very close. The day brightened considerably.

Early in my life I found that it was better to give food rather than money and direct people to charitable organizations for help. St. Francis Center handed out free sandwiches at noon to the street people who stopped by. Some shelters still existed around town, most operated by charities. Often, these were full because the demand was far greater than the supply. It was becoming greater every day.

"What are you thinking?" Sharon asked, breaking my reverie. "You've become very tense."

"Have I?" I laughed.

"Don't tell me otherwise," Sharon said. Your muscles have tightened like steel traps."

"You know much about me," I said.

"Lots of people make fun of sensitive males, either because the guys are really wimps, or they're just pretending to be sensitive," Sharon, said. We stood at the counter inside the Market. Sharon ordered two almond coffees. She held out her hand for my wallet.

"And?" I asked. "I know there's more." I removed my backpack, reached into it, and handed my wallet to Sharon.

"You're the only sensitive male I've met," she said. "One of the few genuine human beings too." She paid the barista. She laughed, openly, without subterfuge.

"I guess that's why I try not to advertise," I said. "People take advantage."

"All the sociopaths come running," Sharon replied.

"To say that I'm sensitive seems too much like an excuse."

"That's why you let me do it," Sharon said. She carried the cups over to the table inside. There were no sidewalk tables. "See, even though I'm one of the best salespeople in my company, I can still do traditional wifely things for my man." She even pulled out our chairs.

"Um, I think that's a husband's task traditionally," I said.

"Who the hell cares," Sharon said, giggling. "You're attracted to Afghans," she said, "because you're so much like them."

Again I laughed, pondering her notion. "Let's see, a hybrid of dog, cat, and horse. Super-sensitive, high-spirited, owned by no one, but lending oneself as a companion—if there's a true bond."

"Don't forget true clowns."

"So graceful, yet so clumsy. Yup," I said, sipping my coffee.

"High maintenance."

I rolled my eyes at that. "I'm such a poodle," I said.

Sharon winked. "Good doggy," she said.

Chess

If I were high maintenance, as Sharon had said, I did not know what to make of her. On December sixteenth, she stopped by my office to say she'd changed her mind about where we should spend Christmas. I'd first recommended Rome "Because I've been there several times, and I love Italy." But Sharon wanted Egypt. So we decided on Egypt.

"I don't want Egypt," she said, sitting down across from my desk. "I want something more exotic."

I looked up from my book. "India?" I asked.

"We ought to spend Christmas traveling the Amazon," she said. "I want more danger."

I didn't know if she was pulling my leg or not. "I've never been to Egypt. I have mixed feelings about it," I said. "But I think we'd better stick with it. The tickets are booked, and I've reserved the Hotel Nile to start with. I figure we can find hotels as we go along. That's what I typically do."

She looked into my eyes. "I worry that Egypt will be especially dangerous for me."

"The ancient sites should be wonderful," I said, "but I've heard it's a spiritually oppressed place. You're particularly vulnerable."

Sharon nodded. She leaned forward in her seat. "I'll have to be especially careful to protect my psyche," she said. "Substance abuse opens people to all kinds of Dark forces."

Although I could have taken more than two weeks, I thought the shorter time was perhaps a godsend. I hoped my own psyche didn't suffer too many onslaughts.

"Egypt is a Muslim country," Sharon reminded me. "Christian holidays are not publicly celebrated. "The Copts celebrate Christmas holidays in private, and the places that cater to Western tourists also put up modest decorations, but you won't see crèches or crosses." She nodded my way. "See, I've done my homework."

"Ok," I said, "we'll have fun."

"Maybe I could find myself a little brown baby in a basket floating down the Nile," she said, her eyes brightening. She rocked an invisible baby.

"Your own little Moses," I said.

"His name would be a derivative of Mohammed," she replied. "Maybe Hammed. I'm feeling maternal these days."

"I just don't want you to clutch an asp to your bosom and give it suck, like Cleopatra," I said.

One of the joys of our relationship was that we both were verbal. We were infinitely sensitive to the multiple levels of reality. We were bound to reflect and influence each other.

"These are our salad days, Mister," Sharon said sternly. "And I do not expect you to let them rot. We will find our brown baby in the reeds of Egypt, at least metaphorically."

"And we can eat, drink, and be merry, but not die, except in that other, better, sense," I said. "No jumping this world for the one to come." I winked. "Oh *petit mort.*"

She leaned toward my mouth.

"Could you make the sounds for me?" I asked. "Just let me hear them, please," I begged, laughing.

Sharon laughed. But she managed to make the proper orgasmic noises.

So loudly, so expressively, that Louise peeked in the door. "Is everything all right?"

Break Up

The next day, a bright but crisp December morning, Dan appeared at my office door. He didn't knock. I looked up and saw him. "I see you're really feeling like Christmas," he remarked, commenting on my lack of decorations. He looked distraught, his shoulders slumped. "Rick left me," he began, coming in.

"When? Why?" I asked.

"He just told me. For someone else," Dan said. They'd still never had sex. "We weren't sure our relationship was solid enough. At least that's what I thought. That was my reasoning. But, it turns out Rick was screwing somebody else all along," Dan cried. His breathing labored, he dropped into the chair opposite me and put his face into his hands.

"Are you sure of that?" I asked. "Things aren't always what they seem."

"He told me," Dan said, speaking to the floor. "Now I know why it was so easy for him to wait. He wasn't horny. He was getting all the sex he wanted with an old boyfriend. They'd broken up, except for sex, which they were having regularly."

"Lots of modern relationships are messy, and gay ones often more so," I said.

"Damn it Ted, I come to you for help and you tell me gay relationships are messy? Do you really think that's what I want to hear?"

"I'm sorry," I said. "I can't tell you something I don't believe. Would you really want that?"

Dan calmed down. He lifted his face and looked directly at me. "No," he muttered. "You know I wouldn't." He looked back down at the floor. "I need some place to stay. I gave up my apartment and moved in with Rick on the first." He began crying again. "We were going to surprise people with a getting together party." I wondered out loud if maybe moving in together had caused Rick to bolt.

"Is Sharon having sex with you now?" Dan asked, looking directly at me.

"As you know, I've certainly never found straight relationships easy either." I was extremely uncomfortable with the question. I avoided eye contact.

"I thought not. You're a great one to give advice on intimate relations," Dan said.

"I am better than many who would advise you precisely because I don't pretend to understand the difficulties of trying to be intimate with someone who has serious problems," I said.

Realizing that he'd wounded me, Dan apologized. "I'm sure that's true. If I had been molested I would probably never be able to have sex again."

"With another person anyway," I added. I thought I shouldn't have said that.

Dan laughed. He grew more serious. "I think Rick was also molested."

"Nothing surprises me," I said, shaking my head. "It seems that abuse of children is much more widespread than people ever imagined."

"Could I stay with you until I find a place of my own?" he asked.

"Sure," I said. "You can stay in the guest bedroom. Then I won't have to find a dog sitter while Sharon and I are away."

"Dogs are at least faithful."

"To the very end," I replied. "Now, you need to disappear for awhile. As you can see, I've got a ton of papers to grade," I said, pointing to the stacks of research papers and final exams on my desk. "We're at the end of the term, so the heat is on. I've got to get everything marked and my grades turned in by Friday."

Dan left to pack his car with his things. All he had to do was show up that night and settle into the guest room.

When I felt his hand shaking my shoulder in the night, I gained consciousness and muttered, "I thought you were going to dog sit, not need baby sitting."

"I know, but I'm scared," Dan said. "And cold. I haven't slept by myself for days. And this is a strange place."

"It gets stranger by the day," I remarked, telling him to get in on the other side of the bed. "I don't give up my side for anyone."

Dan jumped in and snuggled up near me.

"You're poking me," I said.

"Oh," he pulled back. "I was having a nightmare about Rick boning his old boyfriend." "From all evidence, it must have been exciting," I remarked.

"Well," Dan began. "It was. Upsetting as well."

"*O tempora! O mores!*"

"Don't speak Greek. I don't know it."

"I don't either," I said. "That was Latin." I rubbed Dan's head affectionately and said," You can sleep up close, but I don't want to get poked. Not even by your elbow." I paused. "True love waits. Remember?"

Ghosts

Two days before our flight, Sharon stopped by the house. I mentioned that Dan was staying with me.

"Oh, he is," she said, her happy voice gaining an edge.

"Dan had just moved into Rick's, but then they broke up. Seems Rick was dating someone else all along, so he needed a place. It's simple, you see," I said, feeling myself wince. "I offered Dan my guest room."

She ran up the stairs to see if indeed the guest room looked used. When she turned around, her face looked less troubled. "I guess I shouldn't be upset. I was projecting my own issues onto you and Dan."

I shrugged but said nothing.

"I certainly can't claim to have been faithful to anyone for long. I've been true to you longer than everyone else," she added.

I still said nothing but led her back downstairs.

"I can't promise that it's going to last," she said.

"It had better." I decided to try to get hold of the situation with humor. I winked, although I meant it.

"My demons take over," she said

"I know."

Dan was sleeping soundly each night in the guest bedroom. Tray, as usual, slept on the floor beside my bed. Sharon faced no threat from Dan.

The morning that we were scheduled to fly out of Denver to New York then on to Cairo, Sharon called to say that she'd have to meet me a few days later. "A family crisis has come up so that I have to postpone my flight. Don't worry, neither death nor hell can prevent my being with you," she assured me.

She wouldn't tell me what her family crisis was. I didn't pry. I looked at the clock, hung up, and called a taxi.

I wondered if I could count on Sharon to keep her promise that she wouldn't leave me in Cairo on my own. Quickly, I sat at the computer and composed a note to Dan. I explained what had happened. "I'll see you in a couple of weeks. "I'll catch a taxi home. Don't let yourself get too lonely. Tray isn't bad at snuggling, although you'll have to lift her up onto the bed. Please pray for me. From what I hear of Egypt, I'll need lots of spiritual shielding."

The connections were exhausting. I had to run down the ramps at Stapleton to get to my plane on time. I got to the gate just as they were about to close it. When I arrived in New York, I spent three and a half hours waiting in La Guardia for the flight to Cairo. I remembered that I didn't tell people at the Cathedral that I was tired of being a slave. "Oh well, I've left Egypt for Egypt." I laughed. I shrugged. "The story of my life. Boy, oh boy."

At the Cairo airport, I was surprised at the laxity of the guards. It was an unimpressive structure by international standards. Officials didn't seem to worry about a thing. Blithely, they asked for twelve Egyptian pounds, about four American dollars, for my thirty day visa. They stamped the paper and placed it in my passport. I found my bags waiting for me and walked outside. It was sunset. The weather was fairly warm, but not hot. Easily, I hired a taxi to the hotel.

The din, dust, crush, and smog of the darkening Cairo streets struck me. I emerged from the taxi on a street running alongside to the hotel on my left. I heard an internal voice saying, "I know this place. I do not like it." I heeded the voice, but I also remained skeptical, just in case it stemmed from my imagination. I had prepared myself to enjoy Egypt and Cairo, not to disdain them.

I glanced at the Nile, which stretched out before me like a silver ribbon. It was not impressive, not so wide as I'd expected, at least not in the heart of Cairo. I thought it might be more so out in the desert where only pyramids and sphinxes looked on.

The hotel lobby's furnishings—overstuffed couches, chairs and wood tables, lamps with dim light bulbs, pull chains and soiled lampshades—had once been new and luxurious. Perhaps as recent as 1950, although in style they looked like they dated to Agatha Christi's times. By now, things were shabby and threadbare. Everything looked dusty, which didn't surprise me. This was the Sahara.

The desk clerk was dressed in a tattered brown, baggy suit. He wore a mustard yellow shirt with a faded, old tie of some color that I couldn't distinguish. He was an older, heavyset man, his hair and moustache turning a yellowish grey. I noticed how large and leathery his hands were, like his face. "Do you like Cairo?" he asked. His English was good.

"I haven't seen much of it. Just the streets on the way from the airport and the Nile—all in the light of the setting sun," I said.

"Here the sun is always setting, so to speak," the man said. "There is to be another person, a woman, I believe?"

"She'll arrive in a couple of days," I said.

"Oh," the clerk said. He turned around and shuffled to the pigeonholes where the keys were kept. Few keys appeared to be gone. The man looked the slots over. Finally, he took a standard hotel key out and handed it to me. "The room is on the second floor," he said.

I decided to take the curved marble staircase. The staircase was wide, with threadbare leaf-patterned carpet that seemed as if it had once been maroon running up and down the center of the steps. A long while ago, the staircase had been grand, I imagined.

Sharon and I had been promised a large room overlooking the Nile. This one was small, dark, and had no view. The one small window looked out onto other buildings in the back. This wasn't what we had been promised. I knew very well that, while I might make the best of it, Sharon would be very unhappy. She would never accept it.

I decided to trudge back to the desk clerk with my bag to ask if he did not have another room on the Nile side of the building, as we had been promised. With labored breath, the clerk took up his room chart and, with much hemming and hawing, handed me the key to another room. "I'll come up to your room after I get off work tonight for a tip," he said.

His English was perfect. I hoped that this time a cigar was just a cigar, although I wondered what exactly he meant. I'd not been to Egypt before. Perhaps the clerk was just making some silly remark. However, I decided there'd be no tip from me. I'd been told we'd have a nice room facing the Nile. The clerk hadn't done anything special in giving me the room that had been promised.

On the way up the stairs, I continued to wonder why someone would come up to my room for a tip. Why not ask for one right there? The statement seemed rather provocative, although nothing in his manner suggested it. Perhaps I was reading too much into his statement, and asking for a tip later, after work, was the Egyptian way.

At least the new room at the front of the hotel was spacious, with three large picture windows overlooking the Nile, as promised. I unpacked and went to bed. Exhausted, I did not sleep well. I was cold. Although some sort of heat and air conditioning unit stood in the corner near the windows, I could not figure out how to turn on the heat. I wondered if the heater even worked. I doubled the blankets on the bed by folding each in half and not moving so that I kept them on top of me. Soon I fell asleep again.

Nightmares plagued me. I was not sure whether I worried about Sharon, or Egypt, or both. I could remember only the most vivid scenes of the dreams the following morning. I recalled struggling in sandstorm after sandstorm, and people's hands reaching out from all sides to take all the money that I had. Even when I showed them my empty wallet, they grabbed it, searching for more, and then tossed it aside. Jumping on me, they emptied my pockets, hands, hands, hands—still demanding more.

When I woke the next morning, I did not feel rested. It was more than jet lag. I decided I'd better have breakfast, with coffee, before I left the hotel. I walked to the hotel restaurant on the top floor. It was open to the air.

An old, weathered, man, dressed in dusty looking dark pants and white shirt that was yellowing with age, shuffled over to take my order. He was wearing old brown shoes with the backs of the heels walked down.

"Would you like an American breakfast?" he asked. Again, his English was good.

I was served a glass of something like Tang (the waiter said it was orange juice), a small metal pot of strong coffee with grounds in it, a couple of cold pitas, with pats of butter, and little plastic tubs of red jelly on the side. The jelly tasted of some kind of berry. I wasn't sure what.

"Would you like eggs?" the waiter asked.

"No, thanks," I said. Not terribly fond of eggs anyway, I was afraid these folks would make them more tasteless than ever.

As I walked to the Egyptian Museum off Tahrir Square, a middle-aged Egyptian man with a heavy black mustache approached me. He was wearing a Western style brown polyester suit and maroon tie. The suit was ill fitting and baggy. The tie looked stained.

It was almost nine. I wanted to be at the museum as soon as the doors opened.

The man began chatting in good English. "Where are you from? How long will you be in Cairo?" he asked.

I answered pleasantly.

"Where are you going?" he asked.

"To the Egyptian Museum," I answered. I'd read the museum was huge. "I want to have time to look over everything," I said. "I can go back tomorrow and spend more time on things I want to examine more closely."

I wasn't quite sure how he did it, but I soon found myself following the man away from the Museum across a busy street thick with crazy drivers honking horns, where I was sure we would get hit, over sidewalks, and through several winding alleys toward his dimly lit, but cool, multi-roomed shop. I'd never seen so much junk piled everywhere, on counters, strewn across the floors, everything covered by sandy dust, as if little had been touched, or cleaned, for centuries.

"I really don't have much time. I want to get back to the Museum," I said, fidgeting. I didn't know why I was so compliant. I was in no mood to buy, especially not junk.

The shopkeeper nodded. "Relax. I assure you that you will be at the museum by ten. "It is only nine. The museum will not open at nine. This is Egypt. It is winter. It will not open until ten," he said. "You will have plenty of time for the exhibits." He made an air-patting gesture up and down, made by his right hand, as if to tell me to be seated on an old wood chair and remain calm.

"I read that the museum opens at nine," I said.

"In the winter it does not open until ten," he said. "You're like all Americans, preoccupied with schedules. Besides, there is always tomorrow. There's much old junk in there, and it is much disorganized. Egypt is fading into the past. That is our only glory."

I wondered about the shopkeeper's own denial regarding himself and his merchandise. I sensed that I was being conned. But I decided to give him fifty minutes.

He began hauling out his papyruses. I'd read that this could be expected. The man displayed some very finely painted copies of murals found in the ancient tombs, mixed with many that were only mediocre. I figured that the shopkeeper would show me his perfumes next. However, a dozen or so of his nicest, most deftly painted papyruses, struck me as very pleasant. The brush strokes were careful, precise—in rich golds, browns, emeralds, ochres, blacks, reds, and turquoise. They would make good gifts. Some I could frame for myself. So I haggled a little. While I did not try to go for his throat, I did not want to pay the exorbitant prices that he quoted.

The man then showed me a brass and copper bas relief of Akhenaton. It was well crafted and pleased my eye. I bargained for it. The shopkeeper followed with couple of traditional Egyptian copper and brass pieces of men holding water jugs that I thought would make nice gifts. I realized that they were ash trays.

"Yes, they were very popular here in the past. True relics," he said.

Like most things in Egypt, I started to say, as if getting the hang of things. But I thought better of it. Because this was the homeland of these people, they could talk of Egypt's fading glory, but that might seem too much of an insult from an outsider.

Since my dad was a smoker, I knew that these water carrier ashtrays would be just right for him. If he didn't appreciate the artifice, which he probably would not, he could value their utility.

At last, the shopkeeper pulled out a dozen pint-sized bottles of dark perfumes which were adorned with gold-colored paint. The bottles had little plastic stoppers. The man blew off a coat of heavy dust. He wiped them with his hand. "These are most precious. Traditional Egyptian perfumes," he said.

I found the scents heavy and the liquids inside very oily. They stained my skin. I'd read that at banquets wealthy ancient Egyptians tied waxy perfume cones on the tops of their heads, which then melted down over them as the evening progressed. These seemed updated versions of the old thing.

"I'm really not fond of any of these," I said. "I don't want to buy perfume."

The shopkeeper looked downcast, as if I'd hurt his feelings. "These are Egypt's finest," he cried. "All over the world we are known for our perfumes," he argued, offering me a better price.

"No, thank you."

Then his price got better. And better. He took no heed of my dimming protests.

Finally I agreed to buy four bottles of the stuff. I could find some use for four bottles of the two fragrances that I didn't mind.

At noon, I emerged from the cool darkness into surprisingly bright and hot sunlight with several used plastic bags of a hundred and sixty American dollars worth of merchandise. I realized that somehow I had paid an awful lot for those bottles of perfume, and the things that I actually wanted. On this, my first morning, I had bought enough gifts for most of my friends and family. I would be left with objects for myself as well.

I could see those hands, reaching, reaching, fingers clutching at my wallet and then at every pocket, constantly searching to see if I didn't have more money tucked away somewhere. I would have to be wary.

Because my packages were heavy and bulky, and screamed *tourist*, I decided to take them back to the hotel before proceeding to the museum again. As I wended my way back, I wondered if the voice that I'd heard as I stepped from the taxi was that of my guardian angel or the Holy Spirit?

I also needed lunch. I had eaten no breakfast and was starting to feel a little shaky. I was also feeling fatigued. Perhaps some food would help.

After an unremarkable lunch of pita bread, tomato-lentil soup, falafel, and tea in the rather seedy and unswept restaurant at the top of the hotel, I realized that I was too worn out to go off to the museum. Jet lag had caught up with me. I would not have even two hours before closing, which was at four.

I decided to take it easy. I would nap and think about what to do when I woke up. The afternoon was surprisingly hot, probably in the high nineties. I'd heard that the nights dropped forty to fifty degrees. I remembered how cold I'd been the night before.

I had to remember to ask for more blankets and how to turn on the heat. The room seemed to stay cool enough in the day that I would not need air conditioning.

When I woke up, it was night. When I went downstairs, I was able to catch another desk clerk. He was young and very accommodating, his eyes bright and his face animated. He was dressed in a better fitting, and newer looking, navy blue suit. "I will take care of the heat. You will not need more blankets. The air conditioning is always on during the day," he said. That surprised me. He explained that cooled air did not come from the unit in the room, as I'd thought.

Nor did this desk clerk ask for a tip, or say that he'd come upstairs for one later. To suggest it, I decided, was not a typical Egyptian notion. I could now remember the earlier scene as rather humorous. For his help, and his decency, I handed him a ten dollar note.

Flight

I visited Old Cairo and several Coptic churches. One had been built over the site where Mary, heavy with child, and Joseph, were said to have rested on their flight from King Herod. They were wise to flee. Herod soon slaughtered all the children in his kingdom, afraid of the prophesied Messiah born to free his people.

Mary and Joseph reiterated the flight of their ancestors into Egypt, where they would escape death, although earlier it would have been by starvation, rather than the fury of Herod. *Guest workers*, as the Egyptians thought of the Hebrews, or *slaves*, as they considered themselves, were forced to make choices that better times would have allowed them to avoid. At least they saved their skins.

In Old Cairo, a policeman came from the shadows, his weathered hand holding his crotch. "Psst," he said, nodding at me. He seemed to want me to follow him.

I looked away and walked on. "Just what I wanted," I said, barely audible.

I walked past the graveyard, where thousands and thousands of homeless Egyptians make lean-tos from pieces of cardboard and metal, held up by a plank of termite infested, decaying lumber. If they can't find cardboard or metal, they try to make a space the size of a couple of coffins with some rags, empty cans, and trash. This is home.

As I thought about the signs, this scene seemed significant of the entire country. Every Egyptian I'd met complained that his country held only former glories and kept sliding deeper into the sands of oblivion and corruption. A vast graveyard littered with millennia of monuments.

Here in Old Cairo, I noticed that the churches had clanging bells like those that I'd heard so many times in so many places. I could not escape them. But, because everything in Egypt was miserable, with death, disease, and starvation on every side, these bells did not strike me as comforting. No wonder the disembodied voice had told me he knew Egypt and did not like it. Had he lived here in some past life, now being doomed to wander, to work out his sins in some sort of purgatorial existence, still searching for paradise?

I found a hotel and phoned Sharon. I wondered if she'd left. I reached only her answering machine.

I decided I'd better use my *Let's Go Egypt* and find a cheaper hotel, one used by seriously budget minded tourists. If I were going to be there on my own, I needed to be even more careful. I told the clerk that I liked at the Hotel Nile where I was going.

"If Sharon calls me, or arrives, please tell her where I'll be for the next few days." I gave him a tip and said I'd give him more if he did as I asked. "Just let me know if you hear anything."

He thanked me. "I assure you I shall," he said. He told me he had a graduate degree in sociology. Like many people working as desk clerks and in low paying jobs throughout the country, he was educated. "There are no jobs," he said, "not ones that require an education. Like poor orphans, we wait for someone to die. Then perhaps one of us will be lucky enough to take their vacated position."

At the backpackers' hostel, I arranged a day trip with several tourists out to the Pyramids at Giza. On the mini bus, I began talking with John, an American graduate student. He was short and shaped like Friar Tuck. He had a sharp wit about him. The others went off on their own. John and I explored the sites together.

Most of our guides wore robes, often brown, and bedroom slippers with worn down heels. Outside of Cairo, such garb seemed the norm. Even though people were forbidden to use flash cameras inside the chambers, because flashes faded the exquisite colors covering the ceilings and walls, almost every one of the guides offered to let us take flash pictures anyway—so long as we paid them money. Some tourists did just that. John and I refused.

"I can understand the need to augment their incomes," John remarked. "They might stave off starvation another day."

"But at the cost of destroying Egypt's greatest assets," I answered. "What a quandary. Starvation or destruction of the country at large."

"Either way, the result is the same," John said. He shook his dark head of hair and began to scratch. "I wonder if I've got lice," he said.

"The ancient Egyptians shaved their entire bodies, including heads, because of lice infestations," I said.

"The dangers of reading," John quipped. "We know too much. Better to be ignorant."

"Yeah, and then we fall into the pit with everyone else."

"They pull you there anyway," John said.

"I have nightmares about that," I said.

I liked John. He made me laugh. That took my mind off Sharon.

When we descended into one of the underground chambers, it struck me as so hot and close that I could only think of getting out of there. Usually I was not claustrophobic. John did not seem to react the same way. "I keep hoping we'll see some spirits or something," he said.

"I've seen spirits," I said, "but the ones we'd probably meet here aren't ones I want to hang out with."

When I was a toddler, just learning to write, I often scribbled Yaamat on lamps and walls. My mom would get upset with me and my "invisible friend," as she called him. In my early days, I was always aware of him. I swore I saw that name written on the wall. I looked again, but I saw only hieroglyphs. "I don't read ancient Egyptian," I muttered to myself. But I was sure it was the same name I'd scribbled growing up in Colorado. I wondered what that meant. Was Yaamat my invisible friend, the same one who said, as I stepped onto Cairo streets, that he knew this place and didn't like it?

When John and I finally got out of the underground chambers, I felt relieved. No sooner did I have a chance to breathe than three men with camels met us. The oldest of the men, with a huge boil on the side of his neck, wanted us to ride. I had a hard time taking my eyes off the boil. I again began ruminating on the poverty and disease of this ruined empire.

John eagerly got up on top of the camel that was kneeling for him. I reluctantly got on mine. "I know I don't like camels," I said. "They're too stubborn and, when upset, make ear curdling noises. I know I don't like the way riding them feels."

"How do you think they've survived for centuries?" John asked, his camel getting up, swaying side to side. John almost fell off. The camel herder had to prop him.

I laughed. "What did I tell you? I know I don't like them. I don't know why, but I know it."

When my camel rose, I was prepared. I'd braced myself. I found the ride hard and bouncy, just as I'd surmised.

Every day, I continued to find a phone and call Sharon, always with the same result. Only the answering machine. Never a person. "Dammit, Sharon, what's going on?" I'd ask, placing the receiver back in the cradle.

Although I'd been able to walk off my anxiety, it kept rising.

One the sixth morning, John decided to travel to Alexandria. I wasn't ready to go there yet, although I wanted to see the fabled sea port and where the world's great library had once been. Early Christians were rumored to have burned the library down because they wanted to prevent the dissemination of knowledge that they didn't approve of (probably another myth, I'd read). I was sick of Cairo, but I kept thinking I'd better stick around, in case Sharon showed up or phoned.

That night I decided to splurge on a nice dinner at a good restaurant with table cloths, waiters dressed in black pants, ironed white shirts, and clean ties. I sat down, put the linen napkin on my lap, and suddenly realized I needed to find a restroom. I jumped up, asking a waiter where to go.

I barely got my pants off and started to sit down on an American style toilet (with a seat, unusual, even when I found an American pot). I experienced a bout of violent diarrhea that sprayed all over the toilet and the wall behind. Hardly anything went into the bowl. The room and fixtures had previously been spotless, white.

It was impossible to try to wipe up the mess with toilet paper. The chore would require a bucket, mop, rags, and disinfectant.

On my second day, I'd experienced a little diarrhea. I ate yoghurt, and it soon stopped. I continued to eat some yoghurt every day. I surmised that this episode was because of my worry over Sharon, as much as anything.

Red with embarrassment, I returned to my table. I gathered my courage and alerted the waiter. Surely it wasn't the first time a tourist had fouled their restroom.

After I finished my meal, I left a large tip, not only for the well balanced meal without the usual fatty meats and overcooked vegetables that I found everywhere, or kushari, the cheap mix of boiled lentils and rice, but for the mess I'd made. I was glad I had a shot of hemoglobin before I came. I hoped it'd had time to take hold and protect me.

That night in the hotel I sat in the bed with ten wool blankets over me and looked over my *Let's Go*. I'd seen the major sights of Cairo and nearby. Everywhere, there were beggars, lechers, men and boys with boils the size of baseballs on their necks, and those with amputations, including their right hands, probably as penalties for theft, and infected looking wounds. I rarely saw women, and then only in the company of men. I saw only a few children, most of them in the graveyard of old Cairo. "Nothing like being born and reared so near your grave," I thought. No wonder my stomach was so queasy.

By then, I didn't think Sharon would make it. I hoped she was alright, but even that I didn't know.

It was said that the ancient Egyptians thought death even more important than life. Most of the monuments were meant for the dead, ways to keep the afterlives of the rich and powerful comfortable. No one gave a whole lot of thought to improving the afterlives—or the present lives—of the poor and oppressed. Nothing had changed.

Sick as I was of the country, I had eleven days before my flight out. I had to knuckle under and make the best of things. I wanted to go up the Nile to see Luxor and its temples, as well as those of Karnack, which had once been connected by the three kilometer long Avenue of the Sphinxes. Across the Nile from there stretched West Thebes, with the many monuments, tombs, and temples. The vast Valley of the Kings and the Valley of the Queens lay there, many of the tombs not yet excavated.

So many horror movies, with actors like Boris Karloff, Vincent Price, and Christopher Lee, that I'd loved as a child had been set there—*The Mummy*, *The Mummy's Tomb*, *The Mummy's Curse*, *Mummy's Revenge*, and so on. Some I saw only on TV, some at Saturday afternoon matinees at my local theater, years after they were first released. Boy, did I love such tales, even those set in Transylvania and other eerie locales, even the United States—where the classic and chilling *The Black Cat* was set. My mind, my whole being, had long responded to the supernatural. Even when overdone, the paranormal seemed normal to me.

I also wanted to see the famous dam near Aswan, especially the ancient temples that had been moved from now-flooded lands to the island of Abu Simbel. I'd watched documentaries about this huge project and found them fascinating. If possible, I wanted to take a bus or taxi over to the Red Sea that the Hebrews were said to have crossed when they fled Egypt. There too rose Mount Sinai, where Moses was believed to have received the Ten Commandments, written by the Finger of God. I'd wanted to take a quick trip to Alexandria, which I'd read was nothing like the fabled seaport and center of learning that it once had been, but it was north. Everything else was south and southeast.

Early on the seventh day I decided that I had better tell Sharon—rather, her answering machine—that I was headed to Luxor, Karnak, and environs. I'd phone to say where I would be staying, once I'd figured that out. I would again leave word where I was going after that. By then, I doubted that Sharon would show up in Egypt at all. I walked over to the Hotel Nile to inform the desk clerk. The one that I liked was behind the desk. He wished me well and said he'd be sure to tell Sharon where I'd gone.

I hired a driver, who quoted me a very good price. He seemed honest, humble, and came highly recommended by the budget hotel staff. I figured he could steer me clear of most problems. He did not speed or take stupid chances in traffic. For that I was grateful.

Once in Luxor, I found a budget hotel near the train station in the town center. I stashed my bag, and walked down the street, then took a walk along the Nile. Every ten yards, a boat man or a policeman stepped out from the deep shadows of the little tin and mud-brick shacks along the river. They clutched their crotches and signaled for me to go with them. I wanted to bolt and immediately move on to Aswan. "What the hell," I started saying aloud, and in a vicious tone, just as I did when facing down a coyote while hiking in Colorado. I had been trying to practice good manners, but the aggressiveness of certain men was overwhelming. Good manners did nothing to stop them.

Arriving at the temples of nearby Karnack, I met an old man, dressed in a soiled robe that once had been white. He wore tattered leather sandals, again broken down at the heels. He beckoned to me. "I show you things. Most tourists not seen," he said, his English a little fractured. I'd heard that story before and kept refusing the bent, little man. He looked to be ninety. He had a very inflamed boil on each side of his neck, one the size of a pigeon egg and the other the size of a goose egg. He was missing all but two front teeth, one upper, and one lower. He kept pestering me, so I allowed him to lead me away from the main paths to what looked like an archeological dig. I could not make much of anything there. Since the guide had little English beyond what he'd said when trying to rope me in, he could not explain what he wanted to show me.

I gave him some dollar bills. It was Christmas Eve.

He started leading me off again, this time to a little cot placed under a tin and wood lean-to as a respite from the sun. He motioned for me to sit down, which I did, thinking that I would rest for a few minutes. Then he motioned for me to lie down. I moved my head sharply to the right and downward to indicate "No." The man sat down beside me and placed his hand on my thigh.

I thought for a couple of minutes, then rose, knocking the man's hand, which was moving upward, off my leg. "I've got to go," I said, wondering out loud why so many of the men— especially in the Luxor area, seemed on the make. This was not something that *Let's Go Egypt* warned of. The writers cautioned women, especially single women travelers, to be very careful. But they did not warn men. Boy, would I write them about that when I got back to Denver.

I entered the great Karnak Temple, dedicated to Amun. In the hypostyle hall, large enough to accommodate Paris' Cathedral of Notre Dame, I came upon some other single tourists, all male. Without a guide, they were walking as a group.

Since Christmas was at hand, most of us seemed to be feel a longing for others from Judeo-Christian cultures. We found nothing to remind us of the holiday except a few strings of lights and perhaps a few strings of gold or silver tinsel hung under the ceilings of hotels that catered to Americans.

After walking awhile with the tourists, I got my courage up and asked, "Are you guys having problems with come-ons?"

Several nodded. "You're not alone," one tall, blue-eyed American named Mark said. "Egyptians especially like us," he replied.

'One very tall guy with a Dutch accent introduced himself as Hans. "All the buildings here, except the ancient ones, are short, like the people, so it is reasonable to like height. They reach for past glory."

"Reach is right," I said.

My fellow travelers laughed. Many of us noted that no women seemed to appear in public by themselves. Women from other countries were warned by every tourist book we'd seen never to travel alone, and to stay at all times in the company of a male.

"Many European and American males travel to Egypt as sex tourists. They go by themselves, rather than in groups or with their wives and girl friends," a man named Nigel remarked. He was a sociologist from London. "The assumptions of many Egyptians aren't without foundation. Egyptians are sensualists by nature. They have been since ancient times," he said.

I laughed. "In other words, they're willing to comply?" I asked. "In ancient times they were sensualists, and Durrell certainly paints those of Alexandria as sensualists in modern times, but I have a hard time thinking of the desperately poor as sensualists at any time. I'm thinking, however, that ancient Egyptians might more properly have been termed *materialists*, even in religion."

"Probably so," Hans said.

It didn't seem that the others cared to engage in this discussion. So I asked, "Where are the rest of you staying. I'm curious."

"Club Med," Hans said. "Most of us stay there."

"Talk about materialism," I joked. "The reputation of Club Meds as safe havens for sensualists is worldwide."

"No no," Hans said. "I assure you, the Luxor Med is very nice, safe. The food is great. So are the amenities. It is situated in one of the finest parts, along the Nile."

I was always amazed at what good English the Dutch I'd met all over Europe, and now here in Egypt, spoke.

Those of us who weren't staying at the Med decided to have a look for ourselves. Instead of walking back to Luxor, our entire group broke into smaller units and took the horse and donkey carriages. "These are so much more colorful than taxis," I remarked.

At Club Med, I asked the owner of the Luxor Med about their reputation. He assured me that this one had never been trashy. "In fact, many Club Meds are trying to separate themselves from that stereotype," he said. He spoke perfect English with a slightly French accent. "That is not been a good representation, especially in the Muslim world. Here, images of the West as corrupt and oversexed are like the sands. We do not want that reputation."

Those staying at the Club Med invited us to the New Years Eve Feast to be held there that night. "It is only twenty American dollars for the entire all-you-can-eat banquet, including wines and desserts," the owner said. "Originally it was only to be for hotel guests, but we have excess food, so you are welcome."

Egypt required lots of sacrifice as far as comforts and amenities went, so I was game. My non-Med companions agreed. We decided to go back to our own hotels, shower, and try to dress up a bit for the feast that was to begin in a little over an hour.

"We've corrupted these people, not the other way around," a French guy who joined our table at the Feast remarked.

"You must be American," I said.

"I swear I am not. I am the son of the owners," he said. "My name is Jean Luc." He wore two Egyptian silk scarves wrapped and tied stylishly around his neck in what I remembered a typically French manner. "I learned American instead of British pronunciations of English," he said. Eating pieces of a honeydew melon, he took up the idea of corruption. "Good Muslims do not have sex outside of marriage."

"Good Muslims," I said. "But I've read T.H. Lawrence. He found plenty of sex outside of marriage in Arabic countries, certainly with Muslim men. Several French writers did too."

Oh, the food was good. Everything I tried was wonderful. The chickens, beef, lamb, and even ham were well cooked and seasoned, but never fatty. I saw no boiled lentils, although I did see fluffy rice. I found no okra, or something like it, gooey and in some sort of bland tomato sauce. That seemed a typical vegetable in Egyptian restaurants. All kinds of fruits and salads heaped the tables. Only there would I dare to eat lettuce and spinach salads, which the owner promised to have had flown in from Europe. What a luxury. I'd forgotten how starved I'd been for good food.

"Recently, I read about a venerable Persian custom. Older married men, especially the wealthy, take boy lovers," I added, taking a break from tasting everything on my plate. "The boys, usually poor, enjoy the benefits of the older man's money and protection, in exchange for love. The wives know. While it was an old Persian practice, it probably spread to other Muslim countries."

"But they won't admit it, not unless they're remarkably honest, and unafraid of their Mullahs," a German secondary school teacher with thick, round spectacles remarked. He held a hunk of roast chicken to his mouth and bit in, the juices running down his chin.

"It's probably made worse by putting women on a pedestal and treating sex as though it's something to be engaged in only in marriage," Mark said. He popped a bob of fresh sweet cherries in his mouth and spit out the pits after he'd eaten the flesh. "They say that's the case in Latin countries, which are largely Roman Catholic."

"I am gay, Hans said. "All men are like that. As long as you don't receive, you are a male. If you do, you are a woman and worth little." He laughed, breaking a croissant in half. He popped first one half, then the other, into his mouth. "I shall not tell which I prefer." He smiled coyly and sipped red wine.

Most of us concluded that, whatever the cause, we were made uncomfortable by the constant come-ons, hasslings, and hustlings for money, termed *baksheesh,* or alms. Toasting the New Year, we decided to try to stick with a buddy for the remainder of our time in Egypt.

That night, soon after I went to sleep in my very modest room in Luxor, Sharon appeared at my bedside. Such appearances had not happened for months. Again she was shaking. I feared the worst. Instead of getting into the bed beside me, she disappeared, leaving me wide awake, worrying.

Finally, I got up and tried to call her but got not even her answering machine.

The next morning I put a call through to Dan. "Tray is fine," he said. "So am I. I hope you are too."

I asked if he had heard anything from Sharon.

"No, nothing," he said.

"She appeared to me last night while I was sleeping," I said. "Will you try to find out what's going on and let me know?"

Two mornings later Dan called to tell me, "No luck. I was able to talk to a woman at her realty firm. She said Sharon hasn't been heard from since December the twenty-first," he said. "She couldn't—or wouldn't—give me any more information."

"I plan to go to Aswan next," I said. I gave Dan the number of the hotel where I was going to stay. I still had five days before my flight left. I wanted to make the most of my time. Even if I were in Denver, I could do nothing—not if Sharon wanted to remain incognito.

None of the men that I'd met in Luxor wanted to go to Aswan yet, so I hired another driver to take me there. I would go alone. I had heard from male tourists in Luxor that people didn't seem so aggressive and dishonest in Aswan. I'd stick to budget hotels, even though the Club Meds were inviting. I had to watch my pennies.

At Aswan, I sat down in a restaurant for lunch. Before I could order, a decently dressed young Egyptian man of perhaps twenty-five approached me. I'd grown suspicious of all Egyptians. I wondered what he was up to. "Hello, my name is Mohammed," he said. "Could you read please a letter for me?" He handed me the letter, still in the envelope.

It was from a Norwegian woman, postmarked the week before. She'd written in English.

"My spoken English is good, but I cannot read it," Mohammed explained.

The letter read,

> Dear Mohammed,
>
> I am sorry, but it is impossible for me to invite you to Norway. I do not know you well enough for that. I cannot marry you as you want.
>
> I had a nice time while I was in Aswan.
>
> I want to thank you. I wish you well.
>
> Yours truly,
> Julia.

Mohammed was distraught. "She didn't say anything about love!" he cried. Despite the heat and bone dry air, his tears left wet streaks down his blue shirt. I wondered how he could cry so much. He had seen the girl as the way out of his plight. I could not blame him for trying. Nor could I blame the girl for being cautious.

"It's rare that real love happens on vacation," I said. I tried to explain the complications of such involvements to Mohammed in terms that would soften his views of the woman as a traitor who had ruined his life.

He thanked me. He was still weeping profusely. "I have to find a way to a better life!" he cried.

After I was finally able to eat my meal, I walked out of the restaurant into the dusty heat of afternoon.

Another shopkeeper approached me on the street. He also asked me to read a letter to him.

"Today must be letter reading day," I said, mostly to myself. The man invited me into his nearby carpet shop. He handed me a glass of hot mint tea that a waiter brought in on a copper plate. A little bowl of brown sugar crystals sat on the side of the plate.

"No sugar," I said.

"I need your help. Could you read a letter for me?" the man asked. He handed me what appeared a rather worn and yellowed missive. No date appeared on it.

Again it was from a young woman—an American—thanking him for the time that she'd spent in Egypt. "You were very sweet showing me around Aswan," she wrote. "But I'm so sorry I cannot marry you, as you wanted."

This man seemed saddened, but, unlike the Egyptian in the restaurant, this one did not seem distraught. He shrugged, "That's the way things are with women," he said. "None of them can be trusted."

I said nothing.

Then the shopkeeper began showing me his wool carpets. He kept finding new ones. Some were very nice, but I really did not want one other bit of merchandise to haul around. "I must make my rent," the man said. "Do you not like any of them? Is there not one you can buy? Then I will be able to stay in my shop." he said, barely pausing to take a breath. "I am already two months behind."

I did spot a rug that I especially liked. It was a medium sized wool carpet with a typical Egyptian village scene of little, mud-brick houses woven into a camel background. Some stylized blue, green, and yellow birds flew overhead.

The man told me, "Sixty dollars for this. It is a bargain," he said.

As we went on, with me resisting, the man desperately lowered his head. He looked down, as if distraught. "I will let you have it for twenty-five," he said. "You have been so kind to read the letter for me."

Folding the carpet tightly, he tied it tightly with string.

I paid him. I liked it well enough. Twenty-five dollars did not seem exorbitant, although it was probably a huge sum for Egyptians. Aggressiveness and dishonesty did not bring out my sympathy, however. *This guy at least had had a better script*, I thought, wondering why the letter had borne no date. *Was it made up to gain the sympathy of another naïve tourist?*

Sympathetic as I was, I did not want constantly to be confronted in this, or any other, manner. I was willing to admit that Americans shared some responsibility for the plight of the poor in the world. We took from the world what we wanted, so that we might not just survive, but live well. However, I certainly couldn't support or save the whole planet. It felt as if that's what was being demanded, my nightmare of all the hands reaching for me and my money still ringing true. Some of the Biblical Patriarch Joseph's most powerful dreams had come to him in Egypt, perhaps because he was in captivity, so far from home.

Days before, I had come across a young man of maybe sixteen dressed in ragged jeans and an old, red Polo shirt that came from an American charity, I figured. He tended three adult goats in the alleys of old Cairo. He was holding a brown and white baby goat.

"May I take your picture?" I asked.

He nodded. To my surprise, he asked for nothing, even in broken English. I opened my wallet and gave him several Egyptian pounds. "That's all that I have with me," I explained. "I haven't been to an exchange for awhile. I don't have any dollars with me."

At first refusing, the young man finally accepted the pounds. "Thank you," he said, his eyes lowered. He held the kid close like a baby.

Another shopkeeper who befriended me there in Aswan over the course of the few days that I was there seemed honest. He never asked for money, never asked me to buy a thing. He told me about Egypt and said he had a degree in sociology. That seemed a popular subject, especially of those employed in shops and hotels. He wanted to know all he could find out about the United States. He asked me to the one room flat that he shared with six other Egyptian men. He boiled bottled water in an old metal pot for tea. There were two stained mattresses on the floor, which all of the men shared. I spotted two ragged, filthy blankets.

I was experiencing another bout of diarrhea, although this one was mild compared to the one that I had on my second day after arrival.

The man motioned me down the hall to a grimy bathroom with a toilet bowl full of black water. The bathtub was also stopped up with black water. I wondered how in the world anyone used the facilities.

I backed out, holding my nose. I wanted desperately to forget what I'd just seen. I would force myself to wait to use the toilet. Eating only yoghurt and kushari, a dish of rice and lentils, for awhile would help. After that display, I thought that I also could hold my bladder for hours, maybe days.

If I'd not met some Egyptians who were kind and honest and not at all aggressive, my view of Egypt would have been terrible. To be born there, to try to survive there, would not be something I'd have wished on anyone. Those tourists who took carefully guided tours that avoided real interactions with indigenous peoples could keep their picture postcard views of the place intact. They could brag about what wonderful time they had, how gracious the Egyptians were, how marvelous the sights.

My understanding was less superficial. In the real world, our only hope is our concern for one another, but as they really are, not as we wish to see them. By being realistic, we might work things through. We might learn to love one another. At least I hoped so.

No Brown Baby, No Cleopatra, No Anthony

My driver waited in Aswan for me. At first, he wanted to stay in my room with me. He didn't seem one of the Egyptians who was looking to take advantage. "I am a good Muslim," he told me—in a way that seemed genuine all the time that I was with him. Still, I wasn't too sure about his sharing my room. "I will make other plans," he said. "No problem." Evidently he found some work in Aswan while he waited for me. He certainly wasn't charging me much to chauffer me wherever I wished.

He took me out to the temples, which had been moved for preservation to the Island of Philae in the backwaters of the great dam. Just outside the Temple of Isis, I joined a tour because the guide stuck me as very knowledgeable. The bas reliefs were remarkable, the colors still bright, the lines clear, the scenes moving. I was particularly interested in the ancient Egyptian attempts to depict "The *ka*, something akin to the soul," said the guild. "The ka can be separated from the body and has a kind of materiality of its own." Everything about the ancient Egyptians expressed that materialism.

My mind naturally compared these concepts to historical Christianity, which can be seen as rather materialistic, but, more squarely, incarnational. God's taking on flesh exhibits the basic goodness of creation—and the potential redemption of all that is fallen. Judaism also emphasizes the basic goodness of life and all that God has made. In Judaism, there is nothing else outside of God and his will. Even Satan tests God's chosen, as he tests Job. It seems hard, especially for someone of the Western world, to imagine a totally spiritual, non-physically expressed, religion—or existence. That said, certain strains of Christianity, especially as practiced by our modern evangelicals, had become grossly materialistic. According to their televangelists and those inspired by them, God wants all believers rich, powerful, and well. Satan must constantly be warred against, for he threatens to take over all of creation in spite of God. This strain is present in historical Christianity, but never fully expressed. Following the lead of Judaism, historical, mainline Christianity has argued that nothing is outside God's will. He permits evil—but always so that good might come of it.

The guide, shining her flashlight on the well preserved carvings in the temples, innocently referred as them as "eternal ruins." Memories of Rome, eternal city, sparked, I stepped aside and found a blank page in my tour book. On it I composed some lines to commemorate the death of one of my friends:

> Accretion upon accretion,
> everyone builds
> on that which came before.
> Even the ever-present graffiti
> recall those who come later.
>
> A friend, who made no claim
> for the timelessness
> of self, or work,
> invited comparison
> by writing of a photograph
> of her sitting
> on the Pyramid of Cheops—
> "a girl in a spaghetti strap gown."
> Her voice oddly prophetic,
> she returned to Rome.
> In exchange for ten dollars
> and a few thousand lire,
> a hoodlum
> signed her throat
> with the blade of his knife.

My time in Egypt was at an end. I could take no more. Aswan had felt fairly safe, at worst, annoying. My sensibilities, my person, were not so assaulted as they had been in Cairo or Luxor. Perhaps the reason was not, however, that it was a better place, but that I was more experienced, and those who would take advantage sensed that and left me alone.

Regardless, I wanted to get back to the United States where things bore some semblance of civilization. Right after formulating this wish, I heard the same internal voice that I'd heard on my arrival. *"Semblance of civilization,"* he said. "All empires crumble. America's too."

My driver seemed about to cry, as I tried to explain myself without damning his country, without saying that my senses, my intelligence, my conscience, my guilt, my sense of morality and ethics were constantly stirred up in Egypt. Although he had driven me from Cairo, I did not want to go further to the Red Sea before returning. "I'm sorry. I've had enough."

Finally, my driver accepted his fate. He concluded, "I am a good Muslim. It is God's will."

I wondered what I might do to help the Egyptians in real ways, as he drove me back to Cairo.

"Business this season is very slow. Many tourists do not coming because they are afraid of terrorism," he said.

"I can imagine," I said. "I also worried about terrorism, but I decided to come anyway. My woman friend wasn't worried about it."

"Oh, you have a woman friend?" the driver asked. "Where is she?"

"She wasn't able to make it."

"Usually I make enough money during this time to take care of my family for the year," he said. "This year will be bad."

My mind jarring with conflicting emotions sparked by the kaleidoscope of experiences in Egypt, I said goodbye to my driver. I had little cash left, but I was able to give him a little extra money.

I found a cheap hotel, caught several hours of fitful sleep, and boarded my flight out of Cairo at four a.m. After a few hours layover in Paris, I would take a connecting flight to New York, where I would again spend a few hours in the airport before heading to Denver. At least the jet lag traveling with the sun would not be so bad as going against it. That, anyway, had been my experience in the past.

Sitting in the airport in Paris, I wrote myself a few reminders of things to do when I got home.

A teacher of agricultural science who moonlighted at the hotel in Aswan had asked if I could contact my local agricultural college and have them send whatever research they had on sheep breeding and diseases. I would call Colorado State University in Fort Collins about it. I would ask that they send other materials if possible. I would help to defray the costs. That I could do.

An elementary school teacher, who moonlighted as a desk clerk in my hotel in Luxor, had asked if I might get my sister, who also taught elementary school, to have her students write letters to his students. I promised that I would ask. I hope that my sister and her class would befriend those poor students who attended second grade for a couple of hours each morning. "Many do not go much further than that," the teacher said. "They must support their families, just I must work this job after completing my teaching in the morning."

I paced the De Gaulle/Roissy Airport. Even though I wanted to get home, I wished I had enough time to leave and go into Paris. But I didn't.

I sat down to read. I opened an article I'd picked up in Egypt, saying the ancient Egyptians believed colors to hold special properties. Green was the sacred color of protection. Children were entombed with green stones. They also wore green eye liner for that reason.

"I should have worn all my malachite rings," I remarked, laughing to myself. "But I was afraid to show any outward signs of wealth."

I thought of modern Egyptians. I'd talked to no Egyptian women whatsoever. So many men I'd talked with had university degrees. A few held positions in their professions. But to make ends meet most seemed to moonlight as clerks in shops and hotels and waiters, hoping for something better in their areas of expertise. Sadly, the more mature said, "This dream will remain but another phantom, but it gives us hope."

I found myself meditating on dreams. Some are illusionary but give us hope. Some scare us. Some are prophetic. Some seem a mix of all.

I thought of the Biblical Joseph, another dreamer and interpreter of dreams that I knew of from my studies. Joseph's youthful dream of his brothers' sheaves of wheat bowing down to his sheaf made them angry. They had no intention of bowing down to him. They decided to kill him instead. But one of the brothers, Reuben, talked them into throwing him into a pit and selling him to traders.

Pretending that Joseph had been killed by a wild beast, they told his father, who wept but refused to be consoled. His brothers had sold him to Ishmaelite traders, who then sold him to Potiphar in Egypt, officer of the Pharaoh, and captain of the guard.

Because Joseph refused to commit adultery with Potiphar's wife, she lied and said he'd tried to rape her. So Joseph was thrown into prison. There, the Pharaoh's chief butler and his chief baker related their dreams. Joseph said the butler would be restored by the Pharaoh, but the baker would lose his head. This proved correct.

So did Joseph's warning of seven years of famine to follow seven years of prosperity in the entire region. Because the Pharaoh listened and followed Joseph's advice by storing up grain for the famine, Egypt—and by extension, Joseph's family back home—did not starve. They did what many Hebrews did. They went down to Egypt for help. Because of

God's favoring Joseph with wisdom and discretion, the Pharaoh had honored Joseph by putting him in charge of affairs, just beneath him.

In Egypt, Joseph, was reunited with his family. He saved them from certain doom. So they bowed down to him, acknowledging his rightful place of honor. The brothers' sheaves, and, the sun, the moon, and eleven stars did indeed bow down to him, just as he'd dreamed before his brothers sold him into slavery, over twenty years before.

A chain of events had been set in motion, with people doing what was expedient and egocentric, although God, in his providence, turned everything to good. Some say, God *meant* everything for good, a slight shade of difference, for this version implies some sort of predestining, whereas the other suggests that God turns the evil that people do into good. Either way, I was certainly glad to know that God was in the midst of it. I hoped I could believe it too.

When I landed at Stapleton Airport in Denver late that afternoon, I found the weather cool. I was glad I was wearing a sweater. That was enough.

I located my car and decided to see if I could discover what had happened to Sharon before I went home. Then I stopped at her company office downtown. It was a little before five, and nearly dark. I was told by the receptionist at the outer desk that no one knew what had happened. I kept thinking that, if I to talked to the right person, I'd get more information. So I walked back into the offices to try talking to others that I found there at that hour. I found a middle-aged male. "Sorry, I don't know a thing," he said, straightening his tie. I wasn't sure that I believed him. I asked an older woman. "No sorry. I haven't seen her for weeks." I struck out. Sharon had disappeared. That was the common response. She had neither returned to work nor called. Strange. Disconcerting, in fact. I couldn't imagine that no one there had any idea what was going on.

I walked outside to my car and decided to drive over to Sharon's condominium. I rang from the directory in the foyer. No answer. I couldn't tell much from there. I tried walking outside and looking up at the windows, but I couldn't see a thing. It was rather chilly. I wasn't wearing a coat, so I didn't want to walk around outside too long. I saw no one to ask. The building had always seemed quiet. Nothing looked amiss.

I headed home. "Looks like we didn't have any snow," I said, noting how dusty and dry everything looked, even in the streetlamps and headlights.

I didn't know Sharon's family, so I didn't feel that I could look them up. From what she'd said about them, I wasn't sure I'd find out a thing anyway. Her brother wasn't speaking to her. I didn't know if her parents would know what was going on. I surmised that the entire family suffered from cutoffs and denials of every sort. I decided to try that avenue only if everything else failed.

Surely I would hear something before long. Sharon had dropped out of sight before.

All of this made me acutely aware that I had very little knowledge of drug problems and the course of recovery. Nor did I know much about sexual abuse issues. I'd read about them, of course. But firsthand, in-depth knowledge was beyond me. Besides, I kept telling myself, I was not Sharon's therapist. I did not want to be her therapist. I wanted to be her lover.

I turned the key in my door and called out to Dan and Tray. "Anyone here?" Neither answered. The place was dark. I figured they were off walking and would return soon. I realized how much I'd missed them, how much I'd missed my bed, my desk, my comforts.

Classes would begin in a few days. I had to prepare. I saw the stack of mail waiting for me on the dining room table. I looked through it. Nothing important. I was glad I'd not waited around to see if I would get job interviews over Christmas. The few universities and colleges that responded to the handful of applications that I'd sent out said their positions had fallen through, or "Thanks, but we will not be pursuing your candidacy further." Most hadn't responded at all.

"Exciting news, isn't it?" Dan said, as soon as he entered the room and saw me reading my mail. Tray made her way over to greet me.

"Oh yeah, I couldn't live without it. How come you didn't pay the bills?" I asked.

"I didn't want to forge your signature," Dan said. He laughed. "I'll get dinner. I'm sure you need to dig into all the work you've left behind."

I thanked him. Tray followed me up the stairs to my study.

I'd made the right choice by taking a vacation instead of anxiously waiting around Denver, wondering if I would be called for an interview at that year's Modern Language Association meeting.

When I visited campus the next day, although few people were around, I managed to hear rumblings that the university would be forced to cut classes and positions because of worsening budget deficits. People in non-tenure track positions, part time and full time, would be the first to suffer. The few full timers would be cut back to part time, and the many part timers would have their hours pared as well, some to nothing at all. Support staff would be pared back. Everyone doubted that administration would suffer much; they never did; rather they always multiplied like rabbits and continued to wangle raises.

As I walked around campus, I felt the desire to escape. How about fleeing to another country? Unfortunately, I'd not yet found one where I'd wish to live instead of the United States. At least here I was familiar with the language and the people and the systems. In another place, I would only encounter new challenges.

How about another life, another time? I envisioned a train jumping tracks to ones that went in another direction, then another, and another, each unsatisfactory, blockaded, torn up, defective.

That, I feared was what Sharon, and others like her, were doing, at least on the subconscious level. In my own way, on a lesser level, I did it too. I was exploring other countries, other times, in my love of literature, and my world travels. I never did so totally.

As I walked to the library, I toyed with the idea of drawing up a new course on the literature of the urge to live versus the death wish that haunts us all. It would cover the range of human responses to dissatisfaction with one's lot in life. I knew that I'd never get it off the ground, however, now that I had been kicked back to teaching writing only. That spring I had one advanced writing course and an introductory writing course. Not a good use of my talents and skills. But I still had a job. And a small income.

I knew my being pushed down to teach writing classes only, and ones that were stuffed to the gills with students, many of whom were under-prepared, was to punish me for failing to give Spet what he wanted. Spet's underling, Ron, went along. He dared to do nothing else.

I wondered for a moment, as I sometimes did, what things would have been like if I had been more like Tom Jones, the Fielding character who finds himself in all kinds of compromising positions but, because of his happy nature and winsome ways, makes it through them pretty much unscathed.

Unfortunately, Fielding had not constructed my script. Besides, as a judge in his private life, Fielding's outlook on the world grew increasingly dark with age. His own life was not nearly so happy as the books he penned.

Standing before the card catalogue in the library, I wondered what McDougal was up to. Probably, he too was going about business as usual—cruising the parks, making dubious pastoral visits, taking prospective stable boys to fancy lunches and dinners. At least Spet seemed to prefer people of at least eighteen years old. I'd heard that McDougal didn't seem terribly concerned.

I went to the stacks to locate the books I needed. I wondered how long it would be until McDougal was caught. Because he wasn't at all discreet, he surely would be.

"Thanks, I said," taking book after book from the librarian as he checked each out for me. I managed to get all seven of them stuffed into my back pack.

But Spet, I wasn't so sure about him. I hadn't heard that he hung out at Cheesman or other gay haunts. Spet was far more careful about his dalliances and his methods of bending people to his desires. He was much smarter than McDougal, and therefore more treacherous.

I hurried out the door of the library to my car parked in the St. Francis Center lot. I had only a few days to get things ready for classes. I almost tripped going down the steps. I reminded myself that I'd better not break something. "Even sprains I can't handle. I don't have the luxury," I said.

I wondered where Sharon was. Would I really be able to help her, as her grandmother's ghost had believed and demanded? I glanced over at St. Elizabeth's. "I'd really like to talk with you, Mrs. Ghost," I said. "But then, I'm not sure that being passed over necessarily gives someone any more knowledge or wisdom than they had on this side."

I wondered where I was. I wondered where I was going. "Home," came to mind. "I hope that doesn't mean death. I'm not ready for that," I quipped out loud.

Reporting

After classes began and I felt that I was finally getting up to speed, I got up the nerve to phone Sharon's mother. I didn't want to call from my office, so I phoned from home. I could make sure I had complete privacy there.

"Hello," she said.

"This is Ted Jones. I don't know that you know me." I was very nervous. I glanced out the window of my study to the flowering crab tree down below in the common area, now barren.

She was silent.

"I'm a friend of Sharon's," I said.

"I've heard," she said. She wasn't forthcoming with any information.

"I'm trying to find out if she's ok. I haven't heard from her for weeks."

I didn't want to say much, since I wasn't sure how much she knew about Sharon and me, or Sharon's situation. Surely, she knew about Sharon's drug problems.

"Do you know how she is?" I asked. I turned on my little Sanyo computer. I had to write up syllabi for my classes. I'd met parents who were so shut down they denied their children's abuse issues of every kind. Sharon had maintained that her mother would never admit that she'd been right about the sexual abuse.

Her mother still didn't say anything. For a moment, I thought she was going to hang up. But she didn't do a thing.

I fidgeted. I felt supremely uncomfortable. I had to type up some class handouts too. "Thank you," I said, finally. "I'll let you go."

"Goodbye," she said, and the line went dead.

"Cold woman," I said, placing the receiver down on the cradle. I hoped I was wrong. "I looked out the window again. "Is there any warmth for Sharon underneath that icy manner?"

I had little time to spend trying to track Sharon down, especially when she didn't seem to want to be found. I had even less time or inclination to figure out what her iceberg of a mother was about. I had class lessons to prepare for and a never-ending stream of papers to grade.

At the end of January, my old student and friend Laura Cameron called. "How are you, Darling? How are your classes going?" she asked.

Sarcastically, I said, "Oh, I find teaching writing classes, and writing classes alone extremely stimulating. Because of budget problems, class size has been bumped up again."

"That's not good for you or the students," Laura said.

"How am I to spend the time on each student when the enrollment in my Basic Writing course has been upped again—this time to twenty-nine students—and my Advanced Writing course has been upped to thirty-seven?" I asked. "I don't expect you to answer. The question was rhetorical."

"I guess you should be grateful not to have two courses with thirty-seven students on the roster. But you'll find the way to help them," Laura said, encouragingly. "Your administration knows that. I'll bet, if you check, that not everyone, especially the squeaky wheels, got so many students put into their classes."

"I'll bet you're right."

"I told you, darling. They know you won't like it, but you'll put up with it because that's your nature. You'll always be conscientious about your work."

"It's like being stuck teaching toddlers to walk forever and ever."

"Or, like being kept in kindergarten as punishment for being good," Laura said.

Since my thirty-fourth birthday had occurred in the fall, her remark made me laugh.

"I hate to add more bad news," she said, "but Brad has talked Sharon into moving back in with him. Sharon looks like shit. I'm sure she's doing too many drugs and getting beaten. She had a bad black eye when I ran into her the other day. Her whole face was swollen."

My face went hot, my chest leaden. The heaviness spread downward and outward from there. "Who's beating her?" I asked.

"Brad does that now and then. Especially when business isn't going well and he's taking too many drugs," Laura said.

"How do you know this?"

"People in this neighborhood know a lot about each other, especially the dark stuff," she said.

"What can we do?"

"You need to stay out of it. I know from past experience. Involving yourself will backfire. Sharon will leave and get help only when she's ready. She has to hit bottom."

"Did Sharon lie to me about having family problems at Christmas?" I asked, the wheels grinding. "Or do you know?"

"I think that was true," Laura said. "Her brother and she got into it again. He accused her of breaking up the family. Things escalated. Nobody was talking to her. By the time Brad got hold of her, she was vulnerable."

"And I was in Egypt," I said. I glanced down over at Tray lying on the floor a few feet from me.

"Having a good time, I hope." Laura grew more serious. "Darling, you don't really want to get mixed up in such a complicated situation."

"It seems I'm already involved."

"I mean more involved, completely inundated. You have a career you need to tend."

"I'm not sure which one of them you're talking about—the ministry or the college teaching," I said. "Both seem to be faltering. I'm not sure how much care-taking will help either career about now."

"It's too bad you keep finding yourself in mine fields. It must be your karma."

"Just remember that we can't always view trials and suffering as deserved," I reminded her. "I've got to put my nose back to the grindstone."

"All right, Darling. Your nose can't take lots more grinding though," Laura said. "It isn't very long."

I hung up. I turned to my bookshelf, found my Harper Study Bible and opened it. For some reason, I felt prompted to review Joseph's dreams. I opened to Genesis 37 and found an old slip of paper dating to 1974. On it, I'd recorded one of my angelic experiences. "An Angel of the Lord came to me and said, 'Open your Bible and begin reading at Genesis 37, the trials and dreams of Joseph.' The angel disappeared." I was in the midst of my first divorce, which followed upon the heels of being fired from my first teaching job at a Christian college that struck me as not very Christian.

Over my years of wandering in the wilderness, including loss of my home, this experience sustained me like manna. In fact, I'd grown so used to such wandering that I'd almost forgotten my angelic message.

The phone rang again. It was Laura. "What you need is a rich wife. She can take care of you. Then you can write," she said. She laughed, not meanly but pleasantly. "However, I am already taken. It's Bud's money anyway. And Darling, guess what, I am pregnant, at last!"

"You are?" I asked.

"I just heard."

"Congratulations."

"Well, you know how hard we've been trying. All we do is fuck. It wears you out being there on your back day and night with some man thumping between your legs. I swear, I don't know how whores do it."

"You always manage to shine a comic light in the darkest room," I replied.

"I keep telling Bud how sore he made me," Laura said. "But he refused to let me try anyone else to see if his sperm might turn the trick."

I chuckled. Laura's words had been carefully chosen. "Then you'd have to have paternity tests to determine who was the real father," I said. I put the Bible down on my desk. I left it open so I could think more about Joseph's dreams.

"That's what Bud kept telling me. I told him we'd know whose little bugger it was," Laura said. "The competition would make his little fellas try a lot harder."

"Maybe that's what did the trick," I suggested. I looked out the window and saw a sparrow on the sill outside. I wanted to change the subject. I could handle only so much of the scurrilous before it started feeling oppressive.

I promised to have lunch with Laura in two weeks and hung up.

Everyone had problems. I knew that. I had become acquainted with a number of them in my life because people always talked to me. I listened. Probably no one had real security in his or her personal or professional life. Yet, some certainly seemed to enjoy more stability than I. Being philosophical about things helped only so much.

I had to think long and hard about Laura's advising me to let go of Sharon. A few days after our phone conversations, I called her to discuss it in more detail.

"I knew you'd never make it without talking till lunch," Laura said. "You're too anxious about my news, aren't you?"

I laughed.

"I meant my being preggers news," Laura said. She laughed. "Darling, I know you like a book. I know very well what's upsetting you."

"Laura, you of all people ought to understand this," I said. "I've had lots of paranormal experiences, but none like the ones I've had with Sharon, starting from the outset. Ones with her have been ongoing, whereas none of the others have. Those with her have been deeply bonding."

"I know. Her dead grandmother came to you and said you were soul mates."

"Not exactly," I said. "She wanted me to help her grandbaby." I paused, fiddling with the button on my cuff.

"You and Bud spent all that time pursuing the spiritual life with Rajneesh—"

"And others," Laura said. "Bud and I were young then. We had our lives before us. Now, we're older and wiser. We've traded in spirituality for materialism. That's the American way."

"The New Jerusalem turns into the Merchandise Mart," I said.

"Honk, honk, what a parking lot," Laura exclaimed.

From the start, my relationship with Sharon seemed so much more significant than one where you merely take up with someone you meet without the insights of a dead grandmother who chooses you out of all the population of Denver to help her grandbaby. More significant, maybe you are chosen by God himself, or the universe, to work through things left unresolved from past ties.

"Only when you're free will you find someone more suitable. Someone more stable," Laura advised. "And some other career—one that still suits you," she added, just before hanging up.

I could not forget Sharon so easily. I knew about the high rate of recidivism among addicts. I also knew that the abused often return to their abusers, another type of addiction.

But still, dammit, still. Sharon and I were connected, with a bond stronger than any I'd ever experienced. Could I love her wisely, without allowing myself to be devastated?

When one of my ministry team members, Viv, walked by and asked if I was all right—"You're looking stunned"—I realized I wasn't doing so well. When you're trying to understand a complicated and upsetting situation, it takes awhile to realize how you're reacting.

Viv came into my office and stood in front of my desk. She didn't sit, but said, "I'll take you out for a cup of coffee. Remember to breathe," she ordered. "You appear to be suffering from a lack of oxygen. I have big shoulders."

Viv was a Lutheran minister who had been fought by her Bishops from the beginning. One of them had even told her he didn't know how her husband could stand her, she was so pushy, so castrating—qualities that I'd never noticed, and I'd gotten to know Viv pretty well. Because of past experience, I quickly reacted to castrating women.

"It certainly would be good if people could develop discernment, even a little, and judge more truly what people are made of," Viv said. She added, wistfully, "But it wouldn't be life on earth."

"Maybe I should marry you," I teased.

"I have a husband of many years. He really does appreciate me," she replied.

"How about if I get appointed as your Bishop?" I asked. "I could smack 'em and whack 'em, and support your every move."

"Great idea!" Viv exclaimed. "I wish things worked like that." She motioned for me to grab my things, including my coat. "Let's get out of here before Louise manages to come see what we're getting up to."

We walked off to get coffee somewhere in LODO. "I think we should avoid The Market, just in case," I said.

Viv nodded. She knew why. Viv and I talked. I'd filled her in on some things as they went on.

"This is such a difficult situation," Viv said. "You feel bonded to her as you've never felt to anyone before, and yet she constantly lets you down, some might say, betrays you."

I didn't want to hear it put so bluntly.

We pulled our coats against a gust of cold wind from the northwest. The bleak days of January were upon us. This was the Winter of Discontent, once again. I so preferred Januaries of hope, although I'd experienced few.

As we began to cross Speer, I started thinking of The Market, which was still one of my favorite cafes, Viv's too, and so near. "I've been thinking about the Market," I said. "I haven't been there for awhile."

"It is the best place around for a quick cup of good coffee and a snack," Viv said. She knew exactly how my mind was working.

"I hope it doesn't bring back too many painful memories," Viv cautioned. She knew that Sharon and I had often had coffee there.

Viv and I walked on. I mused on painful memories. All I could think of was Sharon, how we'd met, her genuflecting there on the curb after getting away from the Camaro that careened out of nowhere and almost ran her down. I remembered how alive everything had begun to seem, the colors vibrant, the birdsongs melodious, the beauties of earth revealed.

"You're awfully distant," Viv remarked.

"I guess it's just my mood. I'm trying to sort things out." I tried to remain distant.

"I know you don't want to talk about Sharon, but I'd like to help," Viv said. She smiled but didn't push. That was Viv's way. Direct, supportive, insightful. Never castrating.

"I don't want to talk about Sharon. I know that." I shot a quick glance at Viv.

She smiled. She raised an eyebrow.

"Yet, she's all I want to talk about. Our affair doesn't feel over. I have no sense of release. I don't know whether that's because I'm still caught up emotionally," I said, releasing a torrent of thoughts, "or whether it's because there are deeper ties that haven't been broken."

Viv nodded, thoughtfully. "Only you can answer that." She was not in the habit of dispensing popular nostrums. She wouldn't breezily remark that I had to forget Sharon and move on. She knew that sometimes people are brought into our lives for a greater, deeper purpose than appears obvious. She'd told me before and reiterated again this time, "We must obey those leadings, even when they take us into the valley of the shadow of death. Even in Sheol, thou, oh Lord, art with me." She held the door for me. I was too distracted to notice that I'd almost walked into the glass.

I walked inside to a seat near the front window. "I don't want to get too far into the cavernous place. I can distract myself with passersby near the window."

"And not give me your full attention," Viv said. She took off her coat and placed it on a chair. I could tell from her tone and manner that she was teasing. "I do worry a little about your saying you don't want to get too far into the cavernous place. That strikes me as rather Freudian."

"Yes, caverns and women," I said, thinking aloud about the implications of my statement. "Perhaps I was thinking about Sharon, not wanting to get further involved in her problems."

Viv nodded. "What about mothers, the deep caverns from which we all emerge?" she asked. "Because we come from their bodies, we are tied to them throughout our lives. Their issues become our own."

I felt sick, about to vomit. I'd certainly known women who were unable to separate themselves from their mothers. They either ignored the issues, trying to get away from them through various means, especially men, or addictions. Many failed to work through their issues in their lifetimes.

"It isn't just a female issue, you know. Males have to work on their mother issues too."

I set my backpack down beside the table. "Let's talk about you," I suggested. I felt that Viv was suggesting my own attraction to women whose issues with mom in some ways mirrored my own. I held Viv's chair and motioned for her to sit. "I want to talk about Sharon, but I just don't think I can."

"You know," Viv said, "it's a much nicer day that either of us had thought. The sun is shining, and it really isn't that cold. Our psychological states have so much to do with our perceptions."

I nodded.

"I want you to know that I'm being replaced by a new campus minister," Viv said, "one who'll fit the expectations of my higher-ups."

"A male?" I asked.

She shook her head. "Do you think that they would do something so politically incorrect in a university setting? You can be sure, however, this woman won't say, or do, anything controversial. Not even remotely so." She had not had much theological training, Viv said. "And what she has had was from a weak school. She had not been encouraged to ask difficult questions, theological or otherwise. She probably doesn't even know they exist."

"Apparently, that's what they want. What will you do?"

"I don't know. My husband is safely employed with a good company. He doesn't invite trouble. He doesn't discuss the issue of whether Jesus was claiming to be God in the flesh or whether his revelation of the Father was metaphorical."

"I know what you mean."

"Nor does Stan tell people that the Christian concept of Messiah is different than the Jewish—
that Christianity is not just completed Judaism, as many Christians are now convinced. His chief interests are not philosophical and theological but scientific," she said. "He is not me, after all."

"You mean he doesn't point out how theological and political agendas have influenced belief systems?" I joked.

"Nor how belief systems have influenced political and theological agendas. The answer is simply no. Stan doesn't walk that path."

"I knew you were my kind of woman," I replied.

At least I got Viv laughing. "And most of all, Stan never informs people of the many ways that the Reagan administration is ruining the country, by decimating the middle class and creating a divide between the rich and the poor."

"I suppose he doesn't talk about the disastrous consequences that all his deregulations will bring," I added.

Viv shook her head no. "I'll take an almond coffee and a chocolate croissant," she said, handing me a five dollar bill.

I balked, but she insisted.

"I said I was buying."

As I stood to place our order from the barista, I spotted Sharon, off in a corner in the back. She was sitting alone, sipping a cup of coffee, staring into space. I wondered how long she'd been there.

I looked away, and then slowly, carefully, glanced her way again. She did not seem to see me. Had she just come in? Had she been there when we arrived? Physically she looked put together, her colors coordinated, her makeup carefully and beautifully applied, her hair well done and shining. But immediately I tuned in to her psyche. She wore her emotional pain like a shroud.

Feeling as though I'd been kicked in the stomach, I turned away and carried our coffee cups to the table. I sat down across from Viv. She immediately knew something was wrong. "You forgot my croissant," she explained.

"Oh," I said, jumping up to get it.

I returned and told her I'd spotted Sharon inside. "She's sitting by herself in a far corner, staring into space," I said. "She looks good outwardly, but I know she's in pain. I can feel it. I know it as well as I know my name."

"I'm so sorry," Viv said. "You know you can't do much until Sharon wants, or can accept, your help. "But," Viv began, thoughtfully, gently. "You can pray for her," she reminded me. "God still works in mysterious ways."

I wondered why Sharon had chosen The Market. "Was she hoping to run into me? She knows I don't go here often. In fact, I stopped going here without her, once we started a serious romance."

"Maybe she was hoping to glimpse you," Viv said. "But my thought is that most of all she's wanting to connect with good memories somehow, memories of you and her and your happiness together."

It was all that I could do to nod and not burst into tears.

"Did you not know, on some deep level, that this was the reason you'd suggested going to The Market, when you'd not been here for months?" Viv asked.

I nodded. "I suppose you're right."

"Addictions are terrible. They control your entire life. Shaking them is not easy. Many people end up dying from them."

"Suffering from sexual abuse as a child, and from an adult in a position of trust, a priest no less, is nothing to smile at," I said. I wasn't sure that I'd told Viv that piece of the puzzle.

But I must have. "I know," she said.

"Did I tell you of the deadening lack of support and disbelief that Sharon has gotten from her mother and the rest of her family?"

Again Viv nodded. "To think of my troubles over not knowing who wants my knowledge and you over who wants yours," Viv responded, "seems very small by comparison to Sharon's plight. Sharon has knowledge that she never desired, knowledge that no one desires and she has been unable to share with those closest to her."

"But she needs to," I said. "It's been awful, I know, but she's shared some of it with me."

"We do not know what the future will hold," Viv reminded me. "That's why Jesus taught us to pray God's kingdom come, on earth as it is in Heaven."

"That's why things can look worse and worse, even though we are inwardly growing," I said. I frowned, on purpose.

"We certainly hope so," we said, in unison. We were both struck by a note of silliness and began giggling.

I spotted Sharon standing at the coffee counter. I felt my heart leap out of my chest, almost literally. I knew she'd seen me because she glanced away, just as I was about to catch her eye. She stared intently at the specials handwritten on the chalkboard behind the barista.

"Viv, she's here—there at the counter," I said, whispering. "We shouldn't laugh so loud. We're making her uncomfortable."

"If she had any idea of the pain our laughter stems from," Viv said. "You're as white as fresh snow."

"About as cold too," I said, realizing that I was shivering. I pulled my coat close, although I knew this was an emotional reaction.

"Drink your coffee, young man," Viv said. She attended to her cup. "You need the warmth."

Spet walked by, keeping his face turned and his shoulders bent forward, as if he hoped I wouldn't notice him. He was with Ron, the Director of Writing, "who also appears to be conspiring with him," Viv whispered. Surely they'd spotted Viv and me sitting there and were avoiding us. More and more, Spet looked like a weasel, not an observation that I liked making, but true nonetheless. In fact, the more Ron hung out with Spet, the more he too acquired a similar demeanor, with darting, suspicious eyes that all too quickly stared down his nose at the world.

When I'd first met Ron, he was so unassuming—fresh-faced, open, innovative, without being trendy, like many contemporary academicians. It was Ron's first year too. In my mind, I viewed the scene at the party that he and his wife had thrown for all English Department faculty and staff at the university. In the past, such parties had been open only to the full time, tenure track faculty, with no part timers or staff being invited. Ron said he desired to treat everyone fairly and justly.

Ron and his wife were the beaming, proud parents of a sweet and dimple-cheeked toddler with another baby on the way. I'd been optimistic about my career at the university then. It was a pleasure working with someone genuinely intelligent and real.

Again, I began to tune into Ron's son and feel danger surrounding him. Again I saw him grow tall, then fall down like a rag doll. I could not shake the resultant anxiety.

"Great, another foreboding. All I need," I said to myself, my anxiety like an iceberg shooting further up the Arctic Ocean. I really wanted to push my chair out and approach Sharon. I wanted to cry out to her, hold her, and tell her she was mine. She was not going to be abused anymore, not by anyone. I wouldn't let it happen. We'd get through this, together.

But my being felt frozen in place, an ocean away from where she stood.

Fae

When Viv and I got back to our offices, I found a copper haired woman named Fae, sitting in a chair in the hall outside my office. I was surprised to see her. It had been several years since we'd dated briefly. She'd moved to California, quipping, "I'm drawn there naturally. There are two places known for fruits and nuts. California is one of them."

"Aren't you glad to see me? I'm in Colorado for the holidays," she said. She batted her eyes and smiled. "Mother is ailing, and Daddy isn't doing well, especially not with Mother reminding him of everything he's ever done wrong in his entire long life," Fae said. "If Mother is going to die before Daddy she will make him pay every last farthing. That's what she says, reminding him how Jesus warns that all shall be made to pay the very last farthing."

"But Jesus is talking of God's function as Divine Judge, not your mother's," I replied.

Fae harrumphed. "Since when does Mother separate herself from God?"

I had seen Fae's mother in action. Last time I was around her she was publicly threatening to get her long overdue divorce from "that beast," even though both were in their late seventies. Fae said, "She's always been that way. No wonder the poor man had an affair at the start of their marriage. He couldn't bring himself to seek a divorce or annulment. He hoped to find comfort in his secretary," Fae said. "If I had married the woman that he married, I'd have sought succor elsewhere." Fae leaned over and whispered, "I think I have AIDS."

I tried not to act shocked. Despite Fae's vast storehouse of experience, she'd not told me all yet. I'd heard many stories from her, which ranged from the comic, to the bizarre, to the genuinely tragic.

Fae had been in a monogamous relationship with a bar tender for years. "At least I think it's monogamous, but you never know about men," she said, trying to lift the pall that had fallen over the conversation with humor. "He'll never marry me. He tells me he's beneath me. But I know the truth—he's too intelligent to make such a mistake." She smiled, one of her forced smiles that I remembered well.

"Why do you believe you have AIDS?" I asked.

"*Might* have AIDS," she corrected. "I'm afraid to get tested, although all my friends insist that I should."

"Do you have any symptoms?" I asked.

"Well I get night sweats. That's supposed to be one of them. It's also a symptom of the change."

"Yes," I nodded, although I thought that she had probably a decade to go for that.

"I'm scared to death that God is going to punish me," Fae said.

I remarked, "So you believe in God now?" She never used to, not in any real way. She took pride in saying, to whomever inquired, "I've rejected the faith of my fathers, and my mothers, because it's too demanding, too judgmental."

She replied, "I still prefer the Eastern philosophy of one of my old boyfriends. Everything is part of the whole. This world is only *maya*, illusion."

"That isn't quite what I understand *maya* to mean," I said. "Maya means *less than real*. That isn't quite the same as *illusion*, but it is less than the ultimate reality," I said. "That's very much what St. Augustine taught as well. For him, and mainstream Christianity, which followed his teaching, evil has power, but it is less than real," I said. I paused, hoping this complex material would sink in. "Reality is only experienced by participation in God, since He alone is real. He is the ultimate reality. When we stay in communion with God, we enjoy true being," I remarked. I scanned Fae's face to clues to her mental processes. But her face didn't register much. I went on, "Otherwise, we become shadows, participating in a superficial, illusory creation. That's where Satan and his followers dwell."

As always, Fae drew back. Her jaw hardened. I knew what that meant. She did not like my complex views—any more than her mother liked her father's. She rejected the notion of a personal God, still involved with his creation.

"Look," I said. "I don't want to get into an argument." I could feel it coming, just as it always did. If Fae could not steer every relationship, every conversation, like the captain of a great ship, she began a fight. When she dated men who were beneath her, such as bar tenders or janitors, she knew she had the upper hand and could be the good mother, supportive girlfriend. Then she didn't connect with her mother's hatred for her father. She'd come to see parts of these truths. She'd termed such relationships, "Ones of the S & R kinds. Better than S & M, which happens when I get into it with a man who reminds me of Daddy," she said. "Like you."

"So what makes you believe you might have AIDS?" I asked.

"Well, it's probably my guilty conscience. You know how many men I've had. Or who've had me. I'm trying to check out each one of them and see if any of them is sick or dead. That way I won't have to get tested unless it's clear that I need to."

"That's a pretty roundabout way of doing it."

"You know me," Fae said. She smiled. "Roundabout Fae. Men drive around me, and around me, but never—well seldom—turn right in. When they do, they zip right out again."

Again I laughed. "Have you tried stand-up yet?" I asked.

"No, I know you and others think I should," she said. "But I'm too shy. I'm trying to remember if you and I had sex. It's been so long ago I can't remember. I know you didn't really want me. You reminded me too much of Daddy, and you picked up on that, even without me telling you."

I nodded, trying not to call up too many memories from those stress-filled days. Fortunately they did not last too long. I had the good sense to cut them short.

"So we had sex," Fae intuited.

"Once," I said. Pausing for emphasis, I added, "over a decade ago." I paused again and looked directly into her eyes. "Do I seem sick?"

"Well, no," Fae said. "But nobody knows for sure where AIDS came from. I've heard some say it was a germ warfare experiment performed by powerful white men on the poor, ignorant blacks of Africa. By mistake, it got carried into the rest of the population."

"And some think a monkey may have bit someone and infected him with a virus that mutated into something deadly," I said. "Smallpox began as a mild skin disease that lots of people had. But then it mutated into something fatal and got carried into the general populace elsewhere. There it proved fatal." I still scanned Fae's face for anything seismic that might be coming.

"My friends and I run whenever we see a mosquito," Fae added, off on another tangent. "We're afraid we might get it from mosquito bites, since they suck blood," Fae added.

"I knew the fears and tendency to panic," I began, "but we have to try to live our lives as well as we can. That requires being centered."

"Cold comfort that is," Fae snorted. "Telling me to be centered is like telling a meteor to locate an orbit."

I remembered the rampages to which Fae was subject. I wondered if I should get ready to make some excuse to leave my office. I tried to turn the conversation in some more pleasant direction. I asked, "Are you going to be able to stay long with your parents?" I said, "I'd guess you can do a lot to help your dad. Underneath it all, your mother will appreciate your being there. You can also help to keep her on track— that is, from attacking your dad."

"Just as I always have," Fae responded. She sighed. Tears welled in her eyes. "I am so sick of it all. Sometimes I wish I had AIDS just to be done with it. But I'm afraid I'll go to hell, or have to come back to another worse life on earth—as a monkey, maybe a mosquito, depending on my karmic debt," she said.

I couldn't help but laugh. "That's why I've always thought, no matter how bad things seem, that I'd better do my best and not try to jump this world for the life to come. At least not before my time. Even subconsciously," I added, leaning forward to hand Fae a Kleenex. I hoped this gesture would help to make my point. She was intelligent enough to understand it, even if she rejected it and continued to embrace her own little S&M scenario.

Fae thanked me for listening to what she called her "drivel." Partly disclosing my complex range of emotions, I told her, "It's good to see you again." I embraced her and wished her luck. I meant it, but I did not invite her to keep me informed of her progress. I could not take on someone else's burdens at this time, especially the burdens of those who didn't really want to move forward.

No matter how much Fae protested—and she always did, when confronted—I did not believe that she really wanted to work toward any resolution, or true growth. To gain some insight was all right. That gave her more to talk about, more ways to go around and around the problems. *That* was how she was Roundabout Fae. It wasn't just men who drove round and round her, but herself.

With my whole being, I knew if she were to find a good and intelligent man who would marry her, she would stick to him to the bitter end. Preferably his bitter end—although her own would be more fulfilling than nothing at all.

Auto-Immune Diseases

Viv poked her head into my office and said, "I just heard a rumor that you have AIDS. Is it true?" she asked.

Since Fae had just been there a few days before, and was not known for her ability to keep her mouth shut, I figured she must have been the source.

"I heard the rumor from Louise," Viv replied. "Louise was concerned. She won't spread it." Viv took a chair across from my desk. "Louise knows Fae was worried. Fae added that you hadn't had sex with her in years," Viv said. "I don't think Louise takes her seriously. She quickly figured her out."

"Maybe Spet cooked it up, part of his character assassination tactics."

Viv replied, "I wouldn't put it past the Dean of the Cathedral either. I'm sure McDougal's enraged that you took off for Egypt instead of singing in all those choir concerts."

"Yes, and I told him I wouldn't help out with the Arts Festival, or anything else, if he didn't get the rent paid and me some salary."

"Both McDougal and Spet swim in lots of waters. They're known as sharks that devour little fishes that happen nearby."

I envisioned waters dyed with the guts and blood of innocent fish. "What do I do about it?"

"Be you," Viv advised. "Anyone who knows you, knows that you're transparent. You don't hide things. You'll discuss anything."

"But will those who don't know me even bother to find out the truth?"

"Probably not. Certainly not, if they want to believe it."

Only the day before, Ron, the Director of Writing, spoke to me at the English Department mailboxes. Trying to be friendly, I'd asked, "How are you?"

"I saw your letter in *The Denver Post* this morning. How in the world do you find time to fire off all those letters to the editor, along with your other projects?" he asked.

Dumbfounded, I stared at him. "I don't write letters to the editor," I said.

"They're signed *Ted Jones*. They're always about gay causes and intolerance."

"Ted Jones isn't an unusual name," I reminded him.

Ron shrugged. He started ripping open his mail and discarding what he didn't want.

The conversation was over. That's how I was treated around there.

I went to the library and looked over the past four months of *The Denver Post*. Sure enough, I saw probably three letters a week on average, all signed, Ted Jones. Each one of them could be thought of as gay activism. Before that, I'd merely glanced at letters to the editor, scanning certain letters that caught my eye. I had so many other things demanding my time. I'd just never noticed.

The letters definitely were not mine, even though this Ted Jones spoke of sometimes teaching and gay political stands. I certainly agreed that gay people were entitled to equal rights and humane treatment, despite conservative Christian notions to the contrary. But all of this Ted Jones' concerns were not shared by me. My passions lay elsewhere.

When Viv left me, stirring up memories of those letters, among other things, I decided to open the phone book and see if I could locate epistolary Ted Jones. There were four of us. The first two phoned weren't home. The third was. He was the right one. "Yes, I'm the Ted Jones who fires off letters to the editor whenever I can," he said.

"We have a problem. I also teach. People are confusing me for you. I don't totally mind it. I share many of your concerns but I want to stave off such confusion. It's causing me problems."

He seemed receptive. "I don't want that either," this Ted Jones answered.

I wondered if he perhaps he had AIDS, and that was how the rumor had spread to me. I decided, however, not to ask.

"Do you think you could make it clear that we're not the same person? How about using your middle initial?"

He promised to use his middle initial.

"That was fairly easy," I said to myself. I closed the phone directory and put it away in the bottom drawer of my desk. "I wonder if it will do any good."

When I got home that night, I found a letter from my mother waiting in my mail box. After the usual chitchat about the weather and the family, she said that she was going to disinherit me if I did not become a conservative Christian again.

"Again?" I asked out loud. I paused to question whether I had ever been a conservative Christian. Well, I guessed for a few years when I was married years before I could have been called a conservative Christian. I was searching for a faith of my own, trying to sort through the fundamentalism of my ex wife and her family. Even then, I held some radical views that would have made me suspect in rightwing circles.

As I learned more, thought more, studied more—and experienced more—I distanced myself from conservative theological positions in general. My mother was lucky that I didn't abandon the faith entirely, as many scholars do. Because Christianity was not a natural extension of Judaism but was a hybrid religion shot full of Greek philosophical thought and strains of mysticism it was not necessarily an invalid religion. To me the hybridization made it better, and certainly more attractive. "Just keep me away from dogmatic and doctrinaire lines and let me embrace the mystical, as I've always been prone to do," I said aloud. Only Tray was there to hear. "All I need is more mother issues shoved in my face about now," I said.

My mother could not begin to understand such complex ideas. With age, she seemed to need more definites, specifics, to grasp onto like a life jacket. That her conservative pastor was growing more and more fundamentalist in his notions, and ever more aggressive in his campaigns to eradicate the liberalism and paganism creeping in to our society, often through the educational system, did not help what seemed a growing rift between my mother and me. We didn't talk often, but I often felt her presence there at the back of my mind.

After walking and feeding Tray, and rustling up some leftovers for dinner, I went to the computer to compose a brief letter telling my mother that some notions are silly and mostly a waste of time. "Some however, are dangerous. For you to consider yourself a conservative Christian is all right in itself, although I can't understand how you square this with your earlier habit of encouraging me to explore various paths—in science, in theology, in philosophy—during my formative years."

I paused to remember better days. "Remember the butterflies, the rocks and crystals, the bird bones, the flower collections? The books of Greek and Roman mythology?" Such stories fired my imagination far more than the book of Bible stories given to me by my great aunt.

My mother had spoken highly of tolerance when I was growing up. I recalled her reminders that we had separation of church and state written into the American Constitution because of Roger Williams' firsthand experience of religious intolerance. The early colonists had chased him and fellow Baptists from place to place because they did not conform. She spoke of him as some sort of freedom fighter, and indeed he was, at least in that sense.

"Not that one would now recognize Williams' influence on many modern Baptists, I remind you. I promise you, however, that I can—I will not—ever become a conservative Christian myself, even though *fundamentalist* is the more proper term, negative as the connotations (for they are earned)—no matter how manipulative your love might prove." I was laying it on pretty thick.

"So, I guess that if anyone were to disinherit someone," I added, "I would have to disinherit you, just as Jesus asked rhetorically, "who is my mother," when his mother Mary attempted to control him."

I stood up, paced the room a bit, and sat down. "As your son, I believe it my duty to warn you that you are being brainwashed by your pastor. I have thousands of years of good theology on my side. Your pastor, however, has read so little that one could say his is a case of the blind leading the blind."

Mean as my response was, I had had enough of these manipulative tactics. My mother had tried them now and then, but never anything so treacherous as threatening to disinherit me if I didn't change my belief system, as if that were possible. Maybe someone can change behaviors, especially ones not deeply embedded in one's life, but beliefs? I shook my head in disbelief.

The war between factions even within the church was heating up. The televangelists were out to control, not just Americans, but the world. If they could get Armageddon started, they would welcome it. To their way of thinking, that would only force God's hand by causing the Rapture and ushering in the Millennium, when true Christians—that is, themselves—would rule.

Never mind that the Rapture is a recent doctrine cooked up by fundamentalists who insisted on finding proof texts in the Old and New Testaments, another example of following their own theological and political agenda. The historical church never told us God would rescue us from our tribulations. Rather, God tells us that we must go through our troubles, be tried by them. We will be given the grace to endure, if we will—and if we are chosen, if predestination is the case. In all things, God's grace is sufficient.

That is the Gospel. Not the pabulum desired by an infantile theology.

I felt rather guilty berating an old woman, and my mother, but she knew how to upset me. And upset me she did. She knew me well enough to know that I would fire off a strong retort to veiled threats.

With my letter, I packed up a copy of poet priest George Herbert's book of poetry, called *The Temple*. It is a book about Everyman's journey entrance into the Church, from baptism through sanctification. The poems are deceptively simple, but full of riches to be discovered the more one digs. In sum, it is a lovely and profound book lending insight into the mainline historical Christian faith.

I was reminded of Sharon's mother's lack of support, her unwillingness to trust in her own child's take on things. No wonder I didn't feel any warmth toward that woman. She seemed related to my own mom, but even more treacherous. She disowned her child from an early age. Mine only threatened to, and at an advanced age.

No wonder my identification with Sharon had deepened as I found out more about her. On some level I too was abused. Not to the same degree. But abused by those wielding power, nonetheless. Although he never understood me, and did his share of abuse, my dad had in his way tried to be supportive. My values weren't his. But he never tried to force me to change my beliefs. Treacherous, deeply betraying, no, not him.

A Good Priest

Jack, one of my creative writing students, came to talk with me. He'd made a late afternoon appointment through Louise, instead of just dropping by. He was agitated, his face flushed. I just knew that he was going to tell me of a bad experience with McDougal. He was in his mid-twenties, lithe, doe-eyed, and baby-faced—just the sort that McDougal would romp around the Cathedral after, or worse. I knew that Jack had started attending services there because of me.

As we talked, and Jack could speak a coherent sentence, it became apparent that McDougal was not his concern. He had been reared a Roman Catholic and attended Catholic schools through high school. He'd served as an altar boy in his home parish.

The priest who had taken a special concern for him from elementary school through college had just died. He had willed some of his personal affects to Jack, including his big gold ring with a bas relief of a Celtic cross. Jack was wearing it on his right ring finger. Jack had wrapped the bottom of the ring with tape so it would fit him. He held out his hand so that I could inspect it.

The priest had also ordered that a sealed envelope be sent by certified mail to Jack after his death. "In the letter inside Father Mark said he loved me. He'd always loved me," Jack said.

I nodded.

"He said he would have done anything for me, even die for me," Jack said.

I nodded.

"I don't want someone to die for me," Jack cried.

"Well, traditionally, it's not an unusual vow to make to someone you really love. After all, that's what the Christianity teaches that Christ himself did."

Jack nodded. "But Father Mark wasn't meaning he loved me with the pure spiritual love of God." His gaze blazed into mine.

I was beginning to understand. "Spiritual love is hard to separate from physical," I said.

"But he was my priest. He was like the father I never had. You don't expect your priest or your dad to want to kiss you all over and make love to you as he said in his letter." I agreed, although my face must not have made my position clear.

"Well, do you?" Jack demanded. He was distraught.

"No," I said. "But your priest was a man with needs and desires. He was probably lonely. He loved you," I said. "He was not your blood father. At least I don't think so, from all you've said."

Jack laughed a little. "Well, knowing my mom, you never know."

"Do you think you can recognize the real love that Father Mark had for you, which he showed you again and again, and let the sexual aspect be whatever it may be?" I asked. I paused, standing to look out the window at the chickens in the friary yard below. "I'd say Father Mark was a good priest. He did not take advantage of you, did he?"

"No," Jack replied. "He never let me know a thing about his desires while he was alive. He helped me in every way he could. He even sent me money for college, from his private account."

"His was a real burden to bear in silence," I remarked. I turned to look at Jack's face. "Do you think you could keep your love for someone quiet for twenty some years?" I asked.

Jack snorted, "But he was gay."

"Do you think God didn't love him?" I asked, searching Jack's face. I could tell that he was warring inside. "Father Mark did the best he could, given his character and situation in life. He never molested you. He had never laid a finger on you in any way that could be considered dubious. Sure, there were arm squeezes, hugs, pats on the back and arm, but never anything untoward."

"I guess you're right." His face looked less troubled. "I was lucky. Thanks." Jack got up and walked down the hall. His stride was straighter, less troubled.

Many of the priests and ministers that I'd known were honorable, decent, men and women. I was glad to hear of someone who had triumphed over temptation. I'd encouraged Jack to see it that way too.

I began packing up my things for the night. "If people can't talk about the process, about the real pitfalls, the loneliness, the longing, the anger, the fear, and frustration, how could anyone learn to face temptation and resist it?" I asked, as if speaking to an imaginary audience. I locked up my office and walked down the hall. Everyone had left for the night. "Denying that such temptation exists, as those who insist that people keep silent, only magnifies the problem. We must struggle with the texts, and with each other," I said, walking down the stairs. I stepped from the foyer into the night. It was five-fifteen and twenty degrees.

I wondered what direction the churches—not just the Roman Catholic Church, but all of them—would go. Would they do a better job embracing openness and dialogue—or would they go in the opposite direction and close down, pretending that such discussions only defamed, and thus, harmed, mother church? "As so many people do with their mothers," I thought, recalling the common notion of *Mother Church*. "Without the Church as your Mother, God cannot be your Father," one of the Church Fathers had argued.

I headed off toward the little house where the English Department was situated, looking up at the steeple of St. Elizabeth's on my left. "We are but Mother's extensions. We must do as we are told. And believe only what she says we must believe. All else is heretical. That will get us damned forever."

Knowing American culture, and its tendency to swing from extreme to extreme, rarely, if ever, being able to place sexuality and religion into any kind of balance, my guess was that the church—no matter the denomination—would try to slam the doors on all such revelations. Most were no more ready to deal with sexuality than they were the ordination of women. And if they ordained women, as Lutherans and Episcopalians had begun to do, and others further away from the historical faith did, one could be sure that women too would be expected to tow the party line, their belief systems, or suffer the consequences. Women disowning parts of themselves. Of course, arch-feminists would argue that it is men who stand behind all this, directing the female to do so. Somehow, though, I thought such critics missed the collusion so often involved.

I came upon Viv. She was headed back to her office. "Your mind appears to be going a hundred miles a minute," she said.

"I thought you'd left."

"I've been trying to, but you know the wicked. No rest, no rest for us at all."

"I'm having an internal argument with various texts," I said. "Picturing myself snorting the next time someone argues that political and theological agendas don't really affect us all."

"As a former English teacher, as well as theologian, of sorts," Viv said, "I must ask if you are meaning *affect,* or *effect,* or *infect?*"

"The first and the last," I replied, "but they *effect* us too. So, maybe all three."

"A trinity again." Viv laughed. She hurried on, leaving me on a humorous note.

I longed for spring—the crocuses, the daffodils, the tulips, the hyacinths, bird songs, and longer days. I set my backpack down on the sidewalk and buttoned my coat. It was colder than I'd thought.

Sharon's mother. My mother. Her dad. My dad.

I realized that I really didn't know a thing about Sharon's dad, or his place in the family at all. My dad and mother were finally divorced, after many years of his threatening to make their separations final. Ironically, it was my mom who filed for divorce—three days after her mother died.

My sisters and I hoped that this signaled her progress in breaking free from her mother's control. After all, good Christian folks did not get divorced. They endured to the end, the very bitter end.

I opened the door to the English Department house. In the foyer stood Spet, Ron, and a few other male faculty members. They were engaged in a lively discussion.

A couple of them, but neither Ron nor Spet, acknowledged me.

"Yeah, I hear he's also checking out the alternate lifestyle," one of them joked, while another mumbled something inaudible.

Spet caught my eye. "At least in the academy, unlike the churches, we discuss issues," he intoned, looking down his nose, as if to blame me for what the church failed to do.

When I entered the mail box area toward the back of the house, I found Jill, the department secretary sobbing. "I've had it with Spet and the others," she cried. "I've asked for a transfer."

"What's wrong?"

"Spet told me I couldn't have a framed copy of the *Serenity Prayer* sitting on my desk. 'It's a violation of church and state separation,' he said."

I gave her a puzzled look.

"I told him it's my desk, my space, and I have the constitutional right to have it. It reminds me not to take out my machete and go whacking when I witness what I do. See, I keep in there in the second drawer on the right."

I laughed. I understood too well. "I think he's pushing things pretty far."

"He's always pushing things too far. He hates religion."

I nodded. I recalled some of his offhanded remarks not long before when he was giving the unasked-for advice that my writing was too sexual. And too religious, he added.

"Someone, who shall remain nameless, told me Spet could teach Machiavelli new tricks."

I shrugged. "Oh, I'd guess so."

"I have to take the calls from his latest little hussy and put her through no matter what he's doing. He could be taking a pee and I'd have to hold his penis while he talked to her on the phone. Today, he was in a meeting with the Dean. I had to call Dean outside so Spet could hear her news. I even lied for that man and told the Dean it was an emergency," Jill said. "You want to know what the news was?"

I shook my head.

"His hussy's been accepted into the graduate program at Boulder, even though no other graduate program the country would accept her," Jill said. "You know how that happened, don't you?"

I whispered, "We'd better keep our voices down. Spet and the others are not that far away."

"Frankly, I don't give a damn. Not at this point," Jill fumed.

"A lot of that seems to be going around," Ron said, his voice coming through, loud and clear. I wondered if he was responding to Jill, or to someone else.

I helped Jill gather up her purse, papers, and coat. I grabbed my mail, stuffed it into my backpack, and walked her through the group of male faculty members to her car.

She thanked me. She said, "They'll probably be saying now that you and I are having an affair."

"But the latest rumors seem to be that I'm gay, with AIDS," I added.

"You know academics," Jill said, trying to imitate Spet by looking down her nose and talking in an affected way. "Nothing is fixed. Everything is open-ended. Not that I care, you understand. I stay above the fray. I look at the evidence and make judgments." She laughed cynically. "I am an excellent reader of all things. I deserve to teach in a far better university than this! I have a Yale Ph.D."

I'd heard all of this before. I shut Jill's car door and waved goodbye. I tried to smile, as if not to take anything too seriously. I took note that I'd better stay humble and avoid more drama.

Jill rolled down her window to thank me. "Watch your back. They're saying you like boys."

"Be philosophical," I advised myself. "Be faithful." I paused to catch my breath and center. "And be optimistic," I added, trying to put on a happy face. I wished that I could remember the rest of that song. Shirley Temple sang it in one of her cheerful childhood movies.

To make me smile, in real ways, I decided that it was time for me to break totally with the Cathedral and return to my old suburban parish. There people had made no lavish promises to see that my ministry was fully funded. But they did what they could to support it. The women of the church had continued to send me a small check now and then. It paid for coffee and supplies.

I would fulfill McDougal's wife's prophecy that way. Last time I saw her, in passing at the Cathedral, she mentioned that she'd heard, "A rumor that you won't be staying around much longer." Her face was expressionless.

"Oh," I replied and moved on.

"That's what I heard," Mrs. McDougal called after me. She seemed like some snippy junior high school girl exercising her power.

I glanced back at her. Mrs. McDoo, as I thought of her now, wore an insipid grin. I wondered
if she really believed everything she was told. Or was she in cahoots with her husband? No wonder some of the kids at the Cathedral were calling them the McDoos, or Doodoos, for short.

I'd already cut back on attending church services at the Cathedral, going only now and then, as if trying to break a bad habit. The place made me sick.

I looked at my watch. It was seven. I wondered if Dan, who was still staying with me, was home making dinner. I hoped so. We'd gone through all our leftovers. I dreaded the thought of having to cook.

I didn't want to think of his moving out. His moving in was temporary. We'd agreed on that. But I needed someone, a person, on my passage through troubled seas. My ark was being threatened on every side by winds, lightning, hail, icebergs, and everything else that could be thrown my way.

Evidence

It was the morning of Friday, February the fifteenth, going on a year from my introduction to Sharon outside St. Elizabeth's. Another Valentine's Day had been gotten through with no valentine. The weather was cold but dry. Everything looked dead.

When I got to my ministry office I found a note from Louise that my office rent was over three months past due again. My old suburban parish had always paid the rent. It was only fifty dollars a month, a burden on no one. The Franciscans, who owned St. Francis Center, were threatening to evict me. "They don't want to keep sending overdue notices," she wrote.

Immediately, I got on the phone to ask McDougal what exactly was going on—just as I had to do in the fall. At that time a check soon arrived to catch up back rent. I'd hoped he'd also sent enough to pay some months in advance.

"The Dean is busy right now," his secretary said. "Please leave your name and number and the nature of your business, and he'll get back to you."

"Please have him call me back," I said. I slammed the receiver down. She knew very well what I wanted.

The Dean didn't return my call.

That afternoon, Rob, one my students, walked into my office. "I need to talk," he said.

"What's the matter?" I asked. It was obvious from Rob's fisted hands that kept punching each other and red face that he was upset.

"The Dean of the Cathedral knocked on my apartment door this morning. He said he'd come to make a pastoral visit. He looked like a priest, standing there, dressed in black pants, black shirt, and wearing his priest's collar. So I invited him in."

"Oh no," I muttered. I glanced out the window. This was not the first time I'd heard about McDougal's infamous pastoral visits. He really was busy in the morning when I'd called.

"I told him to have a seat and I'd make some coffee," Rob said.

I urged Rob to sit down.

"Before I knew it, he was standing behind me grabbing my crotch and herding me into the bedroom. He pushed me onto the bed and tried to unbutton my Levis."

"What happened next?"

"He grabbed my dick. I knocked him off onto the floor and punched him a few times. 'Even if you are a man of God, you aren't acting like one," I yelled. I kicked him in the side."

"You've got to go to the police. Have you done that yet? And you've got to report this to the Bishop," I said.

"No, I just want to forget about it. I don't know why he thought I was gay," Rob said. "What did I do to make him think so?"

"Frankly, I don't think it matters much, not from what I've heard," I said. "You're an object. That's how he thinks of you and everyone else."

"He makes me feel so dirty, so ashamed. I just want to forget the whole thing."

"You really must report it," I said.

"Why don't you?" Rob's eyes searched my face.

"You'll have to go to the police yourself," I said. I'll go with you, if you like."

"No, I don't want to get the police involved."

In those days, few would have dreamed of taking such matters to the police, not unless the case was clearly criminal—and, even then, most would have hesitated a long time. Police were said not to look kindly on males who reported other males for sexual impropriety. We were weak, and asking for it—if they believed such a misdeed had even taken place. I was, however, angry enough to help Rob report it, and I'd back him up. "Perhaps we can get the police to investigate. I'll supply other names."

"No." Rob shook his head. "That's exactly what I don't want. You can report him to the Bishop," Rob said.

I nodded, although I'd been advised not to do that. "You'll get the tables turned on you," my friends had warned. "Stay out of it. You have more troubles than you can take on as it is. He'll find a way to get back at you—worse than he's doing now."

I began hearing that McDougal was telling folks I was uncooperative—that's why I wasn't getting funding from the Cathedral.

Well, to one way of looking at things, he was right.

I was sick of having male students come to my office, both angry and ashamed, to say McDougal wouldn't let go of their hands when he shook them and chased them around the Cathedral, as he'd dogged Dan. Now this. This topped everything.

While the choir members joked about living out an English sex comedy, my students did not take matters so lightly. I could no longer recommend that any of my charges attend the Cathedral unless they liked that sort of thing, or were old, or female. I urged the students who had been molested that they needed to report the problem to the Bishop, for he had authority over all Episcopal priests in Colorado. I had tried to talk with McDougal myself, but never to any avail. His staff remained in denial.

When I even hinted at McDougal's proclivities, I would be asked, why was I so angry? Why was I making disgusting lies up about this poor man of the cloth? I found myself feeling guilty, as if I were responsible, as if I too were a molester. The Dean was doing great things in the city, putting Denver on the map. The lines might as well have been recorded. He was bringing in all kinds of grants, pledges, and funds, expanding the Cathedral and offices, seeing that the building stones were cleaned for the first time in decades, starting a care center with housing for AIDS victims, leading the community in all sorts of musical and arts programs. He would be remembered forever as one of the Great Deans, because he paid attention not only to building projects but to people. Under this Dean, the Cathedral was prospering in every way. Finally, the Cathedral had even begun to contribute as much money to the Diocese as my old suburban parish, one of the top contributors. Soon it would surpass it.

"Would your Bishop, because of the revenues and fame rolling McDougal's way, be more willing to turn a seeing eye to the suspicious activities than McDougal's staff had been?" Viv asked. Of all my confidants, her advice was the soundest.

"You're probably right."

My day had been wearing. I decided to pack things up and head home. It was four and still light outside. "What you meant for evil, God turned to good," again came to mind. I hoped the scripture was inspiration, but I was afraid it might only have been but wishful thinking.

Instead of going west, I decided to drive east to Cheesman Park. I had the sense that I'd run into McDougal. He was often there.

McDoo was sitting in his car, as he was apt to do, his priest's collar unbuttoned, and flopping onto his black shirt. The man had no shame. His window was rolled down, even though the weather was chilly. He could talk to tricks that way. His face looked bruised. I parked my car behind him and got out.

"What in the hell do you think you're doing?" I demanded as I walked up to him and peered in.

He just smiled, as if he didn't know a thing. "Are you cruising again?" he asked.

"I'm here to confront you, not just over what you did to Rob, but your entire sexual hypocrisy. Actually, it's bigger than that. Your general hypocrisy in everything."

"Most people are stupid. They're dazzled by glamour, the P. T. Barnum syndrome," McDougal explained. It was as if he'd done nothing wrong. "If you get caught, you invoke the

Lord, and then you tell them that you've repented, experienced firsthand the glory of the Lord and are speaking in tongues, hallelujah," he said, grinning. "In this Diocese they forget everything else. You've been filled with the Spirit, the sign of God's forgiveness—his stamp of approval. It's in the Bible."

"Kind of like Jimmy Swaggart," I remarked. If he remained oblivious to my disgust, McDougal was stupider than I'd imagined.

"You can always cash in on the proceeds from your best seller, much of it exaggeration and fabrication, of course," he said. As far as I was concerned, he could worry about getting writers to come in for his Arts Festival—or find another sucker to do it.

That night, I still fumed. Dan and I decided to get away from the complications of city life by driving into the mountains the next morning.

"McDougal is such a piece of shit," Dan said. "But then, so are Spet and Ron."

"I'd hate to have their karma," I said. I tried not to think of losing everything, as seemed immanently probable.

"I know what you're thinking," Dan said, as if reading my mind. "Don't even go there. You'll figure something out. Another door will open, if you look. Maybe it will be only cracked, and you'll have to push. But you'll find it. You'll always have me to remind you."

"Remind me of what?" I asked.

Dan smiled coyly. "Just remember, I don't have anyone either."

"I'm lonely," Dan said, appearing at my bedroom doorway just as I was about to fall asleep. "Can I sleep with you tonight?" he asked.

I laughed. "Spending Valentine's Day without someone special has that effect," I said, laughing. "Get in."

The next morning, we woke early, rested. My anxiety felt miraculously lessened.

Dan made a pot of freshly brewed coffee, strong and black. "This will put hair on your chest," he said, handing me a mug.

"I don't think I need more of that, but you, Son, could use a little more."

He laughed and drank heartily.

When we stood at the car, ready to jump in and head to the mountains, Tray seemed to have trouble jumping up into the back seat of my car. She would hesitate, aim, jump, but not be able to get her front legs in such a position that she could pull her back end up onto the seat.

Dan and I both offered to lift her up, but she insisted on pulling back and starting over. She made several attempts. Finally, she managed to get herself up on the seat.

We couldn't help but admire her spirit.

As I drove off, I mused on the fact that I'd never had a dog live long enough to go through the natural process of slowing down, falling apart, and dying. To think of Tray's death, or having to be put down, deeply upset me. I didn't want her to be hit and killed by a car, as my other dogs had, but I didn't want to witness what was the inevitable end of a natural life.

Dan and I sat in silence. Tray's labored breathing filled the vacuum. Dan reached to turn on the radio. It was set to a classical station. Vivaldi's *Four Seasons* was playing. It was cheering.

"What do you think about S and M?" Dan asked, his manner casual.

For a moment, I took my eyes off the road to look at Dan. I thought he was being funny, trying to distract me from thinking about Tray's end. He knew me well. So I said, "Well gee, isn't that what most people do anyway?"

"I'm being serious," Dan said. "I know you're sad, and I am trying to distract you, well sort of, but I'm curious."

"Curious about S and M?" I asked. I glanced quickly at his face and looked back to the roadway. I glanced into the rear view mirror to glimpse Tray in the back seat. She was sitting up with her head resting on the edge of the window ledge so that she could see everything that we passed. "Ok," I said, "are you talking about the heavy duty pain that some mean by S and M?"

"Well, I mean more like spanking or a light whipping with a belt or whip. I think that could be kind of fun."

"As long as it's done in good fun and no one gets too serious about the pain, I'm all right with it." I paused. "Were you feeling a need to be spanked, or to spank?"

Dan blushed a deep, rosy red.

"I mean, if you feel the need to be turned over the knee, I suppose I could do that for you, just as soon as we return to the house," I said, my tongue in cheek.

"Rick and his partner are deeply into the S and M scene."

I looked at Dan.

He was staring out the window. "They belong to an S and M club downtown. It's equipped with dungeons and torture equipment."

"Well, I suppose in that case maybe you're better off not being hooked up with him. Do you think their involvement is serious?"

He nodded. "There's serious pain involved, but they're not into scarring or blood or feces."

"How do you know this?" I realized my grip on the steering wheel was making my knuckles white. I made myself relax a bit.

"They invited me to join them. Rick talked with me about it."

"When was that?"

"A few days ago."

"Are they into drugs too?" I asked.

"Nothing heavy, at least that's what Rick says," Dan replied. "But they do poppers and coke for play." Dan paused. "My guess is, they do a fair amount of those drugs when sex is involved."

"I repeat. You can be glad you're not involved."

"How do you know I'm not planning to get involved?"

"I think I know you well enough to know that you'll stay away from it—and from them," I said.   From the heavy weather that seemed to lie ahead, I wondered if we were going to get into a snow storm. No storms had been in forecast. But things looked awfully dark.

"Sometimes I feel left out. Everyone I know is into sex and partying with drugs."

"Am I?" I asked. "Follow your own path, the beat of a different drum."

"But I feel so alone," Dan complained.

"Well," I answered. I pulled the car off into a side road that adjoined a large meadow where we could get out and walk. "From the looks of things ahead, I don't think we ought to go further into the mountains. If the weather starts to turn, I want to make a fast trip home."

"I agree. Always thinking ahead. Too bad preparedness doesn't let us escape the troubles of the world."

"Tell me, Dan, if you knew most of the world was going to hell, would you follow just so you could be counted as one of the sheep?" I turned off the motor and opened my door. "I feel that I've lectured enough."

"I'm not brave, Ted. I'm really pretty afraid," Dan said. He opened the back door and let Tray out. She began meandering. "I'm not even that intelligent."

"You're brave enough, and intelligent enough." We followed the trail.   Tray never strayed far.

"For what?"

"To muddle through."

"But I don't want to muddle through. I want to be in a relationship. I want to love and be loved. I want to have a good career, to be known in my field."

"Here's a field," I said, gesturing around us. "It's beautiful. You can be known to all that matters, right here—the earth, the sky—famous among foxes."

Dan smiled.

"Thatta boy. I don't blame you, Dan, but I would ask, what price is your soul?" I asked. I looked directly into his eyes to pierce his consciousness.

"My soul isn't for sale," Dan said. The firmness in his voice had returned. He'd woken from his trance.

"Good." I quickened my pace. Tray took off running like a puppy again. I was amazed at how much energy she was able to muster, especially since she had seemed barely able to get into the car a little while before. Puffing a little, Dan caught up with us.

"Bet you didn't think two old dogs had it in 'em," I said, laughing.

"I figured Tray did." Dan laughed.

"Do you prefer being turned over the knee with your pants on or off?" I called back to him, running after Tray to the next hill. Seeing me, she came back made a little bark, and then ran on, as if playing catch me if you can.

"I've been thinking that over," Dan called. He caught up to us again.

What had been a breeze turned harsher. The wind was blowing from the northwest. Even if it didn't snow, the wind was cold and unpleasant. All three of us raced back to the car.

There, Dan and I pulled burrs and pieces of dead, dry leaves and twigs from Tray's hair. We hopped into the car and started off again. Suddenly the sky cleared. It seemed that the wind had moved the storm out.

Dan wanted to have lunch. I too was famished, so we thought we'd stop in a still-quaint little mountain town called Victor at a restaurant housed in an old hotel.

After I excused myself to go to the bathroom, I returned to find a couple of cowboys standing over Dan, seated at the table. Their voices were raised.

"So, what's up?" I asked.

Dan said, "Nothing."

The men said not a word. They left just as the waitress came over to take our order.

We ordered two bowls of chili and a couple of glasses of water. Some Colorado restaurants did not automatically serve it, since we often had droughts. Our water tables dropped every year.

After the waitress left, I leaned across the table to ask Dan what the cowboys wanted.

"Just the usual bullshit," he answered. "They asked if I wanted a date."

"Oh," I replied. Since I'd known Dan for years, I never really looked at him as an outsider might. I examined him, trying to be objective. I didn't notice anything that would mark him out. He had nice chiseled features, clear, blue eyes, good muscles, nothing that shouted *queer*. Since he'd been working out, he didn't look at all wimpy. He was wearing a plaid shirt and jeans. That also should have satisfied the cowboys' notions of masculinity.

"I told them I was here with my dad," Dan said. "They thought that was funny and started making jokes about it." Dan paused. "Maybe they believed it, once they saw you."

I laughed. "The age difference isn't that marked. At least I hadn't thought so."

"The stress is aging you fast," Dan said, straight-faced. Then he laughed.

"For a moment, I believed you." I waited until I was sure no one was watching. I leaned over and whispered across the table to Dan, "Bare bottomed. OTK. That means—"

"I know what it means, Daddy," Dan said, laughing.

On the drive down winding one-lane highways, lined with steep precipices and huge boulders looking as if they were about to tumble, I thought about ordination. The integrity that I'd worked to obtain over the years would be threatened by "joining the club," as McDougal had referred to the ordained clergy of the Church. I would be expected to toe the party line, whatever it was.

Straight ahead were two big boulders blocking the left lanes. I barely missed a car that had swerved from the left lane into mine to avoid them.

Waiting for my adrenaline to stop surging, I thought about Dan, how he'd recently become a member of the United Church of Christ. Dan swore that leaving the strict Calvinists of his family background freed him. That was part of his process of maturation, I thought. He felt able to explore his sexuality.

As far as wide-ranging sexual play for me went, who was I kidding? My own family Puritanism often peeked through, Puritanism that colors the entire history of our country. We mustn't even joke about sex, because the temptation might overwhelm those tempted.

"You know, I'll bet there are lots of boulders about to break loose," Dan said. "I've heard there have been several avalanches in the back country this season."

"Don't remind me," I said. "I don't want to think about more dangers in my life."

Dan quieted. I went back to thinking about temptations. I was glad that temptation had yet to overwhelm me. In fact, I could make the argument that joking about serious issues— and discussing them openly—was the remedy to acting out. We can explore safely many of the issues through joking and talking, not just in superficial ways, but with some direction, some depth, in mind. That was my counseling training at work. I distrusted most those who hinted darkly at their desires.

Openness, however, makes plenty of people nervous. It exposes them and their own unresolved problems. That's why I held to the necessity of forcing ourselves to confront the Shadow. No one can do that for us, although they can point up the need for it.

Masters like Shakespeare were fond of placing comedy squarely in the midst of their tragedies. The court jester, the wise fool, has a long history in Western culture because he can tell the truth that others cannot. Often the so-called normal folks cannot see what the fool sees, because he stands outside the institutions, yet is connected with them. Native Americans and aboriginal cultures have also revered their holy fools. Comedy helps to dissipate aggression. Interspersing comedy into tragedy makes the issues stand out, helps watchers and readers to examine problems from various angles.

I wished that such theory could be turned into an article for publication. I was always on the lookout for possibilities. But none of it was my own. It was common currency.

I glanced in the rear view mirror to notice that Tray had something black between her paws. She was rolling it around and chewing on it. I mentioned it to Dan.

He turned around. It was a baseball cap that she'd found somewhere and decided to play with. Dan placed it on her head. She sat up and looked around as if to show off her new cap, the brim to the side. "It gives her a kind of sappy look, my old, black-masked, blonde Afghan, wearing a jauntily pitched baseball cap."

Dan laughed. "Sure does."

So how then does the fool make a living? That was the question. And how does he, or she, avoid being killed for telling the truth? Societies have long liked to stone their prophets. Perhaps the comic element, the laughter provides the redeeming quality, allowing the fool to escape, sometimes by just a hair.

I wondered if my sense of humor would save me.

The Disappeared

I realized that I hadn't seen Viv around St. Francis Center for a few days. I went to check her office. It had been cleared of all personal effects.

"She'd been placed on furlough," Louise said, "without pay. Employment by the church is not like being employed by the government. The churches feel free to behave like dictators." Louise tilted her head toward the elevator. The doors were just opening. "Meet Viv's replacement."

Standing in the middle of the elevator was a massive, middle-aged black woman named Betty. Her presence filled the void. She stepped out. She smiled and extended her hand. It was leathery.

Louise started to introduce us, but before she got past, "Ted, I want—" Betty had introduced herself.

"I'm the Episcopal chaplain, mostly volunteer," I said. "And maybe not that much longer."

"Honey, I know all the buzz words Lutherans want to hear. Using them puts folks into a trances state, makes them receptive. They don't have to think," she said. "People don't like that, no matter how much they say they do."

I nodded. "I'm sure there's truth in that," I said.

Louise also nodded and tilted her head to me. "You could learn from her," she said, *sotto voce.*

"Kuhn is big right now as a theologian, so I refer to him often, just as I'm doing now." She paused, looking me up and down, as if assessing me as if I were a bull going to market. "I'll tell you more. I don't hail from Lake Woebegone, but from Alabama. I've long been active in civil rights."

This seemed puzzling to me, since Lutherans in Colorado seemed to want someone who would toe the party line. "I thought you—"

"What are your buzz words?" Betty said, interrupting. "What theologians do you refer to?" Betty asked.

We walked back to my office. I flipped on the light.

"Afraid you won't be able to see me in the dim light?" Betty asked. "My complexion is pretty dark."

I laughed. "It never occurred to me." I motioned for her to take a seat. "Take a load off, you'll need it."

She laughed. "Good to meet someone who can dish it back," she said.

"To answer your first question, I try to avoid buzz words. That's my training in literature. We're taught to avoid jargon."

"Mistake," Betty honked. "You can't be too scholarly and be a minister. Nope. Doesn't work."

"As for theologians, I refer to Augustine more than anyone."

"Oh you Anglicans like that classical stuff, don't you," she said.

"He's very wise. I also refer to other Church Fathers, and to poets, especially seventeenth century English poets like Milton, Donne, Herbert, and Vaughan. I also refer to Shakespeare and Chaucer."

"He's a really old guy" she said. "I see why the church doesn't support you." She turned to look at my bookshelf. "*Complete Writings of the Saints*," she said, "multiple volumes." "Highbrow stuff, right."

"I find them full of wisdom, so yes, I refer to St. John of the Cross, Julian of Norwich, St. Teresa of Avila, and others. I also like C. S. Lewis quite a bit. He gets to the heart of Christianity. He's practical and imaginative at the same time. I don't slavishly follow anyone, however."

"Boy, we need to lighten you up."

"My skin's pretty light as it is," I said.

Betty laughed. She squinted up her eyes as if taking a closer look at me. "You know, Ted, I think I like you. I can imagine you challenge lots of folks, but I like you."

"I'd guess that's a good thing," I said.

After talking with some of my fellow campus ministers over the next few days, I decided that the Lutherans figured, if they were to have a woman as a campus minister, they'd really do it right, take a chance—with an activist, of color to boot.

"Betty tells her higher ups what they want to hear, and in language the average pew-stuffer can understand. She poses no threat. At least not yet," Father Norbert, the head of the Franciscans who ran St. Francis Center, told me. He sat beside Louise at the reception desk, his favorite perch. "We aren't racists in Colorado. No, we definitely believe in racial equality, and women," he added. Father Norbert's blue eyes twinkled. His white beard made him look like Santa Claus. I understood his drift.

I glanced at Louise. She smiled away, absorbing every word of wisdom.

The media loved Betty. Over the next few days, a number of articles popped up in local newspapers. At least one of the local television stations conducted a half hour interview of this "new campus dynamo brought in by the Evangelical Lutherans of America," as billed by Channel 9.

Father Norbert and I were evidently the only campus ministers who mentioned Viv and how much her intelligence, her truly good character, and wit would be missed. Those comments rarely seemed, however, to find their way into the published articles or interviews. It was as if Viv had been wiped from the slate, *disappeared*, to use the language of South American regimes. We North Americans did not seem much better at core than those oppressive regimes that we so readily condemned. "After all, pointing the finger at them makes us feel superior, righteous, true to our North American heritage," Father Norbert said to me. "We outwardly support freedom, fairness, and individuality."

One day, at the end of February, Betty referred openly to me as "a honky," and I admitted it, telling her the story of how one of my sisters referred to our mother as a honky right in the midst of a Denver store, "Where a couple of black women were shopping. They looked at my sister, and then at my mom, and back at each other, then at my mom again, and then at my sister," I said, building my story. "In unison they laid into my sister for showing no respect for her mother. In other words, Betty I respect you and know you will also respect me—unless we do something to destroy that trust," I said. "I have always said good things about Viv because she is truly a good woman. I should like the privilege of saying the same about you."

After that, Betty never referred to me as a honky again, even though I would sometimes refer to myself as one, in a way that gently reminded her that I owned my whiteness.

By March, which blew in with a blizzard marking the first day of the month, Betty said, "I've just about finished Uncle Tom-ing my Bishops and the leaders of other churches, now that I've secured my position."

I raised myself in my chair. I glanced outside at the heaps of snow on the roofs and ground. It was morning and still snowing. My estimation of Betty shot up considerably. "Oh Mama," I exclaimed. I wondered just what we had on our hands.

That afternoon, Betty stomped back to my office, throwing snow everywhere from her coat, scarf, gloves, and hat. "I told you my real self was gonna come out. I just got back from the Bishop."

I told her to sit down. "You will anyway," I joked.

"When I went into his office, I shut the door quietly. He told me to sit down. I shook my head. He gave me a quizzical look." Betty reached over, grunted, and shut my door. "I moved toward him," she said. "My manner remained neutral, non-threatening. Then I reached out and grabbed him by the balls."

I jumped. I'm sure I looked shocked.

"As the Angel Gabriel said to the Virgin Mary, be not afraid," Betty said. "I'm not planning to do that to you."

"Whew," I said, wiping my brow.

"I told him, if he ever said anything that even implied his usual demeaning attitude toward people with minds, I'd twist those little fuzzies right off and toss them to the dogs. I meant it." She paused, laughing. "Not only that," I said, "but I'll call in the media and accuse you of sexual harassment, racism, classism, sexism—and everything else I happen to think of. Then you can watch your career and retirement get flushed right down the crapper." She slapped her thigh and laughed.

"Sistah, I like you more all the time," I said.

She reached out to high-five me. I finally figured out how to respond (with a little prompting on Betty's part). She'd put a big grin on my soul.

"When I left the Bishop's office, I was careful to be seen by his secretary adjusting my blouse and skirt, as if I'd been molested," Betty said. "His secretary said nothing, but her eyes followed me out the door. I know those visuals planted the seeds of suspicion—in case I need to go harvesting later."

I'd always thought Betty did quite well before that, but, by the next morning, she had Kacey Fine Furniture hauling a new, deluxe, electronic massage chair into her office. I saw it going down the hall. "Viv should have done the same thing," Betty remarked, coming to my office to tell me all about it.

"Viv never would have thought of it," I replied.

"You've got to jerk the rug of power right out from under these jackasses," Betty said. "I'll offer you the same free advice as well. That's something you decent academic and religious people don't understand."

"I don't know that I could ever be that bold," I replied. I stood up to look out the window. I wondered how the poor chickens were doing down below in their yard still heaped with snow. "I think too much about various courses of action and their ramifications. I don't want to hurt anyone, not unless I'm certain they deserve it." Maybe the Franciscans had moved them inside for awhile.

"Hesitation only gives them time to get hold of you again," Betty said. "I've got to go get my hair oiled." She smiled. "Guess who's picking up the tab?"

I shrugged. I knew well who she meant.

"I told him I needed a full day at the spa. 'All this stress from working for you has really dried out my hair and skin,'" I said.

As Betty sauntered off, I wondered when the snow would melt. "Can spring be far behind?" I whispered.

Snow

March had blown in with a blizzard. The snow and ice had not melted, even though it was now five days later. Already I felt near despair. Lack of sunshine really affected me. In Colorado I expected it. Overcast days rarely bothered me so much in England, where I expected them.

The spirit of Sharon stood in the doorway of my bedroom again, waking me at two a.m. I looked at the dial of my clock radio on the night stand. She seemed scared but didn't come close. I tried talking to her, but she remained silent. Then she disappeared.

The next night, with snow heaped everywhere from the ongoing winds, I was awakened by the doorbell a couple of hours before dawn. At first I vaguely heard it but rolled over and tried to go back to sleep. The room was cold and drafty from the wind blowing through the ill fitting, old windows of my town home. I pulled up the covers.

But the bell rang again. It was pressed not just once but several times in a row. Then came a long pause, with the bell sounding several times again. Finally, I rolled out of bed, dodging Tray, and went downstairs to see who was ringing at four in the morning.

My feet freezing, I opened the door to find no one. I walked out onto the stoop in the midst of blowing snow and tried to have a look. I could not see far. The porch light was swallowed up in snow. I saw nothing.

When I saw Dan—who had decided to become a roommate instead of a guest, thus helping with my financial distress—later that day, I asked him if he had heard the doorbell around four in the morning.

He shook his head and said, "I didn't hear a thing."

As far as physical evidence went, nothing had turned up. I decided that I must have experienced another form of psychic impression from Sharon.

A few nights later, I was wakened by the Virgin Mary standing at the foot of my bed. I didn't need to ask who it was. I knew. I heard her voice telling me, "Stay close to Sharon. She depends on you more than you know."

Okay, I thought, wondering what that meant. How do you stay close to someone who will not let you near, at least not for long?

Just as quickly as the Virgin had appeared, she disappeared again.

I decided to call Laura and ask if she knew anything about Sharon.

She went through her usual Darlings and how are yous. Finally she said, "Sharon's moved from Brad's again, back to her condominium. Brad's left to continue his drug use on his own," she said. She didn't know anything more. "Please darling, stay away from her," Laura advised. She'll only hurt you more." She paused and added, "I wish I'd never told her about you in the first place."

"Oh, so you were behind our meeting?" I had no idea. "I'd thought our meeting was an accident, well not exactly, her grandmother seemed to be helping pull the strings."

For a moment, I thought, scratching my head. I was trying to reconstruct our first meeting. "Every now and then Sharon did seem to have some knowledge of me and my work that was more than what she'd gained just that day."

"Darling, I knew you two would hit it off," Laura said. "Sharon needed an example of a true priest, not the typical black shirt and dog collar hypocrisy. I told her she might just happen to walk near St. Francis Center now and then, and see if she might happen upon you. She knew what you looked like. I showed her a photo of you standing beside me, one Bud took."

More pieces of the puzzle were sliding into place. "You know I'm not ordained," I replied.

"Darling, I said *true priest*. Men don't ordain those."

I agreed. While Laura was right about Sharon hurting me, I still believed that I had been given a higher command by someone beyond this earthly sewer.

What did staying close to Sharon mean? Was I to seek her out? Or was I to let her come to me in the flesh? Was I meant to stay spiritually close to her, regardless of what happened in the physical world? Was she ready to be helped if I made the attempt?

As usual, my mystical experiences raised as many questions as they answered. I scratched my head at those pop psychics whose observations and experiences seemed cut and dried, simplistic. Were their lives not messy? Were their insights so clear, so easy, as they made them seem?

I decided to take Tray and drive by Sharon's condominium. I said nothing to Dan about it. He wanted me to leave her alone. He didn't approve of my getting involved again. "That's that," he'd said, refusing to argue about it.

I saw nothing extraordinary from the outside. I couldn't tell if someone lived there. The windows always looked the same, not just in Sharon's unit, but in everyone else's. They all seemed to have vertical blinds that were partly closed.

I parked my car and got out. I walked to the front door of the building and found Sharon's name on the directory. I started to dial her number but couldn't do it. If I didn't time things right, I could make matters worse.

I turned around and walked away from the door. I needed some sort of sign that I should call on her rather than wait for her to approach me in the flesh.

A few nights later I got a hang up call. Then another, the following night. The phone rang again the next evening. When I answered, the caller hung up. Although I had no proof, I was certain that Sharon was on the other end.

This time I took action. I drove back to Sharon's condominium. This time, I dialed her number from the directory in the lobby. She buzzed the door open without even asking who was there.

I decided to take the stairs rather than the elevator to help work off some of the adrenaline that had my heart pounding. My gut was clenching, even though I'd just taken another Librax to relax my colon.

Sharon was waiting for me at her door. She was pale, with dark circles under her eyes. She made fleeting eye contact, and then looked away, as if embarrassed. Her shoulders slumped even more.

I reached out, trying to hold her, but she backed away. "I'm not a good influence," she said, insisting that I not touch her. "I will only ruin your life."

"You've been visiting me again at night," I said.

"I don't care who's been visiting you. I don't want to ruin your life." She was insistent.

Even though I didn't want to hear it, I worried that she was telling me the truth. I started to turn and leave, but my feet held fast to the floor. I wanted to hear that we could get on the right track, work through the pain, and find happiness together. My stomach cramped, enough to make me want to bend over in pain.

I shook my head. "I think you're wrong. The Virgin Mary has told me to stay close to you—
you depend on me more than I know."

"Jesus, I can't even get the mother of God off my back." She backed up and shut the door in my face.

I walked down the hall feeling as if the entire building were collapsing about me. When I got outside, the polluted air struck me, making my eyes burn and my nose stop up.

In my mind I replayed more of what had transpired in Sharon's condominium.

I got out of the car and strode back to Sharon's building. I kept pressing the buzzer until she let me back inside.

"You aren't demanding in the usual ways," Sharon said.

"Except for just now," I said, hoping to make her smile.

"You couldn't care less about the usual crap regarding how much money your mate makes, and whether she's turning it all over to you. You don't care about the right labels or the right cars, the right social contacts, or any of that."

"Well, I do appreciate quality."

Finally, Sharon smiled. "Of course you want someone to look their best. But," she paused, "you're far more concerned about their thinking, their internal well-being, meaning that they really struggle with issues, that they're always mindful of the bigger picture—that they act with integrity," she said. She stepped away from me, and then turned to say, "You don't seem to realize how hard that is."

I noticed her shoes. She always wore such nice shoes. These had a little strap and elegantly cut heels, medium-height, curved like a miniature of the calf of her leg. "Well, I think I do. I've struggled my whole life to see the bigger picture and act from *agape* rather than *amor*."

Sharon bit her lip, so hard that she drew blood. "Ted, Ted, Ted, most people have never even heard of *agape* versus *amor*."

I again tried to reach out to her. She backed away.

"Being around you makes people aware of their failures. You take me right back to Catholic school and my Jesuit university experiences," Sharon said. "I'm remembering them now. Even if the nuns and priests and lay teachers *said* nothing, we *knew* what was expected. We breathed a higher purpose in the air," she said, shaking her head. "We drank *agape* at every meal. We were constantly reminded of the communion of the saints, both the living and the dead." Sharon paused again, then said, "If deep down I thought it was a grand delusion, it wouldn't be so awful." She looked away from me for a moment, and bent forward, as if to wretch.

My stomach was feeling the same way.

Then she looked into my eyes again. "I'm such a wreck because I know in my heart that it's right and true. I do believe. But I can't be holy."

"That's a lie!" I yelled. Like a volcano, the words just came up from inside me.

"Ted, I cannot live a holy life." Sharon's voice remained controlled, her pitch low.

I was the one sounding hysterical. I wanted to tell Sharon that she had to stop trying, and let God work through her, grant her grace, but I could not. It all sounded so clichéd. But in my experience, it was true. But at that moment, the cliché sounded hollow. I still had to work on myself to let go. That was the idea of sanctification. "You might die trying, but grace isn't cheap," I cried. "In *The Cost of Discipleship*, Bonhoeffer speaks eloquently of the process. You've got to go through the process!"

Sharon fell to the floor like a rag doll and wept.

I dropped down beside her. She still wouldn't let me hold her.

For someone who had been so severely abused, the process might not be like that. Lots of therapy would be necessary to get to the place where one could work through the issues enough to let go. And perhaps that would never happen, at least not in this life. The damage might be too grave. I turned to leave. I noticed again how leaden I felt, not just heavy, but shapeless, grey.

How was I to stay close to Sharon? If the Virgin Mary were near, I'd ask her. I'd also be glad to ask any saint, or God himself. But the heavens remained silent as a blue stone.

This time I said goodbye. I knew I had to go.

As I drove off, I glanced at my watch to see that I'd only been there an hour. It seemed so much longer. A weight of sorrow had replaced my earlier anxiety. For the moment, the cramping in my gut had lessened. I knew, however, that I'd better take another Librax for it just as soon as I got home.

I knew Sharon was right. She'd been too damaged to enter into any kind of stable relationship, with me or anyone else. I was demanding. I knew that.

As I drove down the street toward home, I felt like running head on into oncoming traffic. I could take out at least another car.

I was left with questions that unraveled into more possibilities, more questions. I was left with the mystery at the core.

Esoterica

Shortly thereafter, Sharon's spirit began coming to me in the night and slipping quietly into the bed beside me, where we slept peacefully. She did not come to me in the physical body, but in the soul's perceptible form that the sensitive can see and feel, just as the body is known to grosser, more earthly eyes and sense.

She didn't speak. She didn't need to. I knew who she was. I knew how she felt, how she moved, how close she snuggled in the curve of my body, my arms around her waist. Although some speak of noticing odors during such experiences, my olfactory sense wasn't wakened.

I believed I was giving Sharon some strength, some comfort, so that she could work through her trauma when she rejoined her body.

One night, I heard her whisper my name. I answered.

I asked why she had not spoken before.

"I had nothing to say," she said. "We've been together before, in earlier lives."

I did not know what I believed about reincarnation.

I toyed with the idea that Sharon and I had been together before. I wondered why she knew this in the spiritual body but not in the physical.

"Some knowledge is available to us here that is not accessible on the physical plane," she remarked.

Seven days later, in mid-March, with the birds chirping and singing wildly in budding elm trees, I drove over to Boulder for a spiritual retreat. I was hoping that perhaps I could gain some insight into my paranormal experiences with Sharon. Maybe I could gain some clarity. Why did we have such soul ties that seemed to transcend time and space?

"You were meant to be together in this life. That was your soul contract," a woman named Doris told me. "I'm a psychic spiritual adviser," she said. "Not the phony kind that takes peoples' money and gives them poison, but real." I'd not asked Doris to read me. She came up and started talking about a woman she saw, "Teaching with you in some sort of Far Eastern, maybe Tibetan, temples in ancient days." Doris paused, looking at me to see how I was reacting. She was a middle-aged woman with red, frizzy hair and brown eyes. "Sometimes she was a man, but usually she was a woman. Most of the time, you were a male, although you were also a woman at times."

I said nothing. I didn't know what to say.

"This woman is above all others your soul mate, your equal," said Doris. "You've been together through many trials, many lives. This woman was often dressed in silks and satins, oranges and lemons, pomegranates, blueberries, cherries, and limes, the hues of sherbets. She is quite advanced spiritually."

Doris spoke quickly, hardly pausing to take a breath. She seemed to want to get out everything she saw.

I was fascinated, so I didn't try to stop her. Doris noticed that I was looking at the energy above her head, as if a small sun stood above her to impress my inner eye. I'd seen nothing like it before.

Doris said, "You're noticing the fissure in my aura. It came about as a result of a serious blow to my head in a car accident."

"Oh," I said. I wasn't sure this was really what I was seeing, but I'd learned that my take on reality didn't have to be exactly like someone else's.

"This woman has fallen under something in this life that has clouded her vision, and her soul," Doris went on.

I found myself nodding.

"It's very dark for her. She depends on you," Doris said. There it was again. "She depends on you."

Such a strange dependence. I looked out the window of the Spiritual Retreat building. The rolling hills around us were starting to come alive with wildflowers of blues and whites. I thought of Emily Dickinson's metaphor, used in one of her poems, of her life as a loaded gun:

> My Life had stood—a Loaded Gun—
> In Corners—till a Day
> The Owner passed—identified—
> And carried Me away—

Sharon presented new challenges to every spiritual or psychological paradigm that I knew. Evidently, one could depend upon someone spiritually yet not show this dependence in the physical world. Here she seemed to operate on her own, or at least without showing dependency on me. Yet, like Dickinson, and most traditional women, she was deeply dependent upon a male-dominated system, which had come early to rule her life. I was not one to say that blame should necessarily be assigned to patriarchy in general, but a tainted form of it, since matriarchies could also be perverse.

Dickinson's poem ends:

> Though I than He—may longer live—
> He longer must—than I—
> For I have but the power to kill,
> Without—the power to die—

Finding herself totally dependent upon the man, as if an extension of his will and force, she could kill for him. But she could not die for herself, sexual punning on *petit mort* included.

Was I enabling Sharon in some negative way? Or was her spiritual dependence upon me helping her to become whole, to undo the damage done by the corruption that had come to dominate our culture?

Would our relationship be more aptly classed as one of interdependence, rather than co-dependence? I certainly enjoyed Sharon's presence as much as she enjoyed mine. Because we had slept together in my bed at night, even if only in a spiritual sense, I woke up happier, more able to face the trials of the day.

All these questions, and more, bombarded my mind, as I drove home from Boulder. I felt in my shirt pocket to make sure the card that Doris had given me was still there. "Just in case you need to talk further," she said. She never asked for money. Maybe she knew how poor I was.

That night, during sleep, it seemed that I left my body to follow Sharon back to her condominium just before dawn. I was aware of the arrangement of her bedroom and her most intimate apparel. I began to notice her bed shaking. I noticed my hand feeling between my legs, as if I were opening, wet and eager. I realized that I was joined with her. She was masturbating.

I decided to join her more fully, as if we were making love. I put my energy into her. I heard her calling my name, even as she came. I knew that she had never felt a deeper release than she had that morning.

She certainly had the power to die. Now, if we could bring that power back into our physical relationship, we would really move forward.

Somewhere in the warm bath that she took afterwards, my consciousness departed from her and came back to my room. I became aware of the growing light of early morning.

I thought about Sharon throughout the day. Finally, I decided to brave giving her a call.

When she answered, she seemed very close, not at all distant, as she had been so many times when I had tried to reach out to her.

"Do you know I was with you this morning?" I asked.

Sharon didn't say anything. I wondered how much she consciously knew.

"You've been sleeping with me every night—" I began.

"I know."

"I was there with you this morning."

"I felt you," Sharon replied. "I knew your love. Why do you think we're so united now?"

I wanted to ask when she was coming back to me in the flesh. But I did not.

Suddenly, she said, "I have to meet a client—I can't talk any longer," and hung up.

I didn't want the conversation to end. But Sharon's hanging up did provide some relief. Trying to talk about things that so few have experienced, so novel to us both, was difficult. We lacked the vocabulary even to begin to express what we knew had happened. The emotions were intense.

That night, when Sharon arrived in my bed, she turned to me and offered to show me how her soul could also join me in my body, alongside my soul. "Is that all right?"

"I cannot—would never—object," I answered.

When Sharon's soul entered, sliding into me with a barely perceptible motion, I felt as if I were a sea, and a dolphin had entered to swim. She began to play. The notion of possessing two souls was something that I'd come across in esoteric literature now and then, but I'd never personally experienced it.

The Kabbalah, I'd heard, speaks of this, although I'd not yet gotten around to perusing the Kabbalah myself. It speaks of reincarnation. Noah was reincarnated as Moses. He had to return to learn the necessity of offering himself to save creation, not just his family and what they needed to survive. I'd also heard that some shamanic aboriginal traditions referred to two souls sharing the same body. The shaman, sometimes she, sometimes he, has both a male and female soul sharing the same body. These twin spirits endow that person with true androgyny and special powers. This being of two spirits, sharing one body, becomes something beyond the normal human, a kind of intermediary between humanity and the gods. People sought them out for advice and healing.

Since I had only heard of these traditions, and not read of them in reliable, that is, scholarly, documented, sources, I could not be sure of their total accuracy. But my own experiences were showing me that there were some truths there.

There in my bed, in the hours of early morning, I could feel Sharon. She showed me how her soul could turn slowly inside my body, while I was still lying on my back. I felt her, as if dolphin were turning over and over inside me, a sea. She turned faster, playfully. She reversed and turned in the opposite direction. It tickled. Was this how the sea felt when dolphins recreated?

After that, this became her—rather, our—preferred mode of sleeping together.

I was reminded of *Paradise Lost*, where the archangel Raphael instructs God's new creatures, the Parents of us all. His signs are strewn about Adam and Eve like the rose petals that adorn their marriage bower. Raphael says that angels enjoy a higher form of joining. They step inside each other, their spirits blending, just as Sharon showed me.

Although we were the fallen children of Adam and Eve, Sharon was revealing more of herself, as well as God's universe. It felt good. The Promised Land lay beyond the materialism of Egypt, just over the ridge—there. It was spiritual—paradise—meant for all who dared to follow.

Our souls in union, communion, Sharon and I were moving there.

Torture

Dan could hardly walk. When I looked closer, I could see deep bruising up around the back of his neck where the shirt collar didn't cover the skin.

"What happened to you?" I asked, following him from the hallway to his bedroom.

"I'm all right," he answered. He sat on the bed to put on his socks. He was getting ready for work.

I noticed bruises about Dan's wrists. They were dark, lightening to greenish browns about the edges. I stood in front of him. I asked, "What in the world have you been up to?"

"I met a Master for some S and M. He had his own fully equipped dungeon," Dan said. "He even has a cross for mock crucifixions."

"My ex's little brother was also interested in those," I commented, "a recapitulation of his overly pious upbringing during his reactionary period."

"The Master's dungeon has three slings, torture instruments, an Iron Maiden, tit clamps, butt plugs, electrical stimulation, and toys of more kinds than I'd ever dreamed possible," Dan said.

I couldn't tell if Dan he was positive about it all, or what. His voice and manner seemed neutral, but then he was dressing.

"When I find myself on a cross, I prefer to sing, 'Look on the Bright Side.'" I began a little rendition for Dan. "If I could tap dance, I would."

Dan started to laugh but caught himself. It obviously hurt to take anything but shallow breaths.

"I guess you need to explore suffering in more depth, since you haven't had enough of it in life," I commented.

Again Dan had to catch himself and stop laughing before he winced more. Putting on his shoes required stretching and that hurt. "I think the world of dominance and submission is more aptly about power exchanges," he said.

"And you see S and M as part of that scene?"

"Most people do, I think," Dan said, as if not entirely certain.

"Perhaps you can learn about these issues by volunteering to do some sort of charity work in a war torn area of the world. The setting would be more real, not something artificially set up. You could learn about real suffering, see the victims up close, and the works of those who victimize them." I paused. "Also, the dangers to your entire being—body, mind, and soul—would be real."

"I've thought about that," Dan said. "Could you please help with my shoes?" he asked.

"Yes, I remember." I bent to push his shoes on his feet and tie the laces. "I'm reminding you," I said. I felt like pushing him back and slapping his face.

"Thanks. I just wanted to explore it a little," Dan said. "Rick got into it, remember?"

"So you're trying to keep up with Rick?" I asked. I wondered what dependence and co-dependence issues were being explored there.

"Please—"

I knew I had to let Dan explore. He did not need to plead with me. "I understand exactly how a concerned father must feel."

Dan nodded. "I know."

"Are you making sure always to have safer sex?" I asked.

"There's been no sex involved," Dan said. He stood up. "The Master only barebacks. He knows I won't do that, so he won't fuck me." Dan paused. He added, "He told me I'm not worthy of his cock anyway."

I noticed that blood seemed to be streaking the back of Dan's shirt. "What in the heck goes on with your back?" I exclaimed.

Dan turned to look at his back in the dresser mirror. Unbuttoning the shirt, he removed it and threw it on the floor. He had at least a dozen long, deep welts across the width of his back. Many of them were seeping blood.

"I wonder if those wounds will get infected."

"I soaked in the bathtub after the session. I didn't notice any blood then, just welts."

I didn't know what to tell him, or what to do. "This is new territory for me," I said. I'd read that scientific evidence has been found for the efficacy of having dogs lick people's wounds. That was traditionally done in Western countries, and is still done in third world areas," I added. "Something in dog's saliva promotes healing." I paused. "Tray," I called, "I know you're not much of a kisser and less of a licker, except occasionally, but Dan could use your tongue."

"If I wanted someone's tongue, I'd ask you," Dan remarked.

His face was a puzzle. I could not read it. I smiled.

"Maybe Noxzema would take some sting out and medicate the welts without seeping through your shirt," I said. "I suggest that you'd better wear an undershirt for the next few days, even though you don't usually do so. You don't want people to think I whipped you or something."

"Maybe you should," Dan said. "I mean, maybe you should turn me over your knee when you see me heading for trouble." He began to whimper a little. I knew he was in pain.

I tried not to tune into it. I needed to remain objective.

Passing Tray, who was slowly making her way into Dan's bedroom, I went to get the jar of Noxzema in the bathroom. When I opened it, it looked as though it hadn't been used for years. The edges near the top of the jar had turned rather crusty and yellow. I scraped it off. Underneath the cream looked fine. I made Dan hold still and try not to yell while I gently, very gently, applied the medication to his wounds.

Dan asked if I realized how much Tray was slowing down. "She almost always limps a little, especially when she gets up after sleeping," he remarked.

"I guess I should be glad she's made it this long, considering her early history of almost getting killed on Federal Boulevard," I said. "She's no young pup any more."

"Kinda like you, Daddy," Dan replied.

That made me laugh. "As I've told you, I'm not that much older than you. I would have had to father you at eight."

"Six," Dan said. "You're not very good at math."

"One of the neighbors, a woman, referred to me as your partner the other day," Dan said.

I said, "I wonder just who she thinks Sharon is."

"A friend, who drops in now and then," Dan said, smiling like a Cheshire cat.

"Even though she's spent the night, and has sometimes left with me," I commented.

"Well, I'm around more than she is, especially now," Dan said.

"But if they paid attention, they'd notice that you and I, for the most part, lead separate lives. The lights in your bedroom often go on and go off at different times than the ones in mine."

"The operative phrase is, 'if they paid attention,'" Dan reminded me. "Besides, we might be trying to fake them out. You know that's what lots of gay couples do."

"At least the neighbors are fairly liberal."

"On some things," Dan reminded me.

"You're certainly getting saucier the longer you stay here," I commented.

Dan reminded, "With you I feel the freedom to pour on the sauce." He said, "It really is too bad I can't feel sexual about you. After all, you're reliable. You'd never hurt me."

"Well, at least not on purpose. Besides, how do you know I could feel sexual about you?" I asked, turning the tables.

"I just know," he said, smiling. His smile was so innocent, so disarming, that I had nothing else to say.

Scripts

"Ted, Ted, you'd better get in here," Dan called from my study. It had once been the middle bedroom. "Something's wrong with Tray. She can't seem to hear me and won't get up."

It was seven a.m. in the morning. I was in the bathroom. I jumped off the pot, pulled up my pants, and rushed into the study. I got down on my knees. Tray was alive, but she seemed dazed. I massaged her gently. In a couple of minutes, she came back. Slowly, awkwardly, she dragged herself up and wagged her tail a little. Timidly, she sniffed at me and then at Dan.

"I wonder if she's had some kind of seizure or a little stroke," I said.

"We'd better haul her off to the vet again."

I handed Dan the phone. He called his workplace to say he'd be a little late. "We've got a dog emergency."

We'd been at the vet's only a month before when we became afraid that Tray was losing her sight. Dan had noticed that her pupils seemed rather cloudy, and she didn't seem to be seeing well, especially if the light wasn't good.

At that time, Dr. Leach had assured me that she was just getting the typical clouding caused by cataracts in aging dogs. "She doesn't have glaucoma. She can see. Low light makes seeing hard for all of us who are getting older," he said, referring to his own graying hair.

I asked about her hearing. "That also seems less than sharp," I said.

Dr. Leach walked behind the examination table so Tray couldn't see him. He clapped loudly.

She reacted by tensing, her eyes opening a little wider. The smell of Pine Sol wafted my way. My senses were also opening.

"Hearing loss is a bit hard to ascertain in an Afghan," Dr. Leach said. "They seem to have selective hearing."

After examining Tray this time, Dr. Leach pulled his stethoscope from his ears and remarked, "Her heartbeat is a little slow." He put Tray down on the vinyl floor and watched her as she walked a little haltingly around the room.

"Is she all right?"

"She'd probably had a little stroke. She seems okay now. Just keep an eye on her and don't push too hard. Some dogs do fine after a little stroke. If she has more, we need to watch out."

On the drive home, Dan and I discussed Tray's health. "Tray has been deteriorating in little, almost imperceptible, ways," I said. Dan was holding Tray on his lap. She was leaning against him, her head on his chest as she looked out the window. "We have to face the fact that she's going to die or have to be put down," I said. "I don't know which is better."

"I'd hate to have to make the decision to end her life."

"But I can't stand to prolong her suffering when we know how it's going to end," I said. "All my earlier dogs were hit by cars or trucks. That was traumatic too."

"I can imagine," Dan said.

"I went years from high school until my divorce till I got another dog," I said. "And that was Tray." I glanced out the window at five boys playing in their yards.

"I had never had to face up to being responsible for ending any of my dogs' lives," I said. Thinking of it upset me tremendously. In fact it made me cry. Euthanasia, *good death*. I recalled Richard Wilbur's lines that "love calls us to the things of this world." To love is to become involved. We cannot have it any other way. Not to love is to fail to embrace life.

Love is painful; through it, our souls are enlarged. The loss of the beloved, even a cat, or a dog, is not forgotten. But all losses, all gains, find themselves caught up finally in God.

Alone in my book-lined study that evening, I was catching up on some reading. Tray was asleep at my side. I thought of Doris, whom I'd first met at the Boulder Retreat. I'd run into her again only the day before on campus. "Oh good, I knew I'd find you here, but I wasn't sure how," she said. Evidently she didn't know I was a chaplain who could be found at St. Francis Center. "I would warn you against letting Sharon's soul come into your body for too long. It could become a crutch," Doris said.

She glanced up at a hawk soaring in the sky above us, calling it to my attention. "So beautiful," she said, "to be able to soar above the world like that."

I nodded in agreement. "While these happenings give you both comfort, they could become a way of escaping the lessons you must work out in the physical world. For Sharon, it's becoming a kind of escape."

I hated hearing that. But I understood what Doris meant when she'd said we could fall into a partial, and, therefore distorted intimacy—"one not meant for incarnated souls. We have bodies to experience things on many levels, not just in the realm of the soul," Doris said.

"The soul is the center of our beings, but we take on bodies to house our souls, to give them expression, and to bring home lessons we must learn," I said, cementing my own knowledge of the subject by verbalizing it to Doris. "Only when we leave our bodies in death, are we free to live in the realms of the soul alone."

I put the article I was reading down.

Doris was right. My relationship with Sharon had started from a soulful place. I was called by her dead grandmother. It was centered there. Laura Cameron had also had something to do with it. The physical world had taken part.

I opened a book of poetry to John Donne's Holy Sonnet, "Batter my heart, Three-Personed God." How could I be sure that, at least for the time being, my intimate relations with Sharon's soul at might weren't serving a larger purpose, one that no one saw fully? After all, the Virgin Mary had told me to stay close to Sharon.

I would have to have a clear sign that we had to stop joining, or at least more peace about ending it than I had gained by this time.

Everything was complex. Nothing was simple. That's the life of someone who thinks—someone schooled in the richness of possibilities and various, sometimes conflicting, meanings.

Do we choose the scripts of our lives? Do we write them? By ourselves? With the help of others—God, our angels, spirit guides, those with whom we will incarnate this time, or perhaps the next time around?

How fully written are those scripts before we enter this world? Are only certain events, like markers, established beforehand, the rest left to evolve as we live among others and love?

Is everything left to chance, to accident? Or is all pre-destined? And if so, by whom?

I stood to pace the room. I bent to pet Tray.

I pulled down various books from the book-shelved wall, glanced at them, and then placed them back on their shelves again.

And what about this ability to glimpse into what we normally call the future? Can we truly step out of earthly time, as we normally perceive it, into eternity and begin to see as God sees? From this perspective, what we choose might appear to be chosen already, since there is no past, and no future. All is present.

Still pacing, I almost stumbled over Tray. "All I need to do is fall on you. That would take care of things. I'd not have to worry about euthanizing you then," I said. The dark humor of the thought made me wince.

Yet we must choose. Again and again we must make choices. Or we do not live. Otherwise, choices get made for us. And we fail to become fully human. Created a little lower than angels, we are meant through the process of learning to make good choices. Slowly we are then lifted into the divine, as the Eastern Church puts it. The Bride and Groom are crowned, their divinization advanced through the sacrament of Holy Matrimony.

For a moment, clear, and radiant as the sun breaking through after a terrible storm, I knew Doris was right. I must not allow Sharon to use me as a crutch. To do so kept her from making the choices that she had to make in her waking life.

She was welcome to join me in body as well as soul. But we could not continue to join only in soul for long.

Doing so would not help me either. Because I felt so comforted by Sharon, even though only at night, I might not get on with my life and my own lessons.

"Tray, let's go to bed. Dan's long been passed out, tired youth that he is."

She heard me, stumbled up, and followed me to the bedroom. I noticed that she had a rather sour smell.

That night, when Sharon's soul arrived, I told her that we had to stop meeting, joining, as we had. "You can't do that," she pleaded. She cried so hard that I let her enter my body. I felt her turning inside me, strengthening me by her joining.

I couldn't deceive myself into thinking I didn't love that experience. I couldn't send the best thing that had ever happened to me out into the darkness on her own.

When the time was right, we would join in body as well as soul.

"We'll do it together," Sharon promised.

"Yes, together," I said.

We lay in agreement. Our souls made a pact. She turned inside me, and turned again.

News

Even though the sun had risen several hours ago, the rooster in the friary yard outside my campus office was crowing proudly. I went to the window to watch him strut and do his little wing-flapping and turning dance for the hens. He was glad for spring and hoped they'd be receptive to the renewed amorousness of all.

I held an anonymous newsletter to faculty and staff of the University in my hand. "So far, the State of Colorado has paid at least three million dollars to settle University of Colorado sexual harassment cases outside of court. The State can expect to pay millions more, once more cases worked through the system."

Names of those who'd filed sexual harassment complaints were listed at the back of the newsletter. I read down the list to see only women's names, some I'd heard of. A few had garnered stories in the media. Some had very complicated cases, such as the Fine Arts faculty member who began a mutual affair with her Chairman, then broke it off, to suffer career sabotage. Some cheerleaders claimed that they'd been gang raped by the football team. That story was everywhere.

I wondered if people—even intelligent and informed faculty—believed that men didn't suffer sexual harassment? Only recently, was society getting over the old notion that women invited violation. "What were you doing to get yourself raped, little woman?" they'd ask. "Dressing provocatively? Sauntering down the street in a bad part of town? Are you sure you weren't looking for trouble, little woman? Or maybe a few extra bucks?"

The rooster crowed and flapped his wings with jubilation. He was doing his victory celebration.

Only recently had people come to know they must not ask such questions, or insinuate guilt on the part of the harassed woman. It was not politically correct, even if they held that position.

But what about men who suffered similarly? I wondered if any of us were speaking up.

The phone jarred me from my reverie.

An Episcopal priest friend of mine named Brian called. "Have you seen this morning's *Denver Post*?" he asked.

"No," I answered.

"Run out and buy a copy. Look on page one of the *Denver and the West* section," Brian said. "A scandal, just as you predicted. See the mice scamper."

I walked to St. Francis Center's reception area. Sure enough, Louise had a copy of the *Denver Post* lying on the counter. It looked like no one had opened the paper yet. The *Denver and the West* section was about halfway in.

Dean of the Episcopal Cathedral Arrested in Sex Sting was printed at the top of a half page article. On Valentine's Day he'd been videotaped in the restroom of a hotel downtown. He was charged with indecent exposure. Because the young man he'd exposed himself to was fourteen, his name was withheld. Because McDougal was a man of the cloth, who promised to seek therapy for his stress related problems, the judge had released him.

Several weeks later, someone tipped off the media and told them to check court records. Sure enough what had been covered up was now exposed. Details were reported in this morning's *Post* and elsewhere.

"I wonder when McDougal will be claiming to have a born again experience with the baptism of the Holy Spirit evidenced by speaking in tongues?" I asked aloud. I put the section back in the right order and closed the newspaper. I put it back on the counter and walked back to my office to have a seat and think things over.

Brian called again. "Have I given you enough time?" he asked.

"Yes, Louise had a copy."

Brian filled me in on details that hadn't yet hit the news. As a priest, he had insider's knowledge carried through the priestly network. "McDougal claims he was under such stress that he began acting out. Nothing like this had ever happened to him before, or so he argued," Brian said. "Bishop Lane believed him. On his recommendation, McDougal checked into a mental hospital for rest and treatment."

"Oh good," I said. I sat at my desk. I wanted to open a book and read, but I knew I had to listen. "I can hardly wait for the fallout. Do you think anyone at the Cathedral will acknowledge the fact that I tried to warn them?" I could see the faces of associate priests and even a secretary that I tried to talk with, only to be dismissed or ignored.

"The Cathedral is in an uproar. Everyone's in denial. No one had any idea that McDougal had been haunting places where gay people go for sex," Brian said. "No one—not one person—had a clue that anything was wrong, everyone swears." Brian sighed. "Everyone knows he did more than expose himself to the kid."

"He had his excuses in mind over a year beforehand. I knew this was the reason for laying them out for me. Just wait. We'll hear he's speaking in tongues."

"You don't really believe he'll try that, do you?" Brian asked. "I want to believe in basic human goodness, even in McDougal."

"I put nothing past the man. He believes people are stupid, so self-centered they'll believe anything that protects them from taking personal responsibility—that is, facing reality," I answered. "What I really regret is that most of his parishioners, and evidently most of the diocese, believe his stories. He was under great stress," I snorted. "All that moving and shaking when he gets the Spirit—I can see it now."

"It'd be great to get that on videotape," Brian said. "I bet he'll get off Scot free. He'll be transferred to another diocese. His associate priests who want to move up in the church will also transfer until the heat dies down."

"No doubt," I said, shaking my head.

"Remember Father Mike," Brian said.

"I'd forgotten about Father Mike," I said. I knew him only vaguely. He was also a married priest. He had an affair with one of his married parishioners. He was counseling her. She later claimed to be irreparably harmed by the affair and sued. She even developed multiple personalities as a result of the trauma. Bishop Lane transferred Father Mike to another parish far away. "Typical dynamics in every denomination," I remarked.

"That one cost the diocese over a million dollars in court," Brian said. "I hope Bishop Lane will be more cautious now. We can't take another big hit like that."

McDoo had been right. He'd told me himself. If you're going to act out, do it so outrageously, so obviously, that people go into denial over it. To see evil actions for what they are, without explaining them away or prettying them up, requires confrontation. We first must confront the uncomfortable recognitions that we too are capable of such wrongdoings. We must sort out what is really evil from what is not, what is just some societal inhibition placed on us. We must also face up to society's restraints that say no, we must operate as a well-oiled machine that admits nothing deeply wrong, evil, because that might strip the gears. We keep the machine humming by thwacking at little things, petty violations that satisfy most people's need to believe that they possess a conscience.

In that way, most people do not dig deeper. There they would see that some sort of personal loss is always at stake for possessing clarity of vision—all the way from noses, to eyes and teeth, to reputations, positions, and incomes. Sometimes, their very lives. Evil exists in the world because people ignore it. They allow it to go on, until it multiplies and overwhelms so many that it can no longer be ignored.

Suddenly, I realized that both of my feet had gone to sleep. I had to remember not to allow myself to sit still for long, no matter how well I could concentrate. I managed to get up and hobble around the office, trying to restore circulation, to get back feeling in them. They felt like boards. When the feeling started to come back, they ached.

Brian and his wife Mary asked me to come to their parish on Sunday. We would have dinner afterwards at their house.

"It's been a long time since we've seen you," Brian said. He shook my right hand and placed his left hand on my shoulder. "I don't know why no one believed you when you warned them about McDougal. We thought you were making things up because you were mad at him."

An associate priest was taking the service that day. He and Mary sat with me in the congregation. We watched as a gaudily dressed woman wearing a red sequined cowboy hat, red leather boots, and denim dress dotted with faux jewels the size of robin's eggs paraded down the aisle toward the altar. She was grossly overweight.

I knew that somehow she was going to move into my life "in a big way." When I whispered my premonition to Brian and Mary, they giggled.

"If anyone could do it in a big way, she'd be the one," Brian said. He added, "Even though married with children, she's a man hunter. Rumor has it, her husband's gay."

"She even went after Brian," Mary said.

Brian snickered. "If any guy had any doubts about his masculinity and orientation, she'd clarify that for him."

I laughed.

"Women like her turn me into a hundred and fifty percent hetero," Mary said. She visibly shuddered.

I wondered what this woman's moving into my life in a big way meant. As I examined my inner perception, I felt as if a Mac truck were rushing toward me. I didn't feel I was going to get hit. But I knew that I needed to watch out. She would be speeding along toward me, her headlights and horn blaring.

The following week, this woman soon showed up at my office at St. Francis Center. "I'm Lee," she said, extending her hand. I wondered how she got past Louise. Louise should have buzzed to warn me. "God has directed me to seek your counsel. He says you will understand."

My guard went up. A big pink ostrich feather stuck up from the back of some sort of grey snood she had on. She wore a long, dramatic black gown, cut low to show ample cleavage.

"I'm sorry, Lee, but my contract dictates that I see only students enrolled at the university."

Lee's demeanor went flat, as did her affect. "Oh," she said, plucking a tissue from my desk to wipe the tears falling from her eyes.

Two days later, I got a call from my Bishop. "Lee Roberts has filed a complaint against you," he said. "She says you were counseling her and trying to date her, a married woman with children."

"She stopped by once," I said. I looked at the doorway, hoping no one was standing outside to hear. I got up to shut my door. "I told her I couldn't see her. I never counsel anyone with my door shut. A number of people were around, so people could testify on my behalf."

"Well, she does have a reputation for drama. I'm told she's an actress or singer, something along that line. We have to be very careful nowadays to take all complaints seriously. We also have to be cautious about jumping off the deep end to believe everyone."

"I agree." Even though the Diocese of Colorado couldn't pay me, at least Bishop Lane was a decent and intelligent man. Too bad others in authority over me couldn't be called the same.

Remote Viewing

A few days later, I decided to spend the day at home. I was feeling overwhelmed by so many things crashing in on me—from needing to find another teaching position, to figuring out what to do with Sharon, who was still coming to at night, though not seeing or talking with me in the flesh, to wondering what was going to happen to Dan, who was clearly embarked on a personal, sexual journey, to worrying about Tray's downward spiral.

At home, I hoped to get more work done. I would not have phone calls to take and counselees to try to help. I had reading and lots of paper grading to catch up on. This was always the case now, with all my writing students. Paper after paper after paper, an endless grind. I'd managed to get my Advanced Writing class down to thirty-one students because six saw that they weren't going to be able to do well without better preparation and more time to work on their writing. At the start, I'd warned them. Some of the weak students, however, remained on the rosters, where they stayed angry, ready to help others into their belief that I was just too demanding. My Basic Writing class was generally weak, but I expected that of them. After all, it was Basic Writing. They too weren't happy with me overall. I should have been teaching literature and truly advanced writing classes, after all. My scholarly training and interests were centered there. I was teaching kindergarten.

In the midst of pouring a cup of coffee, I became aware that one of my students, I wasn't sure who, was trying to lead some sort of insurrection against me. I psychically scanned the scene, vaguely aware that someone was going to Spet about me.

This student was soon sitting in Spet's office, in a chair in front of Spet's desk. The student was Al Snodgrass, one of the unqualified students whom Ron had placed in my Advanced Writing course. He was a very poor student, an unkempt, thirty year old, who had a hard time making D minuses, even with all the free tutoring offered by the Writing Center. He'd only taken Basic Writing before, and had passed with a C-. No matter what was said in class, Al seemed to feel the need to counter with his own objections, which easily turned into diatribes.   I often had trouble shutting him up.

In the past, that is, before Spet had become vengeful because I'd rejected him sexually, he would quickly have ascertained that Snodgrass was a poor student and, looking down his nose, quickly dismissed Snodgrass's complaints. Spet would have done so with sarcastic comments, just as he did with other complaints toward people that he liked. If someone were one of the minions who flattered him, and perhaps more, they could get bad student as well as critical peer evaluations, have few publications, poor inter-relational skills, yet remain confident that every negative thing would be glossed over and excused. Spet saw to that.

I was aware, however, that Spet seemed to be hanging onto Snodgrass's every word. He was leaning forward, not looking down his nose at all. Even his shoulders were held up. I'd never seen him anything but bent.

Snodgrass was complaining that I was imposing my own religious beliefs upon my students, something that I was always careful not to do. I certainly did not hesitate to inform them of the religious and spiritual aspects of a literary work discussed for class. Not to do so would have been poor teaching, although I knew that many poorly informed teachers do not realize the religious and spiritual aspects themselves. If they were better informed, some didn't want to take chances, so they didn't do more than skim over the religious aspects and move right along to things less controversial.

In our increasingly intolerant times, however, everything seemed to be getting more controversial. Sex was another hot button issue. Why, I'd even had students who objected to Shakespeare when I pointed out the fact that his triangular love affair in the *Sonnets* seemed between himself, the Dark Lady, and the Young Man.

"Well I don't want to read him then," one Mormon woman said, "not if he's gay."

"Who said anything about being gay?" I asked.

"If he's in love with a Young Man, he's gay."

I felt Spet hanging on every word from Snodgrass's mouth. Snodgrass's wild hair and eyes didn't seem to put him off a bit. He was leaping at the chance to have cause for terminating me, something he couldn't without cause—which he'd not found yet.

Around noon, I was standing at the toilet, peeing. I became aware that my supporters had gotten wind of Snodgrass's machinations and were marching into Spet's office on my behalf. They were telling him that Snodgrass was making things up, distorting the facts. Our constitution guaranteed freedom of speech. I was free to discuss the religious aspects of the literature—in fact, I had a duty to do so—as long as I did not proselytize. They understood that very well and made the message clear.

For the rest of the day, I was aware of some sort of power struggle going on, with a few detractors marching in to support Snodgrass, while my supporters seemed to outnumber and overwhelm them, pushing them back like winds against the tides.

It was a very strange experience. I was glad I was at home. That way I could distract myself from worry by going outside, doing some gardening, cleaning, and walking Tray. Reading and grading papers was too mental and required too much concentration. I needed physical activities to hold my anxiety at bay.

If I had been stuck at the office, I would probably have tried to find my ministry colleague Betty and give her a hard time, or let her have a go at me. She was not only wise but fun. But she seemed to be taking many days off lately. I'd heard she was traveling the country, conducting teach-ins and social activist seminars. I was rather surprised that the regional Lutherans did not try to stop her. But then, they would have had a number of factors to contend with. Betty was not someone to take advantage of. She was too street smart and too well connected.

Just before five, Dr. Spet called to say, "I want to see you first thing in the morning. Some urgent matters have arisen."

I knew what he wanted to talk about, although I thought it best to play dumb. Spet would use anything he could to add to a case for termination. I could imagine his saying that not only was I too religious, my writing too sexual, but that I was paranoid delusional as well, a danger to good people of sanity everywhere.

I walked into Spet's book-lined office, where papers and books were strewn everywhere, on tables, the desk, the floor, the tops of shelves, and even stacked on books on the shelves. Spet had the mini-blinds open only a little, with no lights on. In the dim light, he looked more than ever like a weasel in his den.

His voice was nasal, his manner sneering. "One of your students has come to me with a complaint," he began. He could hardly look me in the eye. He kept glancing furtively at my chest just above the third unbuttoned button.

Without appearing obvious, I kept trying to look downward and catch some glimpse of my chest myself, just to see if something was wrong. Had I failed to button my shirt properly? Had I spilled food or coffee down my front?

"Since the complaints are very serious I told him, or her, that I would talk with you," Spet said. He obviously didn't want to give away the gender of the complainant. When he published, he always used only his first and middle initials, some said, so that no one would know whether he was male or female. That way, feminists might better think he was one of them.

As he was scolding, I managed to turn a little to the side. I ran my hand across my shirt and chest. I felt nothing extraordinary. I glanced down. I didn't see any stain.

How long were the furtive glances and roundabout ways of attacking to go on? None of this seemed normal.

"I know who it is," I said.

"And just how do you know this? Are you psychic?" Spet asked.

I chuckled. "If you say so."

"You think you're Jesus before the Pharisees," Spet said.

"So you've been reading the New Testament," I countered.

"There have been other complaints, you know."

"If I were teaching in my areas of expertise instead of service courses stuffed to the gills with too many students who lack the prerequisites, I'd get fewer complaints. You never hear grumbles from people in my literature courses, do you?"

Spet said nothing. He continued to stare down his nose at me. He was sitting up on the edge of his chair to do so. His shoulders still slumped, as they characteristically did. I began to wonder if he had some sort of pad under him to make him as tall as I. I wondered if he had hemorrhoids and needed a cushion.

The visual allowed me to continue to fire back. "Also, you've rarely heard complaints from my advanced writing classes, ones with decent numbers of students, instead of thirty-seven. And," I paused for emphasis, "ones with students who should actually be there because they've qualified."

I began to realize that Spet must have had a hemorrhoid problem. That's what I was sensing. Thus, the need to sit forward and on a pillow. I finally glimpsed the edge of it.

I noticed that Spet had said nothing about my supporters. He'd had letters from some who'd wanted to praise me. He even mentioned in his letter of recommendation on file a letter from a long- time high school English teacher praising my skills and knowledge. So did Ron in his letter on file.

Now Spet spoke only of my detractors. I was confident that my supporters had come to speak with him about this matter. I'd viewed them psychically.

Adjusting himself in the chair, Spet added, "A few people who seem to like you also stopped by."

I nodded. "I know. I've heard from them." While I hadn't heard from them in the physical realm, I had in the psychic.

As if Spet realized that he'd better be cautious, for perhaps I knew too much, and had too many supporters, he said, "The student doesn't seem to have real grounds for complaint, just personal bias."

Perhaps we were getting somewhere. Or maybe Spet was again hoping to win me over so he could get closer. I could not figure out why he was so attracted to me, if that was the case. I could have liked him as a person, as a scholar—if he had seemed a decent and honorable man. But there was always that edge, that shadow side that darkened everything.

"By the way," Spet said. "I have a good friend at the University of New Hampshire. I understand you applied for a teaching position there."

"I did," I said. "But, I haven't heard from them, although the job description seemed to fit me to a T."

Spet said nothing more about the job, or what he'd heard. His eyes met mine. For a moment, I thought I detected a hint of humanity, of tenderness.

For a moment, I felt that I ought to try to make amends, to talk about why I had ignored his moves in the fall. I'd not meant to lead him on. Nor had I meant to scorn him, if that's how he took it.

Before I could gather my courage, Spet said, "You should apply for training in library science. You're good with books."

I'd heard that advice before. I decided not to give the situation more energy. "Are we about finished?" I asked. I need to get to my office."

Spet rotated his chair and looked over at the infamous typewriter bolted to the little desk beside him.

I was certain this was the typewriter I'd helped carry to his office over a year before. "Have a good day," I said. I picked up my backpack and walked out of his office through the little hallway that led to what had been the living and dining rooms to the entryway and into the brightening air of spring.

Robins were hopping about the greening lawns, pecking diligently for bugs and worms. Crocuses were blooming— yellow and lavender and purple and white. Even the daffodils and tulips had wakened and were putting up buds in the midst of new leaves. Sparrows flitted about the eaves of the buildings, tapping in the gutters.

I was free. I knew that. Free in my own thoughts, able to perceive clearly. No matter what came toward me from outside, no one had bought my soul, nor had I sold it.

I heard the whirring song of a mourning dove as it took off from the ground somewhere near me. Like that bird, I too could fly.

When I met my Advanced Writing class the next day, Snodgrass was absent. Several of the better students came forward after class. I was standing before the table in front. They informed me of what had happened regarding Snodgrass and Spet.

"We want you to know we'll stand by you all the way to the top—if need be," Julia, evidently their spokesperson, said. She put her books and purse down on the table. A middle aged mother of two grown children, Julia stood at the forefront of the mixed group of five, all younger than she.

"More supporters went to talk with Dr. Spet than those Snodgrass managed to pull in," Julia said. "I think he may have had two people go with him," Julia said.

"He has a Burger King, 'have it your way,' mentality," Lisa, another student, commented.

Lyle and Mike agreed. Good students, who wanted to learn and do better, they expressed disgust at Snodgrass, his narrowness, and his often off-topic comments.

"He doesn't belong in a university," Mike said. He was an engineering student with an excellent mind. He could write, and wanted earnestly to hone his skills. "A trade school would be more appropriate for him."

If I'd not been reduced to teaching only required writing classes, students would have enrolled because they desired to be in my classes, not because they had to be. That would have made a huge difference. Spet certainly enjoyed protection from the unqualified, and disinterested. In fact, his courses sometimes didn't even make the required nine students in order to be taught. I'd never heard of one that had more than twelve.

Even though I was certain that this was again a battle in which I held the upper hand, for I was in the right, I was also aware that administrators do not like complaints. It doesn't matter that the professor's in the right. What matters is the distraction from administrators' own work. Get in their way, and you're soon gone.

But I was free. I didn't know the implications of that feeling. But I owned it. I could fly with the mourning dove.

Unlocking

Spring was fully upon us. The fruit trees were budding. If we didn't get a cold snap, they would be beautiful in a couple of weeks. We might even get apples, peaches, plums, and pears this year. Again, if we didn't get a frost while the fruit was trying to start from pollinated blossoms.

I had gone off for some early Saturday grocery shopping. I never missed the chance to see signs of spring. In spite of rotten teaching conditions, and no nibbles from other universities and colleges, I continued to feel supported by some of my better students, like Julia, Mike, and Lisa.

When I returned home, I noticed a mourning dove that appeared to be nesting in the gutter of the roof.

"Oh no," I called, "mother bird, that is not a good place. It's dry now, but what if a big rain comes? You're nest will be destroyed and your eggs washed away?"

She just bobbed her head, looked at me, and went on nesting.

I put my key in the door and walked inside. I called out to Tray. She didn't answer. I went to check on her. She was sleeping when I left, so I decided not to take her with me. She was still asleep, still breathing—I bent down to make sure—so I decided to leave her alone till she woke up. She could go outside then.

I'd found the courage to tell Sharon that we needed to meet to talk things over. I wanted to see her, embodied, not just in soul form. I wanted to hear from her mouth how she was, as well as what she made of our nighttime soul visits.

I phoned. She wasn't home. I was relieved. I wasn't sure what her reaction to my proposal would be. I put away the groceries. Tray wanted to go outside so we went for a little walk to look at the blooming trees and flowers around the neighborhood.

When we returned, I left a message on Sharon's answering machine, asking her either to meet me for coffee at The Market at four or call and tell me she couldn't make it. "You're welcome to leave a message on my machine if you feel you can't talk with me. In about fifteen minutes, I'm going to do some yard work for a couple of hours, maybe sit in the yard with Tray and read," I said. I wanted to give her as much room as possible.

At two-thirty, I checked my messages. I'd left the back door open so I could hear the phone ring. Nothing from Sharon had been recorded. I wondered if she'd be at The Market at four.

When I opened my mailbox, I saw a letter from my mother. She'd sent me one of her "guilting" letters in which she made some offhand remark about my ignoring her, "Since you've disinherited me. I know you'd love to drive up for church on Easter Sunday," she said, "or Mother's Day, and stay for a few days." She added, "Your sisters would be glad to see you."

To work off my anxiety and my anger, I started vacuuming and dusting house for an hour before driving over to the Market. I felt weak and shaky. I'd thought it was because of my emotional distress, but I then realized that I hadn't eaten all day. Both Sharon and I had unsupportive mothers, although hers was worse than mine. Sharon's abuse had also been worse, and she needed nurturing more.

I rummaged around my kitchen. Nothing quick in the fridge. Finally I remembered the granola in my pantry. I poured some into a bowl, added some skim milk, and quickly ate.

I was still thinking of my lot in life when I walked across the wide expanse of Speer Boulevard. There, sitting at a little table on the broad sidewalk outside The Market, was Sharon. She was waiting for me. She smiled.

I wanted to think we could believe nothing had happened, but we both knew that was not true. We could not just pick up where we'd left off, with nothing said about all that had happened since. It was as if we were running on two tracks simultaneously. Our spiritual selves were going along in tandem, while our physical selves were apart. An image of the escaped boob in Woody Allen's *All You Ever Wanted to Know About Sex, But Were Afraid to A*sk came to mind. It was squirting milk everywhere—until folks finally trapped it in a giant bra.

I recognized more than a little anger in me, some of which was for my mother and her contradictory expectations that I was born to save my family and yet I was to show myself the dutiful son who did what his family, and society, expected. Even more was for Sharon's mother, the biggest boob of all. Not that this was such an unusual script, as I'd discovered in my counseling of people. But it is one heightened in the life of the outsider, the racial, sexual, or spiritual onlooker, forced there by abusive experiences.

"Welcome to your destiny," I thought. I sat down on the wrought iron chair across the table from Sharon. We were both outsiders.

"You look tired," she said.

I noticed the dark circles under her eyes. Her face showed not her usual creamy complexion but looked sallow. "So do you," I said.

"Ted, I've got to tell you," she began, "I had my eyes on you for a long time before our meeting outside St. Elizabeth's."

"Laura clued me in, awhile ago now." For a moment, I caught a glimpse of life as a web that we weave, like silk worms spinning the fibers of our lives into our Joseph's coats.

"There's more. That day we met," Sharon began, "I saw my grandmother up near the roof of St. Elizabeth's, just as you did."

"Did I tell you I'd seen your grandmother?" I asked. I couldn't remember. "We need coffee. I'm parched."

"You didn't have to tell me. I knew you saw her. I couldn't tell what she was saying. Even in life, she ignored everyone but the person she was buttonholing. Since she was speaking to you—I knew it from the way you looked at her and seemed to understand—I figured I didn't need to know what she was saying. She would have embarrassed me, just as she often did."

"I thought you were close," I said. Another piece of the puzzle slid into place.

"I loved her dearly, but I hated her too," Sharon said. Tears streamed from her eyes. "I seem to feel that way about most people."

I glanced away to see Spet and Ron walking out the door of an upscale restaurant across the street.

"I know the departed visit us," Sharon said. "I've seen them more than once. However, seeing spirits doesn't mean there's necessarily a God. Spirits might exist on their own."

"I agree," I said.

"As you know, I believe in the soul," Sharon replied. "I'm sure it lives on and is the core of each of us."

I nodded. My mouth was cotton. "I've got to get something to drink." I could hear the hoarseness in my voice. This time I stood. "The air pollution is getting to me."

Sharon nodded. It is me too. "Stress makes us react to it more." She got up to go inside to the coffee counter with me.

"Anyway, I staked you out," Sharon said. At the counter, she placed her hand, warm, intentional, on my hand. She insisted on paying for the coffee. "I've always felt guilty that I never told you."

I shrugged. "I don't know that it matters," I said.

"Maybe not," Sharon replied. "But I've felt even worse for getting you ensnared."

We walked to the door. Someone held it for us. We walked outside to our table on the sidewalk. My coffee was so full I was having a hard time not spilling it.

"Don't," I said, finally able to set my cup on the table. "I've come to realize that some forms of manipulation are good. We get nowhere if we don't take chances and act."

"Because of Laura, I looked up a lot of your work" Sharon confessed. She sat back down with coffee in hand. She was always graceful, not like me. "Actually, I think I've read everything you've published. I even ordered the microfiche of your dissertation." She looked at me and winked. "I got through the whole thing. I had to read and reread many pages."

She made me laugh. "I could have lent you a bound copy, if you'd have asked," I said. "Better yet, I could have lent you various revised and rewritten versions that I've been hawking to university presses. I've lent them to students."

Sharon looked down, rather shyly. She stirred her coffee. "I didn't want you to know." She paused. "It's so much like stalking. Besides," she said, "I wanted you to think that I had learned far more from my education than I did."

"Writers write to be read, just as teachers talk to be listened to," I said.

Sharon laughed. "Yes, you do tend to lecture."

I laughed. "I didn't spend all my life learning all these deep things not to share them." I sipped my coffee. It was still too hot for my palate.

Heaviness still hung in the air between us. Try as we did, we couldn't seem to break through it to find the union that our souls had enjoyed.

"I knew nothing of you before we met," I said. "I'm not sure that I know a great deal now, except on the soul level," I said. "And I'm not sure how much of that is accurate."

"It's true on that level," Sharon said, almost defensively. "You must not try to make that level of reality identical with this one."

I felt rather puzzled. Why not, I wondered. "I thought that was the whole reason of the incarnation, to bring the soul and body, this world and the next, all the rings of creation, into harmony, into unison, so that the multiple voices that reflect and echo the Word might speak as One."

"That's your Christian outlook," Sharon said. "I'm not sure I believe it. Perhaps the soul and the body do not happily join. What if the soul always desires to break free? What if the Manichees were right, and earth is a prison where the darkness wars always with the light?" she asked, her eyes searching my face. "The soul and its realm of light are what we must seek, and seek always, for darkness seeks in every way to extinguish the light."

I had no answer. That was another paradigm, rejected by Augustine and the early Church, as well as centuries of mainline Christian theologians after him. "To embrace such philosophies, would mean that even the beauties of this world, the things that we hold good, are not—for they are but delusions that trap us in physical creation, worse than the traps that are obvious," I said. "Strict ascetics have believed this, for everything physical is to be avoided if we want truly to walk a spiritual path."

Sharon nodded and held the cup still before her lips.

"I believe it's easy to get confused and get caught in the physical world, as if that's all there is. But it's also possible to affirm the physical—for that is the lesson of the incarnation—yet not worship it by turning it into an idol. Indeed, we look to realms of light, where the soul properly dwells. But we must not reject this world to try to do so. That is to reject creation and God's handiwork, thus rejecting God."

Sharon shook her head. "I fail to be convinced," she said.

"But that isn't what keeps us apart physically, is it?" I asked.

"It might lie at the root of it," Sharon said, rather ominously. She stared down into her cup. She set it on the table. She turned the cup and seemed to read the marks made by the froth, as if they were tea leaves.

I was ready to grant that deeply held philosophical and theological positions do determine behavior. But I still couldn't believe that Sharon's uncertainty in these matters lay in our way.

"I don't believe that I'm good for you," Sharon said. With her forefinger she wiped the froth marks from the top of her cup inside. "Actually, I don't believe that I'm good for anyone, not even myself." She paused again. "I don't know whether it was meant to be this way, or whether I got corrupted and turned away from my soul contract, or destiny, or whatever you want to call it. But I believe that I'll bring more destruction to you, if we come together fully in the physical world."

"Why?" I demanded.

"I bring destruction to myself. I want to escape life," Sharon said. "Ted, can't you see that? You don't have to know all about me. You know enough to realize it, if you stop denying the truth. Our adventures in the soul realm, as you've called them, only convince me more that I want to escape this world," Sharon explained. "For years I've tried to shut down my paranormal abilities. Like an explorer, you eagerly open yourself to yours."

I nodded in agreement. "It's in my nature."

"The world is a dark and destructive place," Sharon said. "The beauty, the laughter, the little acts of goodness cannot ever begin to make up for all the hatred, the pettiness, the torture, and power struggles—the evil."

I felt leadenness again in my chest. It spread into my belly, my entire being. While our astral adventures were leading me to affirm this world, to believe in its essential goodness and beauty, they were leading Sharon in the opposite direction.

I put my hand on Sharon's. A car in the street screeched to a halt to avoid hitting a jaywalking pedestrian. Tears slid down Sharon's cheeks, just as they did mine.

"I've really got to get going," Sharon said. She turned her wrist back so she could see her watch.

"Where are you going?" I asked.

She didn't answer.

"Sharon, where do you need to go?"

"I don't know. I need to get out of here," she said. She pushed her chair away from the table and started to hurry off.

I started to grab her and force her to stay, to be with me and her feelings. I didn't like them either, but I knew that we had to feel to get through them. I realized she'd left her purse. "Sharon," I called, you left your purse. I didn't follow. "Your leaving behind something so important as your purse means you really don't want to go."

She turned and almost collapsed on the street.

"Someone call an ambulance," a man at a nearby table called. He jumped up to steady her.

"No, I'm all right, I lost my balance," Sharon said.

I jumped up and helped her back to her chair. "I think she'll be all right," I said. "If she isn't, I'll take her to the emergency room."

Sharon nodded. "Please leave us alone. I'm all right. Really, I am," she insisted.

"Sharon, we must go through the pain," I said.

She nodded. I helped her up. I walked her to my car and drove her home. "We can get your car later."

I got her home, got her undressed and in bed, where she'd be warm. She was shivering and complaining of being cold, although her face felt hot to my touch. I lay down on top of the covers beside her, watching over her until she went to sleep. Because of the lengthening days of spring, it was still light outside, early evening in April.

I heard the door in the living room open. I went to look.

A woman stepped in. She looked like an older version of Sharon. "What are you doing here?" she asked.

"I'm watching Sharon," I said. "I'm Ted, Ted Jones. She's just been through a traumatic experience."

"It's your fault. I know it is," her mother said. "She was all right till you came along and got her all stirred up with ideas of soul mates, astral travel, and psychic connections. All those crazy ideas she had as a child are back again."

I was flabbergasted. I wanted to lash out, but my mouth didn't work.

"I want you out, or I'll call the police," her mother said, holding her hand out, her index finger pointing. "Now!"

Opiates

When I got home, I was rattled. I needed to distract myself from my anger and pain. I had to get some work done. I had to grade papers. I had to send out more job applications. It was twilight. I was glad for the longer days. Before long, night wouldn't come till eight, then nine, before it started coming earlier again.

I grabbed some carrot salad from the refrigerator, threw some kidney beans on top, and went up to my study.

I rummaged through my desk drawers. I could get some work done—I wasn't sure what. I didn't dare grade papers, not in the mood I was in. I'd rip those students to shreds. I didn't dare write job applications either. Even though I had a basic template on my computer, I figured I'd screw something up because of my emotional state.

I was fumbling, hoping to light on something. I ate some salad in between. I happened upon a syllabus for a course I'd taught, called *Spelling God*. I read the introduction to the course. Central themes of my life were still recorded there, like hieroglyphs:

> In a letter of reply to an editorial in the 1897 *Bookman*, American poet Edward Arlington Robinson wrote, "The world is not a 'prison house' but a kind of spiritual kindergarten where millions of bewildered infants are trying to spell 'God' with the wrong blocks." Trying to spell *God* is an old theme, still universal, concerning most of humanity, which has arrived at various spellings, although sometimes none at all. Some would try to give God a rest (another kind of *spelling*) and take over. Some have even tried to cast a spell on God.

Did anything make sense, at least in some ultimate scheme of things? Was there an ultimate scheme of things? Or, were we just meant to endure incarnate life to the end, fueled by the pleasures, the drugs, both licit and illicit, that we manage to snatch along the way?

I had no idea if there had been any movement toward resolution on either of our parts. Our talk had in some ways clarified things. We'd stopped meeting in the realm of the soul. In some ways I felt relieved, as if we'd done the right thing. But an emptiness that I'd not felt for a long time had also risen to haunt even my waking.

It really was not good for Sharon to have her death wish reinforced, and she was not sure that it was good for me to enjoy at night what was proving destructive in general. I worried terribly about Sharon's ability to go through the pain.

I picked up the phone and dialed Sharon's number. Even though kicked out, I had to see if she was ok.

She answered. She sounded awake.

"Is your mother with you?" I asked.

"I got rid of her," she said. "I really hate that woman."

"I understand why," I said.

"Ted, I know I'm keeping you from being open to anything better."

"Some consolation," I muttered. That wasn't what I wanted to hear at all.

She said goodbye and hung up.

I got up from my desk to go to the bathroom and get some water. I had to make myself work.

"Dogs are so much less complicated than people," I said, passing Tray who was making her way slowly through the hallway. I bent down and hugged her. "Life with you is still painful, but not confusing." When I let go of her, she collapsed on the carpet, as if she no longer had the energy to stand on her own. "Tray!" I called. For a moment, I was sure she'd died. I stroked her. I saw that she still drew breath, but lacked the will, or the ability, to stand.

Lots of life required getting through it. I was not naïve.

I again wondered whether I would have to put Tray to sleep, or if she would die on her own. She looked helpless lying there at first. I sat beside her. She managed to reposition herself beside me as if making the best of her resting place. I continued to stroke her.

Did Tray have any idea of what was to come? Did she take everything in stride? All that breathes must die.

I heard the door downstairs open. It was Dan. I knew from the noises he made.

"Dan," I called. "Can you come upstairs?

"I've only got a few minutes," he called. "I'm meeting Rick. We're talking about getting back together." Coming up stairs, he said, "I hope to move back in with him within a week." He saw Tray lying on the hallway floor beside me. "Is she all right?" he asked.

"I'm not sure. She seems ok now but doesn't want to get up. She kind of fell over when I was hugging her."

"Oh great," Dan said. He rushed over to pet her. "I don't think it's going to be long," he whispered to me.

I nodded. "Don't you think you're moving a little fast?" I asked. "Maybe you ought to try dating for awhile. See how things go." I paused, hoping my advice would sink in. I knew I really didn't want to lose him, especially with Tray on her way out. I'd really be alone.

Dan blushed. "Rick now considers me worthy of his cock," he said.

"Oh," I said, recalling Dan's experience with the Master. "Does this mean he's going to tie you up and have his way?" My hand ran into Dan's on Tray's side.

Dan smiled.

I pulled away. I didn't want him to think I was making a move. I was no Spet, no McDoo. "What happened to 'true love waits'?" I asked.

"Well, you know how doctrine is forced to change with experience," he answered.

"We all seem able to justify doctrinal shifts when they're convenient."

"I'm glad you were just pulling my leg," he said. "For a moment, I thought you were serious."

"I was. Sort of," I answered. "But I know human nature."

"You were never sure Rick and I weren't too idealistic. I know that," Dan said. "You told me so yourself."

I nodded. "Are you planning to get into the SM scene?" I asked.

"Well, Rick does like to tie me up. And I enjoy it," Dan said. He stroked Tray's head, and I concentrated on her side.

"I told you, I'd be glad to spank you a little now and then myself," I teased.

"I know, Daddy," Dan said. "But it wouldn't be the same." Dan paused. He looked me straight in the eye. "Rick and I aren't going to move deeply into the SM scene. It doesn't appeal to either of us."

I let out a breath of air. "What a relief." I continued to stroke Tray's side. Her hair had never been thick or very glossy. It had thinned, and its texture had deteriorated considerably over the past year.

"You're often talking about the value of being tested," Dan said. "Remember Aristotle? Virtue is only potential until one passes the tests and incorporates that virtue into himself."

"I understand more and more what it must be like to be a parent," I said. "All those theories which we've held dear seem so much more dangerous when they're tested by our children."

"Or someone you love," Dan said.

Tray let out a moan, as if to let Dan know that he shouldn't stop petting her.

I nodded. "You might, after all, fail."

"Well, Dad, I'm glad to say—" Dan began. He broke off mid-sentence. The phone had started to ring.

I answered.

It was my priest-friend, Brian. "One of Mary's friends happens to work in the mental ward where McDougal went to recuperate," he said. "Guess what," Brian laughed.

"The Dean is claiming to have been born again and filled with the Holy Spirit," I answered. I knew exactly what Brian was going to tell me.

"And," Brian said, "he's speaking in tongues. Just as he told you he'd do."

"I suppose Bishop Lane now believes he's forgiven, and all his wrongdoing is forgotten," I said.

"More likely he figures that's what the church believes," Brian said. "Watch the quick exit to another diocese far away where his being full of it—the Holy Spirit, I mean—" he chuckled, "can be put into practice."

"I wonder how long that will take," I said.

"For him to get away, or to start being more full of it than ever?" Brian asked. "By the way, did you know that McDoo was being considered for the Bishop of North Dakota when the shit hit the fan?"

"I guess he's out of the running now," I said.

"Also, I wouldn't advise returning to your old parish. The rector is screwing his secretary behind his wife's back."

"She's married too, isn't she?" I asked.

"They're all married," Brian said. "I've heard even more about that parish. It isn't much different from the musical chairs at the Cathedral, except their antics are heterosexual, at least I think so."

I shook my head. "These church people," I muttered. "No one seems to know the meaning of being faithful anymore. Brian, I'm sorry to cut you short, but I've got to go." I hung up.

I returned to Dan and Tray. I decided we should continue watchful waiting, since Dr. Leach didn't think there was much to do, except put Tray to sleep. "I couldn't bear that. At least not yet," I said.

Dan nodded and continued to pet her.

I was losing Tray, I'd lost Sharon, and I was losing Dan. What else was I going to lose? I wondered.

Anxiety

A week passed. In the middle of the night, Sharon's soul paid another visit. I had only a moment to wonder why she'd come when our souls had decided not to do this anymore. This time she did not stand at the bedroom doorway and wait. She entered the room, jumped on me, and began making angry love to me immediately. My mouth hurt from the power of her mouth. She rode me as if there were no tomorrow.

I tried to talk, but her mouth kept muffling my words.

I had never seen her like this. At least not in the soul realm. Was she back on drugs, I wondered? What in the world had made her so angry, yet still wanting to make love with me on some level?

When I phoned the next morning, I got a voice mail recording. I wondered when she'd switched over from her answering machine.

I was sure she'd know who called.

I didn't leave a message. I would try again later.

When I called that night, I again got the voice mail.

I decided to wait another day before driving by her condominium to see if I might find her home.

When I drove by three nights later, I saw a light or two on inside. I really did not want to drop by since she'd not invited me, not even in the soul realm.

But I had to know if she was all right.

I parked and got out of my car. I walked up the walk to the building and walked inside the foyer. I looked down the list to her name and began dialing her number. When I got to the last digit, I hesitated. I couldn't finish.

I turned, left the building, and walked back to the car. Tray would be waiting at home. I didn't encourage her to go with me now, and she seemed only to want to stay close to home. I had to make sure she was all right.

When I opened the door, I found her sleeping very deeply in front of the couch. I greeted her, having to pet her hard to wake her, as I often did now. "I wish you could give me some advice," I told her. "Do you contact Sharon, or she you when you are sleeping? Do you soul travel too?"

Tray rolled over so that I could rub her belly. "Should I be more aggressive with Sharon or wait things out?"

I got no answer from Tray. I had not really expected one.

She stumbled up and seemed to need to go outside. I let Tray out into the back yard, while I made a quick trip to the toilet inside. When I got back downstairs, she was at the door. I opened it. She hobbled in.

I went upstairs to grade more papers. On my desk, Dan had left an envelope with a few hundred dollars in it. "A month's rent, since I didn't give notice," he'd scribbled. I opened the door to his bedroom. He'd moved his things out. He had indeed moved in with Rick again.

I walked around the room. I felt anxious and lonely. Dan's being in the house had provided a buffer from the upsetting relationship with Sharon and what seemed Tray's immanent doom.

The phone rang.

I dashed to get it. Maybe it was Sharon.

"Just thought I'd let you know I'm all right," Dan said. "In fact I'm here in bed with Rick now."

"So glad to know that," I said, with more than a bit of sarcasm in my tone. But then I got hold of myself and told him to "be sure and keep in touch. If you don't let me hear from you regularly, I'll have to send over the posse to make sure that you—and Rick—are behaving yourselves."

Shuffling the Deck

I sat grading papers in my ministry office. The light of a late afternoon in May gave everything a warm glow.

Louise buzzed.

I jumped. I hadn't been expecting that kind of interruption. I got up to look out the window. The crabapples were full of rose-colored flowers. The lilacs were in full bloom.

"Just thought I'd let you know Viv will be dropping around to see you before you leave today," Louise said.

"Viv?" I asked, somewhat confounded.

"Yes, the Lutheran campus minister," Louise said.

"You mean they brought her back?" I asked.

"You'll see," Louise said. She laughed and hung up.

Some woman stuck her head into my office and said, "Hello; I'm Viv." She too was middle-aged, blonde, about five feet seven, but rather gaunt. Whereas the other Viv had worn little makeup, this one paid careful attention to lipstick, mascara, and eye shadow. She let me know how enthusiastic she was to be there, having just graduated from seminary. She let me know she was a fan of Kuhn. She knew all the popular Lutheran slogans and tag words.

"I wonder if you will be cooperating with the ministry team soon?" Viv asked.

"I do what I can," I said. "That isn't much. I don't see the Episcopal Church running out to fund campus ministries."

"That's too bad," Viv said. "May I sit?" she asked, mere rhetoric, as she sad down in the chair in front of my desk. "I'm suggesting that people not be considered part of the team unless they can contribute monetarily and physically at least twenty hours per week."

"I guess that leaves me out," I said. I could tell I was going to like this Viv immensely.

After she left my office, I walked down the hall to see Louise. I saw Viv down on the main floor. She was busy arranging chairs around a podium.

"Is she going to give a lecture or conduct a service?" I wondered aloud.

Louise looked up from her desk and smiled.

"I just met Viv, or, should I say, I had a bit of a run in with Viv," I said.

Louise laughed. "She's a real dynamo."

"She let me know I'd be even more marginalized than ever around here," I said.

"She speaks up," Louise said, adding, "in all the right ways." She winked.

"My kinda gal," I said. "If I could wink, I'd wink back atcha," I said, trying to wink. I could never do it well. Both eyes tended to close.

"You ought to see her in public." Louise pursed her lips and waved in a manner that reminded me of Queen Elizabeth II.

"I'll be she looks, well, *interesting* in her crown," I said, thinking Louise's word choice was interesting.

"Viv knows all the right phrases. A little bird told me she makes those in charge feel important," Louise said.

I figured I knew who the little bird was. Father Norbert was an excellent judge of character. He expressed his judgments slyly.

"Have a good day," Louise said. She leaned over her desk to whisper. "You know how noises carry in this building," she said. "Viv has demanded I leave the building to take care of some work for her. So I have to go. Father Norbert says she'll learn the ropes before long."

I expressed my surprise that one of the ministers would expect that of Louise. No one outside the Catholics asked her to do much of anything. After all, the Franciscans paid her salary. We'd always considered Louise the Catholic secretary and receptionist. She did us all a favor by taking our calls. We would not have presumed to ask for more.

This clearly was not the old Viv who took care of her own business.

"By the way," Louise called. She'd followed me down the hall to tell me in a whisper, "You ought to hear the rumors about CU's Athletic Department and their recruiting parties. Makes my ears red just thinking of them," she said and hurried away again. She rushed down the stairs to the outer door. She had to take care of her added chores.

I'd heard rumblings of sex and booze parties to attract recruits for quite awhile. While it struck some as ironic that people in that arm of academe regularly advocated prayer and invoked God before games, it seemed to me but another indication of an institution where people in fact consider themselves above ethics and morality—as well as the laws of society and God.

In my sleep that night, I dreamed of a woman whose identity was familiar yet unknown. I heard her crying and went to search for her. I found myself standing outside her house. Walking up the steps, I carefully opened the door.

As I surveyed the living room I saw nothing, not even much furniture, yet I could still hear the woman sobbing, as if nearby. I began to examine the walls for doors that led to other rooms where she might be.

The walls seemed made of some sort of cream-colored plastic, or plasticized metal, like that of computer cases and monitors. I found a door and opened it. There was a stairway that I climbed. But it led nowhere.

I descended and searched for another door. Finding it, I turned the knob, but there was nothing but another wall, again of the same computer material, on the other side. I tried another door, but it also led to a wall, this time of bricks and mortar.

Then another. But it opened onto a steep drop into darkness. I could see nothing. I stood teetering at the edge, not knowing what lay below. Able to pull back and not fall in, I slammed the door. I noticed a hall. I walked down it, but it turned into a maze. Feeling trapped, I called out.

The woman's sobs grew louder. Following them, I found her lying in a fetal position, her face turned away from me. I knew I knew her, but I still could not ascertain who she was. We were somewhere in the maze. I bent to try to help her up, but she only cried louder. I could not lift her.

Finally, I gave up and decided that I had no place there. I did not belong.

I woke.

I Live Here

As I drove home from campus the next afternoon, I knew that, like the woman in my dream, I too had been trapped in a maze. For too long, I had been trying to find my way out. Instead of lying around in a fetal position, or trying to pull someone uncooperative out of hers, I had to make some sort of drastic move. I'd tried so many doors, so many stairways. Yet, I remained trapped in my life of trap doors, doors opening onto walls, and false staircases.

I resolved to make a major change that summer. I could not go on in a labyrinth. I had hoped that Sharon and I could find our way out together. But that too had been wishful thinking. Miracles happened. I had so wanted one. But there would be none this time. I had to act on my own.

I began placing phone calls to friends who might be sympathetic to my job plight. Maybe one of them could help. People were friendly and said they'd keep their eyes open.

I hoped someone would hear something that bore fruit. "Otherwise, I'm going to be in real trouble," I found myself telling more than a few of them.

During a late June heat wave, I was upstairs in my study working on an article on Donne's *Corona*. It was Friday night. I looked at my watch. It was midnight. I needed to get to bed.

I went downstairs to let Tray in. It was so hot that the only time she wanted to be outside was late at night. She liked to lie on the grass near my back door.

Normally, Tray got up and tottered in when I went to the door and held it open for her.

This time, when I opened the door, Tray didn't get up. She whimpered, so I knew she was alive. I called a couple more times, and then walked out to get her.

Finally she managed to rouse herself. She stumblingly followed me inside. She whined a little, as if in pain.

I turned off the lights and made sure everything was locked up.

Tray refused to come upstairs. She continued to whine softly and lay herself down heavily in front of the couch.

I knelt down to talk to her. I stroked her head. "Are you all right?" I asked. I began stroking up and down the length of her body, trying to send healing energy into her.

She whimpered a little and reached out to touch me with her front paw. I took it in my hand and squeezed. She seemed to take some comfort from that.

I tried to talk her into getting up and accompanying me upstairs. But she still refused or perhaps could not follow. When I bent to lift her, she resisted. She even growled softly, as if to say she wanted me to leave her alone.

Finally, I decided to turn out the lights and let her sleep where she wanted.

I did not sleep at all well. I kept having nightmares about one thing, and then another. Tray figured in many of them. As did Sharon.

I was startled awake just before dawn. I heard a loud thump, followed quickly by another thump, less loud than the first.

Tray must have knocked something over. I turned over and tried to get a couple of hours of sleep in. But I continued to toss and worry.

I got up. I called out but didn't see Tray anywhere upstairs, so I walked down the staircase to look for her. I called. Just as I turned the corner I saw her lying on her side in a fetal position in front of the couch.

She was dead—the spirit had left her body. I walked over and bent to touch her. She hadn't been dead long. Her mouth was open slightly. Her body was still supple. *Rigor mortis* had not set in.

The thumps that I'd heard must have been hers. She'd tried to climb the stairs to reach me but fell. Then she made it to the couch, and fell again, this time expiring.

I was devastated.

Why hadn't I stayed downstairs with her? Why didn't I realize that she was whining for good reason? She was dying. She hardly ever complained about anything. It just wasn't in her. She made the best of whatever came, no matter what.

What a fool I'd been. I began to weep.

Finally, I let go and let out with what sounded like the keening of all the suffering masses of the world. I couldn't help myself. Tray was my dog. She'd been at my side longer than any human.

When I finally gathered my wits and felt safe enough to call a few friends, I called Dan. He burst into tears and couldn't talk. He muttered that he'd be over as soon as he could. Rick took the phone and mumbled something, but I couldn't concentrate.

I also called Brian. Although he wasn't much of a dog person, he said he was sorry.

"Now, you won't have to worry about making another move and trying to find a place that will let you have a dog."

Poor Tray didn't need to be put through another big move. And I didn't want to try to leave her again with my family or friends while I went off trying to figure out what I was doing with my life.

When Dan appeared at the front door, he looked distraught. He rushed inside to Tray's now stiffening body. He knelt to hold her up close to his chest.

While Dan wept, I dialed Dr. Leach's number. I didn't know what else to do. His receptionist answered and said that they would meet me at the side door to receive Tray's body. The cremation service would come by that day and pick her up.

Dan helped me wrap her body in a sheet and carry her to the car.

We got her to Dr. Leach's. We saw the cremation service truck waiting near the side door. I drove around and rolled down my window.

The driver asked, "Would you like me to carry Tray's body to the truck. Or would you rather carry her?"

"You do it—" I blurted. "No, I must do it."

Dan helped me. We almost dropped her trying to get her up to the truck, but the driver caught her just in time.

"Don't worry. People get very nervous over these things," the driver said.

I was dizzy. Dan was too. I glanced at his beet red face. His blood pressure looked high. I figured mine was too.

The driver asked, "Do you want your sheet back?"

I was too confused to respond. I had to think about it. "Yes," I said.

He then asked, "Do you want her collar and tags?"

I nodded. I didn't want them. But I did.

My hand shook. I almost dropped them.

The driver said he would have Tray's remains ready for me by the end of the week. "I'll return them to Dr. Leach. You can pick them up."

I nodded. I really didn't know what I'd do with her remains, or if I wanted them, but I nodded. I realized Dr. Leach's receptionist was standing there. "Is there anything I can do?" she asked.

"No, thanks, it'll be all right," I said. I paused. "I'll come inside and pay the bill."

"You can do that when you pick up the ashes," she said.

I finally remembered her name was Mary. "I have my credit card with me. I'll give it to you. I reached for my wallet. I realized I didn't have it with me.

"Don't worry about it," Mary said. "You need to let me know how you want to receive Tray's ashes within a few days. Do you want them placed in a simple cardboard box, or in something fancier, all the way from a simple pewter box to a silver or gold urn?" she asked.

I needed a few days before I made more decisions. "I'm feeling overwhelmed," I said.

The driver drove off with Tray's body in his truck and Mary disappeared into Dr. Leach's office.

Dan and I decided to go out for breakfast, or at least coffee, since neither of us were breakfast eaters. "I suggest breakfast," he said. "I figure your stomach is as upset as mine." He paused. "Did you call Sharon?"

The sun was starting to hurt my eyes. I shook my head. "I thought I'd better let her alone, since she seems to want it that way," I said. "Calling her would get things going again."

"The bitch," Dan muttered. "She's never around for you when you need her."

"She has lots of problems," I said.

"They're her problems. Not yours," Dan replied. "You should tell her. Let her share your burdens."

"I still don't think it's a good idea. She has enough stress in her life."

"You're protecting her," Dan blurted. Anger flashed in his eyes.

"That's one of the reasons," I said. "I really don't want to start things up again. If I'm going to get out of Denver, I need to be as unencumbered as possible. I don't need any ties to hold me back."

Dan nodded. His face softened a little. "I see what you mean. Are you going to get another dog soon?" he asked.

"I need time to grieve. And time to figure out what my next move is before taking on more responsibility," I said. "Puppies are not easy."

"You could get an adult dog. A rescue." I'm so thirsty. I've got to get some water. "The world pisses me off," he yelled. He began pacing the parking lot.

"I never would have guessed," I remarked.

"Don't tell me it doesn't piss you off too," Dan shot back.

I remained silent.

"You're not contradicting me," Dan remarked.

"Well," I said. "Do you want me to say how amazed and blessed I feel by all of creation?"

Dan snorted.

I recalled that seeing the newscast of that poor little girl who had been sexually abused and left in the sewage pit of an outhouse in the Rocky Mountains of Colorado.

When two women looked down inside the seat openings because they heard what they thought was an animal scuffling and making little noises. They saw a girl standing in the sewage beneath them. They asked what in the world she was doing there.

"I live here," she said.

Upheaval

When Dan and I entered crowded foyer of Racine's Restaurant, I glimpsed Sharon. I tried not to make myself noticeable. I didn't want to know who she was looking for. But she saw me and rushed back. She grabbed the host, who led us to a table in one of the great spaces to the left.

"What's wrong?" she asked me. "I was stepping out of the shower. I had to show some commercial space to a client, when I saw you standing before me. I saw you looking very upset. I knew you were coming here with Dan. What's wrong?"

Sharon reached to place her hand on mine. I noticed how tan it was. How warm. The old electricity was there. Her eyes searched my face.

I could hardly keep from flooding the table with tears.

Dan broke the news. "Tray's dead," he said.

Sharon began to cry. She reminded me that we knew Tray's death was coming. "It was just a matter of how soon, and how traumatic the event would be," she said.

"I heard you calling me a bitch," she added, glancing quickly at Dan. "You're right," she said. She paused. "I am a bitch."

Dan turned beet red but said nothing.

"I can't seem to change that. I've stayed away so I wouldn't make things worse for anyone else," she said. "I hope you'll understand someday." Sharon glanced at the door. "Oh God, this is it." Her face had turned stark white.

"What?" I asked. "This is what?" I asked.

"The scene I've played over and over again in my mind. I keep seeing the priest who abused me and my brother, older but still handsome and charming. He's standing in the midst of a group of people when I attack him." By then her face was beet red, as if her heart rate and blood pressure were rapidly escalating.

She rose from the table. I reached for her hand.

"Somebody has to stop this monster," she said, rushing toward the crowd gathered just inside the door.

Dan and I followed.

"You!" she called. "You! Aren't you Joe O'Brian?" she demanded.

"Father O'Brian, yes, Father Joe O'Brian," the priest said, smiling his best smile, as if ready for the cameras. He had a full head of graying hair, square jaw, wide mouth, and blue blue eyes, as if right out of Hollywood.

"What are you doing back here?" Sharon demanded. Her voice was shrill, shriller than I'd ever heard it.

"I'm serving as a diocesan priest," Father O'Brian answered, his face innocent as the sky. "I was just brought back from Boston. I've served for years there," he announced, as if talking to reporters. He smiled a wide, toothy, actor's smile.

Sharon moved right in front of him and stood. "Do you remember me?" she demanded.

Father O'Brian shook his head. "I don't think so." He paused. Looking her up and down, his eyes grew wide. "Something about you seems familiar." His smile brightened as if real.

"Well, I was about eight when you first knew me," she said. My brother was a year older." O'Brian shook his head and turned slightly, as if to suggest that the interview was over.

"You're not going to brush me off so easily this time," Sharon said. "I'm Sharon. You called me your little rosebud." O'Brian said nothing but tried to start up a conversation with a couple of women standing near him. He didn't seem to know them. They acted distant, as if they didn't want to get involved.

"I said you called me your little rosebud. Then, after I got used to that, you began to show me just what you meant—first with your finger, then two, then three, and tongue. You quickly followed that with your penis. It's only a little bigger than your thumb." With that, Sharon jumped O'Brian and kneed him in the groin. She wrestled him to the ground and pounded on his face and chest.

People were calling for someone to call the cops. We pulled Sharon off O'Brian, although Dan and I were muttering that we really ought to let her kill him. Some patrons began taking up the call. "Kill him! Kill him! Kill him!" they chanted.

A riot threatened.

Five policemen arrived, sirens blaring. "What happened here?" a male officer asked. The others dispersed themselves among the crowd.

"That woman attacked the priest," an older woman said. She pointed to Sharon and then to O'Brian.

Dusting himself off, O'Brian straightened his shirt and pants and adjusted his collar. "It's nothing, Officer," he said. "I don't want to make the situation more than it is. The young lady is upset. I'm a priest. I'll handle this in a pastoral manner."

Sharon said nothing. But she was seething. I felt her anger as if it were my own.

"I forgive you, Sharon. You must have been mistaken." He still looked innocent as a cabbage. "Please let us talk this out in private," O'Brian said to the police and the crowd.

The police left without making any charges, and the crowd went back to whatever they were doing. Some went back to their tables. Others waited to be seated.

"I'm certain I've never met you before. I've no idea what you're talking about."

"Ever hear of a scourge of God?" Sharon asked. "I'm warning you. Justice will be done."

"Let's figure out how to handle this in private," I said.

Dan and I ushered Sharon out the door to my car.

We knew that telling her to calm down was not appropriate. She had every right to be angry. We were just as pissed off as she. Dan got in the back seat and Sharon sat in the front beside me. I drove to my house.

"I plan to slit the fucker's throat," Sharon kept vowing. She couldn't sit still. She paced.

"I know, and then what?" I would ask, looking her in the face.

Dan did the same. "We have to come up with something better than that," he said.

"The police won't do anything," Sharon sputtered. Once inside, she paced the living room, pounding her fists. "You saw how they submitted to O'Brian's superior wisdom in Racine's."

"To help keep us calm and centered, so we can figure out a plan," I said, "I suggest we work in the gardens, especially among the roses. They need to be trimmed."

"I'll start with the Archbishop of Colorado—higher, if necessary. I don't think he'll do a damn thing, but I'm going to demand that he does. Others were harmed besides me."

"We'll go with you," Dan and I said. We opened the back door.

"Here Tray," I called, "then caught myself."

We walked down the steps.

"I'll do it alone, not with you or with Dan. It's my fight," Sharon said.

None of us had much hope of success. We had become aware of how the churches liked to shuffle 'em off to Buffalo and pretend that those who complained were guilty of failing to love the Church.

We stood outside my back door surveying the property. "Does anyone else around here do any gardening?" Sharon asked. "Trees, shrubs, bushes--everything needs to be trimmed."

"I'm the main gardener," I answered.

"The only one, from what I've seen," Dan piped up, loud enough for people lurking inside near their windows to hear.

"They're only too glad to appreciate your work, as long as it's free."

"Seems like everyone I know," I said. I went to get the loppers I'd bought. When I returned, I cut back some overgrown and sparsely leafed branches on the Peace rose that I'd planted, along with others, near my back door.

You should go to the media," Dan suggested. He and Sharon were pulling weeds among the roses there.

"I'm not sure I want to go to the media. It seems a little too public," she said. "But, I'll think about it."

Society was certainly moving in the same direction. People were less and less willing to keep quiet and endure the pain caused by molestation, even when perpetrated by clergy. Although gays and lesbians were the most vocal, perhaps because they had been the most abused and had the least to lose in our culture, others were also heeding the call.

None of us felt that it would be long before the perpetrators were called to account for their abuses. "But how long will it be?" Sharon asked. "How long do people have to keep quiet about the dirty little secrets of the church?"

"It probably won't be the churches that will act to disclose the abuse," I said. "They'll be the last to come clean—"

"And, only then, because of the pressure put on them by bad publicity and law suits," Dan added. He yanked up a big clump of bluegrass that had invaded the flower gardens. It took two hands.

Sharon grabbed it from him and began beating the soil off the roots on the townhouse wall.

"Beat that thing to hell, why don't you," Dan laughed.

"It isn't as though we've got decades to let it all unfold," Sharon said. She tossed what was left of the grass out into the lawn and stretched. She walked around a little, then bent to examine the carnations scattered among the roses. They too were in full glory.

"Roses and carnations," I interjected, have traditionally been the flowers of heaven. "That's why I planted them when

I first moved in. To remind me." I paused. "It's among the roses that Eve tends that Satan first spies the mother of us all, according to Milton. The roses symbolize the unbroken communion with heaven that our first parents still enjoyed."

"But sin enters. First Eve, then Adam, falls, and it's over for us all," Sharon opined, tossing spent flower petals in the air.

Dan joined her.

"Yet, the reminders of what could have been, and what can be, are still there, waiting to be read," I said, catching as many of the petals as I could in my hands.

"Is that why we hold Tradition so holy?" Sharon asked.

"Maybe," I answered, "but Tradition is meant to be but one guide. Reason and Scripture are also important."

Sharon looked at her watch. She decided to go inside to place a call arranging an appointment with the Archbishop. Surprisingly, his secretary was in, even on a Saturday afternoon.

With questions of free will versus predestination, and earthly time versus eternity, swirling in our minds and in our conversation, Sharon asked me to talk with her again about those who believe our souls set up some sort of contracts before taking on bodies. "I still cannot fathom how people can believe that others and I have somehow contracted our abuse," Sharon said. We were sipping some tea that I'd made.

"Karma might also be involved," I said.

"I abused the priest in earlier lives, so in this one he got to abuse me?" she said.

"That's only one of the possibilities," I said. "But it sounds too much like blaming the victim to me."

"Or excusing the perp," Sharon said.

"Since we can't know the truth, or falseness, of these notions, I think they're best left," I said. "We have to act according to what we know—that is, within the parameters of this life."

"I sure wish Tray was here to hug," Dan said. "I really miss her. She was like a teddy bear." Sharon and I agreed.

"Our connections might just be formed in this life, even though they're so strong that they seem like we've known each other before."

"The operative word is *seems*," I said. "That sounds like your psychiatrist," I said. "Let's return to the idea of a contract. If your soul and O'Brian's contracted to carry out this drama before you came into this world, it is possible that your contract was to bring him to justice, because you were brave and strong enough to do it."

Obviously all these questions, all these possibilities, complicated matters even more.

"I still wonder why you and I have the psychic bond we have," Sharon mused, searching my face.

I agreed. "It's possible we come by it naturally," I said. "Because we're paying attention, we're developing the gifts we have."

"I wonder if abuse hasn't brought out what was naturally there," Sharon said.

"A matter that I too have often thought about," I said.

At the last minute, Sharon decided that she did want me to accompany her to her meeting with Archbishop Morgan on Monday. "I want you as a witness," she said. "I want your support."

Dan looked at us both and smiled.

Although cool and businesslike, Archbishop Morgan promised that he'd look into the matter of Father O'Brian. "But you must remember that these alleged incidents took place decades ago. Obtaining proof, investigation itself, will not be easy. People's stories change over time. We forget what the facts actually are."

Sharon and I nodded.

Archbishop Morgan went on. "These are serious charges, and the man has rights. Above all, the purity of Church must be protected."

Instead of spitting on Morgan, as she looked ready to do, Sharon turned to me and suggested. "I think it's time to go." Her voice lacked affect.

As Sharon and I walked outside, I said, "Institutions desperately desire to protect their own. Whether churches, universities, government, those who speak out, get pushed to the edges and viewed as dangers to the body politic."

Sharon kicked a rock on the walk out into the street. It almost hit a car.

"We're like viruses that threaten to invade and destroy the body. It doesn't occur to those who run the institutions that they might be better off if they'd listened to us before things got way out of hand and the dysfunction, the disease that afflicts every part, invades the entire body."

"You need to search for another position," Sharon reminded me. As we walked on, she said, "I'm going to go home to my own place. I'll be all right," she said, as if reading the questions on my mind. "I confronted the Arch-demon of my life."

"Does that mean that we can now get on with our life together?"

"No," Sharon answered. She turned from me. "I'm keeping my vow to protect you from myself."

"I don't want to be protected," I blurted, but she was already climbing into her car and shutting the door. I watched her speed off.

When I got home, it seemed that all the bells belonging to churches in the neighborhood were ringing. I wondered what in the world was going on, maybe a few funerals, all being held at the same time, coupled with some other services, maybe a wedding or two, elsewhere.

I'd not recalled hearing the clamor, the clanging, the discord, the harmonies, reverberating through the air since I'd first moved in. At that time, my ears were exquisitely tuned to new sounds.

But over the months and with so many distractions, I'd grown used to them. They'd begun to be background noise, little noticed, except now and then, when once again I would wake to become aware of them.

Putting Out the Word

My job search was on. Looking for another position, full time, with a contract, and only one, helped to distract me from my anguish over Tray. Once I got through the worst of the grief and gained back some composure, Tray, rather, her spirit, began to visit me in the night. Sometimes she woke me by jumping on the bed and lying down beside me. She did this nightly, starting a week or so after she died. This continued for ten nights. After that, her visits became less frequent, and less predictable. Sometimes, she brought other dogs with her, some of which I knew from the neighborhood. She always seemed happy and well now.

A Buddhist monk in Boulder told me that dogs have to live at least three lives as dogs before they can ascend the ladder and begin incarnations as humans. I said, "It seems wiser to remain a dog."

I'd thought I was about to get a job at Fordham University. Susan Norman, the Chair of the Search Committee, asked for my full dossier. She said they'd get back to me soon.

My hopes were raised. So was my anxiety.

A week later, Jackson Starling, the Department Chair, phoned. "Could you start in June?" he asked. I hemmed and hawed. "We need someone to teach a couple of summer courses. You'll get paid extra, of course," he said.

"Yes, I answered." I didn't know how I'd do that, but I'd do it. Nothing easily fell into place for me, as some people said things should do when they're right.

Starling said I should expect a contract in the mail. "Please sign it immediately and send it back."

The contract didn't arrive. I kept looking for it.

A week later, I put in a call to Starling.

"I'm sorry, he isn't available," his secretary said. "I'll ask him to call you back."

I explained my concern.

She read back the gist of what I told her.

"That's correct," I said and thanked her.

Again, I didn't get a call back.

I called again. The secretary said she'd have the Chair call me.

That afternoon, a letter arrived from Fordham:

We regret to inform you that we shall not be able to hire you.

We regret any inconvenience.

Sincerely yours,
Susan Norman, Chair, Search Committee

I called Starling again.

This time the secretary said, "Dr. Starling is unable to talk with you. The hiring is up to the Dean."

I recalled Spet's telling me once that he had a friend who was a Dean at Fordham. Although I couldn't prove it, I was willing to bet this was the Dean who was Spet's friend. He'd talked with her, and she'd nixed the contract.

Again, I called the friends who'd promised to help. "Please do not to say a word about my search to anyone at the university, or even at St. Francis Center." Some of them thought I sounded paranoid. "I can't take a chance on anything leaking to my saboteurs. I have outside references and will use them only. Perhaps that will work." I said *perhaps* because I'd knew search committees typically consulted one's Chair.

"Do you think your fears are being picked up by hiring committees and that's scaring them?" one of my friends at the University of North Caroline, Ashville, asked.

"Believe me, I wish that were the case. But I know how my Chairman works. He's malevolent."

In July, Bea, a professor friend who taught at Malone College called to tell me that she'd heard of a last minute faculty vacancy at a small Christian college in some little town in the sticks of Iowa. "They say it's Christian, but not in a narrow-minded way. There are no strict doctrinal and behavioral statements that faculty members must pledge to follow."

"That might work," I said. "I know Iowa has a reputation for its excellent educational system."

"Many of those little Iowa towns have their own private colleges," Bea said. "They've always believed in education."

"I remember the Iowa Basic Exams from growing up," I said. "We took them every year." Perhaps I could live with a college like that—as long as I could get away frequently and not be pulled into a fishbowl mentality. It might be nice to escape the pressures and pace of city life. Why, I might be able to ride my bike to classes.

I phoned the college contact, using Bea's name as a reference. The Search Committee Chair expressed interest. "The Chair of our English Department has just taken a visiting position in another state. We have to fill his shoes in a hurry."

In a few hours, the Dean of the college phoned. "Could you fly in for an interview on Monday?" he asked.

Soon my plane was landing in the Omaha Airport, where I was picked up by the departing English Department Chair. "Call me Doug," he said. He took my bag and put it in the back of his SUV.

We drove through a crazy-quilt of soybeans, corn, "and rape—which Americans call *canola oil plants,* instead of using the British nomenclature," Doug said. He laughed. "I'm a specialist in Puritan literature, so I find this kind of thing amusing," he commented.

"I hope I can," I mused.

It seemed that we were driving and driving over two lane highways through nothing but a patchwork of fields, now and then dotted with a house or granary.

"We're almost there," Doug said.

Just over one of the rises, we spotted the outbuildings of a town the size of a postage stamp. Everything was laid out in squares, with a few rectangulars here and there to help break the monotony. Little rose much above the general flatness, however, except a few cylindrically shaped grain elevators of several hundred feet and a water tower that looked like a huge ball standing on long legs. I thought of several science fiction films, *War of the Worlds*, in particular.

Although the town reminded me of my hometown, it was a fraction of the size. We had a junior college. This place had a full four year college. "We've idealized it as a Harvard of the Midwest," Doug said. "It's a Christian institution that embraces the best of culture and civilization, something unusual among many Christian colleges."

Doug pulled up in front of the Student Center. It was a new building, nice, but flat and square. Several students, faculty members, and staff came to meet me. They were very open and friendly in their blond, Midwestern way. They seemed curious, open to talk about most things. That was good, especially considering the pervasive religious atmosphere of the area. They were open about that too. Doug told me, "Some of the locals have turned from mainstream Protestant denominations to embrace those espousing a more pure, Bible only approach. They shun the trappings of tradition and cultural contexts. That isn't a popular position with most of our faculty," Doug added, "especially the younger ones who have come in from outside."

"That's good," I said. "It's hard to be educated and educate, when you must wear blinders."

"Agreed," Doug said, glancing across the seat at me. "To gain a broader basis of support, the college has had to cater more and more to the evangelicals and fundamentalists. Not a good thing," Doug said, "considering the suspicion that evangelicals and fundamentalists cast on culture and learning. They aren't known to value freedom of thought and expression."

"That's what the liberal arts are all about," I commented. I wondered how happy I would be there. Although careful not to oversell the place, Doug was definitely pitching it.

Just as soon as I stashed my bag in my nicely appointed room with a private bath, Doug took me to tour the campus and meet more faculty members. "I hope you aren't too tired," he said.

"Our President is a former college athlete," Bernard Vander Koop, Chair of the Religion Department, said. "Above all else, he stresses the necessity of maintaining a team spirit and acting like a team player."

"Our former President, who was been hired in the early seventies, stressed scholarship." Doug said. "He was an old school German."

"Yes, he almost bankrupted the place," the Religion Department Chair added. He had a wry smile on his face, as if he found the situation ironic. "Now, we've got a popular President, one of the people," he said. "So goes Rome. Bread and circuses. That's what the populace demand."

I liked Doug and Bernard. We seemed in harmony. They didn't hesitate to speak up either. The people who interviewed me—the scholarly core hired by the previous President—wanted someone who had standards to which he or she held.

Was the core of intelligent professors with high standards and open-minds strong enough to protect me? I wondered. Without a tenure track position—and its built-in safeties—again—I would be more vulnerable than those hired in permanent positions.

Doug drove me past the First Christian Church on his tour of downtown. "Onward Christian Soldiers" resounded from speakers in each side of its square bell tower so that the words would spread to the four cardinal directions. George Beverly Shea's old, emotional voice was backed up by a lush orchestra, with every note, every rhythm, overdone, along with extra wide vibratos. The effect was almost surreal. I envisioned the speakers like Uzis blasting at all things in the visible world—and beyond.

"In that store front over there is what we all call The Tipsy Tulip," Doug said, pointing at one of the buildings on Main Street, about all the town had. "It's the only bar in the area. The town fathers had thought to force them out by refusing to renew the lease on their old building just outside of town," he said. "But some outsider, who happened to own this building, offered a good lease to the bar owner, so it transplanted itself and sprang up here." Doug laughed. "Of course many blamed it on the wiles of Satan."

I also laughed. "You never know, although in this case I think I'm on his side."

"You've been reading too much Milton," Doug said. "You can't make people good by making more laws and trying to enforce them."

I thought it too bad he was leaving to take a job elsewhere. I thought I'd like working with him. Fortunately there were similar minds anchoring most of the departments. "To get such faculty, the former President offered competitive pay, reduced teaching loads, and support for our research in both release time and money," Doug informed me. "All of us hold Ph.D.s and actively research and publish."

"Sounds good," I said.

"Even though the older faculty are plodders without Ph.D.s, and few, if any publications outside of church pulp, you'll find most of them nice people who try to be honest and get along."

The ones I met seemed that way. Perhaps this would be a good spot, where I could prosper on several levels.

Doug slapped my leg just above the knee and squeezed.

"I like enough of the people to be interested without needing a personal touch," I said. I was trying to set boundaries yet be pleasant and funny about it.

I recalled seeing many books on or by Allan Ginsberg, John Updike, Alfred Kinsey, and a broad range of sexuality, and sexual expression, on Doug's bookshelves, right out in the open where everyone could see them. For a Christian college, I'd thought, this was remarkable. Actually I'd never noticed anything like that in Colorado either, certainly not in Spet's or Ron's collections at school anyway.

"Oh you mean this," Doug said, still squeezing my leg. "We're a friendly bunch around here. Most of the men treat each other like players on the hometown team."

For a moment visions of the men grabbing ass flashed before me. "Mmmmm," I said, chuckling.

"We don't get overly friendly, though," Doug remarked, as if intuitively following my thought. "None of that ass slapping or ass grabbing that you see on the field." He removed his hand, and I still felt clean. I felt none of the lingering sinister aspects that I had when dealing with Spet or the former Dean of the Cathedral.

"We wouldn't think of doing it to the women, of course. Well, we might think of it," Doug said, "but we'd know better than to carry it out."   "As you've no doubt noticed from my bookshelves, we're pretty open in the college community about sexuality. Many of us manage it by being honest and upfront."

"That's a good start," I replied.

"Unfortunately, the community as a whole is not so open. Divorced people and unwed mothers used to have a very hard time here, until recently," Doug said. "Now, we've got enough of them that most people realize they're not a threat. The kids keep the schools stocked."

I had noticed the word "most" in his observations, but figured that I could not expect better anywhere, really. I wondered how many unwed mothers there were. I asked about them.

"Usually they get married to the fathers of their babies," Doug said.

I had told him somewhere in the interview process that I had been divorced some while ago. I didn't tell him it had been twice, the second being short enough to be annulled. Doug assured me that would not be a problem.

"By the way," Doug added, "people around here rarely lock their houses. If you don't want some friendly neighbor or associate to walk right in, you need to lock up," he said. "It can be a little disconcerting for someone from outside. Often people don't knock. They open the door and walk in, calling your name or Hello."

"The other morning I stepped out of the shower to find the Chair of the History Department standing there in front of me. He handed me a towel so I could dry off, shave, and dress, while we went over some issues before our budget meeting that afternoon. He's a friend of mine."

"Oh," I said, thinking that I would lock my doors, not just at night, but when I was inside, and when I left. This behavior seemed a little too forward for me. But it certainly did open up some new paths of inquiry into homoeroticity in the heartlands. Perhaps I could get a good paper out of it. That's probably what Doug had in mind too.

Before I left town later that afternoon, the honors students in English wanted to meet with me. They were a bright, fresh lot, not well traveled, not experienced in the world, but intelligent and curious, open. I could work with them.

They assured me that Iowans had a good work ethic, even the bad students. "They do what their teachers tell them. Even if it means staying up all night to get their homework done," one articulate young woman assured me.

They students reminded me of myself, as an undergraduate, with a bright future ahead.

Contracts and Cabbages

Doug called a few days later and offered me a contract. "I'll take it," I said. I didn't have to think twice. I knew I had to get out of Denver. Overall, this college seemed a good fit. My only wish was that the position would have been tenure track instead of a temporary replacement. But that didn't seem anywhere in the cards, not in my deck anyway.

I placed a rental ad for my town home in the *Denver Post* and made arrangements to rent a U-Haul truck for my furniture and belongings. Apartment rentals were not easy to come by there in that Iowa town. It was experiencing a bit of a population boom. A few small industries had moved in, hiring people, both local and from the surrounding areas. City dwellers were expressing interest in moving to small towns, where crime was low, schools were good, and one could trust one's neighbors.

The college would find a place for me. They would reimburse my rental truck moving charges one way. When it came time to leave there, I would have to foot the bill myself.

Soon I had suitable renters for my place and got Dan and Brian to help pack my belongings in the truck. For a moment, it seemed as though I were leaving something important behind, but I could not think what. I checked and rechecked the house, but found nothing I'd left behind.

Then I realized that Tray had gone on my moves before. It didn't feel right not to be gathering her into the truck with me this time. But those were the realities. I had to face this move alone.

I would drive straight through to Iowa, stopping only for gas and fast food somewhere in Nebraska. By the middle of

Nebraska, I was used to looking at flat fields of harvested grain.

By the time I hit eastern Nebraska, the terrain changed. The area around Council Bluffs provided some relief from the flatlands with dramatic cliffs rising suddenly, but once into Iowa, the plains returned. Soon, "this little Eden," as some called it, appeared square upon square before me.

Because no suitable apartment had yet been found for me, several men unloaded some of my things in what had been the old college President's house. It too was square, two stories, and build of wood. I had to spend the night on a couch in one of large classroom downstairs, a room to the left the front door. I surmised that it had been the living room. A straight hall led from the front door to the back door. The main bathroom was just down the hall. At the end was the kitchen adjoined by the dining room, sometimes used as a classroom. Across from the large classroom downstairs were two other faculty offices. The four bedrooms upstairs had been turned into offices for English faculty, one of which was mine. It had been the master bedroom.

The next morning at seven, I was woken by several men from the college, a work crew, I gathered. They unpacked all my belongings into the classroom. At least the air conditioning worked. It was early August and hot as hell, and humid, even at night.

Living in a college classroom, sleeping on my own couch, instead of the one that had been moved out, was another adventure. I was never sure who might walk in while I was sleeping. At least my office upstairs with its adjoining bathroom had locks on the doors. I made use of them when I wanted privacy.

I noticed that someone, another faculty member, thin, with one of the darkest tans I'd ever seen, was always walking past my windows, so close that I could open the window and touch him. In fact, I saw him walking all over town, often right outside various windows. He didn't seem to be looking inside, but the behavior struck me as dubious.

Doug had not taken all of his things from the office yet. He left me some empty book shelves, barely enough for my books. "I'll come back some time this fall, probably during Thanksgiving break, to get the rest."

In the closet I found a cache of books that he'd put away, including those with distinctly sexual subjects. I wondered if Doug worried about parading them here or at his new college home. "If I want some reading material that I can't find in the town or college libraries, I can look in my closet," I joked to myself. "Now, if only others would look in their closets and actually read what's there," I said, "pulling out Rechy's *City of Night*." I'd heard of it. It was considered a kind of underground classic of raw gay sexuality.

Dipping into it, I realized it was pretty seedy and descriptive. I wondered if anyone else at the college had any idea what it was. I couldn't quite imagine leaving it out on my own bookshelf. But Doug was known as a rebel. His area was also American literature, so Rechy would be more pertinent to his studies than mine. That he'd been a star athlete while an undergraduate, preserving his tall, sinuous body into early middle age, and had married a woman whose father was a prominent denominational figure, certainly had not hurt. No one was going to be too critical, at least not publicly.

A couple of single women faculty members made their availability known to me.

"You'll soon find the community is not very welcoming of people without spouses," Mara, a female sociology professor of my age, said. She'd invited me to her apartment for lunch, lunch-meat sandwiches on whole wheat bread, with a dill pickle and potato chips on the side. "Better nowadays even to be divorced and reattached than to be single," she said.

I felt increasing uncomfortable, not just because I didn't like to eat lunch meat, but because little Eden was appearing more and more fallen.

"Single people are not looked on as normal. In fact, we're viewed as threats. As a male, you'll probably not feel as much suspicion as we women, but you'll feel it, believe me."

I wondered about telling Mara about Sharon.

"As a sociologist, I can tell you story after story about peoples' peccadilloes," Mara said. "No one admits to them, but the mouths soon spread everything, especially if it's lurid and sexual."

"I can hardly wait," I said. I was glad I hadn't said anything about Sharon. The facts would be twisted and I'd get crucified.

"People constantly talk about shunning idols. But they all have huge entertainment centers where everyone gathers as if around an altar. They are altars."

I laughed. "Yes, I can imagine that. Literalists often miss the noses on their own faces."

"There's no porn here, but people drive to the adjoining towns for that. That's where the sinners live."

"So you can sin, but just don't do it here," I quipped. Boy, was I uncomfortable. I made up an excuse about needing to get my courses in order for the fall semester.

"I've divulged too much," Mara said. She apologized.

Even though I'd been in town for only a couple of weeks, I soon realized how much these people loved to talk, especially if the subjects were sexual and lurid, just as Mara said. No wonder Doug had all the novels of Peter De Vries in his personal library. He wrote often of Iowa swingers and the sexually experimental, often religious. Soon, the townspeople would want to know every detail of my life. I'd probably told them too much already.

When the college finally located an apartment for me, the former renter, a married athlete who was transferring to another college, let me know that as a Catholic he felt pressured to leave or convert. "They won't admit it," he said, "but it's here. In many of the churches they thank God for sparing them the hail storms that wipe out the crops of their Catholic neighbors," he said. "It's supposed to be a sign of

God's sovereign Lordship, another sign that they're not only called, but chosen."

"Oh," I said. I wondered if the athlete's understanding of things was fully accurate. Episcopalians, after all, are in many ways more Catholic than Protestant, and, in many places in the United States, growing more so. I had noticed a number of signs in restaurants and peoples' home around town that trumpeted, *The Lord is God, To Him be all honor and glory,* and *Jesus is Lord, at his name every knee shall bow.* "Onward Christian Soldiers" was no anomaly blasting from the First Christian Church. Nor were other militaristic hymns that these strict Calvinists seemed to gravitate toward. Over three weeks, I'd attended enough church services to realize that.

If anyone were to find out about Sharon and her desire to bring a priest who molested her as a child to justice, that would further fuel their hatred for Catholicism. Her drug and sex problems would turn her into a demon as well. I'd no doubt share her guilt for getting involved with her.

Well, I would be teaching some literature classes again. For that I could be grateful. I'd still have to teach one Freshman Writing course each semester, but the other two classes would be literature. That teaching load, even though the classes met four hours per week, meant more time to work on my own research and writing.

One afternoon, John Roberts, one of my colleagues from the Psychology Department showed me his huge garden.

"You must be an organic gardener," I said, because I noticed lots of insect damage on his cabbages and corn. His tomatoes didn't look too good either.

"My cabbages have been ruined by cabbage worms."

I thought about asking if he had given thanks for the sovereignty of God, who, for some unfathomable but glorious reason chose to destroy his crops that year. Was it a sign, I wondered, of God's disapproval? I wanted to ask, tongue in cheek. Or, were more natural causes to blame?

I decided however to let my musings go unvoiced. In a theologically soaked atmosphere one could easily make too much of things and see signs sent directly by God when they were not. One could also misread the signs, either in one's own favor, or to the detriment of oneself. I did not know John well enough to explain my thinking on these matters. He might not have been swimming in the same channel or one even close to my own.

John and his wife, Joan, invited me to stay for dinner. "We're just having macaroni and cheese and some vegetables from the garden, both cooked and raw," Joan said. "You're welcome to share our humble hospitality," she added. "We live modestly so we can give more to missionary works in undeveloped countries."

"That's admirable," I said. I agreed to join them.

Over dinner, John happened to remark, "The Scriptures all speak with one voice."

I wanted to correct him. I wondered how he thought that possible. Psychologically I thought the idea most dangerous, for it suggested that we had to become robots to show ourselves followers of Christ. Augustine emphasized the multiplicity of voices, echoing the One Word who was with God and became God, somehow identified with the Divine Logos and the incarnate Christ that the Gospel of John speaks of. But how purely, and accurately, those voices echo Christ—who is the signifier, the way to understand all signs, for in him all signs are properly grounded and read—depends on how closely one emulates Christ. Augustine's is mainline, historical theology.

All things ultimately end in God, just as they began in Him, for he is the Alpha and the Omega. So all things—all signs—have roots in Him. What seems paradoxical—metaphors that seem mixed—are not, when viewed rightly. And some signs have been perverted—that is, twisted—from their original rightness in God. Not to realize the difficulties and complexities involved in reading the signs causes grave mistakes.

I wondered if these folks weren't getting far too much from their derivative Calvinist writers than from Augustine, and the great historical theologians and sign theorists who followed in his footsteps. The emphasis on God's Lordship at the expense of his mercy and grace was a grave danger that I had recognized in the commonplace theology around me.

That however was probably as much the fault of those who attached themselves to Augustinian theology—even through Calvin and his successors—as that of the derivative theologians themselves. Calvin, however, did represent a hardening of Augustine's views. For instance he believed in dual predestination instead of single. God, said Calvin, not only chose those whom he would save but actively chose those whom he would damn. Augustine believed that God merely neglected to save those whom he had not elected to receive special, that is, saving grace. That seems a little kinder.

In actual practice these folks did not seem very afraid of damnation. "Of course not," my colleague Sam said. He had been hired the previous year in the English Department. He and his wife Kathy, a dental hygienist, had finally returned from summering at Cape Cod. He was a Lutheran—"a convert," he told me. "People don't worry when damnation is reserved for their Roman Catholic neighbors. It's much better to think of their neighbors roasting in hell than yourself. They smell better when cooking."

Sam's remark struck me as especially funny because Ann Van Haag, the Acting Chair of the English Department, had earlier said, "We wish we'd known about you before we hired Sam in the tenure track position. We like you better. You're more approachable. We would have put him in a temporary position, so you could have had the permanent one." Her husband raised hogs and often butchered them up for those who wanted to buy a quarter or more. We could count on pig roasts if Van Haag's were hosting.

By that time, I wasn't so sure I wanted the tenure track position. Brian was a better fit. He'd come from a fundamentalist background and understood the rigidity better than I. He didn't seem to react so strongly to the strange and confining notions.

Love and Hate

Four days before classes were to begin, the college found an apartment for me. It was the top floor of a huge, two-story, wood-sided old house just off Main Street. It had been converted in the 1970s into three apartments, two on the main floor and one on the top, with a laundry and storage room in the basement.

Each room had a bank of old cast iron hot water radiators to keep the place warm during the notoriously cold winters of Iowa. The apartment was not luxurious by any means, lacking even a dishwasher, but it would be all right.

I discovered that few of the college teachers drank the town's water. They did not trust that the treatment plant got all the dangerous chemicals out, especially those associated with farming in the area. So we bought bottled water from Culligans, either having five gallon bottles of it hauled in, or we went for it ourselves in gallon jugs. Since it gave me something different to do, and see, I decided to fill up my own jugs at one of the water filtration stops in town.

Stimulation was not something easy to come by in a town that covered one square mile. No wonder the natives drove all over the area from town to town with radar detectors, so the endless miles of flat land wouldn't seem so dreary. As Sam remarked, "The dangers of speeding liven things up a little."

For weeks, rolling into dreary months, Sharon seemed out of touch. I phoned. Sometimes I got her answering machine but never her. I left my number and asked her to call. She didn't respond. I wrote a note now and then. She didn't say anything in return.

Adding to my stress were my sinuses, which had never been worse. People said many suffered from allergic reactions, especially in the spring and fall because farmers plowed up their fields then. Dust, molds, pesticides, fertilizers, fungicides, and other chemicals got thrown into the air.

In my sleep, I sometimes became aware of keening that came to me spiritually. When I woke I'd often lost track of it. I worried that it was Sharon, although it often seemed the voices of more than one person.

One of the pastors who befriended me told me that many in the area suffered serious depressions because "They are so constrained by the small town mentality and the narrow religious beliefs that permeate the area. Please don't tell anyone I told you this," he said. "It's a secret that is no secret. Many here live on tranquilizers and anti-depressants. Many more dose themselves with alcohol." He paused. "And more ought to," he added. He smiled rather sadly and bid me good day.

Some of the howling at night might be that of the townspeople, I thought. Still, I worried that Sharon's voice was one of those that disturbed my sleep.

When I asked Dan if he'd heard anything of Sharon, he told me he'd had the same kind of luck. "I hope everything is all right. I know she's still trying to see that Father Joe is brought to justice," Dan said. "She's networking with several others in the area who say he's abused them too. Her brother still isn't speaking to her. He refuses to become involved."

"What about her mother? Are she and Sharon talking?

"I don't know," Dan said.

In mid-October, Sharon called me late one night. She woke me from a troubled sleep. She sounded drunk; she slurred her words. I wondered if she was also drugging again.

"He paid a visit to me. Father Joe found my address," Sharon complained. "I'm not listed and told my company not to give my number or address to anyone, no matter who asked," she said. Her voice sounded more normal. Maybe she'd been sleeping.

By then, I was fully awake myself. I thought about getting out of bed but decided to prop the pillows and listen there. Unlike my town home, this place was always toasty.

"He kept trying to weasel his way in. Finally I gave up and let him inside," Sharon said. "He sat on the couch across from me and seemed utterly devastated by the actions that I've taken against him. He expressed grave concerns, as he called them, over my stirring others up too."

I punched my pillows so I could sit up higher.

"I started feeling sorry for him again, just as I did when I was a child. Pretty soon I started feeling that I really wanted to kiss him and have him screw me."

I held my breath. I knew what was coming next.

"By the time I got him off me and kicked out the door I couldn't handle it. I went on another binge."

"Sharon, are you still seeing your psychiatrist?" I asked. I had to pee.

"Not lately," she said. "I have too much to do."

"Please get back to him."

"What makes me so mad," Sharon cried, "is that I knew I still loved him and wanted him, on some level, even though I hated him more than ever."

I had read that this was not at all an unusual response in those who had been abused. They often suffer high rates of recidivism, just as the abusers do. Their training is hard to throw off. I was not, however, sure that telling Sharon this would be helpful.

"Well what do you think?" Sharon demanded. "Do you think I'm some pervert who just wants to screw my old priest again?"

I decided to tell her what I'd read. "I don't think you should blame yourself. In regard to him, you've got repulsion and desire more tightly bound together than most of us."

"Gee thanks," Sharon said. She burst into another convulsion of tears and rage. "I just don't know what to do. I can't stand it."

"Maybe you ought to seek a new therapist, a good professional who specializes in drug, alcohol, and sexual abuse issues," I said.

"Getting the perp arrested and thrown into prison will be one of the best therapies for me," she said and hung up. She seemed mad at me.

I did not even have time to tell her that I loved her. It would not have made any difference to say that I would keep her in my thoughts or any other platitudes that I might come up with, not then.

She just hung up. I got up to go to the bathroom. I opened the medicine cabinet and found a Librax. As I dug a capsule out of the bottle I thought about taking two. I did not know what two might do. Would I wake up in time for class the next morning? Would my colon relax so much that I'd lose bowel control? The possibilities were not pleasant.

I went back to bed and tried to get back to sleep. I wondered if being so far away from Denver was a good thing. I was not sure that it was bad. I did not know if Sharon would let me help her anyway. I didn't really know what I could do, except to send Sharon positive thoughts and prayers.

All night I heard her howling. I was tuned into her enough that I was certain it was not just something imagined but reality. This was not the voice of the townspeople, at least not in the foreground.

After several nights of this, I decided to tell Sharon's soul that if she wanted to come to visit again that I was all right with it—if indeed it would help. In return she had to promise that she would work on trying to make things better for herself in waking as well as in sleep. I would not feel then as if she were using the soul travel as a substitute for being in her own body. God knows, on many levels I would have loved keeping her consciousness there with me.

I had read, however, that in such cases where the soul really longs to leave its body the body often becomes inhabited by some other soul, or souls, not meant to be there. Some literature called them *walk-ins*, and said that such phenomena account for some marked personality changes in the person that has had the walk-in. Of course, there were other, purely psychological, explanations.

I was no longer sure that I believed in God in the traditional way that so many believe in Him. The souls of people did appear to live on after death. I had too many experiences to deny that, not just with Sharon who was living, but to a lesser extent her grandmother and even the soul of my own grandfather just before he died and my own grandmother on a couple of occasions after she was dead. I had also had a few experiences with Jesus and Mary and a couple of angels over my lifetime.

I say Jesus because I recognized him as Friend and Lord. I would not have dreamed of disrespecting him or his high position in the scheme of things. So in some ways—perhaps in many—the risen Jesus was indeed the risen Christ to me: he was bigger, more than the mere earthly personage named Jesus.

Even Paul suggests that all of creation moves toward a cosmic Christ, one who fills the entire universe with purpose, for God is ultimately to become all in all, some sort of web in which all creation is meant to participate. Change one part of it, and the other aspects also change, even subtly for all of us share in his *carmen*, his poem, his song that is being composed and sung. That was probably what the ancient church had meant in the Apostles Creed when we affirm our belief in the communion of saints, both the living and the dead. For different dimensions impinge upon one another.

But did a personal God actually will what was to happen, who was to be saved as well as who was to be damned? Did God act like some sort of Middle Eastern Despot?

I did not know. I certainly did not like that idea. Was grace given only to some? That seemed too restrictive. I preferred a God who granted grace to all who were willing, who even made the smallest attempt to receive it. Would Sharon be able to do so?

Still, those old questions of fate versus free will troubled me. Sharon surely had not been damned.

God has always been out to smash our idols, our rituals, our rules. Perhaps our notions of reality, of how things work, had to be broken down too, so that only reality—love— remains. Since Christ above all has been held to be love, this was perhaps the reason that my own experiences always pointed to him, the fulfillment of all signs, the way that all signs must be read.

Even then I did not know exactly what I was theorizing, for in certain lights everything looks dim. We see through a glass darkly. Yet my experiences with the souls of the living and the dead remained. My experiences with the risen Christ lay at the center.

And that left me still a Christian. But a Christian without rigid dogma, or ritual, or creed, except for guidance. "When I was a child I spoke as a child," Paul writes to the Corinthians. "Sharon, I hope you can hear me," I said, consciously calling out to her. "'Faith, hope, and charity, these three abide. Yet faith and hope, when we shall see face to face, will pass away,' writes Paul. 'Love only will remain.'"

Love

That fall, I had designed a course, titled, *Love in the Western World*. In it, we would examine some of the central love themes of western literature. I began a section on devotion to the Virgin Mary, by saying, "The Middle Ages went through a humanizing process because of devotion to Mary and Christ. This humanist thrust culminated in the Renaissance, when many discoveries were made. Much of the exploration turned Christianity on its head, splitting it into various and often warring factions, and turning more and more people away from religion altogether."

I purposely avoided the term, "the *Virgin* Mary," because I knew that would enrage the strident Protestants of the area, who rejected the idea of calling Mary a Virgin, since they didn't believe it, not after the birth of Jesus. Jesus had brothers, was their argument. She didn't remain a Virgin, as Catholics believed.

"We'll now look at some medieval lyrics to Mary. They're lovely poems in their own right. They're also deceptively simple embodiments of deeper truths," I said.

Karen, one of my female students angrily interrupted. "Reading this crap is idolatry. It's totally unbiblical to put Mary on a pedestal like that."

"I see," I said, pausing, thoughtfully. I paced the class a bit. "What do the rest of you think?" I was hoping to get others involved in what could become a good discussion where everyone gained some insight.

With a huff, Karen crossed her arms on her chest. "I refuse to participate. I expect other Christians to follow. Stand up for what's right," she ordered. "Let's be Biblical around here, instead of thinking anything goes." She stood up.

I tried another angle. "We really do need to know something of history, something of the traditions to which Western Culture is indebted. It doesn't matter whether we personally believe the doctrines or not," I said. "It is important that we are able to consider seriously thoughts that may be foreign to our way of thinking, especially when they've proved historically important."

"I don't care," Karen said, again taking the limelight. "True Christians should stay away from poison. I won't allow it." By this time, a couple of her friends, both female, were also siding with her. They nodded their heads, and said, "We agree." They stood too and kept interrupting, no matter how many different approaches I tried.

After several attempts to go forward, I threw up my hands in despair. Karen and friends would not let me speak. "I am really disappointed in some of you. Refusing to let your classmates consider various views is not higher education. Whatever you personally believe, I have greater expectations of you than you've shown tonight." I could hardly even hear myself speak because of the uproar the dissidents were causing.

"We'll see about that," Karen fumed, leading her little band of female Christian soldiers out the door, which slammed behind them. "We're marching to the Dean." I imagined them with their rifles, singing "Onward Christian Soldiers."

I wondered if I would hear something from the administration. In graduate school, I'd referred to the BVM in a class that I taught, just as my Dissertation Director did.

"What are you saying?" Maire, one of my female students, asked. She was enraged. "My brother's a priest. He'll have your hide for this," she threatened.

I explained, "There's nothing sacrilegious about the term. It's found in many Catholic devotionals and calendars. BVM stands for the Blessed Virgin Mary," I said.

"I don't give a rat's ass. It sounds like underwear, and you know it."

If Marie took her complaint further, nothing came of it. I had truth on my side.

I locked up the classroom and left the building to walk across campus to my office. The day had turned dark and cold, with a nasty wind blowing snow in my face.

I had planned in this course also to talk briefly about the Courtly Love tradition as another way of looking at love for a lady—albeit a lady married not to you but to someone in a higher position—as inspiration to something higher.

The snow was blowing so hard that I could hardly see where I was going. I hoped it stopped before I had to get home that night. I didn't know how I'd get there otherwise. I hadn't ridden my bike. I didn't want to walk it, even though I lived only ten blocks away. "If worse comes to worst, I guess I can stay in my office," I muttered to myself, my jaw growing more and more unable to move.

I decided to cut the Courtly Love section also, not so much because some students might object but because presenting it would paint a lopsided picture of the times. Devotion to one's lady was akin to devotion to the Virgin Mary. Both required putting aside one's selfish desires to devote oneself to the one that one adored, that is, worshipped, venerated. It too held religious overtones.

As I thought more about it, I wondered if the students really would object to learning about the Courtly Love tradition. I hit something. It was a bench. I didn't fall, just bruised my knee.

They'd go berserk over the idea of venerating and worshipping one's lady, so I'd have to avoid those terms, dishonest intellectually as that would be. But many in the college, both males and females, seemed hooked on soap operas. The giant screen TV in the Student Center wall aired them all day long. There was always a crowd hanging on every lurid word and scene. Did Karen and her friends object to those and mount protests to get the channels changed or blocked? I wondered.

If Karen went to the Dean, surely he would be smart enough to know I was right and support me. But knowing administrators close attention to the bottom line, I knew that one could never be sure of that.

I stumbled into something. This time it was a student, also trying to make it somewhere. I apologized. She apologized. I realized it was a female—I hadn't been able to tell before she spoke. For a moment, we held onto each other, propping the other up then, tried to trudge in opposite directions.

Somehow, teachers were supposed to be good, and popular, or at least non-wave-making. This was especially true in a homogenous community that held itself superior to Catholics forced to dwell in the unblessed lands outside.

Finally. I made it to the English Department and the security of my office. My face felt frozen, not to mention the very fingers of my gloves, iced stiff by now.

By late afternoon, the snow had lessened, and the wind died down to a breeze. My American Literature I Class was able to look at major Puritan Writings and see that, although Christian, the Puritans were Christians of a very narrow and intense variety. These students were upper level. The class had only eight members instead of twenty. They enjoyed comparing the Puritan founders with the more moderate to liberal Christians who came from the Reformed Tradition as most of them did. In fact, it was not unusual to find criticisms of the neighboring Reformed Church members in Puritan writings. My students liked to joke about the more literalistic, strict brands of Christianity, then, and now, since we were experiencing a lot more of it again.

I turned to Nancy, one of my female students who often quipped with me and others. She liked her perfume, necklaces, and ear rings. "You'd better stop wearing those vain adornments," I said. "You know you're mocking God and acting like a heathen."

"Worse than that, if we're to believe the Puritans," she said.

I was able to bring alive the anxieties of those who believed that God has ordained every step of our lives and dictated every action, even the types of clothing and adornments that his faithful must wear.

I turned to others in the class and said, "Don't you agree? Women's adornment is to be long hair, with covered limbs, and a properly submissive attitude to their husbands, as before God."

"A couple of the males caught on and said, "Yes. Submission. We demand it. That's Biblical."

We enjoyed a good laugh. I figured that more than a few of them had heard about my hopeless attempts to teach lyrics in honor of the Virgin Mary that morning. "That kind of thinking goes over well in today's culture, doesn't it?" I paused. "Those dress codes seem pretty petty, at least in the minds of many Christians today."

"Lots of things do, especially to Reformed Church Christians," Neal, a tall blond son of a pastor from Holland remarked.

"Most Christians have dropped such views," I said, "though fundamentalist-leaning types would take us back there."

I thought for a moment, my hand over my mouth. "Yes, this was a good teaching moment. Few Christians nowadays seriously believe that women who wear men's clothing, for instance, ought to be taken out and stoned, as Leviticus commands. Nor did we believe that clothing made of more than one fiber is an abomination before God. Many love their scavenger shrimp and cloven footed pork, 'the other white meat,' as the pig farmers in the area tout it. Mmm, mmm, mmm. After all, this is pork country."

"The Bible beaters raise more pigs than the Reformed Church members," Neal remarked. "They take the Bible literally when their leaders say to."

"Only then," Suzie added. "Remember, Dr. Jones, your Western Lit class is held in Vander Mutton Hall."

I laughed. "I hadn't thought of that. A bad sign."

"Baa baa," Neal said, making the noise of a sheep.

"Leviticus, a very strange book to most of us, says that parents ought to take disobedient children out beyond the city gates and stone them to death," I said, and laughed. "I wonder how many of us would be alive today if our parents had followed that advice."

"I would be, but Leviticus *is* a very strange book," Suzie said.

"I'm not sure if you're being serious about being such a good child." I laughed. She knew I was joking, as was she.

I pushed my mini-lecture further. "Some Christians have affirmed belief only in the New Testament, that is, the Christian Scriptures, because they believed Yahweh incited too much violence in his name in the Old Testament, which really ought to be called the Hebrew Scriptures, out of respect for Judaism. I know that Jews have a different take, as have mainline, historical Christians. Many takes, actually."

"Whew," Neal said. "I'm going to be a pastor. I don't know if I can handle all these complexities."

I refrained from telling them that Christianity is, in truth, a related, but different, religion. It is not merely the completion of Judaism, as many Christians and "completed Jews" now believe, trying to cobble the two together in unhappy ways—mainly relating to the Second Coming, the so-called Rapture, and so on. That's why we really ought not use the terms, Old and New Testaments, although they are traditional.

Even though these students were fairly advanced, every one of them a decent human being, this concept might be too radical even for them. I kept looking at the faces of my charges. I caught myself more than once wondering if I would be perceived as too liberal, a negative term in some Christian circles. They had forgot the true meanings of liberal—*free, tolerant, generous, open.*

If anyone had objected, I didn't sense it in that class. They were a delight. They knew that men's and women's roles were much more complex than a requirement that women submit to their husbands and other male authorities. I left them with, "Milton writes that wives who are more godly and intelligent than their husbands ought to head their households." I paused. "The caveat is that they be both godly and intelligent."

Gathering up my books, I put on my coat and gloves, and walked out of the building. I caught sight of my bike outside. "I guess I did take it." I grabbed it—we never locked our bikes or cars around town because we didn't need to. It was still snowing. Far too much snow lay the ground to ride. I would walk it home.

I was reminded that teaching, if one is honest and well informed, is a minefield. If you really stretch yourself, and want your students to do likewise, you must provoke.

Suddenly, I remembered that I'd invited Sam and Kathy over for dinner. I had to get the brown rice started, and the chicken in the oven, or dinner would be late.

Over dinner in my kitchen—I had no dining room—Sam pointed out, "Provocation is not considered a good thing in this atmosphere. In fact, we are moving into an era when stirring people to think, and then act on their deep, rather than knee jerk, convictions, is not generally considered good."

"I think you need to be careful," Kathy said. She swallowed a forkful of rice with some chicken. "Your chicken on a bed of mushroom rice is really good."

"It takes some preparation time but it's pretty easy," I said. "Oh where is the Holy Spirit, the Comforter, who pushes us forward, brandishing his sword, implications carried by the term *Comforter* in English?" I intoned.

"He's been turned into some cooing thing, only a dove," Sam said, his voice dripping with sarcasm. He laughed and remarked also on dinner. "We must get the recipe."

"I really don't have one, but I can tell you basically what to do," I said. "It's just brown rice with a big can of mushroom soup and a large diced onion mixed in, then baked in a cake pan with cut up chicken laid out over the top so the juices get absorbed. Oh yes, use salt, pepper, and lots of celery seeds on the chicken and on the rice. That's the secret ingredient."

Kathy nodded. "I think we can manage that."

"Except for terming the Holy Spirit *masculine*, rather than *feminine*," I said, returning to our conversation, "as even the Christian Scriptures seem to indicate, I agree."

"That's the trouble with these paradoxes and inter-related metaphors of religious language," Sam remarked. "They are not mixed metaphors, *per se*. You have to keep them all going at once. It's like juggling, not just a few, but many, balls." Sam paused. "That's close to impossible, even when you're smart, well read, and constantly on your toes."

"The Root of Jesse, which is Jesus, the fruit of the Holy Spirit, and the seed of Abraham," I began. "They're all connected in Christian typology. But then everything is connected, since God is the author of all."

"I am trying to figure out if Kathy is a submissive wife," I said. I glanced at both Kathy and Sam's faces. I was feeling a little provocative.

Sam took a gulp of wine. "We don't worry about those things because we get along. We both submit to God."

"We agree on major issues. If we have a problem, we don't fight about it. We work it out," Kathy said. She looked down at her plate demurely. A face so sweet and kind, I thought. Dark hair, dark hairs, pale skin. No wonder Sam cannot help but adore her.

While Kathy always said something, I noticed that Sam typically took the lead. He was the more intellectual of the pair, although Kathy was by no account uneducated or unintelligent. Nonetheless, I always had the sense that Sam was the head of their household. Kathy propped him up and saw that he took center stage.

Nothing wrong with that. I liked and respected them both. They made a great couple. It worked for them.

As Sam and Kathy said goodnight, ready to trudge home in the snow, they thanked me "For the food and fellowship."

"Be careful. I know you both walk on ice better than I, but it's awful."

"We'll let you show us how to walk on water," Sam said, waving goodbye.

I laughed. I had to admit, thinking, as always of Sharon, that I liked more intensity and interaction in my relationships. Not war. Not craziness, but the passion sparked by deep interfacing. To me, that was an outworking of struggling with texts, of learning to read signs properly—of wrestling with the angel of the Lord. By that, I gained a strong and true sense of self.

Eggshells and Families

I could talk with Sam and Kathy about many of the more complex issues that dogged the college, and, especially, the community. They too had been outsiders, although Sam held a tenure track position. I knew he was a better fit than I. He had a wife, who was lovely in temperament as well as physically, and a baby on the way. He was a small man, with a pleasant, intelligent manner. He loved to joke in a folksy way. The students, and more than a few faculty, perceived him as cuddly, sort of teddy bearish. They loved the idea of his holding a baby, as we all knew he would. Sam's coming from a fundamentalist background, although he had moved beyond it denominationally, had enabled him to fit in with the more conservative elements. Sam was more sympathetic to their mindset and chief concerns than I. He also hadn't been burned by marrying one of them when he was young and callow.

As I got to know him better, I saw that Sam, as I'd intuited, still carried patriarchal authority around with him. While he gave his parents trouble over their narrow mindedness, he was careful to avoid being too controversial, too provocative, in the larger sphere. I wondered if he would have taught those medieval lyrics in honor of the Virgin Mary.

"Probably not, at least not until I had tenure," he said, when I told him about my very unpleasant classroom experience over a week before. He'd heard nothing about it, so we assumed nothing would come of it.

"But you have tenure that you can obtain," I said.

"And you need to worry about getting another job, one with tenure, we'll hope" he said. We were standing in the hallway that stood between our offices, talking. "If Sharon comes to visit during the holidays, you shouldn't let her stay at your place," Sam advised.

I'd told him and Kathy a little about Sharon by then. We'd quickly become close, so I figured I could trust them. They weren't gossips, like so many around town.

Joel and I stuffed our back packs with books and papers that we'd need, turned off the lights in our offices, and closed our doors. I grabbed my trusty bike from the foyer downstairs where it would stay warm and dry, so it didn't freeze my butt if I had to ride. I'd walk it home beside Sam, as I often did when we left together. It was wonderful to live within ten blocks of work. October was upon us, and we'd already had three snowstorms. Little snow remained on the sidewalks and pavement. Only patches lay on the grass.

To make Sharon stay somewhere else seemed prudish, since so many faculty and students were actively engaged in sexual pursuits and seemed addicted to sex-laden TV shows and movies. I'd even jokingly asked, my manner innocent, the owner of one of the local video stores, "Um, where do you keep the porn?"

"In the cellar below," he said, pointing to a trap door in the floor. Even though joking, he might have meant it, for all I knew. Little was coming to surprise me.

"People still talk about that incident and say you were looking to rent porn," Sam said. "I just tell them you've watched all of it anyway." He laughed.

"Right. Crucifixion is scheduled for tomorrow at ten a.m.," I said. "Have you heard that people who want to rent porn drive over to adjacent towns, especially Catholic hamlets, to get it? There, store owners assure everyone, with prominently displayed signs, that people who rent there are guaranteed confidentiality."

"Yes, you pointed that out when we drove over to rent some movies, since we can't do that in this place," Sam said. He shook his head. "Ted, you must learn not to see what you see."

"Can I at least comment on it?" I asked. Then I laughed.

Sam shook his head. "I honestly don't know about you sometimes."

I checked some of those stores out on my own. I noted carefully the people whose identities I knew going and coming from the stores. They looked in every direction before they darted in and came back out, with carefully clutched, opaque, plastic bags that hid the contents inside. If they saw someone else whom they knew in the stores, they wouldn't say a word, not even hello. This was but one more shared secret.

When I explored the attic above my apartment one day, thinking I'd store a couple of boxes up there, I discovered a large cache of porno tapes, magazines, and books, along with an old rotary dial phone that must have weighed ten pounds. The porn wasn't all heterosexual. I wondered if I should throw it away or pretend not to have found it. Because I didn't know where to dump it, I decided not to say anything.

At the beginning of November, Sharon finally called at night, after months of saying nothing.

The weather outside was bitterly cold. Ice was everywhere. I'd fallen three times already, landing on my back and even hitting the back of my head. Only the day before, splayed out on the black ice of the parking lot behind the house, I came close to passing out.

"I'm seeing a new therapist, one who specializes in my issues," Sharon said. "I'm making progress."

"I'm glad to know that. Do you want to tell me more?" I asked, grabbing the tube of Minit- Rub, and slathering in on my lower back and my neck.

"I'll tell you more later. I want to remain upbeat."

"Have you talked with Dan?" I asked. I rubbed ointment up into the back of my skull, still sore from the latest fall. I liked the smell. It opened my sinuses. "He's worried about you too."

"He and I are talking about driving over for the Christmas holidays," Sharon said. "If that's all right with you. Rick has to be out of town."

I was happy, excited, and also anxious about seeing Sharon and Dan. The conflicting emotions were strongest around Sharon. In fact, as I looked inside myself, I would be happy to see Dan without any reservations.

"It may seem old fashioned, but you don't want to present an untoward picture of your private life," Sam again advised over dinner in the dining room of his home. "Sharon is welcome to stay with us when she comes to visit. Your friend Dan comes along, he can stay with you. Heck, he could even share your bed, and people wouldn't give it another thought."

I waited for the punch line. I almost laughed. But one didn't seem to come. "Well, since it's me,' I said, "people would probably manage to make something of it, somewhere down the line anyway."

Kathy nodded. "You know, I hate to say it, but I think you're right."

Sam had bought a nice bottle of white wine to go with the chicken on a bed of rice that he and Kathy had prepared, following my instructions.

"This is very good," I said. "Tastes like mine. The wine looks excellent too. At my house we drink what I have," I said, sniffing the bouquet of the wine that Sam poured in my glass.

"To life," he toasted, clinking his glass against mine and Kathy's.

If Sam and Kathy had known about Sharon's drug problems, would they have been so welcoming? I'd not said anything about that to them or anyone in town. I did, however, warn Sam and Kathy in a general way that, because of Sharon's problems, she was not terribly reliable. "Her issues are multiple and serious," I explained. "Her priest molested her when she was a child."

"Oh my," Kathy said. She put down her wine glass. "I've only heard of that happening."

"That is bad," Sam said. He filled our glasses.

"If they don't make it, you know you won't spend the holidays on your own," Kathy said. She passed around braised chicken breasts, brown rice, and spinach salad. "We'd better eat so we don't get drunk."

"You're welcome to join our family" Sam said. "If my parents are around, they probably won't try to convince you to give up your idolatrous beliefs, starting with Christ's Real Presence in communion."

"I should hope not," I said, remarking on the excellent flavor of the chicken. "I might have to convince them that interpretation of Jesus' words ought to start on the literal level. After all, they're literalists, aren't they?"

"Not when it comes to communion. That is merely commemorative," Sam said. His mother was always attacking his "newfangled 'Popish' beliefs and ways." I could spend time with Sam and Kathy comfortably, especially if I avoided contact with Sam's parents. I'd been invited to dinner with several other families and felt more than a little out of place. These were not unintelligent people, but I knew that my views and experiences were just not in the same arena as theirs.

Even if I were further out than Sam and his family, I didn't feel that I could shock them too easily. After all, Sam had read widely and held a Ph.D. from the University of Massachusetts. Although rather Victorian in his personal views—Victorian literature was his area of specialization—he was capable of entertaining other notions. Besides, every scholar knew that the Victorians were, in fact, not the prudes they seemed. Pornography and prostitution had flourished in Victorian England.

Sam and Kathy kept their house at sixty-eight degrees, just as I kept my town home in Denver. I wasn't used to such low inside temperatures anymore. I was glad I'd worn a sweater.

Open as I was with Sam and Kathy, the psychic connections that Sharon and I shared were not, however, something that I'd told them of. Although St. Paul speaks of being with his brethren in spirit and even of seeing what they are up to from a distance, as if doing psychic traveling or remote viewing himself, many evangelical and fundamentalist Christians throw a blanket of condemnation over such behavior. They've personally had no experience like it themselves, nor have they known anyone who did—except for those whom they've decided are "of the devil."

In my *Love in the Western World* course, I'd assigned *The Color Purple*. Doug had recommended that I assign it. "It's an especially good book for these students," he told me when I consulted him on the phone, as I sometimes did, since he was the real Department Chairman. "I manage to teach it at least once a year, and in various courses."

Once again, the hackles of "the Biblical women," as I'd begun calling them, were raised. "My God in heaven, this book is filth," Karen exclaimed, tossing the book across the room. Her friend Martha followed. The two of them stomped out, fewer than had followed the first time.

"I wish you'd stay away," I muttered. This time, I did not dismiss class. I went on, trying to continue with our discussion.

"Ted, some of your students got riled up over your teaching *The Color Purple*, not just because of the sex, which is everywhere, starting graphically on page one," Sam said, trying to help me understand the outrage that others in the community were expressing, "but, even more, because Celie affirms a belief in God but does not specify exactly which God she is speaking of."

"The god, or gods, of her ancestors, of course," I said. "You know people of African heritage, always up to something suspicious—voodoo, Santeria, and other deviltry."

Sam laughed.

Kathy dismissed herself to use the bathroom. Even though she was pregnant, she reminded me of a nature spirit—tall—and I could imagine her as thin.

"Since Walker does not affirm standard Christian doctrines and practices, and she thanks everyone in the book for coming, signing herself author and *medium*, some people believe her God is not just an idol, or figment of her imagination, but Satan himself. To make things worse, Celie, like Walker, has had lesbian experiences, and neither has renounced them."

"Oh," I replied, rather vacantly. "I didn't give it much thought. I do, however, remember the stir that had been caused by the very first page, the graphic descriptions of how Celie's dad, or so she thinks at the time, molests her, gets her pregnant twice, and then kills her babies."

"That's so perverse," Sam said.

I hoped Kathy would return soon. I wondered if we'd have dessert. Often we didn't.

Even though Walker had won many prizes for her novel, including the Pulitzer, Sam did not like the book himself, so he was not terribly sympathetic. He knew that, like Doug, I liked the novel and felt that it was especially good for that community. Incest was not unheard of there as well, from all that various colleagues and my pastor friend had told me. I'd read that one could expect it in communities that are essentially closed—that is, suspicious of outsiders and all they bring with them.

"Being provocative is not considered a virtue in communities like this," Sam reminded me. He told me this fairly often. "There's a little wine left. It was a big bottle. Do you want it?" he asked.

"No, thanks, I'm feeling what I've already drunk."

Sam poured the rest into his glass.

"No wonder so many around here stoke up on anti-depressants," I said.

"I know a good doctor. He doesn't tell the insurance company what he's prescribed. Nor does the pharmacist that he sends you to," Sam said, his voice edged with sarcasm. "That way you can get life insurance and no one has to know that you've got a history of depression."

"And when you have your fatal accident, your loved ones, and cherished institutions, can get your life insurance," Karen remarked, as she sat back down at the table.

I guessed how the script went. "I suppose the community also colludes over birth control pills and devices, keeping silent about those."

Neither Sam nor Karen said anything. They let various cats out of bags, but there was always a little reticence in going too far, too soon. Strong as it felt, our friendship was still gelling.

The next frigid afternoon, as Sam and I were walking home together, one of the families rumored to be stricken with inbreeding among close relatives passed by in their beat-up Dodge pickup truck. Two of the four children were said to be retarded as a result. Not long before, Karen had told about them. If I hadn't heard about this family from Karen, who was non-judgmental, I was sure I'd soon have heard about it from Ann Van Haag or someone else. From Ann, it would have been broached as some juicy secret that she could hardly wait to tell me, on the QT of course.

The entire town was full of such covenants of public silence based upon the will to overlook each others' scandals. But privately, people loved nothing better than to gossip about the various scandals, some imagined, some real. I kept getting glimpses of the real script, the actual playbook used by the major players here.

"You're awfully quiet," Sam said.

"My jaw is cold," I said. "The weather is giving me jaw aches."

Again, I was not sure that this hadn't been the case in my own hometown. Perhaps my family was too much out of the loop socially to make me aware of this when I was growing up. It was also possible that our secrets did not have to be so carefully guarded from public display because we did not share the same degree of religiosity that pervaded this community.

In my hometown, Protestants and Roman Catholics lived side by side. My great aunt had managed to rid me of all my early girlfriends, who were Catholic, by telling me that they worshipped idols and would not make it to heaven because they were not true Christians. They believed in the necessity of good works for salvation, which was wrong. "Salvation is solely by faith. They plan to take over the world by having many many children and following the Pope's orders," she would whisper. Her eyes would glance round us to make sure the Catholics weren't picking up their pitchforks and shovels right then.

However, most of my townsfolk were fairly tolerant, even though perhaps a little suspicious of the rituals and beliefs of the other. My mother and my grandmother had often extolled the value of tolerance, for they said that they believed in a God who looked on the heart and judged us accordingly. "If the heart was right, trying to do good, then God would surely not turn someone away, no matter what he professed," my grandmother had said. I knew she spent her life trying to get away from the fundamentalism of her own father, who was more than a little judgmental.

"Religion," I said, glancing at Sam, "I sometimes think it does more harm than good."

"Better not to voice that opinion around here," Sam warned me. At the corner, he turned to walk to the right toward his home, while I moved straight ahead toward mine. Without Sam beside me, I could lend my entire imagination to Sharon. I wondered often now, if this time our love would finally be able to manifest, even with Dan around.

Making Music

Three days later, Ann Van Haag, stood in the kitchen downstairs in Vander Mutton Hall. She wanted to talk about Shakespeare's sonnets. "I love teaching them. They're so interesting," she said. "I can't imagine that Shakespeare was homosexual, as some gay activists are trying to say. He loves the young man."

"So love can't go with being gay?" I asked.

"Well, he cares too much about the young man. Auden says that in the introduction of the textbook I use." Ann held her coffee cup in her right hand and tried discreetly to stick her little finger into her nostril, not an unusual gesture for her.

She remarked, "Our denomination has been lucky. We haven't had to deal with the issue of homosexuality, as many denominations do, at least not in ways more than theoretical. We don't have homosexuals—at least not here, in rural Iowa. The cities are different; we know that. So are our liberal denominational colleges." Hardly pausing for breath, as if pressed to get all her words out, she added, "A couple of them even have homosexuals on faculty, and homosexuals who live with their gay partners, making no bones about it."

"It's nice and sunny today," I remarked looking outside. I hoped to distract her from her usual hodgepodge logic. Ann had married a local man and taught at the college for at least two decades, with only an M.A. She was one of the more provincial faculty, although she considered herself hip. She wore bright clothes that she thought lit her up and never hesitated to dispense her wisdom like little sugar-coated pills.

"Well I'd better go prepare for class," she said, looking at her watch. By the way, you have a birthday coming up next week. "We always have cake and drinks, like coffee and punch," she added. Do you prefer chocolate or white?"

"I don't really eat cake, except for some carrot cake now and then," I said. "Too much sugar and unrefined flour. But thanks for the thought. The rest of you are welcome to eat cake on my behalf." I didn't drink punch for similar reasons, though I didn't tell her.

Ann excused herself, and I sighed a breath of relief.

Of all the English teachers, Ann had been appointed Acting Chair because no one else wanted the job. "She likes administration. It appeals to her need for power," Doug, with a wink, told me a couple of hours later. We were alone in his, now my, closed office. He'd made a quick trip back to get more of his books. I noticed he concentrated on the ones in his closet.

"When Ann's friends trust you enough to tell you they feel sorry for her husband and sons, you'll understand why." Doug pushed his glasses up on his nose, grabbed a box of books, and lugged them out to his truck. I wondered if he had *City of the Night* in the box. I hadn't yet read it.

These people were far from innocent—they'd had serial affairs, some even adulterous. Some also had homosexual dalliances. I was sure of that. I'd heard talk. I'd seen signs. They were no more monogamous than the rest of humanity. I suspected that Peter De Vries's send-ups of Midwestern swingers, many of whom were religious, were more fact-based than many in the area wanted to acknowledge. Some of the faculty admitted that he'd been educated by the most prominent college of their sister denomination. "We're not too happy with him," Ann told me, though she'd never read anything he'd written. Her favorite work was written by one of her students. "He wrote an essay arguing that women had every right to flatulate in public, just like men," she said proudly. "It's the funniest piece I've ever read."

I'd never met so many gossips as I'd met there. Ann was all too typical. Ann chalked the tittle-tattle up to Midwestern friendliness. I was by nature friendly and outgoing. But I also believed in trying to lead people onward and upward. The complexity of the Holy Spirit as Comforter was real to me. So I was provocative at times. The true image of the Comforter, as C. S. Lewis points out, is to lead us, drive us, onward with the sword of the Spirit that pares truth from deception. True religion forces us to *see* ourselves. That included myself. I knew and owned that fact.

Hoping that Ann wouldn't catch me again, I planned to slip out of the office. I opened my office door and met Vern Strong, one of the music faculty members, with his dad, Vern Senior. He was visiting from Grand Rapids. Vern was introducing him around the college. Standing in the hall, Vern Senior began expressing his opinions about everything—the bad sexual mores of people everywhere, the threats posed by abortion and gays, stupid television shows, and corrupt media that spins everything in liberal directions.

Everywhere I turned, peoples' family issues were rearing their heads. Vern Senior didn't seem to care a bit whom he offended. His son had always struck me as friendly and thoughtful, never one to buttonhole. Vern Senior treated Vern, older than I by twenty years, as if he were still an adolescent with no rights, no intellectual development, of his own. "If you don't agree with me, you're a moron," he said, after one of his pronouncements. I'd stopped my ears after Vern Senior's first few sentences, so I wasn't sure which one he referred to.

I knew I was subconsciously imagining myself with my dad twenty years hence. No growth, no discernable development on his part, and seeing me still as an extension of himself, like everything else.

"You look upset," Vern commented. "Why's that?"

"I don't know." I shrugged.

Vern prodded, as if not believing me. His dad kept opining to the others he'd nabbed in the hallway. He'd gathered a small crowd around him as if he stood at the Speaker's Corner in Hyde Park. He was now oblivious to Vern's and my conversation.

I made something up. "I'm worried about my mom. Her blood pressure is out of control again. It gets that way." While that often happened, it wasn't going on at present, at least not that I'd heard of.

"Oh," Vern said, "my mom has that too." I could imagine his mother dying and his being left to care for his dad. Vern's life would become a real hell.

I excused myself. "I have to get busy. Nice to meet you, Mr. Strong." I walked into my office and closed the door. I felt like slamming the furniture around. I'd pretty much distanced myself from my dad some years before. We got nowhere. I felt as if I were hitting my head against a wall year after year after year of trying to get through to him.

Because my adrenaline was high, I decided to try walking it off by leaving my office and trekking the length of town before heading home.

No one, in all my years, had so completely brought up my father issues the way Vern Senior had done. I could not figure out why Vern didn't put him in his place. He was probably trying to obey the commandment that children ought to honor their mothers and fathers that their days be long in the land (I'd never memorized them according to their proper order myself—too rote for me). Standing up to our parents when they are wrong was, in my mind, giving them honor. You cannot honor someone by kowtowing and fearing to express your own beliefs. Of course, trying to do that had not gotten me any further than it got Vern.

Oh, no, George Beverly Shea was blasting from the First Christian Church again, this time with "Onward Christian Soldiers."

No wonder I was so upset. I saw my future unfolding before me. Vern was divorced himself. He'd not been married long, I'd heard.

I was not advocating taking out the hunting knife and slitting our parents' throats, no matter how much we felt like it, but letting our parents know that we were grown up and they too had to behave like grownups. If God didn't like it and cut short our day, as the fundamentalists loved to warn, so be it. It was all about control—of others more than oneself.

The images such thoughts painted made me laugh, especially when I realized that another church, The First Alliance, was playing "I come to the garden alone, while the dew is still on the roses," from their loudspeaker. It was not so strident as the Fist Christian's hymn, nor was the volume eardrum-bursting. It sounded plaintive and sad. "Jesus walks with me and he talks with me and he tells me I am his own." I lingered a moment there, now that I was starting around the periphery of town.

I didn't have father-son issues with God, even when two of the Trinity were presented as Father and Son. I didn't know why that didn't bother me, but it didn't. If I was wrong, I expected God to correct me. If I didn't like what God was doing, I also felt free to let him know it. If I didn't understand, I let God know that too. Our relationship was much better than the one I had with my earthly father. But my God listened. He didn't think I was but an unthinking extension of himself. Milton's Son was merely an extension of the Father either, I recalled, an important observation that I made in my book. Milton is always taking the traditions and making them his own, individualizing everything.

My approach to sacred texts was similar. I walked past another Reformed church. It was silent, without a loudspeaker than I could tell. So what if the Bible contained various stories glued together from many sources, some more seamlessly than others? So what if the scriptures spoke with differing voices, which in some manner echoed the one Word, God? So what if the writers got some facts wrong, or even contradicted one another in their many and varied attempts to speak of the ineffable? Did these problems invalidate their attempts?

Only if you had to believe the Bible was perfect, without error, without contradiction, at least in the original version, a caveat favored by evangelical Christians. I could argue with the texts and wrestle with the angel of the Lord, just as Jacob and the Jews did. I could look for the patterns and find the wisdom embedded in such texts.

All these family issues, along with my other difficulties, threatened to open up like a giant sinkhole and swallow me. I wanted to change these folks, just as I wanted to change my family. I knew that desire stemmed from my being brought up to save all those family members who didn't really want to be saved at all. The first child's double bind.

Near my apartment, I saw Mr. Tan, the nickname I'd given the faculty member who walked the town, day and night, winter, summer, spring, and fall. He was striding awfully near the windows of the apartment building across the street. Now and then he stooped to pick up a paper cup or plastic bag in the bushes. With no sense of irony, Ann always said he was helping to keep things around town clean.

I walked up the stairs to my apartment. I looked at my watch. Three hours later, my anger had lessened. I no longer wanted to slit someone's throat. I looked forward to Sharon and Dan driving back for Christmas. At worst, we would give people more to talk about, lighten up their winter doldrums.

I doubted that anyone there would suspect Dan was gay. If Sharon were on her best behavior, people would think she was great. After all, she was beautiful and could be charming. She had to be warned, however, not to tell anyone she was Catholic, lapsed or whatever she was at the time. As an Episcopalian, I was too close to Roman Catholic myself, according to the gossip I'd heard.

No wonder I looked forward to their visit with a strong mix of jubilation and anxiety.

Thanksgiving

The day before Thanksgiving, Dan and Sharon drove to Iowa together. They'd told me, only days before, that they were coming, not for Christmas, but for Thanksgiving. I wasn't sure they'd make it. Dan could be counted on, but not Sharon. They left early that morning. The weather all the way from Denver to Iowa was supposed to be clear and sunny. They ought to make good speed, though the drive still took nine hours if you stopped only for gas and the restroom.

"Don't drive too fast," I cautioned Sharon on the phone at six a.m.. "I don't want to hear that you've been wiped out."

"Dan will drive," she laughed. I'm always in a hurry."

Although they would soon be on their way, I still wondered if something would come up to keep Sharon from making it. That seemed her pattern. I knew it all too well from Egypt the previous year. If she couldn't come, would Dan drive out alone? I wanted him to, but I wouldn't blame him if he got cold feet. He wasn't as adventurous as I.

I'd spent holidays alone before, so I could handle it. Sam and Kathy had issued an open invitation, "Just in case you need it."

At five in the afternoon, I greeted Sharon and Dan at the outer door downstairs. "This is the arctic!" Dan said.

"Get inside. It's like the Sahara in here."

They refused to take off their coats yet. They shivered from the cold, but both of them looked well.

"We left at seven, stopped only to get gas and use the bathroom, and the drive still took forever," Sharon said, huffing up the stairs to my apartment. "I've got to go to the bathroom," she said, taking off to the destination I pointed out.

"Sure is colder than Denver," Dan said.

Be glad everything isn't covered with black ice, or you'd be down on your backs," I said. I asked Dan where Rick was spending his holidays.

Dan ignored my query. As far as I could tell, he and Rick were still together.

"This place, your apartment, is certainly quaint. Fixtures dating to farmhouse of the 1950s," Sharon said. "Is anyone here in the 80s?"

"Well, I'm certainly glad for a breath of fresh air," I said. "This place can be stifling. At least I know you both can be critical with me."

"Along with you?" Sharon asked. She smiled.

I knew she was teasing. My feelings about her were mixed, I realized. I wanted to see her, and more—yet I didn't. She complicated everything, and had from the beginning.

"We've noticed all the religiosity," Dan said. "You can't escape it." He'd already taken note of the hymns blaring from the First Christian Church. "George Beverly Shea, no less."

"I think it's even worse than visiting my ex-wife's parents," I said. "The old mother in law just played that crap on her stereo all the livelong day."

"No wonder you got a divorce," Sharon said. "I noticed all the little wooden shoes and tulip motifs everywhere. Oh yes, and the cutesy lace curtains on all the windows."

"Don't forget the little wooden windmill standing in the park," Dan said.

We went to the kitchen to stand near the stove. We could smell the turkey and stuffing, the baked potatoes and scalloped corn in the oven. I poured us each a big glass of red wine.

"What's going on with you and Rick?" I asked Dan.

After gulping most of the glass, Dan said, "Rick's spending the long weekend at some Body Electric Workshop in San Francisco."

"I've read of those workshops. Rick'll come back with a whole kit of new sexual techniques," I said. "They center on Tantric Sexual Practices. Energy work is very powerful."

"I'd be happy if we just enjoyed some plain vanilla sex for a change," Dan complained.

"You mean he's too wild for you?" Sharon teased. She opened the oven to check on the turkey. "Looks quite done to me," she said.

"I'd like to say I've been done too," Dan said. "We hardly have sex at all, now we're a committed couple," Dan said.

"That's hardly unusual," I said. "Besides, what makes you special? Do you think I'm getting all kinds of sex here?"

"Don't leave me out." Sharon said, shooting me a fiery look. "The last sex I had was with you, way back last summer."

"Rick and I both feel so guilty about being gay, and having so-called unnatural sex, we've almost stopped having a sexual relationship. At least with each other," Dan remarked.

"You mean you're swinging?" I asked. Having just read another De Vries novel, the term was on the tip of my tongue.

"*I'm* not," Dan retorted.

Sharon and I knew what that meant. We looked at each other and away again.

"I hold out hope that the weekend retreat is Rick's attempt at trying to revive the sexual relationship between you and him," I said.

"He might be learning how to get better at sex so he can dump me," Dan remarked.

Again, Sharon and I looked at each other. Dan had a point. We all knew it. I felt as if Sharon and I were functioning as a couple. I was feeling much warmer toward her now, and she toward me. I touched her hand. She played with my fingers.

I could feel my heart chakra opening and flowing into hers, and back. It was as if we'd taken up where we left off—not just in the physical but in the soul realm.

At dinner, Sharon slipped off her shoes. She rubbed her feet on my legs. "Turkey and stuffing," my kind of repast," she said, smiling. I thought of the meal that Adam and Eve shared in their paradisiacal bower before the Fall. Milton meant it to signify their as-yet unbroken communion with heaven and all of God's creation. "I can hardly wait to get filled again."

Dan and I giggled. He even spit out a little wine.

That night Dan slept on the couch so Sharon could share my bed. Before we went to our real sleeping arrangements, Dan and Sharon made lots of noise in the bedroom. They rolled around on the bed, so the neighbors downstairs would think they were sleeping there. I called out to them in a disgusted voice from the couch in the living room. "Hey you two, stop acting like a couple of rabbits!" I called. I whacked the couch with my fist, as if angry.

"Try pigs. Iowans understand that better!" Sharon called back in a voice that was loud, too loud. She made an orgasmic sound.

Dan grunted.

"Be careful. Van Haags will serve you at their next pig roast," I called.

After acting out a little more of that scenario, we turned out the lights and went on as we'd intended. Dan sneaked out to the couch and I sneaked into the bed. Sharon had pulled off her clothes. Because of the stars filling the clear night sky and the streetlamp located just outside the uncurtained windows, the bedroom was not dark.

I didn't think the floors were so thin that the people living in the apartment below would know my *sotto-voce* was not Dan's. But I didn't dare speak in a normal volume.

"Be careful with my breasts, Sharon told me.

I was already touching them.

"Something might be wrong with my implants."

"Implants?" I asked, drawing my hands back.

"Silicone leaking into the system is dangerous. My breasts have been feeling strange lately," she explained.

"I had no idea," I said. "About the implants."

"I've had a few boob jobs. I've even had work done below." She paused. "You never noticed how shapely I was?"

"Of course, I noticed," I replied, although I knew I hadn't examined her that closely. Her emotional and mental states always distracted from my doing so. Now I was afraid to handle them for another reason. "I've just never known anyone who had surgeries to make herself over."

"You do now," she said.

I kissed her neck and played with her hair. We hadn't been together physically since the springtime revelation in her condo.

"I wish you'd accept yourself as you are." I tried to lose myself in the odor of her perfume. I knew her behavior wasn't unusual, especially for those who'd been sexually abused. "Did Brad think your surgeries were ok?" I whispered.

"He loved them. The first was his idea," Sharon said. "He wanted me to get a boob job. The second time, he hauled me off to the surgeons, even though I hadn't wanted to go. He stood and watched as they sucked out the fat and broke the bones and put in bigger implants and inserts." Sharon paused, letting the details sink in. "Then he hauled me home, telling me how all the pain was worth it. My improved looks made him want to fuck me even before I healed."

I tried not to express what I really felt, although I was certain Sharon felt the disapproval in my tensing muscles.

"It never occurred to you I had implants, did it?" Sharon asked. She played with my penis.

"I'd noticed your breasts were large, but no, I didn't think they'd gotten that way because of surgery," I said. I started to touch them again, lightly, ever so carefully as if they were parchment.

Sharon laughed. She remarked again, "You're so naïve. Such a funny combination of wisdom and insight—and innocence."

I winced.

"Don't worry. I love that about you. Only now and then does the worst occur to you."

"Nowadays, it occurs more and more," I said.

I told Sharon that for Christmas I wanted to teach her some Tantric sex myself. I'd done plenty of reading on it and wasn't naïve about that. I could feel my own energy flows and wanted to practice.

"What do you think we enjoy when our souls are sharing the same body?" she asked.

"I want to enjoy it when we're wearing our bodies too."

"Fair enough," she said. She mounted me and drew the kundalini up like an expert. "It comes naturally to me," she said. "Dan, you really must learn Tantric too," she called. "Dan," she said, "I'm calling you."

In a few minutes the bedroom door opened and Dan was standing beside the bed, asking what she wanted. He seemed wide awake. I wasn't comfortable with his presence. The room was too well lit.

"Don't lose it now," Sharon instructed, tightening her vagina. "Keep the kundalini moving, always upward till it moves out of the crown chakra, then starts again." She paused, and then looked at Dan. "What do you think about my tits? Did you realize I had implants?"

I could tell Dan was embarrassed. Rightly so. He said nothing.

"Well," she asked.

"They're beautiful. I don't think I've ever seen more beautiful breasts on any woman," he muttered, "whatever the reason." I had to wonder if he'd ever seen a woman's breasts before, at least in person.

Dan excused himself, closing the door behind him. I heard his steps move back to the living room.

"You mustn't corrupt him," I said. "If the neighbors haven't realized who's here in the bedroom with you by now, they won't ever," I whispered. I wasn't at all happy about that, and she knew it.

"I don't want to corrupt him either. Believe me," Sharon said.

I felt her hot tears dropping upon my stomach. "Oh Sharon," I said, silently finishing the sentence with, "I just don't know what's to become of you. Or myself."

"I want to be good. I really do." Her voice was anguished.

Christmas

Soon after Sharon and Dan left for Denver, Sharon and I talked on the phone about Christmas plans. "I wouldn't dream of spending Christmas with anyone but you," she said, warmly. "That way you can carry forward your plans of empire—you know, pillaging and plundering," she said. "My doctors have checked out my implants and said you can go right ahead and manhandle them as much as you like."

It was midnight. I'd just gone to bed.

"Is this my Jerusalem? Anyan, and Magellan, and Gibraltar, my southwest discovery, *Per fretum febris*," I mocked, paraphrasing John Donne's "Hymn to God My God, in My Sickness."

Sharon knew the famous lines. "Feeling sick?" she teased.

"I am in bed," I said. "If you don't hurry up and give me someone to pillage and plunder, I'll have to slit my wrists. This place is getting to me. It snows and snows, and isn't melting anymore. They pile it up from the roads and sidewalks wherever they can. Some of the heaps are so high, you can't see over them. There's black ice everywhere. I've never fallen so much in my life."

"I'd hate the weather. Denver's mild, so I can usually handle it," she said.

I raised myself in bed. I suddenly remembered a funny incident. "The other day I was walking through town with Sam. The streets were decorated with crosses and Nativity scenes—strictly Christian symbols. Not even any Santas or reindeers anywhere. We spotted two Buicks, both a few years old. On the cars' back bumpers were pasted what appeared to be new stickers, or at least well kept old ones, with the slogan, *I'm not Fonda Jane,* on them. I had to laugh. 'Where in the hell did those come from?' I asked. 'They look new.'"

"'The owners must have bought crates of them during the War in Vietnam so they could keep replacing them for years to keep the memory going.'"

"'Unbelievable,' I said to Sam."

"'They need reminders of their deep disdain for Jane Fonda and all others who don't support the United States' effort to make the world safe for justice, freedom, democracy, and the American Way,' Sam answered."

Sharon reminded me, "At least you enjoy the friendship of some good people who actually think about issues and try to do the right thing."

"That's true," I replied. "I have to concentrate on those and try to ignore, or at least not pay too much attention, to the rest. Although far from paradise, this place is the most decent, most ethical, of any place I've taught."

"Don't raise your hopes too high," Sharon warned. "I remember Sam's telling you that people there had turned around St. Paul's command 'to be in the world but not of it. Most of these people are of the world but not in it.'"

I laughed. "He's right." I decided to get out of bed and walk around. I was wide awake.

"I'm making no progress in my attempts to bring Father Joe to justice," Sharon said. Her voice switched to gloom. "The Archdiocese is stone walling my efforts," she said. "I'm not sure I want to bring the law into the situation." She paused. "I just don't know why the church can't come to grips with sex and sexuality issues, discipline their own, and see that justice is done."

"I agree. But hypocrisy is so deeply ingrained in the very fabric of the Church—of every denominational stripe—" I began, "that we're asking far more than can be delivered. To be realistic."

Sharon snorted. "I know you're right, but I don't like it."

"I don't think I've told you about my Denver student Jack. He told me of the priest who'd confessed that he'd loved him, and always had, but never acted on it," I said, having been reminded. "Do you realize how difficult it was for Jack to grasp the notion that his priest had been a good man, one who had been honest and kept his vows? Jack would have been more comfortable believing that his priest was somehow superhuman, loving with a love that is noble and ideal, but never sexual."

"I can understand why you have a fever," Sharon said, referring to John Donne's "Hymn to God My God, in my Sickness," from which I'd quoted several minutes before.

"You're trying to reroute the discussion," I said.

"But you mustn't die from that fever," Sharon said. "That he may raise the Lord throws down." She quoted the last line of Donne's poem.

"Evidently you know that poem by heart," I said.

Along the same lines, I recalled a recent incident at the college where Raymond, one of my gay students, told me how he'd been set up and raped by one of the athletes in an adjacent town. Relating this to Sharon, I said, "I told my colleagues about it. The women were most outspoken in their response," I said, "especially Ann. She and Irma said, as if one person, 'he shouldn't have been so open about who he was.' Ann added, 'Raymond spent a year with Up with People and came back bragging to everyone about his newfound sexual orientation.' These colleagues, who professed to be feminists, concurred that he'd been 'Inviting trouble. People know his family,' said Ann. 'They don't like the shame he's brought to the community.'"

"Wow," Sharon exclaimed. "Unbelievable."

I heard her slam into something. "What was that?" I asked.

"I just kicked a hole through my wall," she said. "I really did." She laughed.

I winced. "I asked, 'Would you have been so dismissive if the student had been a woman who'd been set up and raped. Would you have blamed the way she carried herself and dressed and what she said?" I paused. "Their faces didn't change. Ann just stuck the tip of her little finger in her nostril and poked around, as she often does. She's actually conducted an entire department meeting with a bugger hanging from her nose." I paused. "'Failing to grapple honestly and fairly with sexuality goes hand in hand with failing to gain true spirituality,' I told them. 'You remain on the surface, hypocritical, and conflicted, otherwise."

"Good for you," Sharon said.

"I have to pace a little faster," I said. "I can feel the adrenaline pumping. My butt feels like it's clenching."

"That's appropriate. You're talking about pains in the butt," Sharon said. She laughed. "My foot hurts still. I wonder if I should go to the emergency room."

"If it doesn't stop, you'd better," I said. "I don't know if either of the women saw the contradictions in their pseudo-feminism, as Sam terms it, at all. And I don't know that the men in this case did. They said little."

"You're still my hero," Sharon replied. "I can't live without you."

I wasn't sure I believed her, although the sentiment was nice. "Speaking of gay males, what do you know of Dan and Rick?" I poured myself a big glass of water, drank it, and poured another. "Last I heard, they were doing well."

"Well enough to spend the holidays together," Sharon said. "Because their families aren't supportive and don't encourage them to come around, not if they have to be together, they're planning to go to Cancun, or some sunny coastal resort, where they can be anonymous, out, and relaxed," Sharon remarked. "I think the pain is lessening, in my foot, that is."

"My mother wanted me to come home for Christmas," I said. "I reminded her, as I've done for several years, that I don't visit my family on Christmas or any holiday. It wasn't a time of good memories, or of family functionality."

"I know well what you mean," Sharon said. "Besides, you and I have been spending our holidays together."

"Thanksgiving only," I reminded her.

"I intended to be with you in Egypt, I really did," Sharon said.

And Sharon's family, well, we didn't even talk about their holiday plans. As far as I could tell, since Sharon had started agitating against the Catholic Church and her old priest, her mother and the rest of her family were colder flint than ever. I was not sure if Sharon had spoken with her mother for months. I figured Sharon's agitation opened old wounds. That required more denial, more suppression, and threatened to shatter family relations even further.

Yet we all knew, in some very deep and dark place, that wounds never heal until they, and their causes, are brought into the light, lanced, and all the puss is drained.

"Sharon bid me good night and hung up. I'll see you soon, my hero," she said.

I paced the apartment. To live, really live, scares so many people that they're likely to go into hiding and stay there, tugging everyone back into the holes with them. Our ancestors dug them. They're familiar, *of the family*, still.

I glanced out the window at the big pile of snow taking up a third of the parking lot in back.   It was taller than even the pickup back there.

I thought of the little girl in the outhouse pit. While some have nicer outhouses than others, some are used to being thrown into the holes beneath. Sometimes a human being or two hear and come to the rescue of one of those children.

Coming and Going

Sharon arrived at the Omaha airport three days before Christmas. We'd been having blizzards throughout the Midwest. Although the last one was a few days before, and the roads were plowed, Sharon decided not to drive. On the way back to town, I broke the news that she was going to have to stay at Sam and Kathy's.

Out the corner of my eye, I could see her tense up, her hands clenching in her lap. She didn't say anything.

"Dan's presence at Thanksgiving confused people."

"How did they know about him?" she asked.

"People in this town know more than we know about our lives," I said. "Or so they think. Last Sunday, when I went into my office, I happened upon Maire, who teaches French, in the kitchen downstairs. She seemed surprised. She had big curlers in her hair. At first I thought it was for that reason, but she scampered off as if I were a rapist. My best students like to say, joking, 'This only adds to your reputation.' "

Sharon shook her head. "This is an evil place. I don't care what the holier than thous think."

"Some people are asking where everyone slept. I've dismissed such speculation as silly gossip. I told Sam, 'I did nothing most of them haven't done before marriage, certainly with their intendeds.' But I agreed to have you sleep at his and Kathy's. I need to make it through the year."

On the way over to Sam and Kathy's, Sharon reached up and pulled down her panty hose. Ripping off her black panties, she tossed them out the car window onto someone's snow-covered yard. "There," she said. "You won't get a pound of flesh, but you can have those, you hypocrites!"

When we dropped Sharon's things off at their house, I
didn't tell Sam and Kathy why things between us seemed
tense. They asked us to come in.

We walked into the living room and sat down on separate
chairs. Sam and Kathy sat across from us on the couch.

"I'll have her back by ten," I said, standing to go. I really
wanted to get up and go in case things turned ugly.

"Maybe you will," Sharon said. "Maybe you won't." She
began to cry.

"You seem very upset," Kathy said. She left the couch to
take Sharon's hand. She looked into her eyes. "Do you want
to talk about it?"

"Ok, I let him fuck me," Sharon blurted.

Sam changed the subject by speaking of something
around town. I missed what. I was too shocked to listen.

Sharon clarified by saying, "I didn't mean Ted."

"Wonderful," I thought, "they'll really think you a
whore."

Sam and Kathy said nothing. "I think you need to talk,"
Kathy said.

Sharon shook her head.

So Kathy asked about our Christmas plans. "You know
you're welcome to have Christmas dinner with us, don't
you?"

"Perhaps you'd prefer to drive up to Minneapolis or
Omaha," he said. "You can get a room in a nice hotel and
enjoy the holidays without distraction."

"I was referring to Father Joe O'Brian," Sharon said.
"The priest who screwed me as a child."

"Sam maybe you should pour us all a big glass of wine,"
Kathy suggested. "Obviously, Sharon needs to vent."

Sam got up and went to the kitchen. I heard a cork pop
and glasses clinking. I'd told him and Kathy about Sharon's
predatory priest. They'd expressed sympathy. The news
wasn't absolutely shocking, although Sharon's manner of
telling about it seemed that way to me.

"O'Brian showed up again and started sweet talking me," Sharon began. She seemed glad to talk. She reached for the glass that Sam offered her and began to chug it. "He told me he really wanted to see me naked again, and, 'My, oh my, you have the prettiest set of tits I've ever seen.'"

My face was flushing—I just knew it—in fact, I felt feverish all over—not only from the scene that Sharon was describing but the words that she was using. I too chugged my wine. I'd never be able to drive far. Maybe I'd have to have Sam take me home.

Sam and Kathy, however, sipped from their glasses. They were not used to people who used such language.

"Father Joe always made my knees go weak, even as a child," Sharon said. "He told me I was still the prettiest, most feminine thing he'd ever seen." She paused. "I said, I'd noticed his use of the word *thing*. He blushed and unzipped his pants. His dick was still the littlest dick I'd ever seen on someone older than ten. Evidently he thought it just fine. He suggested I pet it."

"Uh Sharon," I said. "Do we have—could we be spared some of the details? I can't handle them."

"If I can't tell you and your closest friends, who can I tell?" she demanded.

"Go on," Kathy said. "I know it's painful, but you need to talk. We can see that. Ted is a grown man. He's heard all kinds of stories. I'm sure he can handle yours." Kathy paused. "Ted loves you. He wants to make you his wife."

Sharon looked at me, and began blubbering. She asked for another glass of wine.

Sam went to get the bottle.

"I don't deserve him." Still looking at me, her sobbing became more violent. "I let my old abuser screw me. I'm supposed to be Ted's woman. But I let this supposedly celibate and good priest screw me."

"We sometimes do what we do not wish to do," Sam said. He poured the rest of the wine into Sharon's and my glasses.

"I hate myself for it. I knew better—I *know* better. I let him fuck me," Sharon said. "I hate him. I beat him off me again and called him all kinds of names. I told him what a little dick he had. He gathered up his clothes and made a getaway. I threatened to call the cops," she said. "And the newspapers. And worst of all, I feel guilty for shaming him."

"But he shamed you," Kathy responded, "starting when you were a child."

"Still—" Sharon said.

Kathy and Sam talked quietly with each other. "We think you should take some things from your suitcase that you'll need for the night and next day," Kathy said to Sharon. "Put them into a grocery sack. We'll pull the shades and turn on some lights in the guest bedroom for awhile. Then we'll turn them off, as if you're staying here."

"I don't think anyone will know better," Sam said. "Kathy and I will drop some references to your staying with us around town. The wags will pick it up and spread it."

"When I'm really upset, more than anything I want Sam to hold me all night," Kathy related her manner and voice soothing. She took Sam's hand. He squeezed and leaned into her.

Sharon nodded.

"But be discreet at your place," Sam advised. "Don't make too much noise. The people below you are gone for the holidays."

I knew that a number of people in this community were able to put the spirit of the law above the letter. For that I was grateful. Christian community worked—if people operated also from their hearts, not just their heads.

I toyed with the notion of driving to Minneapolis. The roads were clear, even though snow covered the fields and towns through the Midwest. No new storms were expected.

"Well, if you decide to go, come get your suitcases," Kathy and Sam said, walking us to the door. They figured we could always find some place to stay, even with the holidays.

"Some cheap motel in some out of the way spot can be fun. You don't have to spend much time there," Sam said.

Sharon laughed, and then cleared her throat. "I don't plan to spend my time having Ted drive around town."

I was glad to see she was moving past her latest trauma. But serious doubts about whether this relationship would ever work still nagged me. Sharon had been through so much, and was so damaged, that I just didn't know.

It pained me to think of it. More traumatic still, I wondered if I would ever find someone.

"If you want company on Christmas Eve and Christmas Day, you know you're welcome to spend them with us," Kathy said.

Sharon and I walked arm in arm down the sidewalk to my car. A raccoon or some sort of animal scampered across the street.

Sharon commented on what nice folks they were. "They're a little cool on the surface, a little too controlled for my tastes—"

"But genuine, with good hearts," I added.

"This isn't the place for you," Sharon said. "You need a community, but you've got to have more freedom."

"More passion," I added, anticipating our arrival at my place. I told her, "Be careful," and helped her into my car. The bitter night air had sobered me up.

"I was hoping you might just hold me," she said, as I started the motor. "I don't think I can have sex with you now."

I glanced at her. I'm sure I looked crestfallen.

"The incident with Father Joe is too fresh. I can't get his pencil dick out of my mind or the fact that I betrayed you."

I couldn't deny that those images were also near the surface of my mind. But we had to move past them.

"You're the first sort of normal man I've ever had sex with," Sharon said. "You know that."

"I'm glad you qualified your statement," I said, stopping at a stop sign. No one was on the streets. "*Sort of normal* is more accurate than normal."

"You worry too much, Ted. Believe me," Sharon began, "I've known some really abnormal types in my life, starting with Father Joe."

"I wish you could avoid talking about him," I said. "But I know that's probably asking too much."

Sharon nodded. "I don't want to think so much about his cock," she said. "I've tried thinking about yours—even about Brad's."

"Oh good," I said, "someone else I'd just as soon not think about." I thought I'd pop a Librax when I got home.

"Brad had me convinced I could never be satisfied with less than eight inches," Sharon said. "He was thick and really rammed me."

"Thanks for information you've never seen fit to grant me before," I said. All I needed to hear was how she had to have at least eight inches to be satisfied and how Father Joe had poked her with his pencil dick before that. What an insensitive bitch. I shook my head hard, as if trying to clean my mind.

"I'm sorry," Sharon said.

I thought she was going to apologize for being so callous toward me.

"Brad never wanted to come inside me. He had to show me the money shot."

"Sharon—" I pleaded. "This is doing nothing for me." I couldn't believe she was so disconnected from my feelings. But then, she was typically disconnected from her own.

"Oh look," she said, sitting up in the seat. "It's one of the inbred families," she chuckled. She nodded at a mother and father and several children in the pickup next to us. I thought they were the same family I'd seen weeks before. I'd told Sharon.

As I pulled into my parking spot at the back of the house where my apartment was, I said, "I think we ought to drive to

Minneapolis for the holidays. We need to change the scene and, along with that, be inspired, Like Lycidas, 'by fresh thoughts and pastures new.'"

Sharon laughed. She assured me that she could move on. "And will. I don't want to travel more. I'm so tired, weary of it all."

She opened the door and got out.

"Oh no," I said as we walked inside, "we forgot your stuff."

"I don't need it. I'll use your toothbrush and floss. I've got a makeup kit in my purse."

"We can get things tomorrow." I wondered how we were going to show Sharon's having spent the night at Sam and Kathy's. How could I drive over there and have her come out of their house with me? We'd not thought that through.

I decided not to tell Sharon the flaws in our logic. She had enough to worry about.

That night I dreamed of Tray, that she visited and nuzzled my hand. I knew that it was a dream, but it was one of those very clear and real dreams, that portends something that I need to pay attention to. I was not yet sure what that was. Tray seemed to be offering me some sort of solace.

At three, I woke up. I felt around the bed. No one else was there. I stumbled up and looked in the corners for her. There were no curtains to hide behind in that place. I'd gone from a very nice updated town home of 1465 square feet to a dinky, one bedroom apartment with only pull down shades.

I walked to the living room to look for her.

There, curled up, asleep on the couch, she lay. She'd found an extra blanket and pillow. "Boy, oh boy, do I hope you are going to get through this," I whispered.

I decided not to wake her. I walked to the bathroom. I peed, and then I looked at my face in the mirror. I shook my head. I just didn't know what to do. I was deep in the outhouse hole. I'd been mired in what I'd thought was bad before.

In the morning, Sharon sat at the kitchen table with me, sipping a cup of strong coffee. "I think it best that I go back to Denver," she said. "Things just aren't working. We're out of synch."

I put my cup down. "Running is always a good way to work through things," I said, feeling annoyed. No—more than that—outraged.

"But it's my style," Sharon replied, with a strange mixture of cuteness and sorrow. She glanced at the sparrow dancing on the window ledge. "It's so cute."

I agreed. I began to chirp, as if hoping to be fed.

Sharon broke up some toast, opened the window, and spread the crumbs and pieces on the ledge for the sparrow. It seemed unafraid. She put some crumbs in the palm of her hand to see if the bird would sit on her hand and eat. Before long, she had coaxed it into her palm. It sat and pecked crumbs.

"I have quite a way with animals," she whispered, reaching out with her other hand to stroke its back ever so lightly.

She asked the sparrow if it would like to come inside out of the cold. Slowly, carefully, she clutched it in her fingers and brought it in. She talked to it while she stroked it.

It watched with some curiosity.

After a few minutes, Sharon returned the sparrow to the ledge outside. She carefully shut the window and washed her hands.

"Maybe we ought to buy some land and open a habitat for animals," she said.

I was flabbergasted. I got hold of my anger before I took my arm and swept the dishes off the table onto the floor. "I know I have to keep my own options open in case I'm completely marginalized in my chosen profession. Some sort of wildlife or animal rescue would at least be keeping with my interests." I couldn't help but sound sarcastic. I was. I picked up my coffee again and sipped. "Since you've never had problems with selling real estate, I'm surprised you'd even consider such a career change."

"Just because I'm good at sales and make lots of money selling real estate doesn't mean I like selling things," she replied.

I didn't think I'd ever heard her say that before. But, the bitter and the sweet are rarely found apart. I had been thinking the relationship was over, but now I wasn't so sure. Maybe we were ending one chapter and ready to start another.

"Now," Sharon said, as if shifting moods and subject, "I think I should get on the road."

"You just arrived, and we were planning to spend Christmas together," I said.

"I know. But I think I should go," she responded. "It's nothing against you. Please don't start digging. I think I should go."

"I just can't figure you out," I complained.

"I can't either." Sharon opened her purse and handed me her car keys. "Would you please start my car?" she asked and walked off to gather her things.

I was very puzzled. "You didn't drive over. Don't you know that?" I said. "I drove you here from Omaha. You flew in. Don't you remember? And your things are over at Sam and Kathy's."

Sharon looked confused for a few moments, and then smiled, as if she'd been joking. "I know. I was just wondering how you'd react."

I recalled all the confusing signals she'd put out at various times in our relationship, including the night before. Were we regressing? I had no desire to return, for I had never been able to sort out all of what had been going on. My gut was clenching. I'd forgot to take a Librax.

"I'm using again. I need a fix. I know I can't do it when you're around," Sharon confessed.

The blood drained from my face. I could feel it.

"This happens with addicts," Sharon explained. She raised her blouse sleeve to reveal the needle tracks on her arm.

I hadn't noticed them in the night. I took a deep breath. Enabling someone's addictions was not a good thing. Still, I wanted to help her. My whole being felt like lead. "You need to check yourself back into the hospital," I said. I wondered why I'd not somehow tuned into this. Why did I know some things, but not others, even crucial facts?

"I plan to do that when I return," Sharon said. She paused, pregnantly. "After I take a good hit," she added. "I want to spend the entire holiday season out of it."

I meditated on the choices. I decided to drive her back to Omaha and put her on the plane. I could not be around her if she was using. But first, we had to pick up her suitcase from Sam and Kathy. I had no idea what I'd tell them.

Fields of Gold

The drive to Omaha was awful. The roads were clear but everywhere lay snow, now looking like soiled linens heaped everywhere. I felt that I needed a good cleansing myself. So did Sharon, who said nothing the whole time.

Donne's "Hymn to God My God, in My Sickness" started playing in my mind, as if Donne were preaching to me:

> Since I am coming to that holy room,
>   Where, with thy choir of saints for evermore,
> I shall be made thy music; as I come
>   I tune the instrument here at the door,
>   And what I must do then, think now before.

"Are you warm enough?" I asked, glancing Sharon's way. She was shivering, even though the heat was on high.

I figured she was going through withdrawal. I thought about preventing her from leaving, forcing her off the drugs.

> So, in his purple wrapped receive me Lord,
>   By these his thorns give me his other crown;
> And as to others' souls I preached thy word,
>   Be this my text, my sermon to mine own,
> Therefore that he may raise the Lord throws down.

The voice in my mind finished Donne's poem, just as I drove into the airport.

I parked and walked Sharon inside. It seemed one of the longest walks I'd made so far, and I'd trekked some very long, arduous paths.

"Some paths we must walk alone," Sharon whispered. At the gate, she squeezed my arm and said goodbye

I watched as she walked out to the waiting plane.

I wondered if she would ever get straightened out. The possibility that this was the last time I'd see her passed through my mind, like a voice from a ruined choir. I despised the notion, but it remained, suspended in air, somewhere just out of reach.

I kept wondering why Sharon and I had been brought together. I'd thought I was to help her, but I wasn't sure I'd helped at all.

I'd thought she'd helped me. She taught me a great deal about psychic connections, about the astral realm, about souls that seemed so connected that they're known each other through many lives.

Maybe in some ways she did help, but she was breaking my heart and making me question my ability to endure. This was a crucifixion. Mine.

I turned to my car, got in, and sat. It was cold, freezing, in fact. But I let myself shiver. I needed to feel the pain.

"What you meant as evil, God has turned to good," again came to mind, the words of Joseph to his brothers when they sought his help in Egypt. God had meant the selfish and misguided actions of those close to Joseph for greater good.

I started the motor and drove off. I noticed the exhaust cloud in my rear view mirror.

I looked out over the vast expanses of stubble-covered squares. They were wind-swept in patches, but with snow heaped in others.

If I could step out into the future, onto those fields of gold that I'd once envisioned, to know that things would be all right, that we would be well, and all things would be well, my suffering would not be so awful. God showed St. Julian of Norwich a hazel nut. In "this little thing" she saw "three properties. The first is that God made it. The second, that he loves it. And the third, that God keeps it," wrote Julian. "But what is this to me?" she wrote. "Truly, the Creator, the

Keeper, the Lover. For until I am substantially oned to him, I may never have full rest nor true bliss. That is to say, until I be so fastened to him that there is nothing that is made between my God and me."

A red fox ran across the road and disappeared into the barrow pit. It must have had a den there. "Foxes have holes, and birds of the air have nests, but the Son of Man has no place to lay his head," said Jesus.

"Oh, Sharon, if only I could change things. For you. For me. For everyone," I cried. I pounded the steering wheel with my fist.

Though Five Eyes Break

For weeks, no one that I knew had heard a word from Sharon, even at her workplace. Iowa was still cold, dismal in every way, and growing more so. Not even Sam and Kathy's support—and they gave me as much as they could—helped. People were now saying that Sharon, Dan, and I must have had a three way when they visited. "The Smiths probably heard something that night which got their tongues going," Kathy told me.

I decided to try Sharon's mother, but I could never get her to answer the phone. Nor did she return messages. I didn't know if Sharon was shooting up, in rehab, or seeing Father Joe.

Dan said, "You have to let go. I'm tired of trying to help. She's walking her own path. You can't follow."

"I know," I said.

Near Valentine's Day, I dreamed of her again. She was walking on fields of gold, coming toward me, her arms open, ready to embrace me. Tray was at her side, happy, full of life, and whole.

I woke with strangely mixed feelings. I wanted to feel assured.

Tray was at Sharon's side. Was she playing the part of animal guide? I didn't know. I was uneasy. Something about the dream left me with too many questions. Why was Tray there?

The dream kicked up my intestinal problems. They'd gotten worse. I got out of bed and popped a Librax. I was now taking it twice a day, just as I had to in Colorado. "Back to my gut-wrenching life," I said, staring at myself in the bathroom mirror.

I drove back to Denver for spring break and stayed at Brian and Mary's. The weather was clear and temperate, with little smog. Tulips, daffodils, and forsythia bloomed everywhere. Spring was finally coming to Iowa too. The fields had cleared of snow. They and the grass were starting to green.

I checked on my town home to make sure my renters weren't destroying the place. When I walked through the place, I saw that the three young professional women renting it weren't keeping it clean. The walls looked soiled and nicked here and there, but I couldn't say much. I had to keep it rented. At least they were paying the rent and the utilities.

Somehow Sharon heard that I was in town and where I was staying. She phoned. I'd stayed anxious about her, but I didn't call her. I had to keep my distance. By the night she phoned, I'd used most of my vacation seeing family and friends. I had to get back to Iowa a few days before classes began again.

"Ted, I heard you were in town. But you didn't call me. Why?" she asked.

I wondered what the desperation I sensed in her was about this time. I sensed a slightly different edge than before.

I drove over to her high rise. She invited me in. We sat on her living room couch. She gave me a cup of coffee that was too bitter to drink. "I've had stale coffee before, but this tastes like it's two days old," I complained, spitting the mouthful back in my cup.

"It probably is," she said and laughed. "I reheated it."

I made a disgusted face and set the cup on the table beside the couch.

"I've had a hard winter," Sharon said. She crossed her legs. I went cold turkey and got off the drugs without treatment. I knew what I had to go through, since I'd been there before," Sharon said. "And, with God's help, I knew it was possible, without having to enter rehab." She smiled. "I did it. I'm free. I kicked the habit. I'm on my way back."

"I'm relieved," I said, wondering if I really could be assured of her not relapsing.

"My father died of cancer only a few weeks after I left you at Christmas. I wasn't even told until three days after he passed." She paused. "His funeral seems like it was only weeks ago," she said. "I want you to stay the night—and the next."

I didn't know what to say. I really had to get back to Iowa, but I was willing to fulfill her wishes at least that night. She slipped over and sat on my lap.

I carried her to the bedroom where we made love. Our connection spiritually and emotionally was stronger, deeper than ever.

Afterwards, Sharon turned away from me. She faced the cold, white wall. This time, she didn't masturbate. I raised myself to look at her. I saw that her face was wet with tears.

I asked, "What can I do?"

But she wouldn't answer.

After a long wait, she finally let me hold her.

The next morning, Sharon snuggled and whispered in my ear, "Ted, I want to marry you and have your babies. I finally *know* you love me."

"It's taken you this long?" I asked. I was incredulous. "It's been two years since we first met."

"In this life," she answered, pushing her bottom up against me.

I stroked her hair.

"My therapist asked to make copies of some of your poems and letters to me. If she ever really came to love someone, she would want him to say exactly what you said to me," Sharon said. "But I wouldn't let her copy them. Your words were for me. I didn't want her trying to take any part of you from me." She raised her face to see my face.

She couldn't bring herself to say she loved me. Only once had she said so. "Sharon, why have you told me you loved me only once?" I asked. I felt uneasy. I couldn't quite figure out why.

"Usually your saying you loved me made me feel guilty and confused," she said. "I didn't know what I felt. I couldn't feel love, couldn't reciprocate, although I always felt I should." She became silent, thoughtful. But then with a burst of anger, she blurted, "That pig, Joe O'Brian, he tried to convince me he was the one I loved, and always had."

"I don't want you to try to force your feelings or your words," I said. "I hope you know that." I felt a heavy weight in the center of my being. No matter what I did, I couldn't release her from the pain that had so long held her in bondage.

I stayed a second night. Iowa could wait. I didn't need to get back more than the day before classes began. Being with Sharon was more important.

On the second morning, I felt like singing an aubade to the sparrows chirping outside the window, blessing the ducks and geese and fish and every creature that flies, crawls, and swims on earth, and in the sky, and beyond. All things bright and beautiful, all creatures great and small. The hymn played through memory, my vista opening onto fields of gold again.

"I need some time alone," Sharon announced.

I called Brian and Mary and asked to stay another night there. I wondered it Sharon would recant.

"Man, I don't like this situation," Brian said, shaking his head when he let me in at noon. When I tried to call Sharon that afternoon, that night, and again the next morning, she failed to answer. She didn't return my calls.

I left for the Great Plains, wondering all six-hundred and ninety-three miles back if my relationship with Sharon would ever gel.

The morning of the epiphany, I had asked if Sharon believed that she and I would be happy together. I couldn't help it. I was certain it would not be so if she kept cutting off communication, as I'd told her more than once.

She answered, "Yes. We will. We will be happy. At last. And forever." She nodded, as if trying to convince herself. She rested her head on my chest.

Perhaps Sharon would be less likely to cut me off if she'd not deeply feared the cost of love, the possibility of abandonment. Sharon had asked me, "Please, never leave me. Everyone I've ever loved has left me."

I didn't respond because I knew realistically that there are sometimes reasons we're forced to go, at least for a time. Our wishes do not always come true. I did, however, note that she had admitted that she'd loved some people, seeming to imply that she did—or *would*, perhaps—be able to include me in the country of her heart.

Again, I felt a twinge of regret that I always had to be so reasonable. No, it was more than regret that I felt. I knew my feelings, at least most of the time. I was outraged, more with myself than anyone else. I needed to be able to react immediately and without having to think about every damn thing, researching the facts and various opinions, arguing with every text, examining every angle before trying to act with full integrity—at least as much as I could muster. I never considered myself a particularly good man. "That's the very reason you are," Brian once told me.

"Fuck it, Brian," I said in my head to him, as if he were sitting in the car beside me. "I'm tired of being so much in control, so reasonable, so good."

As I drove the two lane highway through patchworks of greening farms into the neatly laid out squares of the town where I was living, I noticed the inbred family again, walking down the sidewalk just in front of me. This time all of them were together. They were strolling two behind two behind two of them, children in front, with mother and father bringing up the rear. They were singing a hymn. I'd heard they were very musical and loved to sing four part harmony.

I rolled down my window to listen more carefully. It was the "The King of Love my Shepherd Is," the Twenty Third Psalm set to the St. Columba melody. As far as I could tell, no one around here sang it, yet it was a haunting, winding tune, with lovely words, one of my favorites. "The king of love my shepherd is, Whose goodness faileth never; I nothing lack if I am his, And he is mine for ever." People complained that they could never argue doctrine or practices with such people. They never understood, not even the general points, let alone the finer details.

"Where streams of living water flow, My ransomed soul he leadeth; And where the verdant pastures grow, With food celestial feedeth." Yet mom would look at dad, and dad at mom, and say, "But we love one other," and the kids, even the ones with Down's syndrome, would nod.

"Perverse and foolish oft I strayed, But yet in love he sought me, And on his shoulder gently laid, And home, rejoicing, brought me." They continued to sing. I drove slowly so I could take it all in, and be reminded.

More signs to be read in the light of the City of God, where God himself is the light, as Augustine averred. This community, I was convinced, was no earthly Jerusalem, a reflection of the heavenly city on earth—not from all that I saw—no more than the early Puritan settlements in New England, or the Calvinist settlements that Peter De Vries had painted in his novels.

Although I had not yet been to Palestine, I had been to Ireland. I had talked with people whose brothers and sisters, daughters and sons, and mothers and fathers, had died in the fighting. Always, religious differences were a significant—although not the sole—reason for the seemingly insoluble and endless troubles.

While John Lennon's "Imagine" was a nice song—it was playing on the radio, acting as another commentary on my musings—I could not imagine a world without heaven or hell—or religion of some sort. To me the notion was unfathomable. We are spiritual creatures. Without some sort of spiritual identity which gives us a center, we fall apart.

Trauma and sweetness, beauty and repulsiveness, life and death, sin and redemption. The impulse toward spiritual life is intimately linked to sexuality, rooted in creativity itself, yoked with the impulse toward total annihilation All are dichotomizations of the One, the ever-expandable point, the beginning and end of all, to which everything longs to return.

That we might have the opportunity to grow and move toward wholeness, God comes to us in many experiences, in multiple forms. Without the presence of evil, without those who are suffering, lost, needy, hungry, in pain—whether physical, emotional, or spiritual—we lack occasions for growth, opportunities to learn compassion, and every other virtue, making them our own. Incorporating them in our very selves. We gain a true sense of self by struggling with such angels.

I recalled the last stanza of Dylan Thomas' difficult poem, "In All Love's Countries," only some of which I understood. I would teach it on Monday. I loved the rhythms, the sounds, and the images, despite not knowing exactly what he was saying at every turn. I didn't know that we had to.

I had committed the poem to memory back when I was a freshman in college, sixteen years before—back when I was green and hopeful. It ends,

> My one and noble heart has witnesses
> In all love's countries, that will grope awake;
> And when blind sleep drops on the spying senses,
> The heart is sensual, though five eyes break.

Thomas speaks of the deepened understanding, the stronger sense of self that comes after our five senses are battered and broken, after we have struggled to understand our texts, sometimes failing, sometimes succeeding. Only then does the heart really come alive. Only then do we love, love fully and deeply the entire creation, some say, the garment of God. For me, that is a kind of crucifixion and resurrection into a new life.

The words that I'd loved when I was a freshman in college, I still loved. They moved me, they stirred my soul, and they gave me insight, glimpses into the eternal, as the best literature always did. They strengthened me, so that I could go on with my journey, wherever it led, through the valley of the shadow of Death, through green pastures, and sometimes beside still waters.

When I pulled up to the house where my apartment stood, I noticed no spring flowers at all. The grass, plants, and trees were further along in Denver. With Persephone still in Hades, I felt profoundly homesick.

I had no garden to tend here. People farmed, with all available land being tamed, but most did not seem to grow much in the way of flowers besides some tulips in the spring. And those only appeared here and there, mostly on public grounds. I knew that some people had vegetable gardens. I'd visited some. Roses could not survive the terrible winters, I was told.

I missed my flowers. They gave me solace. In spring, they reminded me that hope returns, that the god of the underworld must release his captive. These were signs of renewal and resurrection.

By the time I got my bags and myself up the stairs to my apartment, I was extremely uneasy, even more troubled than I had been on the drive home. This just wasn't home. I was teaching some literature courses. That was a good thing. But, in so many ways, this was a foreign land. Many called it "little Eden," but it was definitely Eden after the Fall.

I could not seem to settle down. Quotes—ideas—from everywhere—seemed to crash in on me like waves. I tried making a pot of Darjeeling tea and sipping it while listening first to classical and then to pop music. I tried TV. I kept switching channels.

I tried taking a nap.

I tried reading to prepare for classes.

I knew I could not concentrate enough to grade papers.

I looked to see if I might have any tranquilizers in my medical supplies. I used to have some valium, but evidently I'd thrown them out.

I took another Librax, knowing that they have an anti-anxiety drug in them, as well as a smooth muscle relaxer.

Dan called. His voice was strange, forced. "Sharon's dead," he blurted and wept.

I could not take in what he'd told me. "What? What are you saying?" I could not seem to understand. I knew that he was speaking English, but it seemed some sort of foreign tongue.

Dan repeated, "Sharon's dead."

I finally heard—but I did not believe him. I refused to believe him. He had to be mistaken.

Moments of silence, full of echoing and conflicting notions, passed between us.

Rick took the phone from Dan and said that he had something to read me. It was a note that Sharon had left at the scene. "Sharon evidently drank herself into oblivion and put the muzzle of a handgun into her mouth, then blew out her brains. The police were called by a neighbor," Rick said. "It happened two hours ago. The police found Dan's number beside the note. 'Call Dan' was scribbled on the top. So a policeman dialed Dan and told him." He paused. We're at her place now.

Rick took a deep breath and went on. "The note reads, 'I cannot live honorably, but I can die like a noble Roman.' Beneath a white space, toward the bottom of the page, she's drawn a circle. These words are inside. They say, 'for Ted:

> With my body, I thee worship.
> And with my body I worship thee—
> I'll wait for you—'"

Rick grew silent.

For a moment, my earthly sight blurred with tears, I glimpsed Sharon and me. We stood on fields of gold, there, where *chronos* meets *kairos,* and earthly time rolls into eternity.

About the Author

One of Thomas Ramey Watson's prominent forebears on his mother's side was Jacques LaRamee. A number of places in the upper Rocky Mountain West bear his name to this day. Laramie, Wyoming is best known. Jacques was a renowned and influential explorer and fur trapper. Because he was just, honest, and treated others, including the often-despised native Americans, well, he was held in high esteem. One winter, the story goes, the native Americans were starving, so they killed one of Ramee's cattle. He told his workers not to say anything—they were hungry. Jacques shared with fellow free trappers his theory that the world was wide and there was room enough for all. He had the courage to live his convictions and followed the beat of his own heart, not what was imposed on him from outside.

One of Ramee's progeny, psychotherapist, life coach, writer, and professor, Thomas Ramey Watson believes that journeying in various realms—of the mind, the physical world, and the soul—is central to enjoying a good life. The insights gleaned from becoming aware of the intersecting planes of existence lead us to fuller and more deeply lived lives.

Thomas Ramey Watson, Ph.D., is an affiliate faculty member of Regis University's College of Professional Studies in Denver, Colorado. He has served as the Episcopal chaplain (lay) for the Auraria Campus in Denver and taught English for the University of Colorado at Denver. He has trained as a psychotherapist and was named a Research Fellow at Berkeley Divinity School at Yale University, a position he did not take, choosing to do postdoctoral work at Cambridge University instead.

He is the author of several scholarly publications, including an acclaimed book on Milton, *Perversions, Originals, and Redemptions in* Paradise Lost. His popular works include his popular memoir, *Baltho, the Dog Who Owned a Man* and two books of poetry, *The Necessity of Symbols* and *Love Threads,* poems that echo more autobiographically the mystical experiences recounted in his novel *Reading the Signs.*

Dr. Watson is available for speaking engagements, teaching assignments, counseling, and coaching. His web address is www.thomasrameywatson.com. He can be reached at trw@thomasrameywatson.com.